LOSN

A006695825

CW00705206

?

COVER FOR A TRAITOR

Sir Rupert Canville, British High Commissioner to Canada, is drowned in a canoeing accident on a remote lake. But is it an accident? British Security, in the person of troubleshooter Dick Fenwick, suspects that the 'accident' was a carefully disguised suicide. His inquiries and 'damage control operation' – if Canville has indeed been responsible for a security leak – lead him to Ottawa, London, Oxford and Warsaw.

The KGB, meanwhile, know exactly why Sir Rupert died, and are arranging a spectacular publicity coup. They haven't expected interference from Hugh Bigrel and Jay Ryan, however. Hugh lost his wife and child in a car crash when somebody disposed of Jay's father Sam, a senior CIA man, with a high-velocity bullet on the motorway. Drawn together by grief and then by love, Hugh and Jay travel to Washington, Canada and Poland in a desperate search for the truth about Sam Thaxted's murder. But they do not realize what danger they are in. There are people in Warsaw who will go to any lengths to stop them uncovering what is potentially the KGB's highest-placed operative abroad – in particular Viktor Krasnakov, who has compelling reasons of his own for protecting the Soviet agent's identity . . .

Intricately plotted and bristling with suspense, *Cover for a Traitor* is an exciting and entertaining espionage novel, written with all the assurance that Palma Harcourt's readers have come to expect.

PALMA HARCOURT

Cover for a Traitor

COLLINS
8 Grafton Street, London W1
1989

William Collins Sons & Co. Ltd
London · Glasgow · Sydney · Auckland
Toronto · Johannesburg

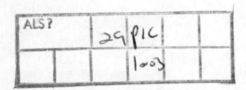

BRITISH LIBRARY CATALOGUING IN PUBLICATION DATA

Harcourt, Palma
Cover for a traitor
I. Title
823′.914 [F]

ISBN 0-00-223429-7

First published 1989
Copyright © Palma Harcourt 1989

Photoset in Linotron Plantin

Printed and bound in Great Britain by
William Collins Sons & Co. Ltd, Glasgow

For Margaret

PRELUDE

He stared across the Ottawa River from the window of his bedroom in the Residence, and contemplated death.

He was not a man who had ever been inclined to delude himself. Normally, in his professional life, he had been prepared to face facts, however hard and brutal they might be, assess them and reach rational conclusions; this characteristic had been one of his major strengths. But now, at this critical moment, he was finding it difficult to consider his own circumstances with any objectivity.

Yet it was essential – absolutely essential – that he reach a decision, and act upon it. Inaction was an impossible course. Dick Fenwick's arrival at the British High Commission in Ottawa was proof of that; he was convinced that Fenwick had remained unsatisfied with his explanation of the events in Warsaw a year ago, and was now determined to ferret out the whole sordid story. And that could not be permitted. The consequences – trial, dreadful publicity, disgrace, dishonour, prison – were too awful to contemplate. He would do anything – anything – to avoid them.

He could, of course, simply confess, admit to being a traitor. Certainly a confession would help to appease Fenwick and his masters, if only because it would save them the time and trouble of mining the truth. But could he trust them to agree to a compromise of some kind, and cover for him? No one, no politician, no senior member of the hierarchy, would want yet another British spy discovered in the corridors of power, but he had deceived them once and they wouldn't like that.

No. A 'simple' confession was not on the cards, he reflected; any such move would involve lengthy and sophisticated interrogation. After the Warsaw episode, they would do their best to squeeze him dry, and there was no certainty that, at the end of the day, the consequences would be other than what he feared. Again he shuddered at the scenario he could so readily visualize.

What was more, even if he were prepared to rely on the authorities for protection, his career was at an end. Inevitably he would be forced to resign. The euphemism 'on grounds of health' might save his good name and protect his family, but that would be all.

And what of Monica? His beloved Monica? He turned from the window for a moment to the figure asleep in the twin bed. Would she be content to live quietly in retirement? Somehow he couldn't imagine it. Not for her boring days in the country. Her life had always been busy, interesting, crammed with a variety of people. No. She would leave him, and without her he would rather be dead.

Dead – that was the word. Subconsciously he had known all along that death was the obvious solution. It was a virtual certainty that once he was safely in his coffin – and he would take great care to make his death appear an accident – the authorities would cover for him. A written confession to satisfy them, and there was every chance that, having nothing to gain, they would let the matter drop with a routine investigation and a quiet damage assessment. Yes, that was the answer. A mixture of self-interest and his family's eminence should ensure that they would bury everything with him.

Part One

ONE

Hugh Bigrel was stretched out on the sofa in the large, comfortably untidy living-room of his North Oxford home, his attention divided between the book he was reading and the television screen. He had turned on the nine o'clock news out of habit, because it was part of the family ritual. But David had cried out, and Lorna had departed to take their young son a glass of water. Alone, Hugh listened to the headlines, which were predictable and dull, and was about to return to his book when the newsreader said, 'We have received a report from Ottawa that Sir Rupert Canville, the British High Commissioner to Canada, has died as the result of a canoeing accident.' She paused, as if feeling she should elaborate on this bald statement, but didn't know how. Then she went on brightly, 'And next, the sports news.'

Lorna had returned to the living-room in time to hear the announcement. With an effort, for she was five months pregnant, she bent to pick up one of David's toys from the floor, and put it on a side table. 'Sir Rupert Canville?' she asked, as she sat down in an armchair across from her husband and reached for the baby's jacket she was knitting. 'You knew him, didn't you, Hugh, when you were in Ottawa?'

'I *met* him,' Hugh corrected her, knowing that Lorna would consider the distinction irrelevant. 'I met Sir Rupert just once, darling. That's all.'

Lorna nodded, and began to knit. She was a fair, pretty girl of twenty-four, eight years younger than her husband. Hugh had in fact been her tutor at St Anne's College, Oxford, until, having made her pregnant, he had married her. And for Lorna it had been a good marriage. She was happy to be the wife of one of the University's most promising dons, she was devoted to her son, she hoped for a daughter and, unlike so many of her contemporaries, had no great desire for a career of her own.

'What was he like?' she asked at length. 'Sir Rupert, I mean.'

Hugh looked up from his book and smiled, suppressing a momentary irritation. He loved Lorna dearly and hadn't regretted a marriage that, at the time, he wouldn't necessarily have chosen. But sometimes his wife would pick endlessly at trivia. Nevertheless, he gave Lorna's question some thought.

He said, 'I remember him as a big man. Big in every way. He topped me by a couple of inches, and I'm almost six feet. And he was broad, thick, solid – an impressive character, pretty sure of himself, as I suppose he had every right to be.'

'Why do you say that?'

Hugh shrugged. 'I learnt a bit about his history – looked him up in *Who's Who* and so on. He was born with a silver spoon in his mouth, as they say. He came from a privileged, wealthy, aristocratic family. I believe on his mother's side he's connected with the Royals. People like that still seem to have a certain inbuilt self-confidence. Others can acquire something like it – but only if they're very fortunate.'

'Did you like him?'

'I certainly didn't dislike him, but I had less than five minutes' conversation with the man. For heaven's sake, Lorna, I just happened to run into Keith Masterson when I was shopping on Sparks Street – Ottawa's main drag. I knew that Masterson had gone into the FCO, but we'd not seen each other since our Oxford days – he was up at Balliol, too. Naturally we exchanged gossip. I told him I was giving a summer course at Carleton University, and he told me he'd been posted to the British High Commission. Then he invited me to a reception there. That was the one time I came across Sir Rupert, and it was no big deal.'

'No. I realize that.' Lorna was impatient; she could never make Hugh understand her interest in public figures whom she was unlikely ever to meet. She finished a row, and inspected the jacket before speaking again. 'Was his wife at the party?'

Resignedly, Hugh put a marker in his book, and shut it. 'Yes,' he said; he didn't wait for Lorna to ask the next question. 'She's a beautiful girl, tall, blonde, elegant. Keith told me she

12

was once a dancer. She's the High Commissioner's second wife, I believe, and about twenty years younger than he is – was. And that, darling, is all I know about her.'

Lorna appeared to accept this. 'It must be dreadful for her,' she said, 'in a strange country and losing her husband so unexpectedly.'

'It's tragic, of course,' said Hugh, 'but perhaps it's not as bad as you think. After all, Canada's hardly a strange country, and she's surrounded by all kinds of official and unofficial help and comfort.'

He swung his legs off the sofa and stood up. Tall and lean, perhaps not conventionally good-looking, but attractive, with a wide mouth, bright eyes and a slightly crooked face, he somehow didn't fit the usual concept of an academic. He stretched luxuriously, not particularly interested in Monica Canville. 'I know it's early, but let's go to bed, darling. I've a hard day tomorrow with meetings and tutorials, quite apart from my lecture.'

But Lorna was still preoccupied with her own thoughts. 'The telly said Sir Rupert had died "as the result of a canoeing accident",' she mused. 'Doesn't it seem strange to you that he should have been canoeing in Eastern Canada at this time of year? It's still practically winter over there, isn't it?'

'Lorna, what does it matter to us? The poor chap's dead, and you'll be able to read all about when and where and why in tomorrow's papers.' Hugh was growing impatient. He was also wrong. Tomorrow's papers would be singularly uninformative, though the media would do what they could with the information available to them.

He held out his hand to Lorna. 'Come along, darling.'

'Yes, of course.' She smiled up at him. 'It's just that I'm curious. I'd like to know what happened.'

A great many other people were equally curious. Among them was one Viktor Georgiyevich Krasnakov. Officially a First Secretary at the Soviet Embassy in Ottawa, Krasnakov in his mid-thirties was young to be additionally a Colonel in the KGB and, on occasions when direct action couldn't be avoided, a political assassin. Outwardly, he was a charming, cultured man, not large, but neat, well-muscled and compact – he made a practice of keeping in training – with a pleasant if cynical face. His suits were expensively-tailored and his nails invariably manicured and, as was only to be expected, he was attractive to women. In spite of occasional warnings from the security authorities in Western Embassies to their staffs, he found himself invited to many small parties.

He had, however, remained a bachelor. For one in his position – in fact for any Soviet officer – marriage to a non-Soviet citizen was out of the question, and in any case there was only one woman with whom he could have contemplated marriage. So he took his sex where he found it. And on occasion, when the circumstances were appropriate, he had no hesitation in almost literally taking it by force.

Krasnakov sat at his desk in his office in the embassy and stared at his telephone, willing it to ring. He was more than merely curious about Sir Rupert Canville's death; he was extremely worried. It was 4.30 in the afternoon in Ottawa – five hours behind London time – and in spite of his belief that he and his sources were aware of most of what went on in the Canadian capital, he had so far been able to acquire few facts to amplify the bald report of the High Commissioner's apparently accidental death.

The phone rang at last, and Krasnakov seized the receiver. 'Yes,' he said, and listened. Several times he nodded as the voice at the far end of the line continued. 'Good,' he said finally. 'Thank you.' The whole conversation, if it could be called that, had been in English.

Krasnakov replaced the receiver and sat back in his chair, a frown marring his usually urbane features. At least he now knew more, though not enough to quiet his misgivings. Indeed, if anything, the reverse was true.

Making a pyramid of his fingers, he considered the situation. Sir Rupert Canville had borrowed from a Canadian friend a cottage on the edge of Lake Naconda, in the Gatineau Hills in Québec Province, north of Ottawa, and had made his way there

14

on Saturday morning, intending to spend the weekend. It was not the first time he had done this. When his duties permitted, he sometimes liked to get away by himself. But it was the end of March. Snow still lay white on the ground in the rural areas of Eastern Canada, unlike the dirty mush in the capital. Krasnakov could visualize the scene. There would be a thin covering of ice on part of the lake, reflecting the pines that came down to the edge of the shore. Undoubtedly it would be beautiful. But it would be cold, too, especially when the wind blew from the Arctic, and his informant had insisted that the cottage was not winterized, and thus only fit for summer habitation.

Krasnakov tried to put himself in Canville's place. It was not easy. He himself was a Russian, a Muscovite. He enjoyed the cold. But, though he was fully aware of the English propensity for eccentric behaviour, he couldn't picture Rupert Canville – and he was well acquainted with the man – relishing any discomfort. So, why had the High Commissioner gone to the cottage at the back end of winter? It could have been for an assignation, but . . .

On Sunday afternoon a canoe had been seen floating upside down in the middle of the lake, and the alarm had been given. This morning divers had brought up Sir Rupert's body. He had drowned accidentally, Krasnakov thought, or he had drowned himself. According to the official bulletin from the British High Commission the death had been an 'accident', but –

All Krasnakov's training and experience had led him to doubt any official announcement without proof or some supporting evidence, and he sensed that something was false here. He could just about imagine Canville sitting in front of a blazing log fire in a cottage, but paddling a canoe through the icy waters of a lake on a bitterly cold weekend, no. At the very least, it was completely out of character. And, even if Canville had decided to take exercise in this odd fashion, why should the canoe have overturned? There had been no storms, no gales, no wind at all over the weekend, and it was a fair assumption that Canville would be reasonably competent in a small boat.

Krasnakov pushed back his chair, and stood up. He went to his window and stared down at the grass below, left brown by the melting snow. Soon, in a few weeks, it would become a lush green lawn. Summer would have come – almost overnight, as usual in that part of the world – and by then . . . He sighed audibly, and rubbed his lower lip.

But that was still ahead. Much could happen in the interval, and he must ensure that events followed a pattern he designed. Just like Sir Rupert some days before, the Russian was facing something of a dilemma. Any overt display of special interest on his part could be dangerous. So, frustrating as it was, he must remain inactive, waiting. He had his sources, and there would be plenty of gossip in diplomatic circles and elsewhere. Rock-cliffe, the élite suburb to the east of Ottawa, where the majority of foreign diplomats and many of Canada's senior public servants lived, would be buzzing with rumours at the cocktail hour. Most of it would probably be garbage, but there might be nuggets among the dross, pointers to official thinking. By tomorrow, with any luck, he would know more. Meanwhile he could only hope that Rupert Canville had indeed been the victim of an accident. Anything else could conceivably be catastrophic.

The man who was best informed about the circumstances of Sir Rupert Canville's death was Dick Fenwick. It had come as a shock to everyone else at the High Commission, but he had been expecting it. He had in fact been warned, though not in time to prevent the tragedy. Canville had made sure of that.

Fenwick was an unusual man, with an unusual job. After a spate of security incidents – even scandals – in British Missions abroad, the Security Department of the FCO had undergone a considerable reorganization. Normally largely staffed by career officers on rotation, a decision had been made to introduce an increasing degree of professionalism and specialization. The result had been the recruitment or secondment of a number of semi-undercover officers – officers of senior rank, who could arrive at Mission, posing as undefined inspectors or experts on organization. Fenwick – ex-army, seconded from MI5 – was one such. In Ottawa he claimed to be a statistician with a mandate to undertake a time-and-motion study, a role which enabled

16

him, with a top security clearance, to ask whatever questions he fancied. Heads of Missions naturally had to be informed of the true roles of the visitors, and there were, of course, whispers of Intelligence, but Fenwick, for one, ignored them. He was, he supposed, a troubleshooter, whose job was if possible to forestall security breaches or acts of treason, and, when that proved impossible, to limit the damage – especially public damage – by whatever means he could.

Inevitably, Fenwick had to operate alone. This suited his character. He had been married, but was long divorced and had seen neither his wife nor his daughter for some fifteen years, an omission he did not regret. He didn't believe in regrets. Nevertheless, he was not without compassion. He had real sympathy for those who, in one sense, became his victims, and for their families. It was a quality that made him good at his job.

It was partly on grounds of compassion that he had resented being posted to Ottawa. He had considered the move unfair to himself and to Sir Rupert Canville, whom he had met during Sir Rupert's previous posting as Ambassador in Warsaw. It had been embarrassing to them both to meet again, though Canville, Fenwick had to admit, had done his best to be co-operative. Now the poor wretch was dead. Fenwick wished he could have prevented it.

He took from his wallet the long letter he had found on his desk when he came into the office that morning, very early, as was his wont. Sealed with Canville's family crest, it had been marked 'Private and Personal', and before Fenwick opened it he had had a premonition of its content. Regretfully he shook his head as he began to re-read the text:

Dear Fenwick,

I write this in the hope that you will use it in whatever way you consider best for our country. I mean this in all seriousness, aware that in the present circumstances it must sound somewhat absurd.

As I am sure you already suspect, I am the cause of the leak that has recently occurred in the High Commission, and which has brought you to Ottawa. I never wished to be a traitor, but

17

I admit that I was more 'involved' in Warsaw than was ever known, and since then I have been blackmailed. This is not an excuse, but merely an explanation.

Once you arrived in Canada, I realized that it was only a matter of time before you would uncover my guilt. I made up my mind not to wait for that to happen. Forgive the drama, but when you read this I shall be dead. I shall be found drowned, and there will be no reason for my family or the public to suspect it was other than an accident. I have several reasons for such a deception. Some you may guess.

First, and most important to me personally, there is my wife. I had a cousin who took his own life, and his wife never forgave herself, though she was in no way to blame. Secondly, my family and friends. Some of my relations would also find reasons to blame themselves, and neither they nor my wife, should the truth emerge, could face the inevitable publicity of my arrest and trial. And, as I am sure you are aware, I have connections in high places.

I sincerely hope that, when the decision comes to be made as to whether or not my death should be accepted as an accident, these factors will be taken into account.

My final reason is the possibility of making some amends for what I have done, by providing an opportunity for what I believe is known in your circles as a 'cover-up operation'. Admittedly this would preserve my own good name which, ludicrous as it may seem, I still value. But, as I am sure you appreciate, it would also be advantageous to the FCO and to Britain. The admitted suicide of a High Commissioner would inevitably lead to rumours of espionage, and yet another public scandal, which we can ill afford. The Americans, on whom we depend so greatly, already distrust our security, and with good reason. But you know this better than I.

So, I can only hope that the right decision will be made. Perhaps it is fortunate that I shall play no part in making it.

The letter was signed with the High Commissioner's full name, and when Fenwick had first read it his immediate reaction had been to wonder how anyone could have been christened Rupert

18

George Peter Alexander de St Vincent Canville. His second reaction was to shake his head in disbelief and sorrow, and mutter, 'Poor bugger,' under his breath.

Re-reading the letter now, however, made him pause for thought. It was an odd confession, primarily because it gave none of the technical data – case officer, drops, tradecraft and so on – that Canville must have known would be of value to the authorities. More importantly, it gave no indication of what information he had passed, and thus would be of no assistance in any damage assessment. None of this jibed with Canville's professed concern for his country.

Fenwick forced himself to wait until the Deputy High Commissioner burst into his room with the announcement that the Québec Provincial Police had been on the phone to say that a body believed to be that of Sir Rupert had been brought up by divers from the bottom of Lake Naconda. Fenwick made the expected sounds of shock and distress, and then asked, 'But why have you come to me, sir?'

'Because – ' The Deputy High Commissioner looked surprised. 'H.E. told me who you were,' he said, 'in case – in case he wasn't available or something – '

'Oh,' said Fenwick, without comment. 'Well, the first thing to do is identify the body, I suppose.'

'Would you – '

'You yourself, or the Senior Counsellor, would be more suitable, I think, sir. Once that's done, London must be told and, of course, one of the ladies must go to the Residence and break the sad news to Lady Canville.'

'She's not there. She's visiting friends in Washington.'

'But the staff at Earnscliffe will know how to contact her.'

'Yes, of course.'

Still the Deputy High Commissioner lingered and Fenwick, who had phone calls of his own to make now that he knew for certain that Canville was dead, had to hide his impatience. 'If I can help in any way, sir – ' he said, leaving the sentence unfinished.

'No, not at present.' The Deputy High Commissioner squared his shoulders. 'I – I was just wondering. I suppose there'll have to be an investigation and – er – a damage assessment, if that's appropriate. There always is, isn't there, when someone like H.E. dies in – er – unusual circumstances?'

Fenwick didn't hesitate. He had already made up his mind to go for a cover-up, and now was the moment to start. He didn't give a damn about Canville's high-placed relations and friends, though he expected that his masters, who would have the ultimate decision, would be influenced by thoughts of them. Nor was he bothered by concern for Canville's wife; he admired Monica Canville's beauty, and he admitted that she had gone out of her way to be charming to him, but he preferred his women to be more casual and less self-contained.

What did carry weight with him, and he was certain would convince the authorities, was the argument that, if Canville's death became known as a suicide, another spy scandal would inevitably follow. And, with Canville's connections, the press would have a field day. As Canville said, this Britain could ill afford.

Fenwick gave a dismissive shrug. 'Of course you're right, sir. Of course there'll be an investigation, and an inquest. But I hardly think a damage assessment will be necessary. No one in his right mind would suspect Sir Rupert of any – irregularity, shall I say?'

Fenwick was an accomplished liar, and he spoke with conviction. He saw the worry fade from the Deputy High Commissioner's eyes, and also felt him relax.

'No, certainly not, but – '

'Well, then – ' Fenwick smiled reassuringly.

But the door had hardly shut behind the other man before Dick Fenwick was reaching for the telephone. He needed his superiors' confirmation that the decision he had reached met with their approval. He got through to London on the secure line quickly and, as he expected, found agreement readily, even gratefully, forthcoming.

Fenwick gave London the gist of Canville's letter, but expressed no comment. That could wait until the full text had been ciphered and telexed. He wondered if any of his colleagues would share his thoughts.

In the meantime, he was grateful that he was not a career diplomat who had to live entirely by the rules. He considered the task ahead of him and did not think it would be difficult, unless the 'cousins' – the Americans: the CIA or the FBI – became suspicious. That, in his opinion, was the major danger.

Fenwick would have been surprised to know that Krasnakov would have agreed with this assessment. British and Russian objectives were hardly identical, but Krasnakov also knew that the biggest threat would come from the United States.

And neither of them had ever heard of Hugh Bigrel. It would be six weeks before they came to know that he existed.

TWO

'We should be leaving in ten minutes,' Hugh Bigrel said firmly.

He had put their bags in the Escort with a sigh of relief. Long weekends with his in-laws were not his idea of fun, though for Lorna's sake he endured them at regular intervals. Now he was anxious to leave, but in the dining-room Mrs Dawson had just poured Lorna another cup of coffee, and David was still playing with his egg.

'What's the hurry? And why get us all up so early?' asked Tom Dawson. He was a builder from the Midlands, now retired with his wife to North Devon. Normally jovial, he was proud that his youngest daughter had been up at Oxford, but had very little in common with his academic son-in-law. 'Can't wait to be shut of us, is that it?' he added.

'Tom!' his wife said reproachfully. 'Don't tease.' She turned to smile at Hugh. 'Pay no attention to him, dear. It's – well, you know, we see so little of Lorna and our grandson, compared to the rest of the family. You understand?'

'Of course.' Hugh refrained from remarking that Lorna's sisters lived within an easy drive of the Dawsons' retirement home. 'But we do have a fair way to go, and if we can make an early start before there's a lot of traffic on the roads – '

'Nearly all on motorways – the M5 and the M4.' Dawson wasn't to be placated.

Hugh didn't contradict him. He looked at Lorna, who finished her coffee and began to encourage David to eat his egg. 'Hurry up, darling. It's time we went home.'

'Don't want to,' David said.

The grandparents exchanged pleased glances, and Dawson said, 'You see, the boy would like to stay, and I don't understand why you can't. It's not as if Hugh's vacation was over. You could easily wait till the end of the week.'

They had faced this argument before, and Hugh didn't respond. It was Lorna who said patiently, 'We told you, Dad. Hugh has work to do, preparing for next term.'

'I'd have thought he knew his stuff well enough by now, without any need for preparation.' Dawson remained disgruntled. He shrugged. 'Still, if you must go, you must.'

Nevertheless, it was almost half an hour before, amid much waving, they finally drove away from the house. David had made a fuss about being strapped into the safety seat in the back of the car, complaining with some justification that it was too small for him, and had wept noisily when Lorna insisted. He had only quietened when Mrs Dawson had brought him a chocolate bar, which Lorna reluctantly let him take.

Then they were off. 'At last,' Hugh said. He was an excellent driver, efficient and careful, and he usually enjoyed a journey by car. But today he was eager to get home. What was more, on a relatively long trip such as this, David was apt to feel car sick, and in her present condition Lorna was not a good traveller.

Indeed it was Lorna who caused the next delay. They had made excellent time, and turned on to the M4, heading towards Swindon, when she started shifting uncomfortably in her seat, and at last she said, 'Hugh, I'm sorry, but could we stop for a few minutes? I need to stretch myself.'

Hugh was instantly anxious. 'Are you all right, darling?'

'Yes.' Lorna laughed. 'It's really not me. It's Gemma. She objects to my seat belt.'

Hugh laughed too. Lorna was determined that the child she was expecting was a girl, and they had already decided on her name. 'Okay,' he said. 'We can't stop on the shoulder, but I seem to remember there's a parking area a mile or so ahead. We'll stop there.'

Later he was to regret bitterly those wasted minutes, and wish with all his heart that he had insisted on continuing to the next large service area, where they had planned a break. Wasted minutes, precious minutes. If they had left the parking area even one minute earlier, they would have been safe. Five minutes earlier and they would have never had any connection with the affair.

Hugh drove fast when they left. Fortunately the motorway was almost deserted. Glancing over his shoulder he saw that David had nodded off to sleep. He was more worried about Lorna, who had been slightly sick when they stopped. He gave her an encouraging pat on the thigh, and she grinned at him.

'Not too long now,' he said.

'I'm all right, love.' She put her hand down beside her and released her seat belt to decrease the pressure on her abdomen. She immediately felt more comfortable, and continued merely to hold the end of the belt in place, hoping that Hugh wouldn't notice. 'Sorry to be a nuisance.'

'Don't be silly, darling,' Hugh said affectionately.

He was to remember those words, but at that moment David woke. 'Bang!' the boy said loudly. Hugh paid no attention. It was an unusually warm day, and the windows in the front of the car were both partially open in order to give Lorna plenty of air, but Hugh wasn't conscious of having heard any untoward sound. There was the steady beat of the tyres on the road surface, and the gentle roar of the wind stream; that was all.

He had rounded a bend on to a long straight stretch of motorway, and had been aware that two cars were approaching fast on the other side of the central reservation, one overtaking the other. Except perhaps for the speed at which they were travelling, about eighty to ninety miles an hour, there had been nothing about them to arouse his special interest.

Then it happened. As if in slow motion the car that had been overtaken swerved to the right, ploughed through the crash barrier on the central reservation and headed straight for the Bigrels' Escort. Instinctively Hugh swung the wheel with all his strength in a futile effort to avoid the collision. He need not have bothered. Metal tore at metal. Glass flew. The grinding, splintering sounds seemed to continue indefinitely. The air about the crash grew heavy with dust and the smell of petrol. But at last there was silence, except for the steady drip of oil and water from the wrecked cars, and the song of a blackbird in a nearby hedge.

* * *

24

'We should have stopped. They may not be dead. I thought – I thought I saw a child in the back and – '

Viktor Krasnakov swore a Russian oath. In the absence of his aide, Igor Galinov – a fellow Muscovite whom he trusted – he had demanded a good driver, and he had no complaints about the young man's driving ability, but he had bloody well stopped on the verge, much too close to the scene of the accident in the other lane. Their car, though an inconspicuous Rover, might well be remembered.

'Get going at once!' he shouted. 'Before anyone comes.'

'I – I can't.'

Krasnakov looked at his driver in disgust. The man was right; he couldn't drive. He was trembling convulsively, as if he had never before seen a traffic accident. His nerve had gone, and for the moment he was useless.

'Get out,' he snapped, 'and let me move across. I'll drive.'

The man hesitated. You're not going to leave me here, are you, Comrade?'

'Don't be so damned stupid. Of course not. We're changing places, that's all. And hurry!'

It was not until they were a couple of miles down the motorway, en route towards Bristol, that the man had recovered sufficiently to speak again. 'I still think we should have stopped, Comrade,' he said sulkily.

Krasnakov swore again. 'Get lost!' he said in effect. 'You'd like us to have waited for the police? Tried first aid, perhaps? Given our names and addresses? And suppose some character had investigated my bag of golf clubs, what would you have said then? "We're going to shoot a few pheasant, officer." Pull yourself together, and think straight for a change.'

The man was a fool, Krasnakov thought angrily, but because of his stupidity he could be dangerous. As soon as they got to London he'd have to be put under restraint and sent back to Moscow on the first Aeroflot flight. There was too much at stake to take any risks.

★ ★ ★

Hugh Bigrel opened his eyes. His first feelings were of something pressing hard against the length of his back, while in front something else pressed against his rib cage. He was conscious of very little pain. He stared through what had once been a windscreen, but was now a jagged hole. There was glass everywhere. At the slightest movement he felt splinters prick his skin. For a long minute his mind became blank again. Then memory returned, but it brought no comfort.

'Lorna!'

Involuntarily he spoke her name aloud. There was no answer, only a dreadful silence. With difficulty he turned to look at the seat beside him. It was empty. Lorna had gone, vanished. But the door on her side of the car remained firmly shut. The thought occurred to him that she had gone for help, but at once he knew that this must be impossible. Tears filled his eyes. He blinked them away and gritted his teeth. David?

He had to make a vastly greater effort to twist his body so that he could look behind him. At once he wished he hadn't. The rear of the car was a shambles. The safety seat had come adrift and been forced forward, squeezing the boy relentlessly against the back of the seat in front. Hugh could just see his son's head, lolling at an unnatural angle, eyes wide open, blood dribbling from the side of the small mouth. An arm was flung sideways, seeming not to belong to the rest of the body.

Choking on the bile that rose in his throat, Hugh turned away from the horror and shut his eyes. He made himself breathe slowly and deeply, and scarcely noticed the pain he then felt. David was dead. There was no doubt about that. But Lorna? For the first time he remembered Gemma, the unborn child, and groaned.

When he next opened his eyes a face was peering at him through the shattered windscreen. It was a thin pale face, with small brown eyes set rather close together, and a sharp nose. Hugh was at once reminded of a fox, but this was a fox with a crash helmet on its head, a human fox who would surely provide help. But the fox made no effort to speak.

Hugh said, 'My wife? Have you seen my wife? A young woman, pregnant?'

'No – o. No, I ain't.'

Somehow Hugh didn't believe him. The man's expression had become shifty and his eyes were flicking around the interior of the wreck, as if in search of something. Clearly he didn't find whatever he sought because he frowned and began to withdraw his head.

Afraid the man would go, Hugh said quickly, 'For God's sake, get me out of here. I don't seem able to do it by myself.'

'I can't, mate. All the doors are jammed. I've tried them. Guess you'll have to be cut out.'

This time Hugh believed him, but he wondered when the man had tried the doors, how long he had been on the scene, and what he had been doing. It couldn't be long, or other people would have arrived. And why had he seemingly lied about Lorna? Had he hurt her? Hugh was beginning to hate the foxy man.

'Then get help,' he said shortly.

'I'm on my bike, mate. There's a service area along the road. I'll report it and the fuzz'll be here in no time. Not to worry. You're the lucky one. The other guy's dead.'

The face disappeared, and Hugh was alone again. 'The lucky one,' he thought venomously. How could anyone dare to call him lucky when David was – was squashed like a piece of rotten fruit? He shuddered and bits of glass fell from his hair and pierced his neck. Then it occurred to him that the foxy man hadn't been referring to David at all, but to the driver of the other car, the car that had caused the accident. Hugh had forgotten his existence. He closed his eyes again, and his last conscious thought was to wonder if he could trust the foxy man to get help.

He was partially awakened by a squeal of brakes, and soon another face appeared before him, though only fleetingly. A voice called, 'There's one here alive, Sergeant. Tell them we'll need cutting gear as well as the ambulances.'

Hugh sighed with relief. The police had arrived. They'd get him out. They'd deal with poor David's mangled body. They'd take care of Lorna. Suddenly relief turned to anxiety.

He made a massive effort, and shouted, 'Hi! Lorna! My wife! Have you found her? Is she badly hurt?'

'It's all right, sir.' This was a different policeman – the sergeant, Hugh assumed. 'There's an ambulance on its way for you, and a doctor. Everything's being seen to. We'll get you to hospital as soon as we can.'

'My wife!' Hugh persisted.

The sergeant didn't hesitate. 'She'll go in the first ambulance, sir. I'm afraid it may take a while to set you free, so that's the best thing to do.'

'Yes.' For a moment Hugh fought to control his emotions. 'She – she's alive then? How seriously is she hurt? She must have gone through the windscreen. You know she's pregnant?'

'Yes, sir. But don't worry about her. There's no need. We'll do everything we can for her. She'll be okay.'

'Thank God,' Hugh murmured.

He was only partially reassured but at least, he told himself, Lorna wasn't dead. And perhaps Gemma would live too, a substitute – no, not a substitute – a recompense perhaps for the loss of David. Hugh's eyes began to close and he was not conscious of the doctor who, leaning awkwardly through the gaping hole that had once been the windshield, cut away his sleeve and jabbed a needle into his arm. Hugh Bigrel slept.

It was twelve hours before Dick Fenwick learned of the accident. He had returned to London three weeks before, and was having dinner in a select and expensive West End restaurant with a potential girlfriend when the maître d' said there was a telephone call for him. He preferred not to take it at the table, and excused himself to the elegant redhead.

'Sorry. Won't be a moment. Business. You know what the property market's like. No idea of off-limits leisure periods.'

The girl shrugged and continued eating. Fenwick hurried after the maître d', who showed him into his private office.

'Fenwick here,' he said into the phone as soon as he was alone. He listened carefully for a couple of minutes. Then he said, 'What's the present state of play?'

'He's in the morgue, officially awaiting identification, though there's no doubt. Luckily the cops who found him acted with exemplary efficiency as soon as they saw his diplomatic passport, and guessed it might be a tricky situation. The US Embassy's been contacted, and they're getting hold of his daughter who lives somewhere over here. They say he may have been on his way to visit her. He's not here on duty, and no one seems to have known he was in the country.'

'That's odd. You'd have thought he'd have reported in.' Fenwick thought for a moment, then, 'They weren't told anything else?'

'No. Killed in a car accident. That's all.'

'Let's hope we can keep it like that.'

'It won't be easy. If the media make a connection – '

'We must make damn sure they don't!' A variety of possibilities flashed through Fenwick's mind, none of them pleasant. Sam Thaxted had become a serious threat to his plans, but he hadn't wished him dead, not like that. He said abruptly, 'The driver of the other car's alive?'

'Yes. He's in hospital, but against all the odds he's not seriously hurt. It was one of those flukes. Apparently his wife undid her seat belt, probably because she was pregnant, and she went through the windscreen. She must have been killed instantly. The boy, too. He was thrown into the back of the seat in front of him and squashed. Nasty. But Bigrel himself seems to have got away with cuts and bruises, a cracked rib or two and minor concussion. He was lucky.'

Fenwick wondered if Bigrel would agree when he was told of his family's fate. He sighed. 'Okay,' he said. 'I'll be along as soon as I can.'

'Not bad news, I hope, sir?' said the maître d' as Fenwick came out of the office.

'A friend involved in a car accident,' said Fenwick. He believed in telling as much of the truth as was possible or convenient. 'I'll just say goodbye to my companion, and arrange for whatever else she wants to go on my bill, and – '

'I'm afraid the young lady has gone, sir.'

'She has?' To the surprise of the maître d' Fenwick threw

29

back his head and laughed. 'Well, I suspect I'm going to be pretty busy for the next few days, so it doesn't matter. At least she's simplified my existence.'

THREE

Hugh Bigrel regained consciousness slowly. Happy, relaxed, indolent, he seemed to float up through fleecy clouds to a strange scene which he eventually recognized as a hospital room. Beside him, on an upright chair, sat his mother. When she saw his eyes open, she took the hand that lay on the coverlet, and he smiled at her. For the moment, he felt safe.

It was with difficulty that Helen Bigrel returned his smile. A tall thin woman, handsome rather than pretty, with iron-grey hair cut fashionably short, she was on excellent terms with her only son, whom she loved dearly. Inwardly, she was shrinking from the task that lay ahead of her. But it had to be done. Involuntarily she straightened her back.

'Darling, you're awake at last,' she said. 'That's good. Do you know, you've slept for nearly forty-eight hours.'

'Hello, Ma.' Hugh made to sit up, and winced as a sharp pain sliced across his chest. Then he remembered. David. And Lorna. He dared not ask. Desperately he turned to his mother, knowing she wouldn't lie to him.

Helen Bigrel responded at once to the unspoken question. 'Hugh, it was a frightful accident, but at least there was no suffering. Little David was killed instantly. You knew he was dead?' She waited for Hugh to nod.

Then she said, 'Lorna's dead too, darling, and the baby. They didn't tell you at once because you were in a state of shock. The police officer said Lorna didn't have her belt done up and was thrown through the windscreen. She can't have known anything about it. Be thankful for that.'

Helen went on talking, though she knew that Hugh had ceased to listen to her. His eyes were shut, and tears trickled down his cheeks from the closed lids. He clutched his mother's

31

hand convulsively. She suffered a little from arthritis and the grasp was painful. She had to make an effort not to cry out.

After a while Hugh relaxed his grip. His tears ceased. He took a deep, shuddering breath that hurt his ribs, and said matter-of-factly, 'There'll be a lot of things to arrange.'

'Yes, but there's no need for you to worry, Hugh. The authorities are being very co-operative over the inquests, and your father's been in touch with the Dawsons about the funeral. Everything that should be done will be done, and by the time you get out of hospital it'll all be over.'

Hugh frowned. 'But – there's nothing much wrong with me, is there?' Tentatively he moved his ribs. 'Surely I'll be well enough to go to their funeral. I *must* go.'

'No, Hugh. It's better that you don't.'

'Why? The Dawsons don't blame me, do they? For God's sake, no one could have avoided that maniac. He was driving much too fast, and he came across the reservation straight into us.' Hugh stopped, breathing hard.

'Darling, don't get so excited. Please! No one's blaming anyone, certainly not you. And it wasn't Mr Thaxted's fault either.'

'Who?'

'The driver of the other car was called Samuel Thaxted. He was an American, on his way to visit his daughter who lives in England. The unfortunate man had a heart attack. The whole thing was just – just a ghastly accident. No one was to blame.'

Hugh absorbed this information slowly. 'I see. Then why is it better for me not to go to the funeral? And, incidentally, aren't the police anxious to get a statement from me?'

Helen Bigrel shrugged and ignored the second question. 'Of course you can go to the funeral if you like, Hugh, but it may not be pleasant. It seems this Mr Thaxted was an important man, a United States diplomat, and we've been warned that there'll probably be newsmen and cameras there, and people waiting to ask you questions. Besides, I really believe the doctor wants you to rest for a few more days.'

'I – I'll have to think about it,' Hugh said, and silently cursed Samuel Thaxted, who had already done him so much harm, and

32

now threatened to interfere with his right to mourn publicly. He wished he could have hated the man; it would have relieved his feelings a little. But he supposed it wasn't Thaxted's fault that he'd had a heart attack.

The next day Hugh was told that he might have a bath, and use the lavatory in the adjacent bathroom. He put on the robe and slippers that his mother had brought him and set off, with a nurse in attendance. It was the first time he had left his room since he had been brought unconscious into the hospital.

Once outside his door, he realized that his room and its adjoining bathroom were at the end of a short corridor, and were therefore isolated from the rest of the building, as if perhaps intended for a patient with a highly infectious disease. This didn't worry him unduly; he merely assumed that he had been given the room because it happened to be available. But then he noticed that, at the end of the corridor, a uniformed police officer was sitting on a hard chair and reading a book.

'What's that policeman doing?' he demanded of the nurse.

'He's to make sure you're not bothered, Mr Bigrel,' she said. 'The doctor didn't want you to be disturbed, and the media can be an awful nuisance sometimes.'

Hugh shook his head in surprise. He had come to the conclusion that his mother had exaggerated the notice likely to be taken of Lorna's and David's funeral, and had decided that by the end of the week he would be fit enough to attend. Now he revised his opinion. And any residual doubts disappeared that afternoon, when he received an unexpected visitor.

His bath had been a treat, but the effort had tired him, and, despite his earlier intention to dress, he was still in pyjamas and gown when the nurse brought in a stranger. Hugh regarded the man curiously. It was somehow obvious that he was not a doctor.

'This is Mr Fenwick,' the nurse announced, smiling.

'And who's Mr Fenwick?' asked Hugh, as the nurse left them together. 'Not a journalist, I hope.'

'On the contrary, Mr Bigrel. Security.' It never occurred to

Hugh to ask for any form of identification, and Dick Fenwick made no attempt to offer any. Instead, he held out his hand.

'I'm sorry,' Hugh gestured helplessly. 'They're still picking the occasional bit of glass out of my hands – and my face.'

Fenwick nodded. 'At least you've got a good excuse not to shave.' He grinned.

Hugh returned the grin, and pointed to a chair. 'You say you're with "security", Mr Fenwick. I can't imagine what security would want with me. I was only saying yesterday that I was surprised the ordinary police haven't found time to take a statement from me. I think that's very odd.'

'Ah,' said Fenwick non-committally. 'That's their business. My problem is that the chap in the other car was a VIP, an American diplomat, over here on a private visit, and the US Embassy naturally wants to know as much as possible about the accident.'

'Well, I don't think I can tell them much. I saw these two cars approaching fast, but they were on the other side of – '

'*Two* cars?'

'Yes. One was overtaking the other, and, immediately after it had been passed, the slower car suddenly swerved across the central reservation and ploughed into us.' Hugh grimaced at the memory. 'I tried to avoid it – but as you know I didn't succeed.'

Fenwick nodded his sympathy. It served to cover his rising excitement. 'The second car – can you describe it?'

'It was fawn-coloured. A Rover, I think.' Hugh frowned. 'You mean he didn't stop? The first person I remember was a man on a motorbike. Then the police – '

'Not so fast, please, Mr Bigrel! This car – the Rover. Is there anything else you remember about it?'

'No. Look, Fenwick, I don't understand – '

'Tell me about the guy on the motorbike. Someone phoned from the service area to say there'd been a bad accident a mile or so back, but he didn't give his name. Anyway, you'd already been spotted by a passing patrol car.'

'The motorbike chap said he'd phone, but I wasn't sure he would. He was an odd sort of character.' Hugh did his best to

34

describe the foxy-faced man, though he couldn't imagine why this factor should be important.

'Did you see his motorbike?'

'No,' said Hugh shortly. He was getting bored with all these questions. He had no wish to relive those dreadful moments, finding Lorna gone, seeing David's mangled body behind him.

Fenwick sensed his impatience, and prepared to leave. He had learnt more than he had hoped. A description of the motorcycle would have been too much to expect.

'There's just one more thing – ' he began.

It was Hugh's turn to interrupt. 'Who was this American that he's so important? Was he an ambassador or something?'

Fenwick hesitated. He knew that Hugh Bigrel was an Oxford don, but he hadn't expected him to be as observant as he clearly was. In some ways it was a pity. He needed Bigrel's co-operation, but he didn't want him to become inquisitive. The police, he reflected, had made a bad blunder in not taking a routine statement from Bigrel, and arousing his suspicions.

Finally Fenwick said, 'No. He wasn't an ambassador. As you may know, American ambassadors are often political appointees. Samuel Thaxted was the next man down, a professional, a career officer, the guy who does all the work, which was probably why the poor devil was ripe for a heart attack. But he was a VIP all right.'

Hugh nodded. He wasn't really interested in Thaxted, or whatever his name was. He wondered why he had inquired about him. 'You were about to mention something else you wanted,' he prompted.

'Not wanted, exactly.' Fenwick had risen to his feet. 'It was merely something I felt I should tell you. Because Samuel Thaxted was a VIP the media are showing unnecessary interest in what happened, and for some reason this has annoyed the Americans. So I hope you'll agree that the least publicity, the better.'

Hugh stared at Fenwick. 'If you mean you don't want me to sell my story to the *News of the World* or the *Sun*, I assure you I won't. I've lost my wife and my son and my unborn child. The last thing I want is publicity of any kind.'

Dick Fenwick gave Bigrel a warm smile. 'I knew you'd say that, but I had to ask you. Goodbye, Mr Bigrel, and many thanks for bearing with me.'

He was gone, leaving Hugh with a vague sense of dissatisfaction. Fenwick's visit seemed to have been quite pointless.

Ten days later the Bigrels collected Hugh, and took him home. By then he was reasonably fit. His skin, though still sore and peppered with small cuts, was free from splinters of glass, and his cracked ribs were no more than an inconvenience. Mentally, however, he still had to come to terms with his loss.

The Bigrels lived in an ugly red-brick house in a quiet street between the Woodstock and Banbury Roads in North Oxford. John Bigrel, who was a master at King Edward's School, had bought it before Hugh was born, and apart from the time he was away at boarding school, Hugh had lived there all his life. It was a big house, and on Hugh's marriage to Lorna had been easily converted into two. The younger couple occupied the ground floor and the basement, which was at garden level at the back, while John and Helen had the two upper floors. With the housing shortage in Oxford being such as it was, this had proved an excellent arrangement, enabling the two couples to live together amicably, without intruding on each other's lives.

Until the moment when John Bigrel turned through the gates and parked on the short gravel drive in front of the house, Hugh had never thought of wanting to live anywhere else. But now, suddenly, he felt an overwhelming aversion to climbing the four steps that led to the front door. He got out of the car reluctantly.

As if she had sensed his feelings, Helen said, 'You'll be staying upstairs with us, Hugh, for a few days at least. I've fixed your old bedroom for you.' It was a statement, not a question.

'Thanks.'

The hall and stairs were neutral ground. All the doors were closed, so that Hugh had no opportunity to glimpse his old life with Lorna and David, and once upstairs he was in his parents' domain. He washed and tidied himself after the car journey. In the mirror over the basin he saw his face. With its criss-cross of scabs and lack-lustre eyes it looked far worse in this setting than it had in hospital.

He hadn't shut his bedroom door, and he heard his father call, 'Drinks when you're ready, Hugh.'

'Coming, Dad.'

Hugh rearranged his features into a more cheerful expression, and went along to the sitting-room. He took the whisky John had poured, and sat beside his mother on the sofa. 'I plan to go into College tomorrow,' he said.

'There's no hurry, darling, is there?' Helen asked.

'No. My lectures and tutorials have all been rearranged for this term, so I don't need to do any teaching. But it's very good of the College. I should at least put in an appearance, and say thank you in person.'

'Have you any other plans? I think you should get away in a little while and have a holiday. Why don't you go up to London, take in some plays, concerts, exhibitions?' John suggested. 'You could stay with Bill and Pam.' The Davidsons were Hugh's cousins. 'They'd love to have you.'

'I might.' Hugh sighed. 'But I don't feel much like enjoying myself at the moment, and first I should go and see Lorna's parents. I'm not looking forward to that, I must admit. I haven't heard a word from them.'

'Leave it for a time,' John advised. 'They're not taking it too well, I'm afraid – especially Mr Dawson. I think he was annoyed that so few people came to the funeral. We'd all been warned that the media would be there in force but, as we told you, there were just some local chaps.'

'And you must have noticed there's been very little in the papers,' Helen said. 'I can't think why that Mr Fenwick made such a fuss about the need to avoid publicity.'

'Fenwick's been to see you, too?'

'Oh yes, we quite liked him – and we agreed about avoiding the press.'

'You've not been bothered?' Hugh said.

'No.' Helen shook her head. 'There was one rather unpleasant character. He said he'd not been allowed to interview you, but he was sure you'd have told us everything and we wouldn't mind passing the story on to him. He hinted there'd be money in it for us.'

Hugh laughed as his mother's voice rose indignantly. 'Cheque-book journalism, that's called,' he said. 'What did you say to him?'

'I assured him that I'd have loved to co-operate, but unfortunately you'd hit your head in the accident, and didn't remember a thing, so there was no story to sell.'

'That must have annoyed him.'

'It didn't seem to. Oddly enough I got the impression he didn't mind in the least.'

There was no reason for the man to mind. He was Igor Galinov and, posing as a reporter, he had obtained the information that he knew would please his master. Indeed, the Colonel was delighted; clearly, Hugh Bigrel was no threat to him and could be set to one side. Though Krasnakov was not to know it, Dick Fenwick had made the same mistake.

FOUR

Hugh Bigrel was alone in the house. His father was at work and his mother had gone into Oxford to do some shopping. It was several days since he had left the hospital, but he had not yet been in the lower rooms, merely making do with the garments and other necessities that had been brought upstairs for him. Now he was beginning to want different clothes, and books and papers. He knew he could no longer postpone going into that part of the house he had shared with Lorna and David, and facing up to the memories the rooms would bring back to him.

He walked slowly down the stairs, across the hall and into the living-room. Superficially it looked the same as ever, but it was not. The well-worn carpet, the comfortable furniture, the television and the video recorder, all were there, but there were no toys on the floor, no books or magazines scattered around, no baby knitting tucked into the side of an armchair. The room was neat and tidy, too neat and tidy, like a little-used front parlour.

Hugh turned away. Quickly, not giving himself time to think, he went into the bedroom he had shared with Lorna. This was equally tidy, but a little more personal. Lorna's cosmetics still stood on the dressing table, with a small jewel box and the silver-backed brush and comb that had been a wedding present. Her clothes, he knew, would be hanging in the cupboards. He would have to phone her sisters and ask what, if any, of her things they could use; the rest could go to some charity.

He collected shirts, ties, underwear, a pair of slacks and a suit, and made a pile of them on the bed – the bed, he suddenly remembered, on which the unborn Gemma had been conceived, in a love-making that, like most of his life with Lorna, had become somewhat routine. But that had been as much his fault

39

as hers. On the whole it had been a good life. They had been happy together. He missed her.

Yet he had to admit it was David for whom he really ached. Standing next in his son's bedroom he looked around at the life-size fairy-tale characters stencilled on the walls, the building blocks piled in a corner, the shelf of carefully-chosen books that the boy had been learning to read, the big wooden box from which toys overflowed, and lastly the little white bed. Tucked under the duvet, their heads resting on the pillow, was a row of bears, David's most loved possessions. One of them, the largest, was missing. It had been destroyed, with its owner.

Tears were beginning to come into Hugh's eyes when he suddenly became aware that the doorbell was ringing loud and long, and probably not for the first time. He had been so lost in his thoughts that he had failed to notice the noise before. He hurried into the hall and opened the door.

'Mr Bigrel? Mr Hugh Bigrel?'

'Yes, I'm Hugh Bigrel. And you?'

'My name's Jay Ryan, Mr Bigrel. I should be very grateful if I might have a visit with you. I appreciate that it must be a painful subject, but – '

'I'm sorry, Miss Ryan. I don't give interviews.'

Hugh made to shut the front door, but found himself gazing down at a narrow foot, shod in an expensive calf shoe, that had surprisingly appeared in the narrowing gap. He looked up at the girl. She had short dark hair cut straight across her forehead, and eyes that matched the jade green suit she was wearing. If her expression had not been so determined he would have thought her attractive.

'Miss Ryan – '

'*Mrs* Ryan. And I'm not a journalist. I don't want to interview you. I want to talk with you. I hope perhaps you can help me.'

'Help you?' Help seemed to Hugh the last thing this audacious young woman needed. 'I don't understand.'

'I'll explain if you'll let me come in, Mr Bigrel. It's difficult on the doorstep.'

'All right.'

Partly because it was the simplest course of action, and partly because the girl had aroused his curiosity, Hugh threw back the door and gestured to her to go ahead of him into the living-room. As she passed him he smelt a sweet, fresh fragrance that could have been scent or soap and, close to her, he realized that she was older than he had at first thought, possibly in her early thirties.

'Sit down, Mrs Ryan,' he said in a businesslike manner, 'and tell me what you want.'

She sat where he indicated, folded one long leg over the other and put her shoulder bag on the floor beside her. Hugh noticed that the bag was made of the same expensive leather as her shoes. And, sitting across from her, he was suddenly conscious of his jeans and old sweater.

'First, Mr Bigrel, I want to say how sorry I am about your wife and son. I truly sympathize. You see, Sam Thaxted, the driver of the automobile that hit yours and killed your family, was my father. As you know, he was killed too.'

Hugh nodded. 'I'm sorry, very sorry, but – I still don't understand how I can help you.'

'Mr Bigrel, all I want is for you to tell me everything you can remember about that automobile accident – every detail, no matter how unimportant it may seem.'

Hugh hesitated. 'But what can I tell you that you don't already know?'

'Please! You were there. You saw it happen.'

Hugh thought fleetingly of Dick Fenwick, but this girl wasn't a journalist; as Thaxted's daughter she had a right to know what little he could tell her. But if she really was Thaxted's daughter, surely – She was looking at him angrily.

'What is it about Sam's death that makes everyone so unwilling to talk about it?' she demanded. 'They all clam up as soon as I ask the simplest question. I hoped that you at least would understand.' She stopped abruptly as if an idea had occurred to her, and began to fumble in her bag. Then she was standing over Hugh, hand outstretched. 'Here you are! If you don't believe me, here's my passport. Do you want a birth certificate, too, to prove I'm Sam's daughter, and not some goddam reporter?'

Hugh took the passport, though he no longer doubted her. He glanced at it, noted that her date of birth made her thirty-one and handed it back. He grinned ruefully.

'I'm satisfied, Mrs Ryan. My apologies.'

'Call me Jay.'

'Jay?'

'That's it. Jay, like the bird.'

The name suited her, Hugh thought. She was quick like a bird, bright-eyed and almost pugnacious. Resigned, he began to tell her about the accident. She stopped him almost at once.

'What other car? No one's mentioned a third car to me. Only Sam's and yours.' Hugh explained. 'And they didn't stop. That's strange.'

'Yes, it is. They must have seen and heard what happened. I don't know if the police have traced them. It's not illegal to leave the scene of an accident if you're just a witness, but I'd have thought that in these circumstances – But perhaps they were in a stolen car, or were desperately late for an appointment, or just didn't want to get involved. People don't always do what they should.'

'Of course not, but suppose the other car hit Sam's and that's why he swerved. It wouldn't stop then, would it?'

'I suppose not. But your father had a heart attack and – '

'No. I don't believe it!' Jay was vehement. 'Sure, I know people sometimes have heart attacks unexpectedly, but nearly always there's some warning, and Sam wouldn't have ignored a warning. He was a sensible man. He wasn't a fanatic, but he took good care of himself. He exercised. He ate the right foods. What's more, the US Government insists that all its senior officers have the most searching annual physicals.'

Hugh hesitated. 'There was a post-mortem, you know,' he said finally.

'Yes, but – Oh, God, maybe I'm being stupid, imagining things, only – ' Jay heaved a sigh. 'I simply don't trust anyone. I went as soon as I heard, but someone from the embassy had identified him, and I wasn't allowed to see him, not till next day, when he'd been all prettied up.' Her voice broke, and for a moment she couldn't go on. 'Then I was told a guy on a

42

motorbike had been the first on the scene, but later the same policeman said he'd been mistaken. A patrol car had arrived first. And somehow everyone seemed to be terribly evasive. But why? Why won't they come clean?'

'That I can't answer,' Hugh said. 'And I'm not even sure there's anything to "come clean" about. But I can tell you one thing. The chap on the motorbike *was* first there. I spoke to him, asked him to get help. I understand he phoned from the next service area.' He described the man with the foxy face, and added, 'I've no idea who he was. He didn't tell me his name. There was no reason why he should. And I know he didn't give a name when he phoned the emergency services.'

'Do you think he actually saw the accident?'

'I've no idea. He didn't say so.'

'Well, perhaps we could trace him.'

'Jay!' Hugh protested. 'Why should we want to trace him?'

'The police lied about him, didn't they?'

'It could easily have been a mistake, a misunderstanding.'

Jay said nothing. The seconds ticked by. Hugh remembered the guard outside his hospital room, and Fenwick's insistence that Thaxted was an important man and the Americans didn't want a lot of publicity about an unhappy accident. And someone, somehow, had been remarkably successful in quashing any except the most superficial reporting.

Hugh looked across at Sam Thaxted's daughter. If nothing else, she had aroused his curiosity. Perhaps, after all, Thaxted hadn't had a heart attack. Perhaps the accident had been his fault. It was unlikely he'd have been drunk so early in the morning, but he could have been suffering from a hangover and taken a drug, or just fallen asleep at the wheel. And, though it would hardly have caused an international incident, the tabloids could have turned out a nasty story about the American diplomat who had killed an innocent woman and child because of his negligence.

If the authorities had reached the conclusion that Thaxted had been to blame, Hugh could understand why it might be better for everyone if the truth were buried. He had no doubt that the

British would have co-operated with the Americans, either to return a favour or to store up goodwill for the future.

He said, 'Your father was an important man in the State Department?'

'He wasn't in State.'

'I thought he was a diplomat.'

'He had diplomatic status. Not the same thing. But he was important, yes. I know I'm breaking the rules by telling you, but he was one of the more senior people in the CIA.'

Hugh gave a low whistle. He didn't know much about the Central Intelligence Agency, though enough to discount half of what was written about it. Nevertheless, he supposed everyone would be more anxious to cover for a negligent or intransigent senior CIA man than for an ordinary diplomat. And if it had been Thaxted's fault that David and Lorna were dead, he wanted to know.

Jay was saying, ' – called me at the weekend to say he'd be over in the UK and he'd be in touch, though he'd got some urgent business to attend to first. He was on an open line, of course, and he didn't even hint at what the business might be – not that I'd have expected him to. Anyway, I can't guess what he was doing on that stretch of the freeway early in the morning.'

Hugh had scarcely been listening. He had been recalling the foxy face he'd seen peering through his shattered windscreen. It was vivid in his memory. Had he been an artist he could have reproduced it. 'It might be possible to trace him,' he murmured, unaware that he spoke aloud.

'What? Oh, the guy on the motorbike. Yes, I wish it were, but how to set about it? It's no use asking the police or anyone like that. The people at my embassy have been kind, but they seem to be convinced it *was* a heart attack. And no one admits to knowing what Sam was doing in England. I've asked people – those who should have known – but they swear they don't. As for you Brits – ' Jay shrugged.

'I wasn't thinking of consulting the authorities,' Hugh said slowly. 'I was wondering about putting an advert in the nationals and a few of the local papers. Granted, Foxy-face may never see it, but there's at least some chance it could come to his attention.

And, if it does, the offer of a reward could lure him. My impression was that he's a somewhat shifty character, who wouldn't say no to an easily-earned five hundred pounds.'

Jay brightened. 'An ad! That's a great idea. We'll share the cost. Do you have some paper? We can decide on the wording at once. Then we must make a list of newspapers and divide them between us.'

Hugh smiled to himself at her enthusiasm. He wondered if she would be so eager if it occurred to her that they might be seeking a witness to her father's insobriety. What Hugh himself didn't realize, until John Bigrel pointed it out to him later, was that Mrs Jay Ryan had neatly involved him in her affairs.

FIVE

'I thought you should see this, sir.'

Dick Fenwick glanced at the newspaper cutting that had been put on the desk in front of him. It was a column of small advertisements from the *Daily Mail*. One, which was prominent in bold type, had been circled in red for his attention.

'A reward of up to £500 is offered for information
from the motorcyclist who stopped at the scene of an
accident between Swindon and Bristol on the M4 on the
morning of the first Monday in April, and later
telephoned for help. In the first instance, the
said motorcyclist should ring the number below.'

Fenwick cursed softly. 'You've checked the phone number, of course?'

'Yes, sir. It's an Oxford number, belonging to J. H. W. Bigrel at an address in North Oxford.'

'As we might have guessed.' Fenwick was sardonic. 'Did it appear anywhere else?'

'In *The Times* and the *Telegraph* and the *Oxford Mail*, of the ones I've been able to check so far, sir. The *Daily Mail* was the first place I noticed it. I suspect it's in the local papers between Swindon and Bristol, too, though.'

'Well, I can't imagine our chummy reading the quality papers, but, if Bigrel's spared no expense, he could easily light on it somewhere. And five hundred quid is not to be sneezed at, certainly not by the likes of Frank Worth. He might be tempted. I'd better go and have another word with him.'

It was a surprisingly warm day for early summer. Central London was hot and stuffy and full of petrol fumes, and Fenwick was glad of an excuse to get out of his office. Once he was free of the worst of the traffic, he opened the sunroof of his car and let the wind blow through his thinning hair. He thought about Hugh Bigrel – and Sam Thaxted.

He had hoped Thaxted's death would be the end of the matter. The 'cousins' – the Yanks – had been completely co-operative, accepting the post-mortem's judgement that the car crash had been the result of their man's heart attack, and happy to have no unpleasant publicity about the incident. It was clear, at least to Fenwick, that Thaxted had been acting on his own, waiting to confirm his suspicions before confiding in anyone. So anything Thaxted had learnt or guessed about Sir Rupert Canville, the late British High Commissioner to Canada, had, with luck, died with the American.

And it didn't look as if the Russians were going to cause any trouble, either. True, they were unpredictable, but with the High Commissioner's suicide they seemed to be prepared to cut their losses. Certainly there had been no attempt to claim Canville as their agent. On the contrary, they seemed as eager as the Brits to cover for him. This made Fenwick suspect that Canville had been more important to the KGB than they wanted anyone to think. But for the moment that was irrelevant.

In fact, things had looked rosy, until Hugh Bigrel had unexpectedly started to get curious. Why? Fenwick asked himself. Something must have started Bigrel down this path – or someone. Fenwick wondered if the motivating force could be Sam Thaxted's daughter. Whatever or whoever, Bigrel's inter-vention was a damned nuisance, and the man must be stopped in his tracks.

But the first priority must be to deal with Frank Worth. Worth kept a garage of sorts in Cowley, on the outskirts of Oxford. It was a shabby establishment, a large shed with a corrugated-iron roof, fly-specked cracked windows covered with mouldering posters, and a couple of petrol pumps in a dusty forecourt. The place was full of used cars in various stages of dilapidation, most of them looking as if they would never be roadworthy again. The youth who worked for Worth was tinkering with one such vehicle in front of the shed as Fenwick drove up.

'Hey, boss!' he called to Worth, recognizing Fenwick from his previous visit. 'You've got trouble.'

He hadn't bothered to lower his voice, and Fenwick grinned savagely, wondering what Worth had told the youth. 'You're wasting your breath, sonny,' he said, pushing past him and disappearing into the rear of the premises.

He found Worth, as he had expected, in his so-called office, a grubby plywood shack of a room at the back of the shed, with a desk, a couple of chairs, some shelves stuffed with car accessories and a telephone. Worth had his feet up on the desk, and made no effort to move when Fenwick came in. Fenwick pulled up the second chair, turned its back to Worth and sat on it, astride, as if it were a horse. He looked Worth in the eye, and said nothing.

'What's it now?' Worth was at last forced to make the opening move. 'I've done nothing. I've never done nothing. I saw a pile-up beside a motorway and, like a good citizen, I phoned for help. That's all.'

'After you'd had a good look round to see if you could sniff out anything useful,' Fenwick replied scornfully. 'But you sniffed out more than you bargained for, didn't you?'

'So what? I told you about it. I didn't have to do that.'

'You didn't volunteer a damned thing. We had to expend a lot of effort on tracking you down. If it hadn't been for that observant girl waiting for you to finish using the phone at the service area, we might never have found you.'

'Well, you did find me, worse luck. Anyway, we went through all this last time you were here, threatening me you'd ruin my business if I didn't keep my trap shut.'

'And have you kept your mouth shut, Worth?'

'Yes, I bloody well have. So what you're doing here again beats me.'

'All I want is reassurance that you're going to keep it shut.'

'Why shouldn't I?'

Fenwick didn't answer at once. In spite of his apparent superiority, his hold over Frank Worth was minimal. From the

48

appearance of the garage, and Worth's shifty expression, he had guessed on his first visit that the business wouldn't bear a close examination, and Worth's reaction to his threats of investigation and exposure had confirmed his supicions. Nevertheless, he knew that his hand remained weak, and he had to play it carefully.

'Why indeed?' Fenwick said, and coughed to hide his sudden jubilation. He had just realized that Worth's feet were resting on a copy of the *Daily Mail*, and that they hadn't budged for the last five minutes. There was every chance Worth had seen the advertisement.

'Why indeed?' Fenwick repeated. 'What about five hundred quid for two minutes' conversation with a certain phone number?'

'I haven't! I swear it! I haven't said a single word to Bigrel, or anyone else. Nor would I. There was no need for you to come threatening me again – '

'Bigrel!' Fenwick interrupted. 'So you *have* called the number. Otherwise how do you know it's Bigrel's?'

'Oh, for God's sake. Look at the advert. It's an Oxford phone code, so I guessed it was him. I knew his name from the papers. All I had to do was check in the book.' He gestured to the telephone directory on the desk beside him. 'But I swear I haven't called him.'

Worth had removed his feet from the desk, and his voice rose in a high-pitched whine. His foxy face was doing its best to appear anxious and innocent. Fenwick didn't trust him, but there was little he could do about it. However, he rose from his chair in one lazy movement, then leant across the desk, seized Worth by the shoulders, and shook him hard.

'God help you if you utter that single word to anyone,' he said.

Hugh Bigrel's advertisement, set by chance at the top of the Personal Announcements column in *The Times*, had also caught Viktor Krasnakov's eye. It was the first Krasnakov had heard of a motorcyclist at the scene of Sam Thaxted's death, though he had read all the news he could find about the accident. He was at once alarmed by this unexpected threat.

Unlike Dick Fenwick, who had known where to find Frank Worth, Krasnakov had nothing to go on but the phone number in the advertisement. This he traced to the Bigrels without difficulty, but that fact by itself was of little help. He could think of no way to make contact with the wretched motorcyclist before the man got in touch with Bigrel.

Indeed, there was only one thing he could do. It would be highly unsatisfactory, but there was no alternative. He could put Bigrel under surveillance, in the hope that Bigrel would lead him to the motorcyclist. Then he could squeeze the truth out of the man, and at least discover what damage, if any, had been done. Forewarned, he might be able to limit it.

But this was the UK, not the Soviet Union. Really efficient round-the-clock surveillance took a lot of officers and vehicles, and the resources were not readily available in England – especially outside London and for any length of time. Krasnakov knew that the best he could do at short notice was arrange for Galinov and himself to take turns keeping an eye on the Bigrels' house, though they couldn't hope to keep even this inefficient operation going for more than two or three days. They must rely on luck, and the fact that Bigrel was unlikely to suspect any watchers.

He drove down to Oxford with Galinov, found the Bigrels' house, and parked the car in a side street almost opposite the Bigrels' drive. They organized themselves into twelve-hour shifts. The officer not on watch could make use of a small safe house the KGB maintained in the Abingdon Road.

It was a frustrating time for them, to say the least, as well as dangerous. Really, they should have made arrangements to use a different car every day, in case the constant presence of the same vehicle became noticed by any passer-by or police patrol. But they were lucky. The local residents seemed totally incurious, and they saw no sign of the authorities.

As far as the Bigrels were concerned, John kept regular hours, but Helen was constantly coming and going in her Mini, and there were frequent visitors. Hugh appeared once in the drive to help his mother with her shopping, but otherwise was not seen.

After three days the Russians, tired and bored, were on the point of giving up. Krasnakov was beginning to fear that the whole exercise had been a total waste of effort, but he was an obstinate man. 'One more day,' he said to Galinov as they changed places, 'then we return to London.'

Hugh Bigrel, waiting for the phone to ring, had been equally frustrated. Nothing happened. Jay had gone back to London, where she worked in a Bond Street dress shop that she partly owned. She called him each evening and, when after three days there was no response to the advertisements, suggested they should be repeated. Hugh insisted on leaving it; he had a vague feeling – he couldn't say why – that too great an emphasis on their search for information might be counter-productive.

On the morning of the fourth day Frank Worth telephoned. Helen answered the phone, and he asked to speak to Hugh Bigrel. He refused to give a name, but waited, breathing heavily, till he heard Hugh's voice.

He said gruffly, 'Saw your advert about a reward for information on the car crash. I can provide it. I'm the bloke on the motorbike. But the money's not enough. I've been warned to keep my mouth shut – or else. I need more to make it worth my while. Much more. At least double.'

Hugh hid his excitement. 'The money's negotiable,' he said coldly. 'It'll all depend on the value of your information to me. But first you'll have to prove you are who you say you are.'

'I'm the motorcyclist all right. I saw you, spoke to you. You were jammed up in the driver's seat, and you couldn't get out because the doors were stuck. Your wife had been thrown through the windscreen. Your boy was dead in the back. Am I right? Is that enough for you, Mr Bigrel?'

'No. You could have read all that in one of the newspapers.'

'But I didn't, see. I was there.' Worth sounded indignant. 'Listen, I was wearing a yellow crash helmet. You remember

51

that? And I've a thin face, sallow-like, and a pointed nose. None of that was in the papers, was it?'

'Okay,' Hugh agreed. 'You've convinced me, Mr – er?'

'You can call me Frank. Now, about the money. A grand?'

'A thousand! I offered five hundred.'

'It's not enough. I told you. I'm taking a hell of a risk in contacting you. There's this sodding guy threatening to ruin my business, or worse, if I don't keep my lip buttoned.'

At Hugh's insistence, Worth gave a brief description of the 'sodding guy'. It wasn't flattering, but it was clear enough for Hugh to be reasonably sure that Dick Fenwick was the man in question. And if Fenwick were prepared to threaten Foxy-face to keep him quiet, his information was clearly worth the money.

'I'll up it to six hundred, and that's final,' he said.

'Done. But on my terms. Now, this is what you do.'

Hugh listened. Then he laughed. 'Don't be a fool, Frank. And don't take me for one. Do you really expect me to drop off a bundle of notes with no more than a vague hope of getting some valuable news in exchange?'

'Yes. You must, guv. It's the only way.'

'Why on earth should I trust you?'

'Two reasons. One, you trusted me to get help.when you were stuck in that car, and I did. And two, you've no option. It's take it or leave it, guv. Which?'

Hugh had been thinking quickly. The loss of the money would be irritating, but not disastrous, and he had no wish to frighten Foxy off completely. Nevertheless . . .

Bigrel said, 'I'll take it, Frank, but there's something you should know. This guy who's been threatening you. I've recognized him from your description. If you try to trick me, I'll be in touch with him. Fair enough?'

There was a long silence. Hugh prayed that Foxy wasn't about to hang up. Then he heard, 'Fair enough, Mr Bigrel,' before the line went dead.

Krasnakov and Galinov sat in their car opposite the Bigrels' drive. Their bags were in the boot. They intended to wait together until evening, and then abandon their vigil and return to London. They had little hope that anything would happen in the last few hours. Galinov, who had been on watch all the previous night, was dozing over the wheel.

It was five o'clock in the afternoon. Krasnakov was on the point of waking Galinov and abandoning the vigil when the Bigrels' front door opened. Hugh Bigrel came out, carrying a thick brown envelope. Krasnakov could see it clearly.

Helen's Mini was standing in the drive. Hugh Bigrel ignored it. He set off at a brisk pace, turning right out of the gate towards the Woodstock Road, and, when he reached it, left towards the centre of Oxford, crossing the road to the right-hand pavement.

At a respectable distance behind him, Galinov drove slowly. This wasn't easy on such a main thoroughfare. Southbound traffic on the Woodstock Road was heavy, even though most people were leaving the city at that time of day as shops and offices closed. A bus driver hooted angrily and a couple of cyclists shook their fists at the Russians when they were forced to stop abruptly. Hugh Bigrel walked on.

Then, without warning, when he had nearly reached St Giles' and was almost past the gates of the Roman Catholic church of St Aloysius, Bigrel turned sharply into its forecourt. Nonplussed, the Russians parked on the opposite side of the road, and waited. There seemed no reason why Bigrel should have gone into the church. Certainly it was not to consult a priest or say his prayers, because within a minute he emerged again and set off northwards in the direction of his home. But he was no longer carrying the brown envelope.

A few moments later a man came out of the church. He was wearing tight jeans and a leather jacket. As he crossed the road towards them, Krasnakov saw that there was a large bulge over his heart, and he guessed at once that it represented Bigrel's brown envelope. Though the Russians couldn't know it, this was Frank Worth.

Worth crossed the road to where a small van was parked illegally on a yellow line. Its back doors were open, and the chances were that a traffic warden would assume the owner was loading or unloading. He slammed the doors, got into the van and drove off.

Galinov had his engine running, but the lights had changed further along St Giles', and a sudden flow of traffic obstructed him. He manoeuvred past a couple of cars, a lumbering bus, a truck and a bevy of bicycles. The last thing he wanted was an accident, however minor, but he dared not lose sight of his quarry. At last he managed to jump a red light, and succeeded in catching up with the van.

Worth drove at a leisurely pace. He had slipped a cassette into place and sang, loudly and discordantly, with his favourite pop star, as he contemplated what he would do with the money in his pocket. The van, which would never have passed a Ministry of Transport inspection, rattled around him. He reached his garage, left the van in the forecourt and went along to his office, quite unaware that he had been followed.

He was alone on the premises, as the youth who worked for him had left for the day. He slipped off his jacket, took out the envelope, and made himself comfortable at his desk. Then he counted the money, six hundred pounds in small notes, nothing larger than a tenner and no sequence of numbers – just as ordered. He grinned with satisfaction; Bigrel had followed his instructions. Now he must do his part or there could be trouble, bad trouble, if Bigrel carried out his threat to set the security guy on him. Frank Worth reached for the telephone.

Hugh picked up his receiver immediately. 'Bigrel here,' he said, hoping but not really expecting that it would be the call he was awaiting. He had already been disappointed when his cousin, Bill Davidson, had phoned a few minutes before; Bill had got off the line quickly, thank God.

Now, however, it was 'Frank', foxy 'Frank'. Hugh recognized the voice at once.

'Mr Bigrel, thanks for the cash. It's okay. Now, you'll forget you ever heard of me? You won't squeal?'

'Of course not. All I want is the information I've paid for.'

'All right. All right. Here it is. I was some way behind you. I didn't actually see the accident happen, but – '

Worth spoke rapidly. Then, in the middle of a sentence, his words tailed away. A strange voice said something unintelligible. There was a crash, as if a chair had been knocked over, and a noise in Hugh's eardrum that made him wince. He guessed that Foxy had dropped his receiver. Obviously at least one other person had come into the office. There were more obscure noises, interspersed with sobs. Hugh thought he heard Fenwick's name. Then someone screamed. Hugh strained to hear. He yearned to know what was happening. All the sounds suggested a bitter argument, a fight, a beating-up. But why? Who? Questions streamed through Hugh's mind. There were no answers.

Suddenly Hugh heard a particularly loud crash, followed by a dull thud as if someone had fallen to the ground. Then silence. A moment later, voices muttering angrily, or so it seemed to Hugh. He couldn't catch what was being said, but he had an impression that it was not in English.

Next came a sharp click. The line hummed gently, and Hugh realized that the receiver had been replaced, and he had been cut off from the scene to which he had been listening. Biting his lower lip, he slowly replaced his own receiver.

Hugh knew that the next thing he must do was to get in touch with Jay Ryan, and tell her what he had learnt about her father from Foxy. But first he needed time to absorb the information, and since he had listened to those shaking sounds of violence he was appalled by the implications.

Krasnakov cursed, and cursed again. The operation had gone wrong. The little shit had been more obstinate in his denials than one would have expected. Then, when he was about to break, Galinov had given him that extra softening blow, and he had fallen, hitting his temple on the corner of the desk. Now there was no doubt he was dead, before they had extracted any information from him.

And there was worse. Krasnakov knew he had no one to

blame but himself. He should have realized that the telephone receiver was dangling loose. In his mind he ran through what had been said since he and Galinov had burst into the grimy little office. There had been threats, but no names had been mentioned, except perhaps that of Fenwick, which was ironic.

No, none of that was important. It had all been in English. Whoever was at the other end of the line, and whatever he may have heard up to that point, it didn't matter. But when the stupid little fool had got himself killed, in their dismay he and Galinov had spoken a few words of Russian. That had been a bad mistake. He wanted no connection between himself or the KGB and the death of Samuel Thaxted.

'Take the money,' he ordered. 'Make it look like a break-in. Then let's get out.'

SIX

Hugh could hear Jay's telephone ringing in her flat off Sloane Square. It rang and rang, but there was no answer.

Next he tried the dress shop. It was not yet seven o'clock and Jay had said that sometimes she worked late. Again he let the phone ring, and was about to hang up, thinking she might be on her way home, when a woman's voice answered peremptorily, 'Yes?'

'May I speak to Mrs Ryan, please?'

'She's not here. She won't be here till Monday.'

'I see. Do you know if she'll be at home later? I have tried her flat, but there was no reply.'

'She's gone into the country for the weekend.'

'Oh.' Hugh frowned. 'Look, I'm sorry to be a nuisance, but it *is* urgent. Could you give me her number?'

'I don't have it. And I'm not sure I'd give it to you if I did. Anyway, I don't know where she's gone. She never bothers to tell me. So I can't help.'

'I see,' Hugh said again. 'Well, thank you anyway.' He found the connection had been broken before he stopped speaking.

Hugh banged down his receiver. When he had spoken to Jay the previous evening she hadn't mentioned that she was leaving London. He told himself there was no reason for her to do so. After all, they had more or less agreed to cut their losses, and forget the foxy-faced man. Nevertheless, he thought she should have let him know, if only out of courtesy. He felt justifiably annoyed.

Suddenly the phone rang and, certain it was Jay, Hugh's spirits rose. He seized the receiver and said, 'Hello.' But it was not Jay and, as he listened to Dora, his sister-in-law, he was surprised at the strength of his disappointment.

57

'You will come, won't you, Hugh? Mum and Dad are a bit peeved you've not been down to see them before. Of course they realize you had to recover from your injuries, but you are better now, aren't you? It would be so nice if – '

Hugh was barely listening; he knew from experience that both Lorna's sisters were apt to talk too much. And he was reproaching himself for not having remembered that it would have been Lorna's birthday on Sunday. This was just the kind of lapse the Dawsons would consider unforgivable. He knew too that he should have visited them ages ago. He had telephoned twice, but the calls had not been fruitful. On each occasion his mother-in-law had dissolved into tears and Mr Dawson, saying a curt goodbye, had clearly blamed Hugh for upsetting his wife, if not for the death of his daughter and grandchild.

'Hugh! Hugh, are you there?'

'Yes, I'm here, Dora.'

'Ah, I thought we'd been cut off. Then you will come down this weekend?'

There was a plaintive note in his sister-in-law's voice, and Hugh Bigrel drew a deep breath. Visiting the Dawsons would undoubtedly be an ordeal, but it had to be faced. 'All right,' he said. 'I'll drive down tomorrow as soon as I can. I'll borrow my father's car.' He still had not bought a replacement for his own. 'I expect I'll be there in time for tea.'

In fact, he failed to arrive until six o'clock in the evening. He was greeted with tears from Mrs Dawson, who gave her husband a reproachful look when he said, 'Well, you've taken your time deciding to come to see us.' And there were more tears when he produced those of Lorna's possessions for which her family had asked.

However, a sherry for Mrs Dawson and a whisky for the two men helped to soften the atmosphere, and supper was a comparatively cheerful meal. The Dawsons talked politics; Tom Dawson was a right-wing Tory, who was anxious to bring back the birch. Mrs Dawson supported his views with items of local news and gossip. Hugh, who secretly disagreed with almost every opinion they expressed, did his best to avoid controversy.

After supper, while Mrs Dawson cleared the table, her

husband took Hugh into the small room, known as the 'snug', that served as his private territory. He unlocked a drawer in a cabinet and brought out what Hugh at first thought was a stamp album. Then, as Dawson riffled through the pages, he saw that it was a scrapbook, a collection of newspaper cuttings.

'I've not shown this to Lorna's mother, Hugh. I thought it would upset her. But you might like to look through it while I go and stretch my legs.'

'Thanks,' Hugh said automatically, finding the book pressed into his hands.

Alone, he turned the pages slowly. To his dismay, he found that Tom Dawson had bought every available newspaper, and collected every possible press reference to the accident. Altogether they didn't amount to much. There were a few columns of print, but most of the cuttings consisted of photographs, nearly all old. Some of the photographs had clearly been provided by the Dawsons themselves. There was, for instance, a print of Lorna in her wedding dress, another of Lorna with David in her arms, and one of David holding his bear; this snap had been taken on their last family visit to the Dawsons, and Hugh had never seen it before. He felt tears prick his eyes, and only curiosity prevented him from closing the book there and then.

But he continued to look and read, though quite cursorily. The text was of little interest. The press had obviously been reduced to making much of the fact that, although David had not been saved by his special baby seat, Lorna might have survived if she had been wearing her seat belt. There was also a plea for stronger barriers between lanes on motorways. Nowhere was there the faintest hint that it had been other than an accident.

Hugh found himself staring at two photographs, juxtaposed by Tom Dawson on facing pages of his scrapbook. One was of Samuel Thaxted, the other of Jay. In their physical appearance, father and daughter were not alike, but their steady gazes and the tilt of their chins suggested that their characters might not have been dissimilar. Hugh guessed that they had shared a lively intelligence, toughness of mind and tenacity of purpose.

He turned the page. He was almost at the end of the book, which was in no sort of chronological order, and found a few more photographs of Jay. One in particular caught his attention, and he read the caption: 'Mrs Ryan leaving Buckingham Palace, where she received from Her Majesty the Queen the Distinguished Service Order awarded posthumously to her late husband, Major Patrick Ryan, killed in the Falklands War.'

Poor Jay, Hugh thought. She had corrected him when he called her 'Miss', but she hadn't told him that she was a widow. He realized that, though he felt he knew Jay Ryan quite well, there was a great deal still to be learnt about her.

Hugh shut the scrapbook, but continued to sit holding it in his hands. He hadn't bothered to read any newspapers until he had been in the hospital for several days, and by then the deaths of Lorna and little David – even of the VIP Samuel Thaxted – had become stale news. Before he had learnt what Foxy Frank had had to tell him, and had seen the cuttings that Tom Dawson had so carefully collected, he had not realized what a magnificent deception operation Fenwick had accomplished.

He felt anger well up in him and he wondered, not for the first time, how Jay Ryan would react to the truth about her father's death – or what he could now tell her of the truth.

Hugh slept badly in the double bed that he had last shared with Lorna. Towards morning, however, he fell into a deep sleep from which he woke, late and unrefreshed. He hurried to wash and dress, and went downstairs. Mrs Dawson was cooking at the stove and Tom Dawson, a Sunday newspaper propped up in front of him, was sitting at the breakfast table at one end of the kitchen.

'Nice part of the country you live in.' Dawson greeted Hugh without preamble. 'Another of those senseless murders. What's the point of breaking into a shabby old garage? They might have known there'd be nothing worth stealing. The kid who worked there said the boss never left more than ten pounds in the till. Think of losing your life for ten pounds.'

'This happened in Oxford?' Hugh tried to sound interested.

He began to eat the bacon and eggs that Mrs Dawson had put in front of him.

'Yes. Cowley. That's a suburb of Oxford, isn't it?' Tom Dawson reached for the toast. 'And why kill the poor chap? Why not just take the money? No, they beat up this wretched – what's his name – Frank Worth, it says here, and left him for dead. It's violence for the sake of violence, that's what it is.'

Hugh had stopped eating. He pushed a piece of bacon around his plate, feeling sick. He told himself that it couldn't be the foxy-faced man; there were probably thousands of men living in and around Oxford called Frank. But he knew the argument was totally unconvincing, especially as he recalled the sounds and the scream he had heard on the telephone.

'Is there a picture of the chap?' he asked. 'I sometimes use a garage in Cowley, but I doubt if it's the same one.'

Tom Dawson passed the newspaper across the table, folded so that Hugh could see the photograph at a glance. It was not a good likeness, but there was no doubt. Frank Worth, who had been beaten up and left dead or dying, was Foxy, the man to whom he had been speaking seconds before the attack had taken place, the man whose death he had probably overheard, the man to whom he had given six hundred pounds. There was no mention of that money. Presumably the thieves had taken it. Thieves?

Hugh returned the paper thoughtfully. 'No. That's not the chap I go to. I've never seen this one.' He lied glibly, even while his mind was racing.

Thieves they might have been, but not ordinary criminals or hoodlums. Fenwick? Surely not. Fenwick had threatened Frank Worth, but Fenwick wasn't a thug. Or was he? Yet, if not Fenwick, who? Had he only imagined that the 'thieves' had spoken a language that he hadn't been able to identify? He could easily be mistaken about that, for the voices had been distorted by the telephone, presumably dangling off its rest. And, if about that, why not about almost everything? Foxy could have been seen through a window counting his ill-gotten gains, and his death be incidental to a casual break-in. After all, coincidences did happen.

Tom Dawson grunted. He had lost interest, having found another more titillating story in his paper.

Hugh forced himself to finish his breakfast, and wondered how he was going to get through the rest of the day, Lorna's birthday, as Mrs Dawson had already needlessly reminded him more than once. He had told the Dawsons that he had to be back home early Monday morning, and so would have to leave immediately after Sunday lunch, but that still left many hours to be endured.

In the end, they passed more quickly than he had expected. Tom Dawson drove him to the local cemetery where Lorna and David had been buried. The Dawsons had wanted Lorna 'brought home' and Hugh had not objected. The two men put flowers, picked from the Dawsons' garden, on the grave. Mrs Dawson had refused to accompany them, saying that she would certainly break down, but it was Tom Dawson who made a choking sound and walked off to be by himself.

For Hugh too it was an emotional moment. Because he had not been to the funeral this was his goodbye to Lorna and David and, he sensed, to a whole chapter of his life. He doubted whether he would ever visit the Dawsons or come here again. If David had lived it would have been different; the Dawsons would have been the boy's grandparents. As it was, he couldn't blame them for wishing, as he felt they did, that he had been killed instead of Lorna.

He turned away from the graves and went to join Tom Dawson, who was waiting by the cemetery gate. They nodded at each other in an attempt at shared sympathy, and walked in silence to their car.

As Mr Dawson did up his seat belt, he said, 'I suppose you knew the Yank – Samuel Thaxted – who killed my Lorna.'

'Knew him?' Hugh grimaced at the absurdity of the question. 'No, of course not. How should I have known him?'

Tom Dawson shrugged. 'I thought you might have met in Ottawa. Lorna said you had all sorts of high-powered friends there, like that top British chap Canville, who got drowned in one of the lakes near the place.'

'No, I – ' It seemed pointless to explain about his casual

acquaintance with the High Commissioner. But he felt it important to make it clear that he had never had anything to do with
Thaxted. He said, 'Samuel Thaxted was an American, Tom, not
a Canadian. He lived in Washington, as far as I know, and I'd
have had no occasion to meet him. I've never been there.'

'I know he was an American. Don't take me for a fool, Hugh.'
Tom Dawson spoke sharply. 'I may not be as clever as you are,
but I'm not stupid. Thaxted worked at the American Embassy
in Ottawa. It said so in the papers. He was a diplomat. He must
have known your man Canville, so you could easily have met
him when you were in Canada.'

Not easily, Hugh thought. But he said, 'I'm sorry. I had no
idea that Thaxted had been in Ottawa.'

'Then you can't have looked at my scrapbook very carefully,
can you?' Tom Dawson said, and hooted viciously at a car that
had overtaken him.

Hugh made no reply. He was thinking how odd it was that on
a visit to the Dawsons he should have learnt so much about
Samuel Thaxted and his daughter, Jay Ryan.

Sunday lunch, to which Lorna's sisters and their husbands came
habitually, often with one or more of their children, had
stretched into the late afternoon. By the time Hugh had said his
farewells and left the Dawsons' house the sky was dark, and rain
had begun to fall. At its best, it was a long drive home for Hugh,
and this evening, with poor weather, heavy traffic after the
weekend and a lengthy and poorly-signposted diversion, it
required a concentrated effort. Hugh was glad to reach Oxford.

Emotionally and physically exhausted, he heaved a sigh of
relief as he turned into his own drive. He looked forward to a
drink, some supper, a bath and bed. Then he saw that a strange
car was parked in front of the garage, and a light was shining
from a ground-floor window. Taking his bag, he carefully let
himself into the house, and even more carefully opened the
living-room door.

'Good evening, Mr Bigrel.'

'You!' Hugh said in disgust.

Dick Fenwick grinned sardonically. 'Yes, it's me. Your mother was kind enough to say I might wait for you here.'

'Look, I've been driving for hours, I'm tired, and – '

'What I have to say won't take long.'

Hugh collapsed into an armchair. 'All right. Go ahead. What the hell d'you want?'

'Mr Bigrel, you put an advertisement in certain newspapers and Frank Worth answered it, though I had warned him not to.'

'Threatened him, you mean.'

'If you like. Anyway, it was for his own good. You know he's dead?'

Hugh nodded. 'I saw it in this morning's paper.'

'Mr Bigrel, if you hadn't advertised for information about that accident, Worth would be alive now.'

Hugh was not prepared to accept this accusation without question. 'If you'd told me the truth about Samuel Thaxted's death I certainly wouldn't have advertised,' he said. Then, more angrily, 'Fenwick, if my wife and child were killed because of some kind of – of gang warfare, don't you think I've got some right to know about it?'

'It was better that you didn't.'

'Better for whom?'

'Better for you, of course, you fool! Earlier, your involvement was incidental – coincidental, even. That's no longer true. You've chosen to get mixed up in something you know nothing about – international affairs – espionage and counter-espionage, if you want to be dramatic about it. And that sort of thing can be just as rough as any gang warfare, and decidedly bad for your health.'

Fenwick was now speaking softly. 'To my knowledge three people, not counting your wife and son, have already died because of this affair. I don't want you or Mrs Ryan to make a fourth – or a fourth and a fifth, maybe. So, keep out!'

'Is that a threat or a warning?'

'If you were wise, Mr Bigrel, you'd take it as both.'

SEVEN

'Shot?' said Jay Ryan. 'Hugh, are you seriously telling me that my father was shot, and that's why he lost control of his car and crashed into you?' Clearly she was shaken by the news, but less so than he had feared.

'Yes, I am. That's what Frank Worth told me,' Hugh replied.

They were in Jay's flat off Sloane Square. Hugh had decided that there were some stories that couldn't be recounted on the telephone, and had suggested he should come up to London. Jay had invited him to supper, and they were in her sitting-room having drinks before the meal. The room, Hugh thought, was not unlike its owner. It was bright and functional, but expensively, if sparsely, furnished.

Jay put down her glass. 'Did you believe him?' she asked slowly, as if giving herself time to examine and analyse the implications of the information she had just received.

'Yes.' There was no hesitation in Hugh's reply. 'I'd swear Worth wasn't lying. Besides, Fenwick as good as admitted the same thing. And – and there was something else I remembered that I haven't mentioned to anyone. I heard nothing at the time, but I believe that David, my son, did. He suddenly shouted, "Bang!" before I saw your father's car swerve across the reservation. I know that's hardly evidence, but – '

He paused, and they were both silent, Hugh recalling those dreadful seconds, Jay busy with thoughts of her father. Then she nodded her acceptance, stood up, went to Hugh and took his hand for a moment in a gesture of sympathy. She picked up his glass and turned to refill it. Her eyes were bright with unshed tears.

Her back to him, she said, 'This guy, Fenwick, is right, Hugh. To go on making inquiries, stirring the pot, could be

65

dangerous, very dangerous. Are you sure it wouldn't be better to try to forget the whole thing?'

Hugh frowned. 'Forget it all? No. I don't want to do that. I don't think I could, now. It's clear to me that, whatever you may have been told, your father came over to the UK on some kind of mission. It went wrong, and British security – Fenwick and his mob, whatever they're called – are trying to cover up for the sake of the CIA.'

Jay was shaking her head in disagreement. She put Hugh's drink on the table beside him, and returned to her chair. Hugh paid no attention to her obvious disbelief in his statement, but continued, 'And I don't see why they should get away with it. Okay, I can understand they don't want a lot of publicity, but I think they owe you and me the truth, instead of their damned threats. At least we should get some explanation of why the man who caused the so-called accident shouldn't be found and brought to justice.'

Hugh leant forward in his chair. 'Jay, you were right when you maintained your father didn't have a heart attack. He wasn't responsible in any way, as I must admit I once half-suspected. He was deliberately killed. Aren't you concerned any more? Why on earth do you suddenly want to forget all about it?'

'It's not like that.' Jay sighed. 'Hugh, honey, you don't understand.'

'What don't I understand?'

'For one thing, you seem to have no idea how difficult it is to shoot even a static object from a moving vehicle. And, if the target's also moving, it's vastly more difficult. Don't you see what that means? It means there's every chance that whoever killed Sam was a trained killer – a professional assassin – and that alters the situation. As I said, I never believed Sam had a heart attack, but I thought the driver of the other car might have flicked Sam's car – nudged it – perhaps accidentally, perhaps as a kind of deliberate stupidity and, because he was an important Brit and the result was so horrendous, the man was being protected. Now I know better – and I may not show it, but I'm scared. Hugh, you should be, too. Let's not forget that Foxy Worth was also killed.'

Hugh regarded Jay Ryan dubiously. His main response to what she had said was irritation. He was annoyed with himself that he had been so much less perceptive than this attractive girl in her scarlet slacks and white shirt, for she certainly had a point about the mechanics of the shooting.

He hesitated. 'You may be right, but I still don't like being pushed around,' he said finally. 'By my government, or yours. And I don't intend to be intimidated, if I can help it. However, there's one small problem.'

'What's that?'

Hugh grinned. 'I haven't the faintest idea what to do next.'

It was the grin that decided Jay. She had intended that their evening together should be the end of her relationship with Hugh Bigrel. She liked him, perhaps a little too much for her peace of mind, but she had no desire to become emotionally involved with him. And, after what she had learnt over the weekend and what he had just told her about Worth, she had decided it was unfair to let him become further embroiled in what was really not his business. Now she changed her mind. She would put him straight. She would tell him the truth as she knew it. Then it would be up to him to make up his mind whether or not to bow out.

'Does the name Rupert Canville mean anything to you?' she asked abruptly.

'The former British High Commissioner to Canada, yes.' Hugh remembered what Tom Dawson had told him. 'Your father was at the American Embassy in Ottawa. He knew Canville?'

'They were – casual friends. They'd known each other before, in Warsaw.'

'I see. But what on earth has Canville got to do with the present affair?'

'I gather Fenwick warned you that, apart from Lorna and David, three people had died as a result of this affair, as you call it: Sam, Frank Worth and one other. The one other was Rupert Canville.'

Hugh, who had been about to take a drink, put his glass down again. 'For God's sake, what makes you say that?'

'A friend of mine called Carol – who worked for Sam at our embassy in Ottawa – is over in the UK on vacation. I spent the weekend with her. In defiance of all the rules, she told me what Sam had told her in strict confidence. Now I'm confiding in you, and I'm trusting you not to let it go any further.'

'All right.' Hugh waited.

'It seems that my father had been worried by Canville's death, that he'd believed it might have been suicide.'

Jay stopped as if searching for the right words, and Hugh said, 'So, what if it had been? I still don't see any connection.'

'This is the tricky part. Evidently, there was a leak of highly sensitive information – Top Secret, if you like – from Ottawa and the US authorities suspected that the Brits were responsible. Hugh, your theory that Fenwick's covering for the CIA just isn't right. It's much more likely he's covering for Rupert Canville. The last thing the British Government – your government – wants at present is another spy scandal – especially a scandal involving someone as highly-placed as a High Commissioner. It would shatter what confidence – what little confidence – remains in the security service over here.'

'Good God, Jay!' Hugh didn't try to hide his amusement. 'You talk about my theory, but what of yours? Because there's a leak of some kind in Ottawa, and Canville got drowned, or drowned himself, you assume the man was a spy. You've no actual evidence for that, have you?'

'No, but – '

'Even if he did commit suicide, there could be a hundred other reasons. That dishy wife of his – what was her name? Monica, that's it – she might have been going to leave him, or – '

'Okay!' Jay interrupted. 'I'm not asking you to believe it, Hugh. All I'm saying is that it makes sense to me.'

'Well, it doesn't to me! Can you really imagine Dick Fenwick shooting your father or killing Frank Worth?'

'No, not in person. But he could have ordered their deaths. As – as far as I can tell, the Brits are no more squeamish than anyone else when it comes to the crunch.'

68

'Nonsense.' Hugh shook his head in dismissal. 'You're letting your imagination run away with you, Jay.'

She was on her feet, glaring at him. 'Don't be so goddamned patronizing, Hugh Bigrel! Someone shot Sam. Someone killed this guy Worth. Those are facts, which you accept. I've not dreamed them up. Any more than I've dreamed up Fenwick's threats, or warnings if you prefer to be mealy-mouthed about them.'

Hugh apologized. He didn't want to quarrel. Nor did Jay. But the evening was spoilt. Hugh left after coffee and a decent interval. He said how much he'd enjoyed the meal, and hoped that Jay would dine with him when he was next in London or if she came down to Oxford. They agreed to keep in touch, and to let each other know if they learned of any further developments. They were polite and friendly, but they made no firm arrangement to meet or phone. The evening ended without even a formal peck on the cheek. And, as the taxi carried Hugh through the London streets to his cousins' mews house in Marylebone, where he was to spend the night with the Davidsons, he told himself that he was unlikely to see Jay Ryan again.

A crowd of people walked along the short path through the lawns that separated St Margaret's, Westminster, from the traffic of Parliament Square. The memorial service for the late Sir Rupert Canville was by invitation only. Cards were carefully scrutinized at the door. The congregation was perhaps not quite as fashionable as the church, but was certainly as superior, and there were many well-known faces to be seen. The circumstances of Canville's death and his social connections had made this service a media event, and television cameras were in evidence, even inside the church. Security was tight.

Dick Fenwick, who had purposely arrived early, thanked his lucky stars that it was not his responsibility. He had come merely to observe, though he was not sure why, or what he might hope to learn. He had found himself a seat by a pillar to the rear of the church, so that by turning slightly he could see those entering. He watched them with cynical amusement.

There were senior members of the Foreign and Commonwealth Office and other top level civil servants, mostly from the
Ministry of Defence. There were politicians including some
from the Cabinet, and a good sprinkling from the Upper House.
The Arts, perhaps in deference to Lady Canville's one-time
aspirations, were well represented. Fenwick wondered if she
would ever have made it to stardom had she not opted for
marriage to Rupert Canville.

Many of the congregation Fenwick couldn't place, though he
had obtained a list of those who had been invited. He put them
down as neighbours, old school friends, business acquaintances,
and their wives. But, like the rest of those come to remember
Rupert Canville, he guessed they would almost all be privileged,
moneyed, influential. Here, indeed, was a good cross-section of
what used to be called the Establishment – that mythical,
mystical, allegedly powerful body that was said to run the
country.

If there had been any doubt of that, the arrival of the Canville
family would have dispelled it. Canville's widow, Monica,
striking in black, was supported by Canville's brothers, on one
side the major-general, resplendent in dress uniform, and on the
other the judge, more soberly dressed as became his calling.
Behind them, the dowager Lady Dorothy Canville, Rupert's
mother, leant on the arm of her cousin, a distant Royal, who
was also representing Her Majesty the Queen. Canville's sisters-
in-law followed them, with a collection of other relations.

The organ voluntary grew louder. Fenwick saw two ushers
about to close the church's great doors. Then a slim figure
slipped in and took a seat in a rearmost pew. Fenwick sighed
with exasperation. He had recognized Jay Ryan, whose name he
was certain had not been on the original list of invitees.

The choir had begun to sing a hymn so well-known that most
of the congregation were able to join in. Fenwick was not among
them. Thinking of Sam Thaxted's daughter, he let his glance
wander around the church, and was cynically amused to see the
Soviet and Polish diplomats who had come to pay their last
respects to Sir Rupert Canville.

The opening hymn was followed by prayers, another hymn,

more prayers. Then came the eulogy, delivered, as was to be expected, by a bishop, yet another Canville cousin. Praise of Rupert Canville as a son, a brother, a husband, Fenwick would not have queried. Nevertheless, it was strange, he thought, that Canville should have been so devoted to his first wife – a semi-invalid about his own age – yet unfaithful to the young and beautiful Monica.

The remainder of the eulogy was a travesty of the truth. The bishop spoke of Canville's career, his integrity and the vital services he had rendered to Britain in the course of his professional life. Rupert, the bishop concluded, had died in tragic circumstances, but would always be remembered with gratitude, not only by his family, who would miss him sorely, but by the country that he had served so long and well.

Fenwick had to suppress an unruly urge to rise and 'forbid the banns', or at least to shake his head at the string of untruths that the bishop had unwittingly uttered. He knew that in the real world he should be thankful for them. In reports of the memorial service, they would be published in the press and quoted in the media. They would help to still any doubts and quash any rumours – if that became necessary. He sincerely hoped it wouldn't. If he had done his job well, the cover-up was by now as complete as could be hoped.

At the back of his mind, his instincts told him that this was not so, that he would be fooling himself if he believed it. The very presence of Jay Ryan in the church could be interpreted as a warning that all was not yet well; she could still cause trouble, bad trouble. Nor did he altogether trust Hugh Bigrel. Dick Fenwick tried to subdue his misgivings as, with the rest of the congregation, he rose to his feet when the choir started on the final hymn.

A few minutes later he hurried out of the church. In his eagerness to get away, he ignored the television camera and crew on the pavement outside.

Helen Bigrel turned on the television set. She and John liked to watch the seven o'clock news while they had a drink before their dinner. Hugh continued to read; he had heard the headlines earlier. Then, just as it had done some weeks ago, the name of Sir Rupert Canville caught his attention.

Because little that could be called newsworthy had happened that day, the television editor had decided to make the most of Canville's memorial service. Hugh watched it desultorily. Unless one were interested in the sight of celebrities, the report was far from gripping.

Then suddenly he sat upright. The television picture had shown the interior of the church and the congregation about to leave. For a fleeting second he had glimpsed a profile, short dark hair, a pert face shadowed by the brim of a hat. Jay Ryan?

'What is it?' Helen asked, startled by his sudden movement.

'Nothing,' said Hugh. 'For half a second I thought I saw someone I knew, but I must have been wrong.'

'If you mean Dick Fenwick, that security man who came here, it *is* him, Hugh. Look!' Helen was pointing at the screen. 'Don't you recognize him?'

'So it is,' said Hugh slowly, watching Fenwick hurrying along the path from the church. 'Yes, I do recognize him – the ubiquitous Fenwick.'

'I wonder what he was doing there.' John Bigrel was intrigued. 'Hugh, do you think there's a connection between Canville and Thaxted? If I remember rightly, I read somewhere that Thaxted was working at the US Embassy in Ottawa just before he died.'

'Yes. Tom Dawson told me that.'

Hugh left the subject there. He had no wish to lie, though he knew he would if he were forced to; he was determined that his parents shouldn't be further involved. He had told them about the advertisement for the foxy-faced man, but not of its results. They had no idea that Sam Thaxted had been shot. They had neither heard of Frank Worth's death, nor of Fenwick's warnings.

'What sort of connection?' Helen asked when Hugh said no more.

It was John who answered her. 'How should I know? But it strikes me, from what I've gathered about Mr Fenwick, that he does very little without purpose.'

Hugh agreed, but he had no intention of mentioning Jay Ryan's theory – a theory he had previously scorned. He had decided that at the first opportunity he would phone Jay, eat humble pie and suggest they meet again.

EIGHT

Hugh Bigrel sat in the garden and tried to read. It was one of those warm early summer days that promised weeks of pleasant heat and sunshine, a promise rarely kept in England. It was therefore a day to be treasured and enjoyed. Hugh had even thought of taking a punt on the river, but any such effort had seemed to be too great – especially alone. Yet he couldn't settle to his book. In short, he was restless.

He still missed Lorna and David, sometimes sharply and unexpectedly, but his health was back to normal. He would have been happy to return to work, and regretted having accepted his College's generous offer of a sabbatical Trinity term. His friends were all busy with their affairs, his father with his teaching, his mother with research for a biography she had been commissioned to write. He alone, it seemed, was aimless and useless.

It was almost a fortnight since the memorial service for Sir Rupert Canville, and there had been no further developments. Hugh hadn't seen Jay Ryan, but he had spoken to her a couple of times on the phone, and had made his peace with her. He had admitted that she was right, that there was probably a connection between the deaths of Canville and her father. However, he had refused to accept that this necessarily indicated – let alone proved – that the late High Commissioner had been a spy or a traitor.

Jay had been prepared to differ quietly. She had also been prepared to accept Hugh's invitation to come up to Oxford for the weekend. By now Hugh had moved back into the lower part of the house, from which the most painful reminders of Lorna and David had been cleared, and it had been at his mother's suggestion that he had invited Jay to stay with the family. She was expected to arrive the next day, and he was looking forward to her visit, which possibly accounted for his restlessness.

Annoyed with himself, Hugh reached a decision. He went inside the house to leave his book, then set off on foot in the direction of the University Parks – that broad expanse of public greenery bounded by Parks Road, the University Science Area and the River Cherwell.

Jay had suggested that he might make some inquiries about Canville in Oxford. She argued that a man's (or a woman's) early life might well provide a clue to their future behaviour, and Canville had been up at the University. So far, apart from attempts to steer conversation on to the subject of the late Sir Rupert in his own Senior Common Room, where they had met with little response, Hugh had taken no steps in this direction. He had found it hard to know how to approach the problem, especially as he had an instinctive dislike of asking personal questions.

However, with Jay's arrival so imminent, Hugh had decided that perhaps he should make another final effort. It was many years since Sir Rupert Canville had been an undergraduate, and by now most of those who had known or taught him had left Oxford, progressed – or failed – in their careers, retired to other parts of the country or simply died. But someone had told Hugh that a don – unfortunately now in his eighties – who had at one time been Canville's history tutor, still lived in Norham Gardens, another road which bordered the Parks.

At least a talk with the old man would show willing and appease Jay, Hugh thought somewhat sardonically as he strode along. He found the right house – one of those solid Victorian mansions which abound in North Oxford – and rang the bell. After an appreciable pause he heard slow, shuffling footsteps, and the door was opened.

'Yes? What can I do for you?'

There was no doubt that he was old. He leaned on a stick and was bent almost double. His big shaggy head was little higher than Hugh's waist. But the voice was firm and imperious. There was obviously no question of senility; he was still mentally agile.

'Professor Moore?'

'That's right. So what is it, boy? Speak up. What do you want?'

Hugh drew a deep breath. He was used to Oxford eccentrics, but he couldn't remember when he had last been called 'boy' or addressed so abruptly. His original intention had been to spin some yarn about researching a book on the late High Commissioner to Canada, but he realized that this would be pointless. The two intensely blue eyes staring up at him warned of an intelligence that would not be easily deceived.

'Professor, my name's Hugh Bigrel.' Hugh explained who he was, and the old man listened attentively.

'John Bigrel's son?'

'Yes, sir.' Hugh was surprised.

'Why on earth didn't you say so at once? Come along in.' He turned and led the way into a room that was obviously a study, full of books but unexpectedly tidy. 'Sit yourself down,' he said, waving Hugh to a chair. 'John was one of my pupils. A bright lad. He should have got a First, but he preferred to get a Blue for cricket. I hope you were more sensible.'

'I got a First, sir, but I missed out on the Blue.' Hugh, amused, had regained his aplomb.

'Good! At any rate about the First.' The old man had at last, with difficulty, managed to seat himself behind his desk. 'Now, how can I help you, young Bigrel?'

Hugh said carefully, 'Professor Moore, I'd like to know whatever you can tell me about the late Sir Rupert Canville. I can't help realizing that this may seem a strange request, but I do have a reason which – which – '

'Which you'd rather not tell me?'

'Yes, sir. I hope you'll trust me.'

'Why not, considering I know no ill of Canville? He was one of those characters born with a silver spoon in his mouth, as we used to say. He had everything in his favour. Physical attraction. An excellent brain. Money. The right connections. A pleasant personality. He should have gone to the very top.'

The old professor went on to speak of Canville's first wife, who had been crippled in a riding accident, and Canville's marriage, on her death, to a much younger woman. 'Not quite

76

his class, the second one, I'd have said,' he commented unexpectedly. Then: 'But beautiful, beautiful. I expect she made him happy,' he added.

Hugh listened politely, but he had already lost interest. He guessed he would learn nothing about Canville that he hadn't known or surmised. Sir Rupert sounded like a paragon. He could imagine Jay saying, 'Too good to be true,' but that was not fair.

'He could have achieved so much,' Professor Moore was saying. 'A pity. A great pity.'

'His death, you mean, sir?' Hugh said.

'That too, of course.' The professor paused for a moment as if paying respect to his dead pupil. Then he went on: 'But it wasn't exactly what I had in mind. I was thinking of the black he put up in Warsaw. Don't ask me what it was, because I can't tell you. I don't know. But it must have been something serious. It didn't exactly ruin his career, but I gather it put it in jeopardy. After Warsaw he must have been hoping for a truly prestigious posting – Washington or Moscow or Paris or something like that. But it was not to be. He'd only done eighteen months as Ambassador to Poland when he was suddenly put out to grass in Ottawa.'

Hugh frowned, and then laughed. 'The Foreign Office may not have seen a posting to Canada quite like that, sir,' he remarked. 'Was there any comment at the time?'

'Not that I heard. There was some talk about stress in certain capitals, and the need not to be hidebound about postings – whatever all that meant. It's true a general shuffle took place around then, a kind of British diplomatic musical chairs. Probably it was due anyway, but it certainly served to cover Canville's move.'

The two bright blue eyes regarded Hugh Bigrel with mild amusement. Hugh was uncertain whether the old man was playing with him, or if he had really tried to be helpful. But Professor Moore, leaning on his stick, was rising from his chair. Clearly the interview was at an end.

Hugh expressed his thanks, and said goodbye. He thought that if he told Jay that there had been some question about Sir

Rupert's departure from Warsaw, he would merely be fuelling her suspicions, and he decided to keep quiet for the present. He couldn't believe that whatever had happened in Warsaw – if anything had – could be important or relevant.

Jay arrived the next day in time for family supper with the Bigrels. She held up her cheek for Hugh to peck as he helped her from her car, and from the beginning she made herself at home, obviously enjoying the company of Hugh's parents, Helen and John. After the meal she and Hugh went downstairs to his own sitting-room. And at once she surprised him.

'I've been trying to find out where Monica Canville is staying, and I've succeeded,' she said without preamble. 'I thought I might call on her. After all, we have mutual friends, and she must have met Sam in Ottawa.' She paused. 'I was hoping I could persuade you to come with me.'

'What?' Hugh was horrified.

Jay laughed. 'It's all right. She won't bite. She's staying with some very rich people in a so-called manor house near Chadlington. I looked it up. It's in the Cotswolds, not far from here. We could drive over tomorrow, say we were in the neighbourhood and – '.

'Get thrown out by the butler or savaged by guard dogs.'

'We'll call from the village first if you're afraid.'

'Okay,' Hugh said reluctantly, realizing that there was no escape.

The weather was holding, and in reality he was not averse to a drive through the Cotswolds in Jay's company. He knew an excellent pub in Charlbury, a few miles from Chadlington. It would be a good place for them to have lunch when, as he fully expected, Jay had discovered that Lady Canville was 'not at home'. However, he was proved wrong, at least on most counts.

Jay emerged triumphant from the telephone box. 'We're invited for drinks and a casual meal,' she said.

'How kind of them,' Hugh replied.

There was an edge to his voice. He was finding the day less enjoyable than he had anticipated. The last time he had driven to Charlbury had been with Lorna and David and suddenly, without warning, he ached for them. It made no sense that he should be here, in these slightly bizarre circumstances, with this American girl whom he scarcely knew.

Jay seemed to read his thoughts. She thrust a sympathetic arm through his. 'Memories, Hugh? I'm sorry. I have them, too, you know. But it's years since Patrick, my husband, was killed in the Falklands and the memories no longer hurt. It'll be the same for you.'

She talked quietly about her brief marriage as they walked back to the car and drove to the Manor, where a Major Peter Lansdowne lived with his wife, Diana. A man in shirt, breeches and boots opened the large wrought-iron gates for them. The drive was long, the house imposing. But there was no butler, and no guard dogs were in evidence. It was a maid who showed them into a long, richly-furnished drawing-room.

Diana Lansdowne came forward to greet them. She was in her mid-forties, pretty and plump, casually but expensively dressed. She told the girl to tell Lady Canville that her guests had arrived. She was obviously American, speaking with a soft Southern drawl. She introduced her husband, a big man with an oversized moustache, who was equally obviously British.

As they were shaking hands a second man, who had been standing by the far window, came towards them.

'And this is Mr Smith, a cousin of my first husband,' Mrs Lansdowne said.

He, too, shook hands with Jay and Hugh, giving each of them a warm smile which revealed perfect teeth. A handsome man, brown-haired and blue-eyed, he might have been a leading film star. He said he was in England on a brief holiday, but neither he nor anyone else offered any further explanations.

Then Monica Canville came into the room. She went straight to Jay and immediately took both her hands. 'My dear, how kind of you to come and see me. I was so sorry about your father. He was such a nice man and a great friend of Rupert's. We saw quite a lot of him in Ottawa.'

Jay muttered something, but no one was listening. Inevitably Monica was the centre of attention. She turned and smiled at

Hugh, who thought how lovely she was. Mrs Lansdowne introduced him.

'Mr Bigrel? But I'm quite certain we've met before. In Ottawa, wasn't it?'

'Yes, Lady Canville.' Hugh returned her smile. 'You have a good memory. It was at a reception at the High Commission.'

'Of course I remember. You were teaching a summer course at the local university – Carleton, that was it.'

The life-style of the Lansdownes was further demonstrated by the entry of a manservant with a tray holding glasses of champagne. Conversation became general, and shortly afterwards Diana Lansdowne led the way across the broad hall to the dining-room, which turned out to be only slightly smaller than the room they had left. Hugh and Jay exchanged wry glances.

The 'casual lunch' was laid out on a long table, buffet style. One helped oneself and sat where one pleased. In a sense it was an ordinary, informal meal. But there was nothing ordinary about the food: smoked salmon, oysters, plovers' eggs in aspic, pheasant. York ham, stuffed veal, an array of salads and cheeses – and to drink, champagne, naturally.

Hugh and Jay insisted on leaving immediately after coffee, in spite of polite urgings to stay a little longer. Major Lansdowne had even suggested they might like a swim in the pool – covered and heated – before they left.

'They couldn't have been kinder,' Hugh said, 'but enough's enough. Do you suppose they eat like that every day? After all, they can't have laid it on for us.'

'They may have laid it on for Cousin Smith.'

'Why do you say that?'

'You didn't recognize him? That was Worral J. Smith, multi-millionaire, Democratic white hope for the next Presidential election, every woman's dreamboat – or almost every woman's.'

'You don't like him?'

'I've nothing against the guy. But generally I'm not too keen on politicians.'

For a while they drove in companionable silence. Jay was an efficient driver, as Hugh would have expected. Unconsciously he found himself comparing her with Monica Canville.

'I don't need to offer you a nickel – a penny – for your thoughts, Hugh,' Jay said. 'I can guess. You're thinking about dishy Monica. Weren't you flattered that she remembered you?'

'Yes, I was,' Hugh admitted. 'And surprised, because I was merely one of a big mob at that reception. But I suppose diplomats and their wives have to learn to remember faces. Incidentally, we went to that place for a reason, remember? What about it? You were talking to Lady C during lunch. Anything interesting about your father?'

'No. She was sweet about him, naturally. She said all the right things and so on. But from our point of view it was a useless visit. Mostly she talked about the awful shock of suddenly becoming a widow. Poor dear! It seems silly to be sorry for someone like Monica Canville, but I was, in spite of myself. I think she must have loved her Rupert.'

'Did you ever think she didn't?'

Jay shrugged. 'Canville had a lot going for him, I admit, but he was twice her age, and she could have had her pick of husbands, as I'm sure you'll agree, Hugh. Still, older men can be attractive. Take Worral Smith, for instance.' She glanced sideways at Hugh.

When he made no response, she added casually, 'As I was saying at lunch, I'll be going back to the United States in ten days or so. Sam was cremated. It was what he wished. But I want to take his ashes home.' Her voice was suddenly tight.

'To – to Washington? I didn't hear you mention it. Are – are you going to be away long?' Hugh stammered in his surprise and disappointment.

'I'm not sure. There are quite a few people I'd like to talk with about Sam. And I thought I might go up to Ottawa. Perhaps I can persuade someone to come clean.'

There was a pause while both were busy with their thoughts. Then Jay said, 'Hugh, why don't you come with me? You'd enjoy Washington DC, though the cherry blossom will be over. I've an aunt who lives in Georgetown – that's a very pleasant residential area close to downtown – and we could stay with her.'

'I'd love to, but – ' For once Hugh searched for words.

81

'Money?' Jay queried.

'No. I could manage – unless you want to fly Concorde.'

'So what's stopping you? Your college doesn't expect you to work this term. Do come, Hugh. I've never been to Canada, and I'm sure you'd be an enormous help.'

Hugh knew he was being pressured, but he didn't really care. He could do with a holiday. Why not go to the States? Surely it was an invitation not to be refused. Whatever else transpired, Jay would be good company.

'Okay,' he said. 'Why not? I'll come.'

'Perhaps Bigrel and the girl could have an "accident", Comrade Colonel.'

Viktor Krasnakov regarded his aide with disgust. 'No, Comrade. They can't have an "accident", as you call it. There have been too many "accidents" already. Don't delude yourself that Fenwick and his colleagues have been taken in by them.'

'But they can prove nothing,' Igor Galinov said quickly.

'That's not the point! Fenwick must not start asking himself why we're suddenly so eager to be helpful to the British. We want him to believe we had our own reasons for eliminating Thaxted – reasons that had nothing to do with Canville – and that Worth's death was merely tidying up the Thaxted business, as indeed it was.'

'I understand, Comrade Colonel.'

Galinov did his best to sound placatory. In fact, he was far from sure that he did understand. He'd been told that Canville had been a Soviet agent-in-place, one of those non-ideologically committed fools who'd been persuaded – blackmailed was an unfortunate word – to serve the USSR. But Canville was dead. Why wasn't that the end of it? Why did they have to cover for him?

Galinov was not a stupid man. Probably he hadn't been told the whole truth, he thought. Comrade Colonel Krasnakov had been unusually tense of late, and he was sure that this mood dated from the time of Canville's death. Nevertheless, it was

82

prudent not to ask too many questions. He looked expectantly at his senior officer.

Krasnakov was pacing up and down his office. 'That the Ryan bitch should go to Washington, I could accept. But not with Bigrel, and certainly not to Ottawa as well. No. There's no doubt they're on to something.'

'But if we can't take care of them, Comrade Colonel,' said Galinov, choosing his words, 'what can we do?'

'Watch them. Encourage them, but with a little disinformation so that they're led in the wrong direction.' Krasnakov turned and gave Galinov a grim smile. 'Deception, Comrade, that's what's needed. We, I think, will head for Ottawa ourselves.'

Part Two

NINE

During his stay in Canada Hugh Bigrel had never found time to cross the border, so this was his first visit to the United States of America. He was hardly welcomed with open arms. Separated by bureaucracy from the home-coming and US passport-holding Jay on their arrival at Dulles International Airport, he had waited in interminable queues for his entry to be processed. Everything was in order, but his stated profession of university teacher seemed a cause for suspicion.

It was about an hour after the aircraft's arrival when, having reassured the US Immigration Service that he was merely visiting their country on holiday, and had no intention of seeking work – in a university or anywhere else – and having had his bag thoroughly searched by an unsmiling customs official, that he was at last formally free to proceed Stateside. With a sense of relief he sighted Jay waiting for him among the jostling crowd in the arrivals concourse.

Jay was talking to a tall, leggy blonde in a smart suit, peaked cap and sensible shoes. The general impression was that she was wearing some kind of uniform. She didn't wait to be introduced but, turning to Hugh, gave him a wide smile and offered him her hand.

'Hi! I'm Betsy-Ann. You must be Hugh.'

Behind her back Jay winked at him. 'We're in luck, Hugh,' she said. 'I was expecting to ride the coach into Washington – it's a long fifty minutes – but I guess we're going first class, courtesy of – what did you say your outfit was called, Betsy-Ann?'

As Betsy-Ann answered, Hugh noted that, back home on her own ground, Jay's accent and choice of phrase were becoming less English and more American. It was only natural, he supposed.

'The Starlight Limousine Service,' the blonde was saying. 'We're new, just starting up. That's why, for the next week or two, we're offering a free automobile ride every day to a couple flying in from Europe. It's a PR stunt, of course, but today you got lucky. You're the winners. All you have to do is have your picture taken with me and the automobile. Say! What about that?'

'Great,' said Hugh, amused. 'Why us?'

'Picked with a pin.' Betsy-Ann laughed, once more showing perfect white teeth. She led them along the concourse, opened the door of a large car for them and, once they had posed for the promised photographer, saw them comfortably settled in the rear seat before putting their bags into the trunk, as she called it, and getting behind the wheel. 'Here we go at last,' she said cheerfully, and shut the glass panel that divided the driver's compartment from the passengers.

'Thank goodness,' said Hugh. 'I was afraid we were going to have the pleasure of her conversation all the way into Washington. Incidentally, I'm sorry I kept you waiting, Jay, but blame the authorities. I should think they'd be used to visiting foreigners at Dulles by this time, but university teachers seem to be objects of suspicion here.'

'Not particularly,' said Jay. 'But, you know – illegal immigrants and drugs and all that. Controls are inevitable, unless you're some kind of VIP. At any rate, let's be grateful for this automobile. It's certainly better and quicker than the coach. And the cost of an ordinary cab's out of this world.'

'It's luxurious, certainly.' Hugh leant back and stretched his legs, as the large American car moved smoothly forward. 'And free, as you say.'

'It'll be nearly all free while we're here. We'll be Aunt Hilda's guests, and I guess she'll lend us an automobile.'

'It's very kind of her to include me. Tell me about her, Jay. Is she your mother's sister?'

'Gracious, no! Aunt Hilda is Sam's half-sister, and ten years older than he was. She was always devoted to him, and when my mother died she suggested he should consider her house his home. She was a widow with no children, so it was an excellent arrangement. Most of the time he was away, of course, but I know she's going to miss him a lot.'

'Do your mother's family come from this part of the States?'

Jay looked at Hugh in mild surprise. 'No. Didn't you know? My mother was originally Polish. Sam met her in New York. She was an interpreter at the United Nations – not for the Polish delegation, but for the UN itself. You know, simultaneous interpretation and all that. As I understand it, it was love at first sight. Her death devastated him.'

'How did it happen? She can't have been very old.'

'She wasn't, but she had something wrong with her heart. No one suspected it, and she just died in her sleep one night. That made the shock even worse for Sam – and for me. But I'd just got married, and naturally it wasn't quite the same.'

Hugh nodded his sympathy. 'You've still got Polish relations, Jay?'

'Some cousins.'

She no longer seemed inclined to talk, and Hugh didn't press her. He was content to look out of the window at the big cars purring along the broad multi-lane Dulles Access Road at a leisurely fifty-five miles an hour. As far as he could see, no one passed anybody, and all the traffic seemed fixed to some sort of moving belt. Maybe it was. In any case, their relentless but unexciting progress was soporific. They had had an early start that morning, and his head began to nod.

Jay woke him as they were turning off the Freeway at a spaghetti junction. 'Have you contacted your friend in Ottawa yet?'

'Keith Masterson? No, I thought it might be better to wait till I got to Washington. It'll sound more casual like that. But I'm pretty certain he'll put us up. He's got a huge apartment for just one man.'

'That's fine.' For a moment Jay gave the impression that her thoughts were elsewhere. Then she seemed to recollect their situation. 'Hugh, you'll be glad to know that in a moment we'll be crossing the famous Potomac River on the Key Bridge – the

Francis Scott Key Memorial Bridge, to give it its full name. Once we're across we'll be in Washington, DC – and on the edge of Georgetown. I'll bet you don't know who Francis Scott Key was.'

Hugh was surprised. 'I've never thought about it.'

'You would if you'd been at school here. He's the poet who wrote the words of *The Star-Spangled Banner*. I think he was Attorney-General for DC sometime in the 1800s.'

'I'll take your word for it,' said Hugh.

Minutes later they drew up in front of a tall, narrow, terraced house, and almost before Betsy-Ann had had time to open the car door, Hilda Avery had come out to greet them. Mrs Avery was in her late sixties, a thin, upright woman – not unlike her house – with an intelligent face. She regarded Hugh quizzically, even while she was embracing her niece.

'Come in! Come in!' She gestured towards the open front door. 'How very nice to see you both. I hope you had a good trip.'

'The flight was fine. Couldn't have been better,' Jay assured her. 'But Dulles International doesn't improve that much. Hugh had to wait quite a while in line-ups at Immigration and Customs. I was a bit luckier – and we got a free limousine ride into the District. You can't beat that.'

They turned to thank the Starlight Limousine Service's driver. But Betsy-Ann had already deposited their bags on the sidewalk and, hand raised in farewell, was drawing away from the kerb. They waved in return, and the next moment forgot her as Hilda Avery welcomed them to her home.

Viktor Krasnakov and Igor Galinov sat in a small bare office in the Soviet Embassy on Charlotte Street in Ottawa, listening to a tape that had been flown up from Washington and staring at a couple of photographs. Krasnakov's handsome face was expressionless, but Galinov could tell he was pleased.

'Fools,' Krasnakov said without venom. 'Would you ever accept a free ride from an unknown taxi company or limousine service, or whatever they call it, Galinov?'

'No, Comrade Colonel.'

'I'm glad to hear it. But let's be thankful that Bigrel and Ryan did just that. Now we're sure they're staying with this aunt in Georgetown, and we know where they hope to stay in Ottawa. Tell me about this Masterson.'

'Yes, Comrade Colonel. Keith Masterson is a First Secretary at the British High Commission here. He lives in one of those big blocks of apartments overlooking the Rideau Canal. He was at Oxford University with Bigrel, but as far as we know they're only casual friends.'

'Is he married?'

'No, Comrade Colonel, but there's no evidence that he's other than heterosexual.'

'Really? Ah, well, I doubt if we'll want to compromise him. What we need at the moment, Galinov, is what the English call a "red herring".' Seeing his aide's blank face, Krasnakov sighed and translated. 'We've got to distract these two from their present pursuit, if you can call it that. But the problem is how. It won't be easy. Jay Ryan's an obstinate woman.'

Thirty-six hours later, the 'obstinate woman', her face buried in a large white handkerchief provided by Hugh Bigrel, was making a tremendous effort to suppress her tears. She had – so she thought – accepted her father's death, even when she had come to believe that it was the consequence of intentional violence – unexplained violence. But now, as they drove back from St Patrick's Church after handing the casket containing Sam Thaxted's ashes to a priest, who had blessed them and placed them in the crypt, she was, suddenly and without warning, overcome by her loss. She wept.

'I'm sorry!'

It wasn't an apology. It was anger at her own weakness, and Hugh needed no explanations to understand how she felt. He made no effort to comfort her. Neither did her aunt who sat, stony-faced, on Jay's other side and gazed out of the car window; Hilda Avery had her emotions well under control.

In the front of the Cadillac the two men spoke softly to each other. The driver was a cousin of Hilda's, a widower about her age, and a relation on whom she had come to rely. He had also been a friend of Samuel Thaxted. His name was Norman Saint. 'Neither a saint nor an angel,' he had said on being introduced to Hugh earlier in the day, and Hilda had at once agreed with him.

'Maybe not, Norman, but you're a good man,' she had said. 'There aren't many who can claim to be that. You shouldn't aspire to more.'

'And I certainly don't claim to be one of them,' the other man had said, offering Hugh his hand. 'I'm Clifford Di Bianco.' A very different type from Norman Saint, he was younger, short, dark, brown-eyed, and with a faintly olive skin. 'I was a colleague of Sam's. Before he retired, Norm here used to be our boss.'

Hugh assumed that Saint had once worked for the Central Intelligence Agency and that Di Bianco still did, and he asked no awkward questions. Jay, he was sure, had vouched for him, or they wouldn't have been so forthcoming. Nevertheless, in spite of their apparent friendliness, he sensed an atmosphere of distrust.

Though he suspected it would be inevitable, it was with regret that he learnt that the two men were returning to Mrs Avery's house for drinks and a light lunch. What hadn't occurred to Hugh was that they would make use of the opportunity to cross-examine him. Nor had he realized how completely Jay must have confided in them.

'So you can't personally confirm the fact that Sam was shot, can you, Hugh?' Norman Saint pressed him. 'This guy, Worth, could have been lying to you, wanting to give value for money, to square his account with you, as it were.'

'Why should he have bothered? He had the money and I had no idea who he was. I couldn't have gone after him or found him again.' Hugh didn't mention his threat to inform Fenwick, who did know where to find Worth.

'Clearly someone did,' Hilda Avery said.

'That could have been chance – sneak thieves, for instance,' said Di Bianco. 'We're only guessing that this guy's death was important because of what he said about Sam. We don't know that for sure. If it weren't true then his death could be irrelevant.'

'And his beating-up? There were two of them. I heard them, remember? If they'd been ordinary thieves they'd surely have taken the money and gone. Now they risk a murder charge – if they're ever caught.' Hugh was becoming indignant, and he didn't care if he showed it.

'Look,' he went on, 'I was an innocent man driving home with my family after a visit to my in-laws. I'd never heard of Sam Thaxted, but because of him my wife and child are both dead. So, what about answering some of *my* questions for a change?'

Hilda Avery hid a smile as Saint and Di Bianco exchanged glances. Jay, who had been watching Hugh intently, openly grinned at his sudden display of aggression.

'Why not?' Norman Saint said affably, and nodded his head to Hilda at her offer of a second martini.

Hugh seized what he sensed to be a temporary advantage. 'First, can each of you look Jay in the eye and say you don't know what her father was doing in England?' he demanded.

'Yes, we can both say we didn't know for sure,' said Saint positively. 'But in my case I'd like to qualify that statement. I saw Sam shortly before he left for the UK. He came down to Washington for a couple of days, as Hilda will confirm – I don't know why – and it was clear to me that he was a worried man. When I faced him with it, he admitted that he was troubled about the recent death of a friend. He thought it could have been suicide.'

'Sir Rupert Canville's?' Jay said involuntarily.

'Yes. He told me something in confidence, and I've told no one till now.' He glanced at Di Bianco. 'Maybe you'll think I should have told the office, Cliff, but I didn't. Anyway, Sam said he feared Canville had gotten mixed up with the Soviets, and had taken his own life because the Brits were on to him. Sam emphasized it was only a hunch, and he intended to keep it to himself till he could get some proof, but I had the impression that he knew – or surmised – far more than he was telling me,

93

and I even – ' Norman Saint looked from one to the other of the four listeners. 'Hell! I thought it. I might as well say it. I even wondered if Sam mightn't have gotten himself involved in some way.'

'Sam!' Jay jumped to her feet, knocking over her empty glass. 'Are you telling me you suspected Sam, my father? You must be crazy, Norman Saint.'

'Calm down, Jay,' Hilda said sharply. 'Nobody's called Sam a traitor, but men – women, too, I guess – sometimes get involved in things through no fault of their own.'

Jay Ryan was not to be calmed so easily. She turned her back on Saint, and swung round to glare at Di Bianco. 'And what do *you* know, Cliff – or guess or surmise or wonder? You've kept very quiet.'

'My dear Jay – ' Di Bianco opened both his arms in a placatory gesture ' – all this has been news to me. But if you want an off-the-cuff personal opinion, I'll tell you. I respect what our English friend here has to say, and I take Norm's point. But I don't believe Sam was shot. I can't see any reason to believe that the Brits weren't right, and that it was a sudden heart attack. After all, British doctors and pathologists are no slouches, and these things do happen. You all know the story of the guy dropping dead on the cardiologist's doorstep just after he's been given a clean bill of health. I appreciate that the result was a tragedy for everyone concerned, but now maybe it's – '

'Best forgotten?' Hugh Bigrel's voice was colder than the melting ice in the martini jug.

'As regards playing amateur detectives, yes!'

The answer had been softly spoken, but it had the effect on Hugh of being slammed into a brick wall. He bit back a retort. He didn't like Di Bianco, and would have bet the American didn't like him much. Nor did he delude himself about the reason. He had seen the way Di Bianco looked at Jay and, ridiculous as it seemed, he found that he resented it.

'I confirm what Norm said,' Di Bianco went on. 'I assure you, Jay, I've no idea why Sam went over to the UK. In fact, I didn't even know he was going. It may or may not have been concerned with what he seems to have told Norm about Canville. Incidentally, as far as Canville's concerned, hasn't it occurred to anyone that, even if he did commit suicide, Sam could have been mistaken about his motive? Canville could have had cancer – even AIDS – or believed his beautiful young wife was two-timing him, or – '

'Yes, of course, but – ' Jay began, then shook her head. Clifford Di Bianco had spoken so reasonably that it was difficult to disagree with him.

'Anyway, I'll tell you one thing I'd stake my life on – ' Di Bianco gave Jay a dazzling smile, which he extended to Hilda Avery and Norman Saint, though by the time it reached Hugh it had lost some of its spontaneity ' – Sam's never been a traitor to his country, in word or thought or deed.'

TEN

'Hugh, do you think there's any chance Cliff Di Bianco could be right? What he said seemed so sensible, so logical.'

Jay continued without waiting for a response. 'If Canville did commit suicide for some irrelevant, personal reason – if his wife were going to leave him, for instance – the Brits might well have thought it best to try to cover up. It's only reasonable that suicide should seem to be tricky or suspicious when people with access to secrets are involved. Anyway, Sam could have started thinking, and jumped to the wrong conclusions. And the accident that caused his death, and Lorna's and David's, could have been just that – an accident. Foxy Worth could have lied and – '

'Could? Could? Who are you trying to convince, Jay – yourself or me?'

Jay stared at him for a moment. 'I really don't know if I'm trying to convince anyone,' she replied finally.

Hugh had never seen her in so despondent a mood. He reached across the table and took her hand. They were in a small French restaurant in Georgetown a few blocks from Mrs Avery's home. Hugh had insisted on taking Jay out to dinner. It was Hilda Avery's bridge night, and neither he nor Jay had particularly wanted to become part of it, in spite of Hilda's encouragement.

So far, in spite of the excellent food and a bottle of good wine – Californian, which Jay had demanded as a demonstration – the evening had not been a success. In his own mind, Hugh blamed Di Bianco, while at the same time admitting that the judgement wasn't fair. The CIA man had had to form his opinion from a second-hand story, and he hadn't been given all the facts. Besides, there was always the possibility that his scepticism had

96

been assumed, in order to protect Jay, and avoid her involvement in what he might fear was a dangerous affair.

Gently Jay withdrew her hand. 'We could just have a super holiday in Washington, and forget the – the crusade,' she said tentatively.

'No!' The determined negative was spoken before Hugh could bite his tongue. Thoughts of Lorna and David and the unborn Gemma flashed through his mind. He remembered Dick Fenwick. He had no reason to trust Fenwick particularly, but he was convinced that the security man's threats, or warnings, or whatever they had constituted, had not been spurious. Fenwick wouldn't have wasted so much time and effort on an unimportant matter.

'No,' he repeated more mildly. 'I'm not prepared to abandon the "crusade" – as you call it – at least at this stage of the game. Di Bianco could be right, but I doubt it.' He was choosing his words with care now. 'His explanations are too – too smooth, too neat. I'm not sure he's in such a good position to appreciate the situation as we are.'

'Why?'

'Well, he'd never met Worth. He never heard him being knocked about, as I did. If he had, he might believe that Worth was telling the truth. And another thing, Jay. Remember there's something that Di Bianco doesn't know. Fenwick as good as admitted that your father had been shot.'

'Yes.' Jay sighed.

Hugh signalled to a waiter to bring his bill. 'When we get back to your aunt's, I propose to phone Ottawa, and see if Keith Masterson can put me up for a day or two. I'd like you to come, Jay – I want you to come – but, if you'd rather not, I shall go alone. Perhaps it won't achieve anything much, but I'll have the satisfaction of knowing I've done all I can.'

'Of course I'll come with you.' Illogically, Jay became indignant. 'Do you think I don't realize that if it hadn't been for me you'd never have got involved in all these doubts and suspicions? I trust Cliff – and Norm Saint. They're great friends, but you and I are in this together. We've got to see it through.'

'Good!' Hugh grinned at her. 'I thought perhaps – '

97

'I know. I'm so sorry, Hugh. I've been terribly low today. It's because of – of being in Washington and – and – no Sam any more. But I'm okay now. Let's go and call your friend in Ottawa right away.'

By the time they had strolled back to the house through the quiet Georgetown streets, it was after ten. The bridge game had broken up early, and Hilda Avery was alone in the sitting-room, nursing a nightcap before going to bed. Jay refused, but Hugh agreed to join her in a whisky after he had called Canada.

As he reached the telephone it bleated, and automatically he answered it. A man asked to speak to Mrs Ryan, saying there was no point in giving his name because she wouldn't know it. He sounded nervous.

'Hang on,' Hugh said. 'I'll see if she's around.' Distantly, over the line, he heard a door slam and someone call out.

'No, I can't.' The voice was tense, suddenly hurried. 'I can't wait now. Just give Mrs Ryan a message. Tell her to be outside the giraffe compound at the Zoo tomorrow morning at noon. Alone. It's about her father.' Then immediately the line went dead.

Hugh replaced his receiver slowly. The following day was Saturday. He and Jay had planned to travel to Ottawa on Tuesday, for she had insisted that while he was on his first visit to the States he must see something of its capital. So the sightseeing might as well include a visit to the Zoo, he thought sardonically.

The next moment he reproached himself. It was difficult to take very seriously such a melodramatic message – a message like part of an incident in a spy novel – but nevertheless there had been that reference to Sam. Undoubtedly Jay would want to keep the rendezvous, and there was no way he could stop her. But he must be nearby in case – in case of what? As he remembered Fenwick's warnings the message no longer seeemed quite so absurd.

Thoughtfully Hugh returned to the sitting-room. Hilda Avery had finished her drink and, asking them to excuse her, said she was going to bed. As she went she gestured to the drinks tray, inviting Hugh to help himself. He poured a whisky, added a little Perrier, and sat down opposite Jay.

'Something wrong?' she asked at once.

Hugh shook his head. 'Not really,' he said, as he told her about the message he had been given. 'I think someone came in and interrupted the guy. Otherwise he'd have waited and spoken to you – and we might have learned more.'

'With any luck, maybe we'll know a lot more tomorrow.'

'Jay – it could be some kind of trap.'

She stared at him, her green eyes wide. 'In front of the giraffes? Surely not. Anyway, you haven't seen the Washington Zoo on a fine Saturday morning.'

Hugh had to laugh. 'I don't think the giraffes would be much help if – ' He left the sentence unfinished, remembering Sam Thaxted and Frank Worth. 'But the crowds might be a good thing, though they might not – ' He stopped suddenly, contemplating the forms an attack on Jay might take.

'You said this caller sounded nervous, Hugh. Maybe it was someone who knew Sam. He had a lot of friends, both in and out of the Company – the Agency. He used to help people with the odd dollar. He was a generous man, my pa – ' Jay caught her breath. 'I suppose it could have been the death of him.'

'What on earth do you mean?'

'Well, as I said, Sam was a generous man – generous in every way. I'm certain he'd have given your Sir Rupert the benefit of the doubt – if he'd thought there was any benefit to give. In other words, he'd have felt duty bound to look for evidence – proof, almost – before he'd have accused him. And maybe it took him too long. Maybe it gave them time. Maybe they got at him first.'

'You've changed your tune from earlier this evening, Jay.'

'And why not? You're pretty convincing, you know, Hugh.'

'I didn't know. But who do you mean by the "them", and the "they" who got to him first?'

'The Brits. The Soviets. I don't know, Hugh. It could even be the CIA. Frankly, I'm confused, hopelessly confused by now

99

but, in spite of what I said earlier, I'm as determined as you are to find out why Sam was killed.'

She yawned and rose to her feet. 'And with that declaration, I'm going to follow Aunt Hilda. What about you? You haven't called Ottawa yet?'

'No.'

'Well?'

'It's a bit late but – yes, I will.'

This time Hugh got through to Keith Masterson without pause or interruption. Masterson sounded genuinely pleased to hear from him. He said that life was hectic at the High Commission, but he'd be delighted to put Hugh up for as long as he cared to stay, providing he'd be responsible for feeding himself.

'I don't want to sound inhospitable, but I'm having a sandwich for lunch these days, and working late most nights. So, apart from breakfast, meals at the apartment are apt to be haphazard, to say the least.'

Hugh assured him that this was no problem. 'There's one thing, though, Keith. I've a friend with me. Her name's Jay Ryan. She's Samuel Thaxted's daughter. I imagine you knew Thaxted at the US Embassy up there in Canada. We've been staying with Jay's aunt here in Washington. I know you've got room, and I hope you won't mind if she comes too.'

There was an appreciable pause before Masterson replied. Then he said, 'Sure. But I must say, Hugh, you haven't wasted much time, have you?'

Hugh laughed. 'Don't get the wrong idea, Keith. Not that it's any of your damned business, but there's nothing between us. Separate rooms, please. I'll pay for the extra bedding.'

Keith said, 'Oh, don't be a fool. Forget it. I was just surprised, that's all.' But, possibly in Hugh's imagination, he sounded disturbed.

Hugh hastened to add, 'Look, we've come over to this continent for a special reason. I'll tell you about it when we see you. Okay?'

'Okay. Tuesday, you said? I'm afraid I shan't be able to meet the Piedmont flight.'

'That's all right. We'll arrange to rent a car at the airport, and I know my way round Ottawa.'

It was a perfect summer Saturday and, as there was no convenient Metro station in Georgetown, they took Hilda Avery's car – a so-called 'compact' Japanese product – and set off for the National Zoological Park at the southeren end of Rock Creek Park in northern Washington. Traffic was relatively heavy, even though most US Government offices were closed for the weekend, but they twisted through the maze of one way streets between Georgetown and Connecticut Avenue without difficulty. It was after half past eleven by the time they had turned left to cross the Taft Bridge, and managed to find a place to park near the Shoreham Hotel, about half a mile from the entrance to the Zoo. Here, after Hugh had been given precise directions, he parted from Jay and left her to follow him.

It was years since Hugh had been to a zoo; Lorna had thought them cruel places of confinement for wild animals, and he had never taken David. This zoo was doing a thriving business and, as he sauntered casually through the crowds towards the giraffe enclosure and watched the numbers of family groups obviously enjoying themselves, he regretted his omission.

The giraffes were popular. On the one hand, Hugh found it simple to hide himself by moving to and fro amongst the groups of spectators, who were in constant flux. On the other hand, it was hard to observe individuals. There were pairs of lovers of all ages – one a white-haired couple, hand in hand – and family parties of all sizes. But, as far as Hugh could see, with the exception of himself, there was only a single lone male. Hugh stood well back and studied this man surreptitiously. He was in his late twenties, wearing jeans and a T-shirt labelled 'Harvard'. He looked strong and muscular, but he was clearly nervous, as he kept checking his watch and glancing around him.

Then Hugh saw Jay approaching, slightly late for her appointment, as they had planned. In a wide, swinging skirt and matching blue shirt she looked happy and carefree. He threw a quick glance at the 'Harvard' man to see if he had also spotted

Jay. Evidently he had, for he was running forward through the mass of people, arms outstretched as if to seize her. Hugh felt cold. Cursing his own lack of planning, he started after the man – and stopped in his tracks as, ignoring Jay, 'Harvard' embraced a plump girl in very tight shorts and T-shirt, who had suddenly appeared on the scene. They walked away, arms around each other.

By this time Jay had reached the edge of the giraffe compound, and was staring at the animals with that air of astonishment they always seemed to induce in observers. The giraffes, unmoved, stared back. Hugh tried not to breathe hard. He was shaken. Jay, he thought resentfully, was better at dissimulation than he was. No one would have guessed from her behaviour that she was here to meet an unknown who might be dangerous.

Danger! Hugh cursed himself for not taking his duties as a bodyguard more seriously. He should surely have made a thorough survey of the surrounding area; after all, there was no guarantee that a true rendezvous was intended. Once Jay was in position, a single shot would be all that was necessary. Escape would be simple in the confusion that would attend Jay's sudden collapse. But why –

Desperately Hugh looked around – and caught his breath. A man wearing a seersucker suit, in his forties, fair-haired and balding, whom Hugh had noticed a few minutes earlier and dismissed as of no consequence because he was accompanied by a pleasant-looking but inconspicuous middle-aged woman, had detached himself from his companion, and was speaking to Jay.

The man seemed to be speaking rapidly and earnestly, and Jay was obviously no longer able to appear unconcerned. Even from a distance Hugh could tell that her body had tensed, and from time to time she nodded as if in acceptance of what she was hearing. Suddenly Hugh became aware that the woman, whom he had taken to be the man's wife, was watching him with as much intensity as he was watching Jay.

At that point, the man turned abruptly away from Jay, hurried to the woman and, taking her by the arm, led her off. The whole sequence of events had taken no more than three or four minutes, and it was most unlikely that anyone had noticed it.

Relieved that his more extreme fears had proved unjustified, Hugh went to join Jay. He was filled with curiosity.

'All right, Jay?'

'Yes. Why not?' She smiled, but she sounded distracted.

'Well, what did he say? What did he want? Was he from the Agency? Did you know him?'

'Know him? No, of course not. Look, let's go, and I'll tell you all about it.'

They had reached the car before Jay spoke again. Even then it was merely to suggest a place for lunch – a sea-food restaurant in Chevy Chase, just over the Maryland Line, famous for its soft-shelled crabs. Infuriated by her attitude, Hugh did his best to control his impatience.

The restaurant turned out to be small and unpretentious. Jay led Hugh through the dining-room and out through wide doors into a pleasant garden, where the plastic furniture was bright with multi-coloured cloths and cushions. She chose a table in the shade, away from a party of businessmen in deep discussion, and a couple who looked as if they were on the verge of an acrimonious divorce. When a waiter arrived too promptly, Jay looked inquiringly at Hugh and then ordered for them both.

'Hugh, I'm sorry, but I've had a shock. That guy was called Bob Harper. He *is* in the Agency, as a clerk. He works for Cliff Di Bianco, but he made me swear I wouldn't tell Cliff he'd contacted me. He said if I did he'd be fired as a security risk, and never get another job.'

Jay paused as the waiter returned to lay their places and plant the inevitable glasses of iced water before them. When he had gone she failed to resume immediately, and Hugh found himself wondering if she were debating with herself how much she should tell him.

'For heaven's sake, Jay,' he said at last, and irritably. 'What is it? Surely you trust me by now. You said yourself that we were in this together.'

'It's not like that.' Jay nibbled absently at the end of a breadstick. 'It's Cliff. I can't imagine why he should lie to me.'

'Perhaps he didn't. Presumably you've only got this new chap's word for it. Jay, what on earth did Harper tell you?'

'He said that a clerk was like a bit of furniture. Sometimes people forgot you were there, and spoke in front of you, or didn't remember to shut a communicating door. Anyway, one evening, he'd overheard Sam and Cliff having what sounded like an argument. It was about a fairly senior Canadian service officer who'd recently been posted to NATO Headquarters in Brussels. Harper refused to give me his name or any other details, but it should be possible to trace the man. As far as Harper could make out, Sam believed that this Canadian had been turned, and was working for the HVA – that's the East German espionage outfit – and it means he was effectively a KGB agent. It seems his mother was originally German, though his father was English. Evidently Sam had little more than suspicions. Cliff wanted him to leave it alone, but Sam was determined.'

Once more the waiter returned. This time he brought plates of soft-shelled crab, bowls of salad with thousand island dressing, fresh bread and tall glasses of Budweiser. 'Enjoy your meal,' he said, like every waiter or waitress in every restaurant in North America.

His presence had given Hugh a moment to think, and appreciate the implications of Harper's information. Here was a possible explanation for Thaxted's presence in Europe, and why someone – or some authority – might have decided to eliminate him. But a lot of questions remained to be answered.

He said, 'It doesn't tally with what Sam told Norman Saint, does it? In fact, it's a direct contradiction. I assume this Canadian would have known Canville in Ottawa, but it's a pretty tenuous connection, and explains nothing.' He began to attack his crab. 'Jay, did Harper give you any idea why he was risking his job to tell you this story?'

'Yes.' She played with her salad, but didn't eat any of it. 'He said he owed Sam. Sam had gotten him out of some hole by lending him money last year, and he wanted to repay the favour. He said he didn't think it was right the Company should lie to Sam's family, and pretend he hadn't been on a mission, when in fact he had.'

'But why should the Company – the Agency – or Di Bianco – lie about it?'

Jay shrugged. 'God knows! He's supposed to work in a mysterious way, too.'

Hugh's smile was sympathetic. 'Is there any means of checking on this Harper fellow without betraying his confidence?'

'Ye – es. I guess so. I could ask my friend, Carol. She's been posted back to Washington.'

'Do ask her! We need to know all we can, Jay. If what Harper says is right it alters the situation considerably.'

'It complicates it, that's for sure. But I still think we must go up to Ottawa, Hugh.'

'Of course,' Hugh said, and wondered if they were both crazy.

ELEVEN

Fenwick tapped on the door of the office, and opened it without waiting for any answering 'Come in'. Keith Masterson glanced up from the papers he was studying. His expression, which had been somewhat surprised but inquiring and benign, became fixed in what he hoped was an acceptable mask when he recognized his visitor. He quickly rose to his feet.

'Good morning.'

'Morning. And a fine one it is, too.' Fenwick perched himself on the end of Masterson's desk and looked up at him. He didn't have far to look. Masterson was short, with a disproportionately large head crowned with a splendid crop of red hair. 'I hope I'm not disturbing you.'

'Not at all,' said Masterson politely.

By now no one in the British High Commission was at ease with Dick Fenwick. In fact, ever since his sudden, unexpected return to Ottawa, the atmosphere in the Mission had been tense. The pretence that he was doing some kind of efficiency audit or time-and-motion study hadn't been abandoned officially, but in reality it had become a joke, except that any laughter about the situation was tinged with worry. There were whispers, vague rumours, that a security damage assessment was taking place but, if this were true, it was a much more subtle and low-key operation than was usual in such circumstances, and the reasons for it were not clear. Nevertheless, suspicions were rife, tempers were frayed, and a couple of secretaries had been seen in tears.

'Do sit down,' Fenwick said, as if addressing a visitor to his own room, 'I won't keep you long.'

'That's – that's all right. I'll be glad to help, whatever it is.' Masterson sat, and found that he now had to look up at Fenwick.

He took off his spectacles and made a show of polishing the lenses on a silk handkerchief.

'You're a chum of Hugh Bigrel's, I gather,' Fenwick said conversationally. 'You've known him some time?'

'Yes. We were up at Oxford together.'

'Close friends, then?'

'Well, we don't see a great deal of each other, but – '

'When does he arrive?'

The question was totally unexpected, and Masterson hesitated. 'I – er, today. They're coming in from Washington, DC on the afternoon Piedmont flight.'

'Are they staying long? And you did say "they", didn't you, Masterson?'

'I – I'm not sure how long.' At first Masterson ignored the second question. 'Hugh phoned from Washington and asked if I could put him up for a few days, and of course I agreed.' Keith Masterson shifted in his chair. He was uncertain how to proceed; Fenwick seemed to be waiting in expectation of further information. Reluctantly he added, 'He's bringing a friend with him. I don't suppose you'd have known Samuel Thaxted. He was at the US Embassy here. It's his daughter who's arriving with Hugh.'

Fenwick nodded. 'Did Bigrel tell you why they're coming up to Ottawa?'

'He just said he'd tell me when he got here.' Masterson was feeling less and less comfortable. He disliked Fenwick's questions. Though in themselves they appeared reasonably innocuous, he also disliked himself for answering them so readily.

Finally he said, 'Look, I don't understand why you should be so interested in my friends and – '

'You don't have to understand.'

Fenwick spoke mildly, but to Masterson his words seemed like a chilling slap in the face. He opened his mouth to protest and shut it again. He stared at Fenwick's back.

Fenwick had slid off the corner of the desk, and gone to the window. Allowing Masterson plenty of time to absorb what he had said, he stared across Elgin Street and Confederation Square at the brown bulk of the National Arts Centre and the curious turrets of the Château Laurier Hotel. He knew the Canadian National Ballet was performing in the Centre, and he would have liked an opportunity to see them. But it was well-nigh impossible to make time for such pleasures.

Fenwick turned round and sat on the windowsill. He regarded Masterson with care, and made up his mind; he would get more from an appeal than he would from bullying.

He smiled at Masterson, as if about to take him into his confidence. 'I don't know if Bigrel told you her name, but the girl who's with him is called Jay Ryan. She's Thaxted's daughter all right, and Ryan's her married name, though she's a widow now. And I've got a pretty good idea why the pair of them are coming to Ottawa.' He leant forward and spoke more slowly. 'For their sakes I wish they weren't. Keep this to yourself, but they're on a wild goose chase – inquiring into events that preceded Sam Thaxted's death – and it could be dangerous. They've been warned off, but it seems the warning hasn't taken.'

Fenwick paused before he went on. 'Masterson, I'm truly sorry to involve you, but it's necessary. I need to know what they do, where they go, what their plans are, what conclusions they reach, if any. All and everything, in fact. I assume they'll confide in you, at least to some extent, and – '

'You're assuming that I'll spy on them! That's what you want, isn't it?' Masterson had flushed to the roots of his red hair. 'Well I damn well won't, Mr Fenwick! I don't know who you think you are, but you've no right to come in here and suggest that I'd be willing to – to – '

Fenwick sighed inwardly, but let Masterson blow himself out. Then he said wearily, 'Oh, but I do, Masterson – have the right, I mean. I've every right to demand your help, and I sincerely hope you're going to co-operate with me.'

'You can hope as much as you damn well like. I won't! What's more, I shall report this conversation to the Deputy High Commissioner and – '

'Please don't be stupid.' This time Fenwick heaved an audible and theatrical sigh. 'Just listen to me, Masterson, he may not appreciate it immediately, but you'll be doing Hugh Bigrel a good turn if – '

'No! I won't listen to you. Why should I? Surely you've got your own thugs to do jobs like this.'

Fenwick was beginning to be annoyed. Keith Masterson was proving more obstinate than he had expected. 'Not here in Ottawa,' he said. He reached into the inside pocket of his jacket, took out his wallet and extracted from it a folded sheet of paper. He tossed it on the desk in front of Masterson.

'Read that!'

It was clearly an order, and Masterson obeyed. Then he carefully refolded the letter, which was addressed 'To Whom it May Concern', and was signed by the Permanent Under-Secretary of State of the Foreign and Commonwealth Office and the Head of Her Majesty's Diplomatic Service. He swallowed hard.

'This requests full co-operation with you,' Masterson said. Then, after a pause: 'I appreciate that, sir, but I believe that in these circumstances I still have a moral right to refuse.'

'I was afraid you'd mount a white charger and say something like that,' Fenwick replied grimly. 'Okay! If that's how you want to play it, you'd better start clearing your desk. You'll be out of here and on your way to the UK before your friend Bigrel arrives in the city.'

'You couldn't do that!' Masterson was astounded.

'Oh, couldn't I? Be assured, I could, I can, and I will, Masterson. Lift the phone and speak to your precious Deputy High Commissioner. By your refusal you've made yourself into a security risk. And I don't need to remind you what effect that will have on your future in the FCO – or anywhere else in Government for that matter.'

'You don't mean it? I can't believe it!'

'You'd better, and bloody quickly. Either give me your word you'll co-operate fully, or start to pack.'

Eventually Keith Masterson nodded. 'And what does that mean?' asked Fenwick.

'I don't really have a choice, do I? I'll co-operate.'

'Fully?' Fenwick was reading Masterson's thoughts. 'And don't imagine you can double-cross me. If I so much as suspect you're holding anything back or trying any stupid tricks, you're for the chop. Understand?'

Keith Masterson stared at Fenwick with something approaching loathing. 'Fully,' he said quietly. 'I give you my word, though I doubt if it's worth much.'

'Good! I'm glad you're being sensible.' Fenwick smiled affably. The confrontation with Masterson had ended as he had expected. He half-sympathized with and half-despised the man, but he had no complaint; he had got what he wanted. He pushed himself off the windowsill and walked across to the door. 'Don't worry,' he said. 'You're doing what's best for Hugh Bigrel – and Jay Ryan – though, even if they knew, they might not agree with me.'

The door closed gently behind Fenwick, and Keith Masterson was left, wondering.

That afternoon Hilda Avery drove Hugh and Jay to Washington National Airport. She urged them to pay her a return visit before they left for Europe, and kissed them both goodbye. Hugh was touched.

'Your aunt and I get on well together,' he said with obvious pleasure.

Jay laughed. 'A wonderful English understatement,' she said. 'Aunt Hilda's definitely taken with you.'

'It's mutual and I'm – I'm flattered.' His voice faltered.

'What is it, Hugh?'

Jay's question was urgent. Their idle banter had come to an end. Suddenly Hugh was staring past her, moving his head as if trying to catch sight of someone or something.

'I thought I saw that girl – Betsy-Ann – the one from Starlight Cabs, or whatever it's called, the one who gave us that free ride from Dulles,' he said slowly.

'So what?' Jay relaxed. 'Maybe she's decided to favour this airport for a change.'

'Maybe. But I'm nearly sure I saw her at the Lincoln Memorial yesterday, when we were sightseeing.' Hugh made a dismissive gesture. 'I expect I was mistaken. It seems fairly unlikely she'd be following us around, doesn't it?'

Jay had no chance to answer. Their flight had been called and in the business of checking-in, security controls, and boarding the Piedmont Airlines Fokker F28, Betsy-Ann was forgotten.

As they fastened their seat belts, Hugh said, 'What? No other formalities? I thought it would be almost as hard to leave the States as it was to get in.'

Jay explained. 'Washington National's devoted entirely to domestic traffic. Theoretically this is a domestic flight as far as Syracuse, New York. That's where we leave the USA. After that it's international into Canada. It's a bore, I know, but it's better than the long haul out to Dulles to catch a direct service to Ottawa.'

'Anyway, it's only two and a half hours,' Hugh said. 'And I suspect it'll take us a good thirty or forty minutes to go through Canadian immigration and customs, rent a car and drive into the city centre. Keith should be home by then, but if he's not there we can get the key from the porter and help ourselves to his diplomatic liquor.'

They were silent as the aircraft gathered speed along the runway, and roared into the sky. With pleasure Hugh let his thoughts wander over the last few days. He had enjoyed Washington, the broad avenues, the splendid monuments, the wide vistas of the city planned by a Frenchman, Pierre L'Enfant, to be both purposeful and beautiful. He had enjoyed climbing the grassy slope towards the towering obelisk of the Washington Monument, its base bright with the flags of all the States. He had enjoyed his tourist visit to the White House, and shopping in the boutiques of Georgetown. He had enjoyed almost everything – and especially Jay's company – so much so that for once he had scarcely given a thought to Lorna or David or his parents.

As if to salve his conscience he reminded himself of his mission, his reason for coming to Washington DC, and he thought again of Jay's meeting with Bob Harper by the giraffe compound in the Zoo. That was an episode he had not enjoyed. Reviewing it in his mind, he was struck by a thought that had not occurred to him before.

III

He had been watching Jay and Harper intently and, as they talked, had become aware of the woman he had presumed to be Mrs Harper watching him with equal intensity. But until now he hadn't asked himself why she should have been interested in him. He was sure his own behaviour hadn't in itself attracted her attention; there were plenty of people around and no reason for her to associate him with Jay. The only answer he could think of was that the woman had expected him to be present, which was absurd; even if by some means she'd known of him, she'd have had no means of recognizing him.

He shrugged away the problem. Perhaps he had imagined the whole incident, though it did suggest another question. He said, 'Jay, you told me you didn't know Bob Harper, but he must have known you. How else did he recognize you?'

Jay gave the matter some consideration. 'I suppose he might have seen me with Sam,' she said at last, 'and I did get a certain amount of local publicity when Pat was killed in the Falklands.' When Hugh said nothing, she added, 'Does it matter? I did ask Carol, my friend in the Agency, and she vouched for Harper. He works for Cliff all right.'

'So we accept what he had to say about this Canadian with an Anglo-German background, though it doesn't seem to jibe with what Norman Saint told us?'

'Yes, I think so. At least we must look into it. Why do you ask?'

'I've been thinking about how much we should tell Keith. I trust him, but he owes allegiance to his masters in the FCO, presumably including the late Sir Rupert Canville. So we shouldn't say anything about suspicions of Canville. And I imagine you don't want to mention Di Bianco or Saint?'

'Certainly not in connection with the Agency. But that's no reason why we shouldn't ask Keith Masterson about this Canadian, is it? I'll think up a way to put it tactfully.'

Hugh grinned. 'Okay. But we'd better agree on our story. Keith's an intelligent man.'

★ ★ ★

Keith Masterson had left the office early and cut a cocktail party at the French Embassy, so he was waiting to greet Hugh and Jay. He had steadied his nerves with a large gin and, at least for their first evening together, had decided to forget Fenwick.

After Jay had been introduced and the usual confusion of arrival had passed, Keith settled them on his balcony, which stretched the width of the apartment and had a superb view, overlooking the Rideau Canal immediately below and the Gatineau Hills to the north. Keith fetched drinks and explained that he had inherited the apartment from his predecessor, who had been married with three children. 'I'm incredibly lucky to have such a large place to myself,' he said.

'And with this outlook,' Jay said. 'My father must have had the same view,' she went on. 'He had an apartment on the Driveway too, a block or so along, and he described the people skating on the Canal in the winter – to and from their work, as well as dancing outside the Arts Centre. I meant to come and visit him while he was up here, but I've been living in London and never made it.'

'That was a shame,' Keith said. 'Your father was Sam Thaxted, wasn't he? I never knew him, though we must surely have met at the many parties there are in Ottawa.'

'Jay's come to collect some of Sam's things from his embassy,' Hugh said. He turned to Jay. 'And you want to inquire about some Canadian, don't you?'

'Yes. A friend in London asked me to look up someone's family. The silly thing is I've forgotten the guy's name, but I know he's a service officer – fairly senior – who's recently been posted to NATO Headquarters in Brussels. I suppose you couldn't help, Keith?'

Jay had lied convincingly, and Hugh was amused when Keith, who had been on the receiving end of an appealing smile, agreed at once.

'Of course,' he said. 'I can get one of our Military Advisers to ask the Department of National Defence here. They're always co-operative. Do you know anything else about this chap? What was his rank, for example?'

'I don't know, but I expect colonel or above – that's fairly senior, isn't it? And if it's any help, his father was originally German, and his mother has English relations.'

'That might be enough to go on. I'll do my best,' Keith said, getting up to refill their glasses.

Jay thanked him, and the evening passed pleasantly. Keith Masterson had taken considerable trouble over the meal, which was mostly cold, but excellent. They chatted and relaxed. Only occasionally was any tension apparent, as when Hugh asked if Sir Rupert Canville's accident had made a great deal of difference to the High Commission, or when Keith seemed especially curious as to what precisely they planned to do the following day.

They had finished coffee, and Keith had suggested a nightcap when the telephone rang. He excused himself and went to answer it, only to return immediately.

'It's for you, Jay. There's a phone on the hall table, or you can use the one in my bedroom if you want to be private.'

'The hall's fine. But what on earth – ' Jay exclaimed. Then, 'My God, I hope nothing's happened to Aunt Hilda.'

Jay was gone several minutes. When she returned she was smiling and composed. 'No panic,' she said. 'Aunt Hilda's fine. That was my friend, Carol. You remember her, Hugh? She got this number from Aunt Hilda.'

'Yes.' Hugh gave the answer that Jay clearly expected. He had never met Carol, but he knew who she was. 'What did she want? Anything important?' He tried to sound casual.

'No, it was silly really. She's just heard that Bob Harper's on leave. He and his wife Mary left for the West Coast over a week ago, so we'll miss them.'

'I – I see. What a pity!' Hugh turned to Keith. 'Some people Jay wanted me to meet in Washington when we get back there,' he explained, and hoped that he hadn't shown his astonishment at the news Jay had brought.

TWELVE

Hugh Bigrel slept badly. He had drunk more than usual, the bed was hard, and his mind was over-active. There had been no opportunity for him to speak privately to Jay, and he couldn't stop himself thinking of the problem posed by the man who had claimed to be Bob Harper. Like a dog with a bone, he worried at it.

It seemed as if two individuals had deliberately impersonated Bob and Mary Harper. Why? Apparently to tell Jay about a quarrel between her father and Clifford Di Bianco concerning a Canadian service officer.

In spite of the impersonation, the story could still be true, and, in some as yet unimaginable way, relevant; the informer might have feared identification – clearly, if he were a member of the CIA, such tales out of school were not within the rules – and have merely chosen another name that could be authenticated. Admittedly he was taking a risk, but he might have calculated that the chances that Jay would check on him were slight. In fact, it was plain bad luck that, even when she did, the deception had been discovered.

That, Hugh thought, as he tossed and turned on the increasingly unyielding mattress, was the obvious explanation. Why not accept it? Because he decided, it over-simplified the ridiculously complicated. The chap in question would have done better to have given no name at all, if all he had in mind was doing Sam Thaxted's daughter a minor service. The extraordinary impersonation made no sense. And why involve his wife – if the woman were his wife?

At last Hugh dozed, but soon he woke again. Through the wall he could hear Keith Masterson's gentle snores. They reminded him that Keith had promised to make inquiries about this Canadian who was said to have been posted to NATO, and he realized that neither he nor Jay had considered what action if any they would take then. If they faced Di Bianco with the story, he could just deny it, and anyway they had no right to take any action which might throw suspicion on anyone on the basis of an unsubstantiated tale told by a deceptive and anonymous informant. If the pseudo-Harper had himself lied throughout, the officer might be totally innocent.

Hugh's mind was once more going round in circles. Why should pseudo-Harper have bothered to create a false scenario? To deceive, yes. But with what purpose? There seemed no logical answer.

Towards morning Hugh eventually fell into a deep sleep, failing to hear Keith get up and leave for the office, and it was after nine before the smell of coffee roused him. He pulled on a robe and went along to the kitchen, where Jay was having breakfast.

She greeted him abruptly. 'Hugh, I've been thinking.'

'Good,' said Hugh, yawning. 'So have I. I hope you've reached some reasoned conclusions, because I haven't.'

'I've come to one conclusion.' She poured him some coffee. 'Eggs?'

'No thanks, Jay. Just toast. Tell me.'

'I believe Ottawa is central to this business. Sam was at the US Embassy here. Canville was the British High Commissioner. And we know there's a connection between them, both because of Fenwick's interest in them, and because of what Norman Saint told us. Now we have another character – a Canadian officer, who was also in the city about the same time.'

Hugh managed to conceal his disappointment at this somewhat unilluminating analysis of the situation. He commented, 'Jay, if the chap you met at the Zoo was a phoney, isn't it likely that – '

'Sure, I know, I know,' she interrupted swiftly. 'But, phoney or not, he still involved Ottawa, didn't he?'

Hugh had to agree. 'So we're back to the late High Commissioner,' he said, trying not to sound reluctant. 'Okay. While you're busy at your embassy, I'll do some checking.'

★ ★ ★

An hour later they parted on Elgin Street, Jay to go up to Confederation Square on her way to the US Embassy, and Hugh to cut across to the Ottawa Public Library on Metcalfe Street. Neither destination was far from Keith Masterson's apartment, and it was easier to walk than to take the car.

The day was hot and humid. Hugh, who had walked fast, was thankful to get inside the air-conditioned building. The Public Library was nearer than either the National Library of Canada or Carleton University Library, and he knew that its reference department would be able to provide him with the material he needed without any formalities.

The senior librarian on duty in the department remembered him and greeted him as an old friend. 'Professor Bigrel,' she said, 'how nice to see you again.' Hugh, who had forgotten that in North America all university teachers were called 'professor' or 'doctor', accepted his honorary rank without comment, and returned her compliments.

Then, to his pleasure and without prompting, she mentioned the tragic death of Sir Rupert Canville. She hadn't known him personally, but a friend of hers, a locally-engaged employee of the High Commission, had frequently remarked how pleasant he was.

'Of course, poor Sir Rupert had no one to blame but himself,' she added. 'It was a foolish thing to do, taking out a canoe alone on a half-frozen lake. He wouldn't have stood a chance; the water was about freezing, and his thick winter clothes would make swimming impossible.'

Her interest and sympathy made Hugh's task that much simpler. Hinting that he was considering a biography of the late High Commissioner, he asked to see the relevant Canadian newspaper files. 'Apart from an account of the memorial service, there weren't many details of the accident in the British press,' he said.

'There was a great deal here,' the librarian said at once. 'The *Citizen* naturally made a lot of it, and so did the *Globe and Mail* – you remember, the Toronto paper – and the *Montreal Gazette*. The French Canadian press, too, for that matter.'

'I'd like to see all of them, if I may. Are they microfilmed yet?'

'Most of them, I think. We try to keep up to date to save shelf-space.' The librarian gave Hugh a warm smile. 'You go and sit over there, Professor Bigrel. I'll get you everything you need.'

She was as good as her word, and Hugh had reason to be grateful. By the end of the morning he had absorbed a considerable amount of new information. He now knew the name of the lake where Canville had drowned, the name of the owner of the cottage that Canville had borrowed, and the name of the man who had spotted the up-turned canoe floating amid the ice and raised the alarm. He made careful notes.

Naturally, much of what he read was of no consequence, though it helped to build up the background. For instance, he was interested to learn that it was not unusual for Canville to go off by himself for a solitary weekend, when his duties made this possible. And he realized that nowhere was there any suggestion that the drowning was other than accidental, not even in one of the gossip columns which made a point of lamenting the fact that at the time Lady Canville was paying one of her 'frequent visits to friends in the USA'.

Hugh thanked the librarian profusely. In a couple of hours he had managed an investigation that would have taken considerably longer without her help. With time in hand he walked slowly from the library to the Château Laurier, where he had arranged to meet Jay.

He found her sitting at a table under an awning, on the open-air terrace at the side of the hotel facing the Parliament Buildings, across the staircase of locks that led the Rideau Canal into the Ottawa River. She was gazing solemnly at the fruit and ice in the tall glass in front of her. He sat down beside her.

'Hi,' he said. He pointed to the drink. 'That looks wonderful. What is it? Pimms? May I have one?'

'Just wave at the waiter.' She grinned at him. 'Then tell me how you got on at the library.'

Hugh produced his notes, and told her what he had learnt.

He had an excellent memory, so it was easy for him to repeat verbatim much of what he had read. Jay listened attentively.

'I'm not sure what help all this will be,' he concluded, 'but at least it's opened up some possibilities. Perhaps we could drive out to this lake, and talk to the chap who found the canoe.'

'Why not? We'll go tomorrow.'

Hugh tasted the drink the waiter had brought him. Nodding his approval, he said, 'What about this afternoon?'

'There's something I want to do this afternoon, Hugh. I'd like to go to the apartment block on the Driveway where Sam lived.'

'For a special reason?'

'I had a long talk with the girl who had been his secretary at the embassy. It was she who packed his clothes and arranged for his possessions to be shipped to Aunt Hilda in Washington. There wasn't a lot. Sam believed in travelling and living light. But it took her over a couple of days, and when she got there the second time, she knew someone else had been in the apartment.'

'The porter?'

'She asked him, and he denied it vehemently. She says she's a meticulous person, which I believe, and various small things had been moved. As far as she could tell nothing had been taken, but it looked to her as if the place had been thoroughly searched.'

'What's the porter like?'

'Hugh, this is a high-class apartment block. The senior porter and his staff will all be bonded; in a way, they're security men as much as porters. In fact, I guess they're employed under contract from a security firm. I agree anyone can be corrupted for a price – and not necessarily in dollars – but I think it's unlikely. And Sam was a careful man. There would have been no money or personal jewellery or anything tangible like that to steal, and the obvious things, like the TV and the video, weren't touched. No, I guess there's not much doubt the apartment was searched, probably for papers.'

'Would Sam have kept any there?'

'Nothing official, but I suppose he could have made the odd note, or left behind something to suggest where he was going in the UK or who he was going to meet there. But if he did it's surely gone now.'

'What about a diary? I never thought of it before, but he must have had some kind of engagement book. Was it on him when he was killed?'

Jay nodded. 'Yes. The police gave it to me with his other things, but it was no help. The week just had a line through it. According to his secretary here he merely told her to cancel all his appointments and flew off. No one seems to know why he went so suddenly. Or if they did they weren't telling me.'

Jay bent down and hoisted on to her lap a plastic carrier bag that had been lying on the floor beside the table leg. From it she took a leather-framed photograph. She handed it to Hugh.

'My mother,' she said simply. 'She was Maria Socha before she married Sam. He kept this on his desk, and they forgot to pack it. He had a smaller one for his wallet.'

Hugh studied the face with its high cheekbones and large luminous eyes, surrounded by dark hair. 'She was very like you, Jay.'

'Not really. There's a resemblance, but she was beautiful.'

Hugh didn't argue. He returned the photograph to Jay and finished his drink. 'Anything else at your embassy?'

'No.' Jay smiled ruefully. 'And I'm afraid the photo's no real use, but I wanted you to see it.' Her voice broke. Then, as if regretting her emotions, she said. 'Let's go have lunch. We can eat in the coffee shop here.'

Viktor Krasnakov had had every reason to be contented with the situation in Washington. To the extent that he could judge, the operation – such as it was – seemed to have been under control while it was centred in the United States.

The American girl, Betsy-Ann, had done her job well, and she could be used again if necessary. She'd now be able to pay off some of the debts she had acquired from her high living, he thought cynically, but even if she became solvent for a while it would make no difference. She was the kind who always wanted more, and would never give up what she'd got.

The Ivanovs were a different matter. They were patriots. Working at the United Nations in New York – he as a member of the international staff, she as an interpreter – they made themselves available for innumerable tasks, often small but of inestimable value, and they were utterly reliable. Krasnakov had no doubt that the report he had received of Boris Ivanov's meeting with Jay Ryan at the Washington Zoo was accurate in every respect. He had no means of knowing if the deception had borne any fruit, but muddying the waters a little could do no harm.

Then, predictably, Ryan and Bigrel had come to Ottawa. It had been simple to follow them from the airport to the block of apartments on the Driveway, and a guess that they were staying with Masterson, who was in the British High Commission, had been easily verified. It was astounding, Krasnakov mused, how unsuspecting people were, and how readily they answered strangers' questions.

So far, so good, Krasnakov thought gloomily. It was since then that things had started to go wrong. Galinov had wasted the morning watching for Ryan to emerge from the American Embassy, and the stupid girl – what was her name? Irena Serenova, that was it – they had borrowed from the local KGB staff to assist them, had somehow lost Bigrel when traffic lights had changed at some intersection.

The afternoon had been an improvement. Galinov had, of course, been able to pick up Bigrel when he met Ryan for lunch. And their visit to Samuel Thaxted's old apartment must have been a complete waste of time. It had, Krasnakov knew, been searched professionally before the American's clothes or possessions had been removed, so this annoyingly persistent couple would have found nothing in the place to interest them.

But at this point Galinov's report had taken a surprising and unexpected turn.

'Are you sure that's where they went, Galinov?'

'Positive, Comrade Colonel. Instead of walking along the Driveway, as was reasonable if they were returning to where they're staying, they cut through to Elgin Street, and went straight to a store called Simond's. It's a dry-cleaning establishment.'

'Dry-cleaning!'

'Yes, Comrade Colonel. Dry-cleaning. And it was shut, with a notice on the door saying the proprietor had died, and this was the day of his funeral. I read it after Bigrel and Ryan had moved on.'

'So? What did they do?'

'Well, I stopped in a flower shop entry a few doors away, and watched them reading the notice. Then they stood on the sidewalk and seemed to be having a discussion.' Galinov shrugged. 'After a couple of minutes they walked off and returned to Masterson's apartment. That's where I left them.'

'Quite right. We can't watch them all the time. With so few to do the job they might get suspicious.'

Krasnakov remained deep in thought, until Galinov volunteered, 'I wondered, Comrade Colonel, if Masterson might have asked them to collect some cleaning for him, but I don't think so. It's difficult to say why, but I definitely got the impression, perhaps from the kind of discussion they were having outside, that – that this was more important to them than an errand like that.'

'I see,' Krasnakov said. 'Or rather, I don't. But I intend to. If you're right, Galinov, they'll be around at that cleaning place first thing in the morning – and you'll be there too. What happens after that depends on you. I leave it to your initiative.'

Galinov bowed his head. 'Yes, Comrade Colonel,' he said, hoping that any failures of omission or commission wouldn't land him in trouble.

THIRTEEN

Krasnakov's guess was proved accurate. Immediately after breakfast the next morning Hugh and Jay left Masterson's apartment and went straight along to the dry-cleaner's. They hoped there would be few customers so early in the day, but found that others had had the same idea. Denied their cleaning yesterday, a small crowd was waiting hopefully on the sidewalk outside the store.

When eventually the funeral notice was removed, the blind pulled up and the door opened, they all stepped inside. The two girls behind the counter were besieged by importunate and hurried customers.

Hugh found himself separated from Jay and, in the small space available, tried to stand to one side. Pressed against a rack of dry-cleaned garments in their plastic bags, he could still see her and hear her.

'Good day. I'd like to have Mr Thaxted's cleaning, please. I'm afraid you've had it for ages, and the ticket's been lost. You called the porter at Mr Thaxted's apartment last week to say it hadn't been collected.'

'Did we? It wasn't me that called, but I'll look. Thaxted, you said?'

Jay nodded, and the girl thrust her way through a door into the rear of the establishment. The remaining girl was quick and efficient. The crowd of early customers soon dwindled, and Hugh became aware of a man standing beside him.

He was of medium height and medium build. His hair was light brown, his face nondescript. He wore brown slacks, a yellow shirt and a check jacket. Hugh would hardly have noticed him, except that he seemed to be making no attempt to claim any cleaning and that, when their gazes met, he smiled nervously and edged away.

Hugh's attention returned to Jay. The girl had come back through the rear door with a plastic bag over her arm. She passed it across the counter and took some dollars in exchange. As she rang up the price on the register, Jay picked up the bag, and Hugh turned to leave the shop and wait outside for Jay. He had quite forgotten the man who had been standing beside him.

'What did you get?'

'Just a pair of his slacks. Nothing important, but then I scarcely hoped for anything.'

'Let me carry them for you.'

Hugh took the plastic bag. The handle of the plastic-covered wire clotheshanger over which the slacks were folded protruded through the top of the bag and made it easy to carry. He swung it a little as he walked.

'Now we get the car and head for the hills, as we planned?' he said.

'Sure. Why not? You have a map of Québec?'

'In my pocket, yes. Naconda's one of the more obscure lakes. We'd never find it without – '

Hugh broke off abruptly and swung round as if he had been pulled on a lead. In fact, he had felt a violent tug which had thrown him off-balance.

'Hugh! What is it?'

'I – Well, I'll be damned!'

Hugh stared in amazement at his hand, which still retained a grip on the metal clotheshanger, and the plastic bag. But the bag was now empty. Its side had been slit neatly, and the slacks jerked free.

Jay had sized up the situation quickly. She pointed to a man, who had dodged across Elgin Street, and was running hard on the opposite sidewalk. Hugh made to follow him, but she gripped his arm.

'It's no use, Hugh. You'd never catch him.'

Even as she spoke, the man turned down a side street and was lost to sight, but not before Hugh had recognized him as the man in the cleaner's. And suddenly he had the impression that he had seen him somewhere yesterday, or even the day before.

'Jay, I don't think he was a common thief,' Hugh said. Automatically they had begun to walk again. 'I think he's been following us around, and he pinched those slacks because they were Sam's.'

'But why?' When Hugh didn't reply immediately, she answered her own question. 'Perhaps it was just an extension of the search of Sam's apartment – they hoped, or feared, that something might be found in a pocket of any clothes left to be cleaned. It seems to be a long shot, but, if I'm right and there was something in those slacks, we've lost it.'

Viktor Krasnakov regarded the navy blue slacks lying on his desk with disgust. They had been thoroughly inspected; their pockets were still turned inside out. But nothing had been found. They were what they appeared to be, an expensive American pair of men's trousers that had been dry-cleaned. The fact that they had once belonged to Samuel Thaxted was obviously irrelevant.

'You took a stupid risk, Galinov,' Krasnakov said angrily. 'What if you'd been caught? It wouldn't have been *funny*.' In the security of their own embassy they had been speaking Russian, and Krasnakov's sudden use of an English word that had so many meanings disconcerted Galinov.

'It was impossible for them to catch me, Comrade Colonel. I picked my moment carefully, there was the element of surprise and I'm a fast runner.' Galinov shrugged his apology. 'At the time it seemed worthwhile, but evidently it wasn't. A pity.'

'Most certainly a pity, Comrade.' Krasnakov was unappeased. 'And most unlike you.' Normally, Krasnakov reflected, Galinov was good at his work, reliable and not given to such extravagant behaviour. 'Surely you realize that in future this man Bigrel will recognize you, so we can't use you as a watcher any more. And, apart from that fool of a girl Irena Serenova, there's no one else.'

'In a car, Comrade Colonel, with the minimum of disguise, he wouldn't know me,' Galinov hurried to reply.

'But unfortunately he and Ryan seem to enjoy going around Ottawa on foot. No, it was enough of a problem before, and now it's – '

'Comrade Colonel.' Galinov dared to interrupt. 'There's something I've not told you yet. When I was about to make the snatch I was right behind them, and I heard a word or two of what they were saying.'

'Go on!' Krasnakov bit off the words.

'It wasn't much,' said Galinov quickly. 'Something about making for the hills – I assume they meant the Gatineau hills – and, believe it or not, Comrade Colonel, Lake Naconda.'

'Naconda.' Krasnakov looked up immediately. 'Naconda! You're sure you're right?'

'Absolutely, Comrade Colonel. It's a distinctive name.'

'Anything else? When were they going?'

'I'm not certain, Comrade. But they did mention getting their car, and I think perhaps they were going at once. I'm sorry. But Irena Serenova was watching. She was in our own car, parked across the street from the dry-cleaning shop, and she will have followed them.'

'That girl'll run out of fuel, or drive into a ditch or commit some folly.' Krasnakov laughed scornfully. Then resignedly he added, 'All right. There's nothing to be done about it. Leave me now, Galinov. And take Mr Thaxted's wretched trousers with you.'

Galinov departed, thankful to escape from his master's presence, and Krasnakov was left with his worrying thoughts. Whether or not Irena Serenova succeeded in following Ryan and Bigrel was really immaterial. They would learn little from peering through the windows of the cottage where the late High Commissioner had spent his last hours, or gazing at the waters in which he had drowned. What was disturbing – frightening was not too strong a word – was their obvious and continuing interest in the circumstances of Canville's death.

Their unexpected call on Lady Canville at the country home of the Lansdownes had been something of a shock, but had turned out to be harmless; Ryan had talked mostly of her father, and Canville had scarcely been mentioned. Probably their true motive had been to question Monica Canville about Thaxted, but there wasn't anything she could have told them. No, Ryan and Bigrel had gained nothing from that visit. On the contrary, Jay Ryan, speaking of her proposed trip to North America, had herself given away useful information.

But now it looked as if they had made a connection between the two deaths – of Canville and Thaxted. Why else should they be so interested in Lake Naconda? A sentimental journey? Krasnakov shrugged, and swore aloud. He had hoped that the story about the Canadian officer would have been occupying them, but apparently not. The only consolation was that they were still a long way, a very long way, from the truth. But they had taken a step nearer to it.

Galinov's report had been accurate enough, but there had been a development of which he was unaware – a development that had caused Jay to suggest a change of plan. So, instead of driving up to the Gatineau, they sat drinking mid-morning coffee on Masterson's balcony and, ignoring the magnificent view, they talked. At Hugh's feet was the metal clotheshanger with the plastic bag that had once contained Sam Thaxted's slacks. And on the table between them was a large safety pin and a small envelope on which had been scrawled, 'Found in pocket'.

Unable to see a suitable litter bin in which to throw away the hanger and its dangling plastic, Hugh had carried it back to the garage of the apartment block where their car was parked in a visitor's slot. It was only when he slung the useless object on to the rear seat that he caught sight of the envelope pinned to the bottom of the hanger's hook, its presence previously concealed by the printed advertising on the plastic bag.

Now they were discussing the contents of the envelope – a slip of paper that could so easily have been lost or discarded.

'Jay, this could be nothing whatever to do with our present problem,' Hugh protested. 'Sam might have made these notes of Polish names and addresses for a hundred different reasons.'

'Sure,' said Jay. 'But it's worth checking on them, isn't it? Hugh, we agreed that that character stole the slacks because he thought there might be something in them worth finding. What he didn't know was that cleaners always look through pockets and send back anything they come across.'

'Okay, but how do you propose we check? Dzolak and Beluch both have Warsaw addresses. I suppose we could look them up in a phone book, and give them a call.'

'Don't be sarcastic, Hugh!'

'Sorry, but I don't see how these names are going to help. We're not even sure of the third one.'

'I think it must be Krasneski. It's a pity Sam's writing isn't clearer.' Jay ran her hand through her short dark hair. 'And Sam's underlined him twice, so he seems to be the most important of the three.'

'But there's no address for him.'

'No, and that makes me wonder if he could be right here in Ottawa – at the Polish Embassy, say.' When Hugh expressed doubt, she continued, 'Look, Hugh, it's a possibility. I think it's worth considering.'

'It's a guess, Jay. Nothing more.'

'But still worth considering,' Jay persisted.

Hugh shrugged. 'What do you want to do? I imagine there's a diplomatic list for Ottawa, just as there is in other capitals. We could ask Keith to check him out for us.'

'We shan't see Keith until this evening,' Jay objected. 'Hugh, why don't we just go along to the Polish Embassy and ask for Krasneski? Right now. Why not?'

'They may not be very forthcoming.'

'Too bad. They can't eat us.'

Hugh discovered the address of the Polish Embassy from the telephone book, and it was a simple matter to locate Daly Avenue, not far from the Soviet Embassy in a district of Ottawa known as Sandy Hill. It was too far to walk in the heat and, followed by a bored Irena Serenova, they drove eastwards across the Canal, and managed to find a parking place close to an unpretentious building at the end of Daly Avenue near the Rideau River.

'Let me cope,' Jay murmured as they went up the steps and rang the bell at the closed door.

'We want to make an inquiry,' she said to the man who opened the door to them.

'Visas? Afternoons only,' the man replied shortly, with a strong central European accent.

'No, no,' Jay said quickly. 'It's about – er – staff.'

'Staff?' Reasonably enough, the man seemed surprised. 'You want job?' he demanded.

'Of course not! We just want to make an appointment to see Monsieur Krasneski,' Jay said.

'Krasneski?' The man was clearly at a loss. Finally, he said, 'Enter. I will find someone.'

They waited, standing, in a hall opposite a desk marked 'Inquiries', while he mumbled into a telephone. Then he said, 'A moment, please.'

He stayed with them until a woman appeared down the staircase in the background. She was in her forties, with a sallow complexion and black hair shaped to her head like a helmet. Irresistibly she made Hugh think of a wardress.

'What is this?' she asked abruptly, taking a seat behind the desk, as if about to interrogate them.

'We would like to see – or make an appointment to see – Monsieur Krasneski,' Jay repeated.

The woman's eyes widened behind her spectacles. 'There is no Monsieur Krasneski here,' she said firmly.

'Are you sure?'

'Quite sure. This is a small Mission. There is no question of a mistake on my part.'

'Then it must be my mistake.' Jay smiled.

Her smile was not returned. The woman picked up the telephone receiver and spoke rapidly into it in Polish. She looked up. 'Your names, please?' she said.

Jay hesitated. 'They're not important,' she said, brushing the question aside. 'We'd have liked to have spoken to Monsieur Krasneski, but as you say he's not here – '

'You still do not understand. He is never here. He is not a member of our staff.' Again she spoke into the phone, then put down the receiver. She looked speculatively from Jay to Hugh. 'Perhaps he belongs to another embassy,' she suggested.

'Perhaps,' Jay agreed. 'Anyway, as we're here, could we see your Warsaw telephone directory?'

This time it was the woman's turn to hesitate. 'To check on Monsieur Krasneski?' she said at last. 'You know his address? There are certainly several people of that name in Warsaw, but – ' She reached into a drawer of the desk and brought out a book.

'Please don't bother.' Suddenly Jay seemed to change her mind. She turned to leave the building, making an imperceptible gesture to Hugh to follow. And when she was at the door, the man about to open it for them, she called back to the woman at the desk in a burst of Polish.

'What the hell was that about?' Hugh demanded, as he half-pushed Jay through the door, and along the sidewalk to the car.

'I didn't like it in there,' she replied, and laughed. 'Did you see that woman's face when she realized I spoke Polish?'

'No, but I can imagine it,' Hugh said, sliding behind the wheel. 'It was a shock to me, too. What did you say to her?'

'I said, "You've been most helpful. We appreciate all you've done". Then *"Bardzo dziękuję. Do widzenia"*. That's "Thank you very much. Goodbye".'

'It all sounds fairly innocuous, if a bit fulsome in the circumstances,' said Hugh.

'Ah, but it didn't matter exactly what I said. What did matter was that she knew I understood what she'd been saying on the phone, or most of it,' Jay said. 'My mother always spoke Polish to me when I was young, but unfortunately it's got rusty in the last few years.'

'Jay, don't keep me in suspense! What did the woman say?'

'She said something like, "I've a strange couple here asking to see someone called Krasneski. The girl's very persistent, but she won't give her name. I suggest you take a good look at them".'

Hugh started the engine. 'You mean someone was coming to inspect us? That's why we left so quickly?'

'I guess he – or she – was inspecting us right then on a monitor,' Jay said. 'No. I didn't think we'd get any more out of them, so we might as well leave.'

Hugh shook his head in doubtful admiration. 'Jay, you're wonderful,' he said. 'But I hope this doesn't mean trouble.'

FOURTEEN

It was rapidly becoming a typical Ottawa summer's day. The morning had been increasingly hot and humid and, by the time Hugh and Jay had had an early lunch with the intention of driving up to the Gatineau immediately afterwards, the sky had darkened to such a degree that the street lamps were shining and the lights in most government offices in the nation's capital had been switched on. It could easily have been evening rather than midday.

Thunder was rumbling and roaring in the distance, obviously coming closer and closer to the city. Soon, there was an occasional particularly loud clap and lightning forked among the black clouds. Hugh and Jay waited with a crowd of people clustered irritably under the portico of the Lord Elgin Hotel as rain began to fall. They had been eating in the air-conditioned coffee shop, and found the outside air so heavy and oppressive that breathing appeared a conscious effort.

The rain fell in great globs, each seemingly the size of an English 10p coin or a Canadian quarter, at first two or three drops together, but gradually more and more until finally it was no longer possible to see across the street. Then a huge crash, which sounded as if it were directly overhead, shook the ground beneath their feet, and at the same time the sky was lit from end to end by a jagged white light.

Hugh was suddenly conscious of Jay's body pressed tightly against him, and her hand clasping his. He glanced down at her and saw to his surprise that she was pale and shaking.

'Jay, are you all right?'

She managed to nod vigorously, 'I'm okay. It's just that I – I hate electrical storms.'

'A good thing – ' Hugh began, but bit back his remark. He

had been going to say it was a good thing that the self-confident and independent Jay had at least one weakness, but he realized in time that any such remark would be inappropriate, if not infuriating. He rearranged his sentence quickly. 'A good thing it's not going to last, then. Look over there. It's clearing already,' he added encouragingly.

Indeed, though the rain was now beating down so fiercely that the drops rebounded from the sidewalk and the roadway, looking exactly like a regiment of soldiers as they moved up and down in step, the sky was lightening. There was a further clap of thunder, but it was neither so violent nor so threatening as the last.

But someone in the group waiting under the portico for the weather to improve took the opportunity to comment, as if in answer to Hugh, 'Sure, the storm's easing for the moment, but it'll come round again. You'll see.'

'Thanks,' Jay murmured, withdrawing her hand from Hugh's. 'We seem to be out of luck, Hugh. This trip to the lake's fated. We can't go in this.'

'No, I agree,' said Hugh. 'Even if we could find the way, we'd probably get bogged down on some minor track. We'll go tomorrow instead. After the storm the temperature and humidity will drop, and it will be quite pleasant.'

'Tomorrow will be Thursday. What do you say we go back to Washington on Friday, Hugh, and spend the weekend with Aunt Hilda? Maybe we can get something out of Cliff Di Bianco or Norm Saint – something about these Poles, perhaps.' Jay shrugged. 'We don't seem to be getting very far in Ottawa.'

'Fair enough,' Hugh agreed. 'Apart from Keith's hospitality I haven't provided much help. I'm sorry, but teaching a course at a local university doesn't open that many doors.'

'No need to apologize.'

Hugh resented the tension that had somehow sprung up between them, presumably because Jay was ashamed of the moment of weakness she had shown during the worst of the thunder. He said, 'The storm's nearly over, at least for the moment. I suggest we fix our flights to Washington and London, then take the afternoon off. Personally, I'd like to go to the

Canadian National Gallery and look over the Arts Centre. Neither of them is very far. Perhaps we could meet at the Gallery in an hour or so?'

He continued as Jay looked at him inquiringly, 'Something's just occurred to me. I'd like to do a spot of phoning first, and see if I can make a Carleton contact who could conceivably be useful. It's a forlorn hope, but still – '

Keith Masterson wasn't yet drunk, but he'd already had more alcohol than was good for him. A boring cocktail party at the home of the High Commission's Cultural Attaché, the British Council representative, who had a house in Rockcliffe, the district of Ottawa where most diplomats lived, had been preceded by an unpleasant conversation with Fenwick – almost an interrogation, Masterson thought angrily. Inevitably he had taken the opportunity offered by the party to forget his misery, and he had drunk far more than usual.

Although he had been asked to stay on for a buffet meal – a spare man was always welcome, he had thought to himself uncharitably – he had declined. But when he got back to his apartment he had no inclination to cook, and found little food immediately available. He had opened a can of soup, eaten some bread and cheese and half a melon, and made himself a cup of coffee, vaguely regretting having refused the invitation to supper.

Afterwards he had turned on the television set, flipped through the many channels, and turned it off again. Then he had poured himself yet another gin and tonic, and brooded about Dick Fenwick. By eleven o'clock when he heard the sound of a key in the lock and the cheerful voices of Hugh and Jay, he'd had several more drinks; he had also forced himself to search the rooms his guests were occupying, though he had found nothing that might interest Fenwick. He made no direct response to Hugh's greeting.

Instead: 'Where've you been?' he asked, his speech slurred.

Jay answered. 'Visiting with an old friend of Hugh's, who teaches political science at Carleton University.'

133

'Really? What did he have to say?'

Jay and Hugh exchanged glances, amused by Masterson's state. Hugh, who had passed a disappointing evening because they had learnt absolutely nothing new about Sir Rupert Canville, said, 'We mostly talked American politics.'

'Not wildly interesting,' commented Jay, though in fact she had been intrigued by the professor's offer to lay odds that the handsome Worral J. Smith, whom they had met at lunch with the Lansdownes back in the Cotswolds, would become the next President of the United States. 'But we had an exciting morning,' she went on.

Between them they told Keith the story of the stolen slacks and the slip of paper with the Polish names they had subsequently discovered. To their surprise he refused to take them seriously. When they insisted, he became aggressive.

'I've heard of nutters who steal women's knickers off washing lines, but this – this is absurd. You must take me for a fool. You've already got me in the dirt. Now you plan to push my face in it.' He rounded on Hugh. 'It's not fair. All I did was offer you beds for a few nights. I didn't want to get involved in your sordid little affairs.'

'What the hell are you talking about?' Hugh had misunderstood; he thought that Hugh was implying a sexual relationship between himself and Jay, and he let his temper flare.

'For God's sake, calm down, both of you!' Jay cried.

Hugh was silent, but Keith was beyond caring. He held up his glass in a mock toast.

'Here's to you!' he said fiercely. 'And your Canadian service officer in NATO – who doesn't exist, any more than do his German ma and his English pa! And, of course, here's to the fucking Fenwick, who's going to destroy me – all because of you.'

'Fenwick!' said Hugh. 'Dick Fenwick. Damn and blast the man!'

But as he spoke he was reminded of Fenwick's warnings. He knew that he – and Jay – had got into waters far deeper than either of them had ever intended or appreciated. They were caught in what amounted to a rip tide, with currents and cross-currents they had as yet no means of understanding; probably they were behaving like carefree fools. They could easily drown, Hugh thought, and take others with them – Keith among them. Come to that, some had already suffered – Foxy Worth, for one.

Nevertheless, Hugh knew that he was committed. It was Jay who had committed him. And there was no way of going back now. He couldn't imagine himself at home in Oxford, giving tutorials, lecturing, researching, writing, as if nothing had happened. He would fret unceasingly about the Canville affair; he knew also that he would fret about Jay Ryan.

'You're tight, Keith,' he said harshly, 'tight as a tick, and you've already said more than enough. I want the rest, too. Just what have you been up to with Fenwick?'

'I – I couldn't help it,' said Masterson. 'Oh, God! I feel awful.'

'I'll make you some black coffee,' Jay volunteered.

By the time she returned with the coffee Hugh was standing over Keith, who was staring up at him in obvious distress.

Jay said, 'Hugh, what have you done?'

'It's not what I've done. It's what my old drunk chum here has done. Fenwick's in Ottawa, masquerading as some official at the High Commission, and he's ordered Keith to spy on us – tell him everything we do, and so on.' Hugh didn't bother to hide his disgust. 'Now Keith's scared because Fenwick's angry and not satisfied with his reports. As far as I can make out, he thinks Keith has tried to deceive him in some way. Evidently, as we suspected, that Canadian officer was a mere figment of the pseudo Mr Harper's imagination.'

'Oh, hell!' Jay looked at Keith pityingly. Then she said thoughtfully, 'at least it's put Cliff Di Bianco in the clear. Cliff didn't lie to us.'

'No. That's one complication less,' Hugh admitted.

Jay offered Keith the mug of coffee she had made and he took it thankfully. He sipped slowly.

'I'm sorry,' he said after a minute. 'Truly sorry. I didn't want to do it. Fenwick threatened me. He said that if I didn't do as he asked, he'd have me shipped back to the UK as a security risk. It would have been the end of my career.'

'Nice guy!' Jay was sardonic.

'He said it was for your own good. He said you'd got yourselves involved in something that could be dangerous.' Keith was almost pleading by now.

Jay looked at Hugh, and motioned towards the door. To Keith she said, 'Would you like some more coffee?'

Keith nodded his head, and winced. 'Christ! I'm going to have the father and mother of a hangover in the morning.'

'Serve you right.' Hugh refused to show sympathy. 'I'll get you some aspirin while Jay makes your coffee. Incidentally, do you have an Ottawa diplomatic list?'

'In the top drawer of my desk.' Keith pointed across the room. 'What am I going to tell Fenwick?' he said, almost to himself, as Hugh and Jay left the room.

Hugh collected the booklet from the desk, and found some aspirin in Keith's bathroom. Then he followed Jay into the kitchen. 'The wretched man's got a point,' he said. 'What in hell's name is he to say to Fenwick?'

'That's just what I wanted to ask you privately,' said Jay. 'Can we trust him to keep quiet about anything at all that we've told him?' She was busy making another mug of coffee.

'I think he'd want to – but no. We can't be certain. In any case, Fenwick would get it out of him. He might as well have the benefit of coughing it up voluntarily. We'll say he can do as he likes. Let's hope that by morning he won't remember the names.'

'Have you found them?'

'In the diplomatic list? Let me look.' Hugh riffled through the pages. 'No, they're not there – not even Krasneski. I'm afraid your guess was wrong, Jay. That dragon at the Polish Embassy told the truth.'

'There may be non-diplomatic Poles in Ottawa,' said Jay.

'None of those names are in the phone book. I looked.'

'Or we might try their embassy in Washington,' Jay added speculatively.

'Or London.'

'Or go and visit those addresses in Warsaw.'

Laughing wryly at the absurdity of the idea, they returned to the living-room. Keith was half-asleep, but they woke him. He drank the coffee and swallowed the tablets, and let Hugh half-lead, half-carry him to bed.

There Hugh assured him that they understood his position, that they had no quarrel with him, and that he might tell Fenwick everything. In addition, he could say that on Friday they were leaving for Washington on their way home to England, their inquiries at a dead end. And when Hugh had left him, Masterson wept maudlin tears of gratitude.

Someone else was weeping into an Ottawa pillow that night. It was Irena Serenova. She was frightened, shaken and sore.

Krasnakov had been furious. He was still furious. Though it was well after midnight and he had retired to the small bedroom that he occupied in the Soviet Embassy he couldn't sleep. He paced up and down, cursing Irena Serenova's folly. The bloody girl had failed to perceive any significance in Bigrel's and Ryan's visit to the Polish Embassy, and hadn't reported it until she returned late in the evening. He had reached for the phone, but realized almost at once that it was far too late for him to take any action that night. He must be careful not to make too much of the affair. Even among one's allies there were dissidents, and a whisper could grow and spread. There was nothing for it but to wait till morning.

It was immaterial that it wasn't the wretched girl's fault, since she'd had no means of knowing that he would have wanted to act immediately. She had no instinct. Betsy-Ann, he had thought, would have guessed.

And, as he recalled a mental picture of the tall, leggy American, desire had overcome him. He took out his frustration with Irena Serenova by pushing her on to his office floor, tearing at her clothes and thrusting himself into her. Irena Serenova knew better than to resist. She hadn't even cried out when he hurt her, but merely whimpered. And when he had finished and told her to get out, she had retreated without protest.

Remembering, Krasnakov felt no satisfaction. It had been a form of physical relief, that was all. He heard a distant clock strike, and counted. Five hours to go before he could decently telephone the Polish Ambassador, and arrange to go to the embassy.

He flung himself on to his bed, and put out the light. After a while he slept. He dreamed of the one woman he had truly loved. It was a happy dream, and he was sorry when his alarm woke him.

FIFTEEN

Viktor Krasnakov decided that it would be best to call on the Polish Ambassador alone, and he made an appointment as early as possible in the morning. He was resigned to the fact that he would be compelled to waste a great deal of time in needless pleasantries.

The two men – the Ambassador and the Soviet KGB officer – were acquaintances, no more, and each distrusted the other. In theory, the Ambassador outranked the so-called attaché, especially an attaché of another embassy, but both officials were aware of the facts of life. The Russian knew for certain, and the Pole – who had his own small UB staff to contend with – strongly suspected, that Krasnakov wielded far greater authority.

As far as the Ambassador was concerned, all this meant that the formalities had to be observed scrupulously until, or unless, Krasnakov decided otherwise. For his part, Krasnakov, seeking the Ambassador's co-operation and unwilling to underline the importance he attached to the inquiries he intended to make, felt it necessary to play a waiting game.

In fact, when tea had been served in tall glasses accompanied by the usual wafer-thin biscuits, and they were alone, it was the Ambassador who decided that he must be the first to broach the reason for the visit. Previously the two men had spoken English but now the Pole, remembering that the Russian had a reputation as a linguist, addressed him in Polish.

'And how can I be of help to you, Comrade?' he asked.

Krasnakov said, 'Ah, yes,' very casually, and proceeded to explain. He had found it impossible to devise a plausible fiction, so he was reduced to an approximation to the truth. He said he wanted to know more about the young couple, the Englishman and the American girl, who had called at the Polish Embassy the previous day – what questions they had asked, for instance.

'It could be a trifling matter, nothing that would interest us. An inquiry about a visa, perhaps. On the other hand – ' He made an expressive gesture. 'Without going into detail I can tell you in confidence that recently these two persons have become over-curious about a minor operation that's no concern of theirs. I'm sure they're not really important, but they could possibly have nuisance value. You understand?'

The ambassador understood perfectly. He was to provide information, but ask no questions. He had no objection. On the contrary, he was glad to co-operate; a favour done was a favour to be returned. Because the American girl had suddenly and unexpectedly broken into Polish, the incident had been reported to him immediately, and he could see no harm in passing on what little he knew to the Russian. Gesturing to Krasnakov, he lifted his phone and gave an order.

When the woman who had reminded Hugh Bigrel of a wardress appeared in the office, he didn't introduce his visitor, but said, 'Please repeat what you told me about that couple who came in yesterday morning.'

There was not much of a story to tell, and she told it baldly. The Ambassador glanced at Krasnakov, inviting questions. For a moment Krasnakov found it difficult to speak. He was badly shaken. Krasneski was very similar to his own name, and indeed he had used it in Warsaw on occasions when he had wanted to pass as a Pole. And Ryan's father had been in Warsaw with Canville –

The Ambassador was staring at him curiously, and with an effort he regained his composure. 'Krasneski's a fairly common patronymic in Poland, isn't it?' he said addressing the woman. 'Was a first name mentioned, Comrade?'

'No, Comrade.'

'A pity.' He smiled at her, and turned to the Ambassador. 'As I said, I don't think it's of any great importance,' he lied. 'I'm afraid I've bothered you for nothing.'

Five minutes later Krasnakov had made his farewells and left the Polish Embassy. His mind was in a turmoil. Perhaps Galinov had been right, he thought bitterly, as he strode along the street towards his waiting car. Perhaps it would have been better if Ryan, at least, had suffered an 'accident'.

'No, I bloody well don't remember! I was drunk, I tell you! If I'd not been drunk I wouldn't have told them about you – sir,' Keith Masterson said angrily, but wearily.

'Okay,' said Fenwick. 'Many wouldn't, but I believe you. At any rate, I accept that you got drunk last night. One look at you would be enough to convince anyone of that. I've rarely seen a better example of the morning after.'

Masterson groaned aloud. He was sitting on his bed, in pyjamas and gown. He hadn't washed or shaved, though it was eleven o'clock in the morning. But he didn't care about his appearance; it was how he felt that mattered, and he felt like hell. His head ached. If he moved other than slowly a sharp pain pierced his eyes, and he was forced to screw them up, which in turn made him want to vomit. His tongue, like a dirty rag, clogged his mouth. He wished, in spite of his troubled dreams, that he could have gone on sleeping. He breathed deeply.

'I'm doing my best,' he said. 'After all, I did phone you, didn't I?'

'At Bigrel's instructions?'

'No! Your trouble is you're too bloody suspicious.' He had difficulty with the last word. 'I called you because – because – '

'Because you were scared of what might happen if you didn't. Right. Let's go through it once more then. You were tight, and in your cups you 'fessed, like the good little public school boy you once were. You told your friend, Hugh, how you'd been talking about him, and Mrs Ryan, to a nasty man.' Fenwick put his hands on his knees and leant forward so that his face was close to Masterson's. 'But, before that, what had Hugh told *you*?'

'I've – I've – ' Masterson began.

'I know, but I want to hear it again.'

Masterson just stopped himself from moving his head sharply to nod agreement. Searching his memory, he recounted for the third time all he could remember: the apparent theft of the slacks, the slip of paper found in the pocket by the cleaners, the visit to the Polish Embassy, the decision to leave Ottawa and go home.

Fenwick continued to hammer away. 'You're sure the name was Krasneski?'

'Yes. They showed me the bit of paper. The writing was a scribble, but – '

'You didn't say that before?'

'What? That the writing was poor? Does it matter?' Masterson was growing more weary by the minute. All he wanted was to be allowed to sleep.

'It might do,' said Fenwick, disguising his sudden jubilation.

Here was confirmation that something he had merely suspected might indeed be true. Previously Masterson had maintained that the name was Krasneski, and the man a Pole. From what had been said, it was clear that Bigrel and Jay Ryan believed this too. But then, Fenwick thought, it was unlikely that either of them had ever heard of Viktor Georgiyevich Krasnakov.

'Beluch!'

The triumphant cry startled Fenwick. 'What?'

'That was one of the other names,' Masterson explained. 'I was trying to visualize that paper, and there it was.'

'Well done,' said Fenwick, though the name didn't seem to have any particular relevance. 'What about the third?'

'No. That was just a jumble of letters. But – '

'But what?'

'You could ask Hugh. He could hardly refuse to tell you, could he?' Masterson wondered why this simple answer hadn't occurred to him before, or to Fenwick himself, for that matter.

'No. I'm sure he'd never refuse.' Fenwick grinned. 'But if they're going home on Friday, as you said, I expect he's thrown the paper away by now. And of course neither he nor Mrs Ryan will remember a thing.'

'You are a – a – '

'A suspicious bastard? Yes. No matter, Masterson. Perhaps

I'll take your advice. You don't happen to know where the two of them have gone today, do you?'

'I'm not certain, but I think they've gone up to the Gatineau. They left a note saying they won't be back till this evening, and they'd take me out to dinner as it was their last night.'

'I see.' Fenwick thought at once of Lake Naconda. 'Well, I'd better leave you. Then you can recover in time for the celebrations. Thanks for your help.'

With a wave of his hand Fenwick left the bedroom. He saw himself out of the apartment, nodded to the porter as he passed through the hall and went down the steps on to the Driveway. Too busy considering what he had learnt from Keith Masterson to pay any attention to his surroundings, he walked slowly back to the High Commission.

It was good news – the only bit of good news – that Bigrel and the girl were returning to the UK, a fact he didn't doubt because it would be so easy to check. They would be safer there, he hoped, though, whatever they had told Masterson, he found it hard to believe they had abandoned what they had probably come to think of as their justified search for truth.

In other words, it was unlikely they'd had the sense to decide to stop making bloody nuisances of themselves. And, reluctantly, as he walked, he reached the conclusion that, since they refused to pay any attention to his warnings, or to co-operate in any way, it would in future be up to them to cope with whatever might threaten to harm or destroy them. He himself had more important things to do.

Hugh Bigrel pulled the car off the dirt road at a place where the trampled grass with its wheel ruts implied a rudimentary parking place. He opened his door, and inspected the wooden notice that had been blown down in the previous day's storm. On the board was the single word, 'Robertson.'

'This is it, Jay.' Hugh thrust the post back into its hole, where it stood a little lopsidedly. He pointed to a narrow, muddy track that meandered up a hillside covered with pines and maples.

'We'd better go on foot, I think. If we take the car it'll probably get stuck, and then we'll be in real trouble.'

'That's okay. I'm wearing solid shoes.'

Jay got out of the car and together they started up the track, which grew steeper and steeper, until they came out on a small plateau. They found themselves beside a cottage faced with cedar shingles, which over the years had mellowed to a silver-grey. It was a simple, one-storey building, with a wide veranda on four sides. And below, beside a boat-house, a wooden landing-stage stretched out into what was obviously Lake Naconda. The lake itself might have been chosen as an example of typical Gatineau scenery. Pine- and maple-covered slopes stretched down to a wide expanse of calm water, which reflected their forms precisely, and on the far side of the lake could be seen other landing places and, amongst the trees, glimpses of other cottages.

The track continued down to the lake itself, but, by common consent, Hugh and Jay, after pausing to catch their breath and admire the view, climbed up the half-dozen steps to the veranda of the Robertson establishment, and quartered the building, staring through the windows. As far as they could see, the cottage included a large living-room, simply but pleasantly furnished, three bedrooms, a kitchen and a bathroom. Hugh pointed to the electricity supply lines overhead, which fed not only the cottage, but also what was obviously a wooden pump-house down by the lake.

'It's not exactly primitive, is it?' he said.

'Far from it,' Jay agreed as they leant on the veranda railing and stared once again out across the lake. 'I wish it were mine. I think it's lovely here, with that blue sky and the blue water with those magnificent reflections. And there are people in the cottages on the other side, so it's private, but not too lonely.'

'Not at this time of year,' said Hugh, 'but it would have been different in March. When Rupert Canville came here for his last visit, the thaw would have started, so the track wouldn't have been deep in snow. He wouldn't have needed skis or snowshoes or a snowmobile to reach the cottage. But it would have been bitterly cold, and that water would have been grey, not blue.'

Jay shivered.

Hugh went on, 'And out on the lake in a canoe – well! According to the newspapers there was still ice on the water, and it was a bleak weekend with little or no sunshine. He had to wear layers of clothing, so of course he'd have found it hard to swim. It wouldn't have been any use clinging on to the canoe and shouting for help. The cold would have got him before anyone could reach him, and anyway, who would hear? The cottages the other side were all shut up for the winter. Canville liked solitude, they say.'

'Poor man! Even if he was – '

Jay stopped abruptly as they heard the sound of heavy footsteps climbing on to the veranda, and clumping around it towards them.

They turned to face the newcomer, who was something of a surprise. He had sounded like a big man, perhaps young and aggressive, but in fact he was small, about five feet four and, to judge from his grey hair and his seamed, weather-beaten face, well into his seventies. But he didn't lack aggression, as he regarded them with rheumy blue eyes that carried a hint of menace. Nevertheless, he spoke with reasonable politeness, and with a strong French-Canadian accent.

'And who might you be, folks? You don't look like police.'

Jay decided at once that this was a moment when charm could save the day. She smiled at the old man sweetly.

'Good heavens, no, Monsieur Legros, we're not police. It *is* Pierre Legros, isn't it? That's who Dr Robertson told us we'd probably see around.' She felt a white lie was justified in the circumstances. 'He said you kept an eye on the cottage for him. My name's Jay Ryan, and this is Hugh Bigrel.'

The old man moved gum from the side of his cheek, and began to chew rhymically. After a moment he spat over the edge of the veranda, and became noticeably more amiable. 'So you're friends of Dr Robertson, are you? I must say, you don't look much like police, or more of those darned reporters. We've had a bunch of them in the past months, though they've left us alone recently. How can I help you? There's not much to do up here at this time of year – except get drowned, so they say,' he added with a curious intonation.

Taking the implied cue, Hugh intervened. 'We're not reporters, Monsieur Legros, we assure you, but we do have an interest in the drowning, as you call it. Sir Rupert Canville was also a friend of ours, and we know that it was you who found his body.'

'A–ah! Now I understand, Monsieur Bigrel. Madame.' He bowed to Jay. 'You've come to see the lake, have you?'

Hugh made no reference to the question of accident or suicide, and merely said, 'Yes. Of course we read about the death in the English newspapers, but that's not the same and, as we were staying in Ottawa, we seized the chance to come up here. Sir Rupert was a famous man in his own country, as I'm sure you know.'

'And in Canada. A good guy, with no side.' Legros had relaxed now, and spoke positively. 'He often came to stay up here, sometimes with the doctor, and sometimes by himself. He liked the lake. He was a fine swimmer and he could handle a canoe real good.'

'Did you see him that last time?'

'Sure did. I was on the roof when he arrived. Those darned racoons do a mighty lot of damage if you don't watch out for them.' Legros chewed ruminatively. 'Sir Rupert left his automobile at the bottom of the track, where you left yours. He was only carrying a rucksack, so I asked him if I could fetch the rest of his stuff. But he said he'd got it all with him, so I lit the fire instead. That was the Saturday morning.'

'And it was the next day you found him?'

'I saw the Robertson canoe floating upside down in the lake down there Sunday afternoon,' Legros corrected Hugh. 'I was worried about those racoons or I'd not have come back. The cottage was unlocked and there was no sign of Canville, so I drove home like stink and called the QPP – the Québec Provincial Police. But the divers didn't get Sir Rupert's body out till Monday morning.'

'Terribly sad,' said Hugh, 'and an awful waste. I can't imagine why he had the canoe out in such weather.'

'Neither can I,' Legros said. 'It wasn't like him to take stupid risks. That's why I'm pretty certain – '

There was a long silence. Jay caught herself holding her breath. Hugh hesitated; if he made some inappropriate remark, the moment might pass. So he waited in silence. The old man seemed to have forgotten that he wasn't alone.

Then he seemed to make up his mind, and continued, 'Look, M'sieur Bigrel, Madame,' he said, 'you say you're not police, and you're not reporters, and I believe you. In any case, it's old history now and the case has been closed and it's dropped out of the papers. But you're not from the British, are you – the British authorities? I wouldn't want that.'

'We give you our words,' Hugh said. 'We're just interested friends – of Sir Rupert, and Dr Robertson.'

'All right. Well, after all these months I'll tell you something I've told no one else. It was partly the whisky, you see. He liked his whisky, did Sir Rupert. Sometimes we'd have a drop together. But don't get me wrong – he was no alcoholic, and yet – He'd brought a full bottle, but when I went back to the cottage to wait for the QPP it was in the hearth, empty. And he'd not been here much more than twenty-four hours, maybe less.'

This time the silence lasted even longer. Eventually it became beyond bearing, and Hugh broke it. 'You've been thinking that for some reason he did have too much to drink, and that's how he came to do a rather silly thing like canoeing on a half-frozen lake?'

'No! That's not what I've been thinking, M'sieur Bigrel,' Legros said sharply. 'There was also the food, or rather the lack of it. He told me he was staying till Monday, but he'd brought next to nothing to eat, and when I offered to fetch him anything he needed from the store he refused.'

Legros hesitated. Then: 'I blame myself,' he said. 'I should have guessed what he was planning. I should have watched out for him. Like I said, he was a good guy. I liked him.'

The old man turned away, his eyes suddenly full of tears. Hugh and Jay exchanged glances. Rupert Canville had received what amounted to an accolade, but it had confirmed Jay's belief

147

– a belief that Hugh now felt he had no alternative but to accept. Canville had taken his own life.

'He didn't leave any kind of note, did he?' Hugh said, following this train of thought. 'Or – '

'No. I looked. There was no note. So I didn't have to tear it up, Monsieur. I took away the empty bottle of whisky. That was all.'

'And you told no one? Why not?'

'Why should I? Nobody, neither the QPP, nor the RCMP guys in plain clothes, nor the English guy from their High Commission or whatever it's called – Fenwick his name was and I didn't like him – who came swarming – none of them asked about the food. And I didn't say anything. Why should I?' he repeated. 'If Sir Rupert wanted to die private-like, that was his business. Nothing to do with these darned prowlers.'

'But you've told us,' Jay said gently.

'Yes,' Legros agreed. 'It's different now – and you're different too, I think. The whole thing's over. And I'm not sure I want it on my conscience, without someone else knowing. I suppose I needed to get it off my chest. But it's between us, remember?'

Jay remained a little nonplussed, but Hugh had learnt enough about the stubbornness and independence of the Québecois in the face of authority, and his ready acceptance of those to whom he took a liking, to appreciate the way the old man's mind was working. He was surprised, however, when Legros suddenly asked, 'Would you like to see round the cottage? I've got the keys.'

For the old man's sake rather than their own they accepted the invitation. They could hope to learn no more. The cottage belonged to Dr Robertson and his family. The furniture was all theirs, the posters on the walls, the books in the bookcases, the games for a wet day, the children's toys. There was nothing to indicate why it should have been here, in this relatively remote corner of Québec, that Sir Rupert Canville, the British High Commissioner to Canada, had finally decided to take his own life.

SIXTEEN

Fenwick had no difficulty in spotting them as they came through the automatic doors at the departures entrance to Ottawa airport. They made an attractive couple, he thought absently. Neither of them was conventionally good-looking, but he noticed that men turned to watch Jay Ryan as she passed, while women seemed quick to respond to Bigrel. There was a certain air about them – of vitality or self-sufficiency, perhaps – that became more apparent when they were together; he assumed they would soon become lovers, if they had not already done so.

He watched them from the safety of a newsstand in the central concourse as they checked in for their Washington flight. In some senses they made him feel his age, but he did not envy them. On the contrary, he was rather sorry for them. But it was not his business to feel sorrow for individuals – or at least to act on such feelings – and he had already done more than he should. He had warned them in explicit terms. It was a pity they weren't stupid, or easy to cow – possibly in the long term a pity not only for themselves, but for everyone involved.

Fenwick stepped out from behind a display of coloured postcards and stood directly in Hugh Bigrel's path. Bigrel showed no surprise at his appearance. 'Hello, Fenwick,' he said. 'Come to see us off? You are kind.'

Fenwick ignored Hugh's comment. 'I just want a word or two with you,' he said. 'I'll buy you a cup of coffee. You've got plenty of time before they call your flight.'

They raised no objections, but followed him to the coffee shop in a corner of the concourse. It was doing a brisk trade, but they were lucky. A man and a woman were leaving a window table, and Fenwick quickly circumvented a couple of elderly ladies to secure it. He ordered coffee and Danish pastries without bothering to ask what Hugh and Jay might like.

As soon as they were served, he said, 'I won't play around. You know what I want. The names and addresses on that bit of paper you found attached to Thaxted's cleaning.'

'Why?' said Jay.

'Didn't Keith Masterson repeat them to you?' asked Hugh.

'Spare me!' Fenwick ignored his coffee and his pastry, pushing the cup and saucer and the plate to one side. He leant across the table. 'Masterson was so drunk that his memory of what you told him is confused, and that's putting it mildly.' Then, suddenly, 'You still have that slip of paper?'

'No, Mr Fenwick,' Jay said. 'I tore it up. There seemed no point in keeping it. As far as we could tell, the names looked Polish and the addresses were in Warsaw. We tried the Polish Embassy here, as I'm sure you know, but we got no joy from them. So what else can we do? That list could have been in my father's pocket for months. It has no necessary relevance to his death – or to any other current happenings.'

Fenwick looked at her speculatively. He was inclined to believe that she had destroyed the paper, but he knew she hadn't told him the whole truth. The mere fact that she had been so forthcoming, so confiding, was enough to demonstrate that she was trying to deceive him.

'Quite likely not, Mrs Ryan,' he agreed. 'Nevertheless, I'd like to have those names. Of course you remember them.'

'Yes, I do, I think. And I'll tell you – if you'll tell me why you want to know them so badly, Mr Fenwick.'

'Right. That's a bargain. You first, Mrs Ryan.'

Jay hadn't expected such instant capitulation. She glanced at Hugh, who signified that the choice was hers. He was prepared to support whatever line she took, and whatever she said, true or false.

'There were three names,' she said slowly. 'Krasneski, Beluch and Dzolak – all Polish, and all common enough.'

'They were written clearly?' Fenwick tried to sound casual. 'For instance, you're sure it was Beluch and not Baluch?'

'As a matter of fact, Sam's writing was ghastly.' Jay shrugged.

'It could have been Baluch. Does that name mean anything to you? Do you know who he might be?'

'I haven't the faintest idea,' said Fenwick, as he thought how easily Krasneski might be mistaken for Krasnakov. 'Now, what about the addresses?'

'There were only two.' She produced addresses with sufficient hesitation to suggest that she was having difficulty in recalling them, and which Hugh recognized as false. 'And now it's your turn, Mr Fenwick.' She paused before she spoke with some formality, 'Why are you – an Englishman, a foreigner – so interested in the contents of my late father's pockets?'

Fenwick regarded Jay with some cynicism. He had a pretty good idea that the addresses she had quoted were spurious. She was a clever woman, he thought, but not clever enough. Her obviously assumed hesitation before producing details that must be engraved in her memory was an adequate indication.

He asked no further questions, but pushed back his chair and rose to his feet. He said, 'Mrs Ryan, I don't intend to keep my side of the bargain, and tell you why I want this information. In my opinion, you've cheated me, so I shall cheat you. Your friend, Masterson, remembered more than you expected. Goodbye, or should I say *au revoir* – or even *Do widzenia*! Anyway, take care, both of you – and I mean that.'

The next moment he was striding out of the coffee shop towards the main doors of the airport. He felt irritated, though the morning hadn't been entirely wasted. He had learnt a certain amount. His belief that Krasneski could possibly be a misreading of Krasnakov had been confirmed. He now knew the third name on the wretched bit of paper, unless of course Mrs Ryan had been lying about that too. And – and this he recognized as the source of his irritation – any hope he might have had that Hugh Bigrel and Jay Ryan had been persuaded to abandon their stupid intervention had been dispelled.

Hilda Avery was waiting to greet them when they disembarked from their aircraft at Washington National. With her was Norman Saint, whom Jay regarded with some disfavour; she

151

had not yet forgiven him for suggesting that Sam might have got himself involved with the Russians. As a result, on the drive to Georgetown, she made their trip to Ottawa sound as if it had been no more than a casual holiday. Hugh followed her lead.

Saint was amused. 'You seem to have had a very dull time,' he said. 'Didn't you learn anything about Sam, or aren't you going to tell us?'

'I thought we'd wait till we got home,' Jay replied coolly.

'You mean, when I've left you?' Saint laughed. 'Don't you trust me any more, Jay?'

Mrs Avery did her best to prevent any further bickering. 'You'll come in and have a drink, Norm? Then we can all hear whatever there is to hear.'

'Thanks, Hilda, I'd like that,' Saint said, 'if Jay doesn't object.'

But when they were inside the house he stopped teasing, and was serious. He asked no questions, but said at once, 'I've not been idle while you've been away. I may be retired, but I've still a lot of contacts, and I've been making a few inquiries myself. I think I've learnt one or two things that may interest you.' He looked Jay straight in the eyes. 'I was very fond of Sam, you know.'

'Yes, I know,' she agreed at once, her earlier antipathy dissolving.

'Well, that understood, and if you'll swap, I'll tell you what I've gathered from my various sources,' Saint said. 'Okay?'

'Okay,' Jay said.

'Well,' said Saint, 'in the first place, Sam was intending to go on from the UK – to Poland.'

'Poland!' Jay and Hugh spoke simultaneously.

Saint made no comment on their reaction. 'Yes, Poland,' he said. 'Sam applied for a visa, but he was refused. No reason given. No reason need ever be given. But, being Sam, he didn't give up. He started pulling strings at State – the State Department, our Foreign Office,' he added for Hugh's benefit.

Hugh nodded. The explanation had been unnecessary. He was thinking that Sam's daughter didn't give up, either. 'And he succeeded?' he asked.

'Yes. He got his visa. But he didn't get to Poland, as we all know. He died in that car crash.' Saint paused to sip his gin and tonic. 'My second piece of information, if you can call it that, also concerns Poland, but I must stress that it's no more than gossip. I had a chat with someone who was in Warsaw when Rupert Canville was posted from Poland to Ottawa. He says the move was very sudden, and seemingly quite unexpected – by the Canvilles or anyone else. There was some talk at the time, not much, but some.'

'What sort of talk?' Hugh asked.

'A rumour that the British Ambassador had become involved with a Polish woman. Apparently she was charming and beautiful, and well-known in Warsaw as a kind of political hostess. Her name was Anna Seschki and – to put it delicately – there were serious doubts about her virtue.'

'And that would be an adequate reason to remove an ambassador from his post?' asked Hilda Avery.

'If the rumour had any basis, yes. And in some cases, even if it hadn't.'

'Was there any suggestion of an actual attempt to blackmail Canville because of this alleged liaison?' said Hugh thoughtfully.

'No, but the risk would be enough – especially in a satellite capital.' Saint shrugged. 'Anyhow, I repeat: this was the merest rumour. My informant said he didn't believe it, and was loath to mention it, but it would jibe with what Sam told me about his suspicions of Canville, wouldn't it?'

'It sure would,' Jay said. 'Anything else, Norm?'

Saint shook his head. Surprisingly he looked slightly abashed. 'I – er – told Cliff Di Bianco what I'd learnt. I felt it was my duty.'

'And why not?' Hilda said encouragingly. She got up and took his glass. 'Let me freshen your drink.'

'Thanks, Hilda. Cliff and I believe it would explain a lot about Sam's actions if, suspecting that Canville had allowed himself to be blackmailed, he went on with his inquiries, but privately. Sam wouldn't want to malign a dead man if there was a chance he was wrong.'

'That sounds typical of what I've heard of Sam,' Hugh

commented. 'But, without being chauvinistic, I can't accept what you're implying – that the British would have had him shot in cold blood, to prevent an accusation by the CIA of yet another high-powered English spy. The risk would have been too great. You Americans would never have trusted us again.'

'If they'd found out about it,' Jay reminded him. 'Fenwick's done his best to cover up everything, hasn't he?'

'Wait a minute!' Saint spoke with authority. 'Look. You won't like what I'm going to say, either of you, but I'm going to say it all the same. Di Bianco and I agree that there's absolutely no evidence, apart from that guy Worth's, that Sam was shot. On the contrary, I agree with Hugh. The Brits wouldn't have risked it, and why should anyone else?' He paused, then added, 'You know, in my experience it's only too easy to become obsessed with one idea – one theory – to the exclusion of any other possibility.'

Hugh saw Jay's chin come up, and he gave her a warning glance before she could produce the indignant reply he knew she was about to make. He said, 'You're quite right, of course. If we discount Foxy Worth we've no reason to believe Sam was shot. As for Canville, in Ottawa we found what could be called corroborative evidence that he committed suicide. Jay will tell you about it, and of course you can tell Di Bianco, but it's nothing to do with us if Canville might – just might – have been an agent, and the connections between him and Sam's accident and the deaths of my family were no more than coincidence.'

He looked to Jay for support, and she said, 'I have to agree. And anyway there's nothing more we can do.'

Hugh and Jay broke off their conversation as Hilda Avery returned to the living-room after seeing Saint to the door. She regarded them quizzically.

'Well!' she exclaimed. 'You're a fine pair of deceivers. Don't bother to deny it. You're not as good as you think you are. You may have convinced poor old Norm that you're satisfied, but you haven't convinced me. I was watching and listening from the sidelines, remember. You still think Sam was shot, don't you?'

'Yes!' Jay didn't elaborate.

'Thanks for not lying to me.' Hilda was sardonic. 'But are you going to trust me?'

'Yes, again,' Hugh said, 'if you'll give us your word to keep it strictly to yourself. We have to ask that.'

'Of course. I understand. You have my word.' Hilda sat down and stared at them soberly. 'So what else did you find out in Ottawa?'

They told her about the stolen slacks and the slip of paper with the Polish names. And Hugh gave their reasons for believing that Foxy Worth had told them the truth. 'Sam was shot, and we want to know why, and who by. That hasn't changed,' he said. 'And we do seem to have a possible lead with these Poles. One of them could be the "who", though the "why" is as mysterious as ever, unless in some way it's connected with Canville. But, apart from checking the names on the diplomatic lists here in Washington and in London, we can't think of any further steps to take.'

'You could go to Warsaw,' said Hilda mildly, 'as Sam evidently intended to do. Except that – you must realize it could be dangerous. If someone was prepared to kill Sam and this man Worth, why not you, too?'

'Aunt Hilda, naturally we've thought of going to Poland. After all, no one's tried to harm us so far, in spite of Fenwick's warnings,' said Jay. 'But there are practical problems – time, for one. I can't abandon my shop completely, and Hugh'll soon have to be considering his next term's work.'

'If that's all that's stopping you, I think you should go.' Hilda Avery was reflective. 'I doubt if you'll be happy unless you do. As regards time, you could sort out your affairs while you're waiting for visas. They may take some while. What about money?'

Hugh looked at Jay. 'I'm sure the exchequer will run to a few days in East Europe,' he said.

Hilda Avery had the last word. 'Don't argue any more then. Just come back safely, both of you.'

SEVENTEEN

Hugh Bigrel was pleasantly surprised to find that he was glad to be back in Oxford. At Heathrow he had exchanged affectionate kisses with Jay, and seen her into the car of an American woman friend, whose first name was Alice; he didn't catch the rest. Hugh and Jay had made such plans as were possible, and agreed when to meet again. As far as Hugh himself was concerned, his mother had brought the car down from Oxford, and driven him home.

He felt as if he had been away for ages, far longer than the summer he had spent at Carleton University in Ottawa; everything was familiar, but subtly changed. He at once re-established himself in the lower part of the house and, though it was true that memories of Lorna and David did return sharply, they no longer hurt him, and he settled in contentedly.

The first morning after his return he went along to his College. He was greeted warmly by the Principal, whom he happened to meet in the Porter's Lodge, and had a lengthy discussion with the Senior Tutor about his second- and third-year pupils, as well as the potential new intake due when the Michaelmas Term began in October. Once more he felt at home.

And the rest of the week passed quickly. He spent many hours in the Bodleian and the College library, picking up the threads of his research work. He wrote long-overdue letters, contacted friends and on Saturday evening, out of gratitude to Helen, who continued to do his housekeeping for him, took her and John out to dinner at the Randolph Hotel.

He had already given his parents an expurgated version of his visit to North America. He had not mentioned Fenwick, or Keith Masterson's betrayal, if that was not too strong a word.

156

Nor had he yet said anything about Thaxted's slip of paper, or Poland. It was over dinner that he broached that subject.

'Warsaw! But you've just come home and – ' Helen Bigrel pulled herself up. 'Sorry, darling. It's not our business. If you want to go, of course you must.'

'It's not all that easy to get a visa, is it?' John said.

Hugh thought of Sam Thaxted. 'I'm told things have eased up considerably. I shouldn't imagine I'll have any trouble. As I understand it, they welcome hard-currency tourists. There's a good travel agency in the Broad. I'll try them. They should know if there are any problems.'

'Will you be gone long?'

Hugh smiled at his mother. 'No. Not more than a week. Jay has some cousins in Warsaw whom she's never met, and we'd like to see the city. And, of course, if we can, we'll try to trace the names on that list of Sam's.'

'It sounds fine,' John remarked, 'especially as you say Jay speaks Polish. That should make things easier for you.' He paused, then added, 'Hugh, I don't want to come the heavy parent, but be careful! Poland isn't England or America, you know. If you start asking awkward questions in the wrong places you could get into a lot of trouble.'

Hugh nodded. 'I'll be careful. I promise,' he said lightly.

But on Monday morning, as he walked along Broad Street to the travel agency, he wondered if the promise had been rash, and might perhaps prove impossible to keep. Nevertheless, he wasn't deterred. His father's had been only the last of many warnings. Yet Jay and he were still untouched. So far, he added to himself.

He left the agency with his mind stuffed with information, and a bundle of brochures and leaflets. He had been right; Poland welcomed tourists, if not with open arms, certainly with outstretched hands, especially if they had hard currency to offer. There seemed no reason why he and Jay shouldn't be included in the welcome.

The same evening he phoned her. He would come up to London with his passport, the completed visa application form, photographs and a money exchange order certifying that he had obtained the necessary amount of currency; such a certificate was apparently demanded by the Polish authorities. Jay, having fulfilled the same requirements, would meet him, and together they would visit Polorbis – the official overseas agents of the Polish Government Travel Bureau.

Hugh had been studying his literature, and they decided that the simplest thing would be to avoid an organized party, and travel together, but independently. Seemingly there was no objection to this, as long as they stayed at one of the official hotels. They also agreed on a departure date, a month ahead, which should allow plenty of time for their visas to be processed.

Hugh arranged to spend a couple of nights with his cousins, the Davidsons, at the beginning of the following week, when Jay said she would be less busy, and he insisted on taking her out to dinner. He found himself looking forward to their meeting with intense anticipation.

On Sunday evening, while Hugh was having supper with his parents, the telephone rang. John Bigrel answered it, and returned to the dining-room. He was frowning.

'Hugh, it's for you. It's Jay. She – she doesn't sound too good.'

Hugh was already half-way to the door. 'Thanks, Dad,' he said over his shoulder as he made for the phone in the hall. 'Jay, Hugh here. Are you all right?' he asked anxiously.

'Yes. I'm okay, but I shan't be able to keep our date tomorrow. Sorry.'

'Why not? Are you ill?'

In his anxiety Hugh spoke more sharply than he had intended. It was clear that Jay was not all right. Her voice had been weak, and he could hear her breathing as if it were an effort to speak. When she failed to answer immediately he repeated his question.

'No, I'm not ill,' she said at last, 'but I had an accident this morning and I'm a bit battered.'

'Battered?' Hugh controlled his impatience. 'What's happened? Jay, are you alone, by yourself?'

'No. Alice is with me – that friend of mine you met at

Heathrow. So don't worry. I'm okay, but I can't talk any more now. Hugh, I'll call you in a few days.'

'Jay!'

Either she hadn't heard his appeal, or she wasn't prepared to heed it. The line had gone dead. Hugh replaced his own receiver and stood, staring at the telephone, for a full minute. He told himself not to be stupid. Jay had had some kind of accident, probably in the house; perhaps she had fallen off a stepladder; that would account for her use of the word 'battered'. But he was not reassured.

Returning to the dining-room, he said, 'Jay says she's okay. It must have been a bad line.'

'So you'll be going up to London tomorrow, as planned?' John said.

'Yes. By the early train.'

Hugh spoke casually, hiding his anxiety. If the fear that gripped him were justified, and Jay's so-called accident had been a deliberate attempt to injure – or kill – her, he didn't want his parents to know. It would only add to their worry about his trip to Warsaw. And anyway he was probably wrong.

Jay herself opened the door of the flat near Sloane Square, and Hugh's first momentary reaction was relief. He had pictured her in bed, scarcely able to move, badly hurt. Then reality struck, and as he took in her appearance he was shocked.

Jay was wearing a kaftan which concealed her body, but the left side of her face was swollen so that the whole was distorted. One eye was almost closed. The bridge of her nose merged with her forehead. Her skin was a yellowish-grey. She looked dreadful, like an old woman; in the street he would hardly have recognized her.

'Jay! My dear Jay!'

Without thinking Hugh stepped towards her, and would have taken her in his arms, but she stepped back quickly, warding him off. 'No, Hugh. Don't! Right now I'm too – too fragile to be touched.'

Dumbly he followed her into the living-room, where she sat

down carefully on an upright chair. She tried to smile at Hugh, but it clearly hurt her. Hugh was appalled.

'Jay, what happened?'

'Yesterday – Sunday – was a lovely day, and I decided to walk to Brompton Oratory. It's a fair distance, but I never seem to get enough exercise in London. I had heard Mass and was on my way home when – '

Jay stopped, for a moment unable to continue. Hugh watched her anxiously. She stroked her left cheek and winced.

'Sorry, Hugh, but it's not easy for me to speak.'

'Jay, have you seen a doctor?'

'Oh yes.' She made an effort. 'I walked home around the back of Harrods and down Pavilion Road – you know, that narrow street without sidewalks that runs parallel to Sloane Street. It used to be a mews, but now it's all up-market terraced cottages. There was almost no traffic, and very few people about. I was walking at the side of the street, when I heard the sound of an automobile coming up fast behind me. I – I turned round, and realized it was coming straight for me. I did what I could to huddle myself against the door of a house, but it hit me. I remember sailing through the air and the road slamming into me. Then I was lying on the ground, with people peering at me, and a police patrol car, and an ambulance that took me to hospital.'

'God! You might have been killed!'

'I darned nearly was!' Momentarily Jay's indignation over-came her discomfort. 'As it is, I was lucky. But I'm badly bruised all down one side. I've a sprained wrist, a hair-line fracture of my collarbone, two cracked ribs and some loose teeth. And you can see what my face looks like.'

'I'm surprised the hospital let you go.'

'I insisted. I didn't want a fuss. They got hold of Alice, and she told them she'd take care of me. She's staying here for a few days, though she's out doing some shopping now. Hugh – ' Jay's single eye regarded him desperately. 'I know it's a narrow street, but there's plenty of room for two or even three automobiles to pass. There was no reason why this – this thing – should have driven straight at me. No reason at all.'

'It didn't stop, naturally?'

'Of course not.'

Hugh knew what Jay was suggesting, but it was hard to accept. In spite of Sam's death, and Worth's, and Fenwick's warnings, they were not accustomed to dealing with violence of this kind.

'Can you describe the car or the driver?' he asked abruptly.

'The police asked me that, and I told them. I thought it was a blue Ford Escort with a single man in the front. Unfortunately there were no witnesses, and the police weren't impressed. They said that unless he'd driven on out of panic, and eventually gave himself up, they were unlikely to catch him, though they'd do their best.'

'Not exactly satisfactory, is it, Jay? And if − if it was a deliberate attack, no use at all.'

'I know,' she said quietly, 'and I intend to take every precaution I can to see that nothing else happens to me before we go to Poland.'

'You think we should still go?'

'Of course. But we'll have to wait till I've recovered a bit. What's more, we'll have to give the matter a good deal more thought than we have. There's no point in asking for trouble. For one thing, I'm not certain that we should apply for our visas together. Can't your travel agency do yours from Oxford?'

Hugh regarded her doubtfully. He wasn't sure what to think. There was clearly no doubt in Jay's mind that the attack on her had been deliberate, but the driver could have been drunk or high on drugs. There was no proof he was in any way connected with whoever had shot Samuel Thaxted.

When Viktor Krasnakov, still in Ottawa, received a report on Jay's 'accident', he was not altogether displeased. If she had been killed the police would have been far more interested and, one never knew, there was always an outside chance that the driver might be traced through the stolen car. Again, even if he were caught it was unlikely that he'd admit to having been paid for his part in the operation, or that he had any idea of the identity or nationality of the man who employed him from time to time, but once more one never knew.

And, Krasnakov hoped, the 'accident' had achieved its purpose, to act as a warning and deter Jay Ryan from any more dangerous inquiries. When he learnt that he had been wrong in this assumption, that he had underestimated Mrs Ryan, he was furious.

'Stubborn bitch!' he said, banging his fist on his desk. 'Stubborn bitch!' His breathing was short, and he was pale.

It was Galinov who had brought him a cable with the information that a request for a Polish visa had been received from Mrs Jay Ryan at the Polorbis office in London, and that a similar request had been made for Mr Hugh Bigrel through a travel agency in Oxford. Now Galinov stood stiffly to attention and waited for the storm to pass. He couldn't recall ever having seen the Comrade Colonel display such a fine fit of temper. As a rule Krasnakov, however angered he might be, managed to show restraint.

Gradually the Colonel regained control of his emotions. 'They're fools – fools!' he said more mildly.

Galinov took his cue at once. 'Yes, Comrade Colonel. Fools. Amateurs. They should have known it made no difference where they applied for visas. They should have guessed they might be on a watch list, though, if I may say so, it was a brilliant flash of inspiration on your part to guess they might try to get to Poland.'

Krasnakov was in no mood for flattery. 'It was a blinding flash of the obvious,' he retorted. 'But I'd hoped that after Ryan's little mishap – The question is, Galinov, what do we do now? Do we let them go, and – '

'Comrade Colonel!'

'What?' Krasnakov wasn't accustomed to being interrupted by his aide.

'Comrade Colonel, I'm sorry, but – but your instructions must have been misunderstood. The visas for both Ryan and Bigrel have already been refused. I suppose they could be told it was a mistake, and if they re-applied the visas would be granted, if – if that's what you wish,' Galinov ended miserably.

'No.' Krasnakov was shaking his head. 'No, leave it. After

all, without visas they can't reach Warsaw. That way is blocked. Maybe they'll give up now, or they'll think of some clever move. More likely the latter,' he continued bitterly. 'If this wretched couple give us any more trouble it'll be the end of them.' Krasnakov's smile was not pleasant. 'We will attend to it ourselves, Galinov. It'll be worth the risk.'

It was chance that suggested their next move to Hugh. Several weeks after the Polish visas had been refused, he was again staying with his Davidson cousins, and one afternoon had let himself into their flat. Back turned, he was shutting the front door behind him, when Pam Davidson came into the hall.

'Hello, Bill. You're home early, darling,' she said. Then, as Hugh swung round, she realized her mistake and laughed. 'How silly of me. I really thought you were Bill. You're awfully alike, you know.'

'Yes. We are, aren't we?' Hugh said slowly, regarding Pam with unusual curiosity.

'What is it?' she said. 'Why are you staring at me like that? Have I got a smut on my nose – '

'I've just had a fantastic idea.' Hugh continued to study her. 'It may not work, but I think it could. I'll phone Jay now, and tell you about it when Bill gets home.'

'Okay, I can wait. Though the suspense will be terrible.' She was amused.

But she was less amused when she heard the details of Hugh's scheme, and her husband was scornful. He said it was a ludicrous suggestion, impractical, dangerous and he would have no part of it. Hugh persisted.

'Why?' he demanded. 'You've both got valid passports. You won't want to use them in September. All I'm asking is that you arrange to go on a package holiday to Warsaw, and then let Jay and me go in your places.'

'All!' Bill was indignant. 'Don't you realize it's a criminal offence to lend someone your passport? You'd almost certainly get caught, and we'd end up in the dock with the pair of you.'

'Or you'd end up in a Polish prison,' Pam said. 'If they've

refused you a visa, they don't want you in the country. Besides, why are you so determined to go there? There are lots of other places for a holiday.'

'Jay's particularly anxious to see her relations, especially now that her father's dead. And we think the only reason we were refused visas is that she's half-Polish, and we were stupid enough to try to make it a private trip,' Hugh lied. 'At least, those are the only reasons we can think of.'

'I see,' said Bill speculatively. 'You could pass for me, I suppose. But what about this Jay? We've not met her. Does she look like Pam?'

'Not much,' Hugh admitted.

In fact, Pam Davidson, though about the same height as Jay, was plump. Her eyes were blue, her hair a medium brown and worn shoulder-length. She was pretty, but without Jay's innate distinction. But Jay had been enthusiastic on the phone, saying that passport photographs were notoriously poor, and she could do a lot to change her appearance.

'Anyway,' said Hugh, 'if you're not prepared to help us it doesn't matter, does it?'

There was a long, uncomfortable silence. Then Hugh began to talk about a concert at the Barbican to which he hoped to take Jay. Bill interrupted him.

He said, 'I keep our passports in the desk in our bedroom. You could steal them, Hugh, and we could swear ignorance. That's my best offer.'

Part Three

EIGHTEEN

As the LOT Tupolev aircraft climbed into the skies above London, Hugh Bigrel tried to relax. There had been no trouble at Heathrow. The small Polorbis group of tourists had gathered at the appointed place inside Terminal Two, and been shepherded by their courier through security and customs. No one had queried the identity of William or Pamela Davidson.

Nevertheless, it had been a tense time, and Hugh suspected there might be worse to come. When they arrived at Okęcie, Warsaw's international airport, in about two and a half hours time, he guessed they would be subjected to a far more rigorous inspection by the Polish officials. And, even after they had reached Warsaw, and were settled in the Orbis hotel in which the party had been booked, they would still have to contend with their courier, who was travelling with them.

The courier – who had introduced herself as Madame Marta Bereski – was a not unattractive woman in her thirties or forties. She was plainly dressed, and seemed superficially co-operative and charming, though she had already made it clear that she was an efficient organizer. Mixing his metaphors, Hugh had an idea that, if an occasion should demand it, an iron glove could emerge from beneath the pleasant veneer.

Hugh had viewed with some suspicion the way in which, when the group had assembled, Madame Bereski had insisted on collecting all the passports of her group and scrutinizing them; to make sure that the visas were in order, she said. She had had to return them, so that they could pass individually through British emigration, but now on the aircraft she was collecting them again, so that they could go through Polish immigration as a group. It could have been Hugh's imagination, or a guilty conscience, but he thought that he had seen her studying Jay's photograph with particular care, surreptitiously comparing it with the apparent original. He glanced sideways at Jay, who was staring out of the aircraft window.

He still found it difficult to accept her changed appearance. Apart from having a shorter haircut than usual, he had done nothing to himself, but Jay had produced a minor miracle. She had changed her hair style and had the colour lightened. She had persevered with coloured contact lenses though she disliked wearing them. And perhaps the greatest change was in her clothes. She had purposely bought garments that made her look plumper and less elegant. Pam Davidson wouldn't have been flattered by the resemblance, but the result was what Jay had hoped to achieve.

Sensing that Hugh was watching her, Jay turned and smiled at him. 'Okay?' she asked.

'*Tak. Bardzo dziękuję,*' Hugh replied.

Jay laughed. 'You've been working hard,' she said.

'I have indeed. You must admit it's an awful language, Pam dear, but I thought a few words might come in handy.'

'Yes.' Jay shook her head. 'It's not easy is it, Bill?'

'No, it's not,' Hugh agreed. He knew that Jay wasn't talking about Polish, but of their supposed relationship.

There were twelve others in their group, excluding the courier. They were of varying ages and occupations, but they had one thing in common. Everyone wanted to be friendly, and exchange personal information – except for Hugh and Jay. *They* needed to be constantly on guard in case a careless word betrayed that they were not William and Pamela Davidson, the married couple they claimed to be. It was a strain. Hugh wondered if, after all, they had been sensible to come on a package tour, but it had seemed the safest way.

And some of his doubts were dispelled when they arrived at Okęcie. He found there were considerable advantages in being marshalled together, rather like a school party on its first trip outside the British Isles. Marta Bereski, who had clearly been through the performance many times before, issued orders, gave directions, answered questions. Obediently, the group complied, and all the formalities – customs, passport and immigration officials and currency control – were simplified.

After less delay than Hugh had expected, the group was boarding a small bus, provided by their hotel, and was on its way to the centre of Warsaw. Jay slid her hand into Hugh's and squeezed it hard. He shared her relief. In spite of the presence of the courier, the party's luggage, which she had caused to be lumped together, had all been thoroughly serarched. This hadn't worried either Hugh or Jay; they had been careful what they packed. But Hugh noticed that, ahead of them, a man travelling alone had been made to turn out his pockets.

In Hugh's wallet were prints of. two photographs. One, provided by Jay, was of her father, Samuel Thaxted. The other, obtained through the good offices of the *Oxford Mail*, was of Sir Rupert Canville. Hugh didn't think they would interest the airport officials, but he had feared that by some unlucky chance Canville might be recognized by a member of the group, and questions asked which could arouse Madame Bereski's curiosity. At least that danger was now past. Holding Jay's hand, he made a great effort to concentrate on what the courier was saying.

'As you know, the hotel in which we are to stay is the Orbis-Solec. It is an excellent modern hotel, like all in Warsaw. Warsaw was of course almost totally destroyed in the Great Patriotic War, but it has since been rebuilt. You will enjoy the Orbis-Solec.' She made her last sentence sound like a command. 'It is in one of the most beautiful parts of Warsaw, near to the River Vistula.'

There was a murmur of appreciation and anticipation from members of the party.

'When we arrive at our hotel, there will be lunch, and I expect you will wish to unpack. Some of you may like to take a short rest after the journey. But there are so many beautiful things to see in Warsaw – buildings, parks, museums – that we cannot afford to waste much time. So later in the afternoon we shall visit the Park Lazienkowski, which is not far from where we are staying. There you will see the Palace on the Water, which once belonged to King Stanislaus Poniatowski. Then . . .'

'God! Are we going to be organized as much as this all the time?' Jay whispered to Hugh.

'I don't know, but we'd better play along for today, though she's right about one thing. Time is short. We mustn't let ourselves be bullied.'

'At least I'll try to contact my cousins. They could be an enormous help.'

Marta Bereski seemed to be staring directly at them, expressing disapproval at their lack of attention to her words, and Hugh bit back the remark he had been about to make. He could see that the courier might represent a major problem, especially as he already had the impression that Jay and he were not her favourite members of the present group.

This impression was confirmed when they arrived at the hotel. It was indeed a modern building, but the accommodation varied. Their party, as was the common practice with tours, had been given an allotment of rooms, but the actual allocation was left to the courier. Last on her list, Jay and Hugh were shown into an end room, somewhat smaller than the others they had glimpsed. It was plainly but pleasantly furnished, with its own shower room, and it had a double bed.

Hugh opened his mouth to protest, but Jay forestalled him. 'This'll be just fine,' she said.

'Why did you say that?' he demanded as soon as they were alone.

Jay looked around and put her finger to her lips. 'What do you think?' she whispered. 'Bugs?'

'Oh, hell, they can't bug every room in every tourist hotel in Poland,' said Hugh. Then, 'Why did you tell Bereski this room's so perfect?' he repeated.

'Because it's next to the fire stairs, and not in the middle of the corridor. You never know. That could come in useful. As for the double bed – ' She looked at him. 'I don't mind, Hugh. Do you? Or – would you be thinking of Lorna?'

'No, I shan't.' Hugh shook his head, knowing that he spoke the truth. 'Neither of Lorna, nor Pam. Only Jay.'

'Good,' she said softly. 'I'm glad.'

* * *

Hugh opened the bedroom door immediately he heard Jay's gentle tapping. After lunch everyone had retreated for a rest before going to the Lazienkowski Park. Jay, rather than use the phone in their room, had gone down to the public telephones in the foyer. She had been some time.

'Sorry I've been so long,' she said as she slipped into the room. 'I had difficulty getting through.'

'But you reached them in the end?'

'Yes. I spoke to Urszula. Needless to say, she was surprised at my sudden appearance in Warsaw. She and my mother used to write to each other quite often, but since mother died I'm afraid the correspondence has dwindled into an exchange of Christmas cards. She's a lot older than I am, and we really don't have that much in common.'

'Surely she was pleased to hear from you?'

'Oh yes. She was most welcoming. What really surprised her was to learn that I'd recently got married again, and my name was now Davidson.' Jay smiled wryly at Hugh. 'In any case we're asked to supper tonight. She says she'll cook us a real Polish meal.'

'But tonight?'

'Yes. She apologized, but it's the only evening this week that Marek is free. As you know, he's a government servant, and it seems he's recently been promoted, and is now working in the Radziwill Palace. I gather that's where the Praesidium of the Council of Ministers meets.'

'That sounds pretty grand.'

'Yes. I think it's about the same as working in the Cabinet Office in Downing Street.'

'I see. Well, he might be able to help, but we'd better be careful what we tell him, Jay.'

'That goes for Madame Marta Bereski too, though I must admit my conscience doesn't prick me about deceiving her. But I regret having to tell a lot of lies to my Polish cousins, when we've never even met. Still – '

To Hugh's surprise he saw that Jay's eyes were suddenly full of tears, and he cursed himself for not having realized that being in her mother's homeland for the first time would be so affecting for Jay.

Hugh joined Jay in the foyer of the hotel. He was grinning broadly. 'The Bereski is not pleased,' he said. 'I told her that it was our wedding anniversary so we wanted to be alone, and not have dinner with people we scarcely knew. I hoped she might be sympathetic, but no. She asked all sorts of questions. How long had we been married? Why hadn't we mentioned our anniversary before? Where did we plan to go? I said the Bazyliszek, because we'd read about their fruit soup and wanted to try it, and she retorted that it was very expensive and, as our meal here was part of the tour, we'd be paying twice.'

'Why should she care?' Jay said.

'To give her her due, she did point out that this was a foreign country, and she was responsible for us.'

Jay shrugged. 'Too bad,' she said. 'I asked at the desk, and they say taxis are scarce, and almost impossible to order in advance. Our best bet is to line up at the nearest rank, so we ought to leave now. We don't want to be late.'

In the event, they were lucky, and managed to flag down a passing cab close to the hotel, so that they arrived a few minutes early at the modern apartment block not far from Warsaw University, where the Sochas lived. The presents Jay had brought from England helped, but it was a slightly embarrassing and emotional meeting for the two women. As far as Jay was concerned, it involved a lot more lies, as she introduced her new 'husband'. For the men it was different; they eyed each other appraisingly.

At first sight, Hugh was not impressed by Marek Socha. Socha opened the conversation by remarking that the vodka he was offering them was superior to Wyborowa, the best standard brand. He went on to explain the importance of his new job, and boasted of his son in the army, and his daughter who was to be a doctor. He spoke good English, though with a pronounced accent, and sympathized with Hugh, who admitted to knowing no Polish, on his lack of skill as a linguist. He was, in Hugh's opinion, both patronizing and unsure of himself.

Suddenly Jay laughed. To Hugh it sounded forced and, when he turned, he saw that she had tensed.

She said, 'Urszula says I don't look as she expected. From the letters she got from my mother, she thought I'd look like her – my mother, I mean – but I don't.'

'Really?' said Hugh, drawling the word. 'That, my darling, is because you've insisted on doing your hair in the latest London fashion. I much preferred it as it was. And you've put on weight,' he added reproachfully.

This time Jay's laugh was genuine, and Urszula joined in it. Marek poured more vodka. Urszula paid a quick visit to the kitchen and, on her return, conversation became general. Then, perhaps inevitably, it turned to a comparison between life in the West and in Communist countries. Marek became annoyed when his wife said that it was often necessary for ordinary people to queue for hours to buy food, though there was always plenty in the restaurants.

'You women exaggerate,' he said. 'Any shortages are because we don't like frozen and packaged foods as Westerners do. Wait till our guests see what we have for supper; then they'll know there's no reason for anyone to complain.'

'It's ready now, if you would be seated,' Urszula said, pointing to the table laid for four at the end of the sitting-room. 'I hope you are hungry.'

'Ravenous,' said Hugh, smiling at her.

Obviously Urszula didn't understand the word. Her English was not nearly as good as her husband's. But she returned Hugh's smile, and at once he saw her resemblance to Jay.

Marek had picked up the vodka bottle, and was leading the way to the table. 'Come,' he said, 'and bring your glasses. There's plenty more vodka where this came from, and it will add pleasure to a meal you'll enjoy.'

Certainly the supper was excellent. Fish marinated in sour cream was followed by roast pork. This, the Sochas explained, when served with pickled plums, sauerkraut and an apple salad, was considered a great treat in Warsaw. The meal ended with *racuski*, sour milk pancakes, and both Hugh and Jay agreed it had been excellent.

Made mellow by their praise, the food and the quantity of vodka he had drunk, Marek became a more agreeable companion. Jay seized her opportunity.

'Marek, I wonder if you'd do something for me,' she said.

'Anything, my dear,' Marek said gallantly, with a small bow.

Jay began the story that she and Hugh had concocted. 'When Sam, my father, was at the American Embassy here in Warsaw he knew someone called Krasneski. I think he must have been a government servant of some kind, perhaps connected with foreign affairs, and I was hoping you might be able to trace him for me.'

'That's all you know about him? No first name? There could be several Krasneskis in the government lists,' Marek said, but he didn't seem to consider the request extraordinary.

'No, I'm afraid I've nothing else to go on,' Jay said.

Urszula asked the awkward question. 'Why do you want to contact this man?'

'Well, Sam often mentioned him, and I got the impression they were good friends. And Krasneski may not even know that Sam's dead. I just felt I'd like to meet him while I'm here for old time's sake, if you like.' Jay was purposely vague. 'It's not terribly important, but – ' She looked appealingly at Marek.

'I'll do my best,' he promised.

'And with your cousin's connections,' Hugh said, as he and Jay went in search of a taxi to take them back to the hotel, 'we really might locate this mysterious Krasneski, though heaven knows what good it'll do us, if any.'

NINETEEN

Hugh Bigrel's first half-conscious thought on waking the next morning was of Jay. He put out a hand to her. The bed was warm but empty, and he opened his eyes. She wasn't in the room but the water was thudding in the shower and, content to know where she was, he turned on his back and stretched indolently. His body felt both tired and exhilarated.

It had been a wonderful, joyful night. Their first love-making had been brief and violent. He hadn't had a woman since Lorna, and Jay's need had matched his. But afterwards they had pleasured each other in a way he had never before experienced, and he believed that she had felt the same.

Jay came into the bedroom, disturbing his memories. She was naked except for a transparent nightdress, and at once he wanted her again. He held out his arms.

'No, darling. We can't. Not now. We're late already. They're going to the Old Town this morning, and we must go with them.'

'I'd much rather stay in bed, with you.'

Jay laughed. 'The Bereski would come and rootle us out.' She began to dress. 'Hurry up, Hugh. We really mustn't annoy her again. Besides, it suits us to play along. One of the addresses we have is in the Old Town, and even if we have to go back there, this visit will help us get our bearings.'

'Okay.'

Reluctantly, Hugh slid out of bed. He showered, shaved and dressed quickly. Nevertheless, they were the last of their party to arrive in the restaurant for breakfast. Madame Bereski was in the middle of a lecture on the architectural wonders they would be seeing during the morning, but she stopped when Jay and Hugh came into the room.

She said, 'The Davidsons will tell you that I do not exaggerate.' She looked directly at Hugh. 'The Rynek Starego Miasta is a fascinating place, isn't it? And you will have seen it floodlit, which is very romantic.'

Hugh hoped she was not trying to lay a trap for them about their destination the previous evening, but he decided the risk was worthwhile, and agreed with her at once. 'It was marvellous,' he said. 'The place, the food, the atmosphere, everything was wonderful and, as you say, Madame, very romantic.' He hoped he hadn't overdone it.

But the courier was nodding her acceptance. 'So you won't mind returning with us today, though not of course to eat at the Bazyliszek?'

'We're looking forward to it,' Jay said.

Indeed, the city's old market place – a large cobblestoned area called the Rynek Starego Miasta – which had been meticulously rebuilt as a duplicate of its original, totally destroyed in the Second World War – was worth any number of visits. And the party was glad to reach it. The day was fine and warm and, after trailing around the narrow, winding streets of the Old Town, listening to Madame Bereski deliver her talks on the architecture and history of the Cathedral of St John and the Renaissance Jesuit Church and other places of interest, it was very pleasant to relax in an open-air café in the centre of the square.

Even here, as if determined that her party should get every zloty's worth from the visit, Madame continued to impart information. She drew attention to the wrought-iron grills, the steep, tiled roofs of the narrow houses, and the frescos on the façades facing the square, and she recounted old legends connected with particular buildings. Hugh let most of it flow over him as he wondered how Jay and he were to escape by themselves.

It proved to be relatively simple. A couple in the party declared that they had done enough sight-seeing for the moment, and proposed to remain at the café until lunch. As they were in their sixties and obviously tired, no one could object. Another couple, who had become friendly with them, opted to join them.

Jay seized her chance. 'Personally, I'd like to shop around

those attractive little boutiques on the square,' she said. 'They look fascinating.'

'Yes, let's,' Hugh said enthusiastically.

Madame Bereski was not pleased. She warned them that they would regret not seeing the Warsaw Historical Museum, but they made it clear they would be quite happy to miss it. So, telling them that they must reassemble in two hours' time at the café, she led off her depleted party. Hugh and Jay only waited for them to be out of sight before setting off on their own.

During their tour of the Old Town that morning they had been lucky enough to spot the name of the street they wanted to visit. It was even narrower than most, scarcely more than an alley, and they had some difficulty in finding it again. But, with the aid of the map in their guide book and a helpful local man, who was delighted with Jay's Polish, they eventually located it.

'Number Twelve,' Hugh said. 'Let's just stroll past, and see what we can.'

They found Number Twelve just beyond the first bend in the winding lane. It was a tall, narrow house, similar to those on either side of it. On the ground floor was a small shop and, judging from the curtains, above was living accommodation. The store seemed to specialize in amber and silverware and embroidered articles. It looked well-established and reasonably prosperous, though easy for tourists to miss.

'We'll buy something,' Jay said firmly. 'Then we'll ask questions. After all, that's what we've come for.'

A bell attached to the door tinkled as they went into the shop. It was quite dark, for little daylight came through the small display window, and the artificial light was dim. As they entered, a woman rose from a stool behind the counter, and bowed her head in welcome. '*Dzień dobry*,' she said. Though she was middle-aged, her figure was trim and it was complimented by a heavily-embroidered blouse and skirt of the kind that a Polish peasant woman might have worn on her wedding day. Jay returned her greeting in English, and asked if she spoke the language.

'One word. Two word. Hello. Thank you. *Proszę mówić wolno.*

177

You speak slow, please.' She seemed to think the question a great joke.

Jay began to look at the goods on display. 'I'd like to buy Alice a small gift,' she said to Hugh. 'She was so kind about caring for me when that wretched automobile knocked me down.'

A small boy in very short shorts came into the shop. It was apparent from his looks that he was not a potential customer, but the woman's son. Although he was several years older he reminded Hugh of his own David.

'Hello,' Hugh said.

The boy regarded him solemnly but silently until the woman said something to him in Polish. The boy nodded in reply. 'Hello,' he said to Hugh. 'I know English. My name is Tomasz.'

'That's splendid,' said Hugh.

Jay had chosen some silver earrings for Alice, and was paying for them, after the price had been written down for her. Hugh took out his wallet and extracted a five hundred zloty note, which he reckoned would represent a modest but sensible bribe. He gave it to the boy, and at the same time showed him the photograph of Sir Rupert Canville. He had no need to ask Tomasz if he had ever seen the man in the picture, because the boy's face was immediately wreathed in a wide smile. Hugh was sure that this signified recognition, but before he could say anything else, the woman was shouting something at her son.

The boy thrust the note into the pocket of his shorts, but took the photograph to the counter. The woman picked it up, and stared at it. In the dim light of the shop's interior it was difficult to know if she had paled, but there was no doubt that her eyes had widened and her mouth become set.

'Jerzy!' she called, turning her back. 'Jerzy!'

A man appeared from behind a tapestry hanging across a doorway at the back of the shop. He was big and powerful-looking, with dark hair and a heavy walrus moustache. He wore jeans, and more hair sprouted from the top of his undervest. The woman handed him the photograph, and muttered something inaudible.

The man's expression didn't change, but he swallowed twice.

Hugh saw his Adam's apple bob up and down in his throat. He pushed the photograph across the counter to Jay, who was nearer.

'*Nie*,' he said, shaking his head. 'Don't know. Never see.'

He seemed to be labouring the point, and Hugh said, 'But you are Jerzy Dzolak?'

The man hesitated, then nodded, and Hugh swung round towards the boy. '*You* know the man in the picture, don't you, Tomasz?'

'*Nie*,' replied Tomasz unconvincingly.

'What you want?' Dzolak intervened menacingly.

Hugh took no notice of the question, but produced the photograph of Sam Thaxted, and showed it to Tomasz. 'What about him?'

The boy was frightened now. '*Nie*,' he cried, and ran out of the shop into the street.

Hugh offered Thaxted's photograph to Dzolak and his wife. They each took a quick glance at it, and Dzolak waved it away.

'*Nie!*' he repeated. 'Don't know! Never see! You go!' He made a threatening gesture, but still didn't attempt to move from behind the counter.

'Okay,' Jay said. 'We'll go.' She picked up the present she had bought for her friend, and at the door of the shop she turned and added suddenly, 'Remember us to Beluch when you see him.'

Hugh followed her out into the alley, and at its bend he glanced over his shoulder, and saw that Dzolak was standing in his doorway, watching them depart.

'Whew!' Jay said as they began to make their way back to the Market Square. 'What did you think of that?'

'They were lying, obviously,' said Hugh. 'I'm sure they recognized Canville from those prints, though probably not your father, and it certainly upset them. They were vehement in their denials. Whatever else, Canville can't have been an ordinary customer.'

'Did you think my mention of Beluch worried them at all?' Jay asked.

'Difficult to tell.' For a moment Hugh was silent, then he

said, 'You know, Dzolak became quite aggressive, but I'm sure it was because he was afraid.'

'Yes, I got the same impression.' Jay sighed. 'It's intriguing, but it doesn't get us very far, does it?'

Hugh thought to himself that it confirmed the theory that there was more than a casual connection between Canville and Thaxted, but he knew that this was a delicate subject as far as Jay was concerned, and he didn't mention it. Instead, he said, 'Maybe we'll have better luck with this Beluch. But we'll have to leave – him – till – tomorrow – ' His voice tailed away.

'Hugh, what is it?'

They had entered the Rynek, and were moving among the café tables to the appointed rendezvous with the rest of their tour group. Hugh had stopped suddenly. He stared into the distance.

'I thought – ' he began, frowning. 'No. It's stupid. I must be wrong. I'm imagining things.'

'What?' Jay was impatient.

'There was a man. I only caught a glimpse of him, but he looked exactly like Dick Fenwick.'

My kingdom for a taxi, Fenwick thought, though he knew that only horse-drawn cabs were allowed in Warsaw's Old Town. He hurried on, paying no attention to his surroundings, beyond thinking them an inferior version of Montmartre. His mind was in a turmoil.

And that was why he'd imagined seeing Hugh Bigrel, he told himself. Of course it couldn't have been Bigrel. It had been someone who resembled the bloody man; certainly the girl with him hadn't been in the least like Jay Ryan. He had made a mental connection with the couple because he had been concentrating on Rupert Canville.

'Damn Canville!' he thought viciously.

On this occasion Fenwick had been in Warsaw for two weeks, officially checking on efficiency at the British Embassy. In fact, he had come to tidy up the Canville affair, if possible. He disliked loose ends, though he accepted that they were often inevitable in the world in which he lived and worked.

Today, for the first time on this visit to Poland, which he hoped would be his last for some time, he had been able to arrange an appointment with Anna Seschki at her apartment. As always, she had been charming and, although she was no longer young, he could understand why Canville had succumbed to temptation and become her lover. Apart from her appearance – red hair, blue eyes and a figure that any man would eye with appreciation – she was an intelligent woman.

They had sipped aperitifs, and she had insisted he should stay to lunch. She had answered all his questions willingly, but with unconcealed amusement and, as in previous interviews, she had given nothing away. The one moment at which he had felt she was genuinely serious was when she was expressing her grief at 'poor dear Rupert's death'.

'Such a waste,' she had said sadly. But later she had added, 'He never told me any of his silly secrets. You ought not to have sent him to that terribly cold country. I've missed him.' Her generous mouth curved into a smile. 'In bed and out.'

Her last remark had jarred on Fenwick, and almost without thinking he had said, 'Canville was good in bed, was he? Better than Viktor Krasnakov?'

Anna Seschki was a fine actress, but not quite good enough. Her expression had remained half-wistful, half-amused; it was her body that had betrayed her. It had become absolutely still – except for her hands, which trembled slightly as she dug her long red nails into her palms. But she had recovered quickly, and when she spoke her voice was free from strain.

'I haven't seen Viktor Georgiyevich for ages. I understood he'd gone back to Moscow,' she had said. Then, laughing, she had dropped her venomous little bombshell. 'You know, you British are stupid. You always accept the obvious. Because Rupert and I were – friends, you assumed I'd compromised him. You forgot that I'm Polish, not Russian. You should have blamed Viktor Georgiyevich for your problems, not me.'

For once in his life Dick Fenwick had been stunned. Questions had flooded into his mind, but Anna Seschki had given him no chance to ask them. She had risen to her feet and indicated that their meeting was at an end. It would have been useless to persist.

What he must do now was get back to the quiet of his office, and analyse the implications of what Anna Seschki had said. He lengthened his stride further. Then, suddenly, he remembered his possible glimpse of Bigrel and Jay Ryan. If Anna Seschki had opened a new can of worms . . .

As Anna Seschki had said, Viktor Krasnakov was back home in Moscow, but he was not idle. He was in daily communication with London, Washington, Ottawa and Warsaw, like a spider at the centre of his web. Most of the reports he received were seemingly of little value, but an item here and another there could help him complete a part of his jigsaw, or warn him of potential danger to the operation for which he was responsible.

His instructions had been that any piece of news, however apparently trivial or unimportant, about either Hugh Bigrel or Jay Ryan, should be relayed to him without delay. Since they had been refused Polish visas, they had dropped out of sight and appeared to be inactive, but he didn't trust them.

And how right he'd been, he thought, as late in the afternoon he stopped briefly to watch a chess game in Gorki Park. The Dzolaks had had the good sense to report immediately on the visit to their shop of a suspicious couple who produced photographs of Canville, and someone else he guessed was Thaxted. The description of one of them fitted Bigrel, but the other was unlike Ryan. However, a few phone calls had confirmed that they were both 'on holiday', and he had no doubts as to their whereabouts. He had urgently initiated inquiries as to how they had reached Poland. He planned to go to Warsaw himself with Galinov, and personally make sure that the girl, at least, was taken off the board.

TWENTY

'She is unwell? Ill? Sick to her stomach?'

Hugh's conscience pricked him as he saw the anxiety on the courier's face, but only momentarily. He guessed that Madame Bereski was thinking mainly of herself, and of the complications that would arise if one of her charges should be in need of an operation, or suffer from some serious – even infectious – disease.

'It's really nothing,' Hugh said. 'A sinus headache. I'm afraid my wife is subject to these attacks if she gets overtired, and yesterday was a bit much for her, with all that sight-seeing during the day, and then the Mazowsze folk dancers in the evening – splendid as they were.'

'I see. You don't think the fresh air would do her good? We're going to Zelazowa Wola today, to visit the birthplace of the great Chopin.'

'No. She couldn't manage it. It's a pity, but – I'm sure you understand.'

'You yourself – you will come with us.' It was a statement rather than a question.

Hugh had been expecting it, but he managed to look surprised. 'Oh no!' he said earnestly. 'I couldn't leave my wife alone in a hotel, in a foreign country, could I?'

'Very well. As you wish, Mr Davidson.' The courier was impatient now. 'I'll tell the maid that Mrs Davidson is not to be disturbed.'

'Don't worry about us, please. We'll be here when you get back. I'm sure Pam will be better by this evening.'

'Let us hope so.'

With a brisk nod Madame Bereski disappeared to her duties,

while Hugh returned to his supposedly ailing wife. Jay sat up in bed as soon as she saw that he was alone. Hugh grinned at her.

'All settled,' he said. 'I'm either a better liar or a more accomplished actor than I thought.'

'Good. By the time I'm up and dressed they should have gone, and we can set off on our own.' Jay was already throwing aside the duvet. 'I'll just have to be careful not to be seen leaving the hotel. If they notice us coming back we can say I recovered quickly. The Bereski may be suspicious, but what can she do? And let's hope Beluch will be more co-operative than the Dzolaks.'

'My turn to buy something if it turns out to be another shop,' Hugh said.

In fact, the address they had on Nowy Świat was not that of a shop. To their surprise, the taxi-driver recognized it as soon as they got into his cab, and said, 'For the lady, yes?' Asked what he meant, he said they had told him to go to Monsieur Beluch's Beauty Salon. It was where all the important ladies in Warsaw went, but he scarcely thought it was a place for a gentleman.

Hugh and Jay exchanged glances. It was difficult to imagine a connection between Sam Thaxted and a beauty parlour. Presumably Sam had been interested in the place in his professional capacity as a CIA officer, rather than in his personal capacity as someone seeking a face-lift. But, as with the Dzolaks, they would have to play it by ear.

Hugh paid the taxi-driver, and they stood on the pavement, regarding the Nowy Świat – a broad thoroughfare, and part of the so-called 'Royal Way', which led, under a variety of street names, from the Castle Square to the south of the city. The salon, when they turned to it, appeared to occupy the ground floor of a corner house. From the outside there was little indication of its purpose. In the window were fresh flowers and, on a small easel, an oil painting of a beautiful girl. The name 'Beluch' was inscribed in gold lettering above the door. The place could easily have been an art gallery.

'Come in with me,' Jay said. 'I'll ask for a manicure. They'll probably insist on an appointment but, if they don't, I'll meet with you back at the hotel for lunch. Okay?' Before Hugh could

184

stop her, she bent down and ran the back of her nails against a paving stone.

'Yes.' Hugh nodded and opened the door for her.

He wished he could have sounded more enthusiastic, but for some reason he had taken an instant dislike to the salon, and distrusted its appearance. The inside of the shop did nothing to lessen this dislike and distrust.

For the interior matched the elegance of the exterior. 'Over-ostentatious discretion,' Hugh thought – those were the words to describe the outfit – a place for assignations; it was no wonder he was worried. The floor was covered by a thick blue carpet, and heavy velvet curtains of the same colour were drawn across an archway which presumably led to the business side of the establishment. A receptionist in a blue dress, which might or might not have been a uniform, sat behind an elegant glass desk, on which were carefully placed a vase of flowers, a telephone, and an appointment book. Against the wall stood two gilt chairs, in front of a table with some glossy magazines in a variety of languages.

'May I help you?'

Not only her appearance, but her voice and manner were in keeping with the décor. Her smile was polite, impersonal. And before either of them had spoken she had addressed them in English. Jay made no comment on this.

'I hope so. I badly need a manicure,' she said.

'You have an appointment, madam?'

'No. I'm afraid not. But I had a slight accident. I slipped against a wall.' Jay held out her hand, showing the broken nails and the chipped varnish. 'I remembered hearing of Beluch. I think it must have been from my friend, Lady Canville; probably she came here when her husband was the British Ambassador in Warsaw. I was sure you'd help me if you could.'

'We have many ladies from the embassies,' the receptionist said. She picked up her telephone receiver and gestured towards the two frail-looking chairs. 'If you would wait, madam, I'll see if we can fit you in. May I have your name?'

'Pamela Davidson,' Jay said firmly.

They perched on the chairs, Jay more comfortably than Hugh,

while the receptionist murmured into the phone. They couldn't hear what she said, not even enough to decide what language she was speaking, but they caught the word 'Davidson' repeated a couple of times.

The receptionist put down the receiver. Another girl, this one in a white clinical coat, came through the curtains. 'If you'll come this way, madam,' she said.

Jay gave Hugh a hurried kiss on the cheek. 'See you at lunch, darling.'

She was gone before Hugh could respond. He hesitated, but there seemed no option but to say good morning to the receptionist, and leave Jay to the tender mercies of the salon. Because the day was fine and he had time to spare and felt restless, he decided to walk back to the hotel. He was within fifty yards of his goal when he saw Jay's cousin, Urszula Socha, emerge from the entrance.

He waved to her and called her name. She stopped, and there was no doubt that she saw him. He expected her to return his wave, and then come to meet him. Instead, she turned and ran across the road, causing several drivers to hoot angrily. Hugh stared after her. He couldn't understand her behaviour. They had parted on excellent terms, and why else should she have come to the Orbis-Solec except to see Jay?

His question was soon answered. He was making for the bar in search of coffee, when he became aware of footsteps hurrying behind him. The hotel concierge was holding out an envelope.

'Mr Davidson! It's for Mrs Davidson, sir.'

Hugh took the envelope. 'Sorry,' he apologized. He had heard someone calling for Davidson, but had paid no attention, failing to connect the name with himself.

He sat at a table in the bar, fingering the envelope which had clearly been delivered by Urszula. If she had behaved normally, returned his greeting, been friendly, he wouldn't have thought twice about it. He would have put the envelope in his pocket, and given it, unopened, to Jay when she returned. As it was, he was tempted.

He bit into a rich cake, of the variety that always seemed to accompany coffee in Warsaw, and the temptation grew too much for him. He was sure Jay wouldn't mind. He slit the envelope and took out the letter it contained.

The message was brief. It had clearly been written in haste, and the ending was smudged. Frowning, Hugh read it through twice.

'Dearest J,
　　M cannot help you. He asked a friend and was told best to forget K. You must. Please.
　　　　　　　　　　　　　　　　　Much love. U.'

Thoughtfully he replaced the letter in its envelope and returned the envelope to his pocket. He could think of only one interpretation. Marek had made inquiries about Krasneski, as he had promised, and been warned off in no uncertain terms. Therefore, Krasneski was a character of importance, and possibly potentially dangerous. Urszula had been afraid – her note reeked of fear – which was why she had avoided him. She wanted no contact with anyone connected with Krasneski, however remotely.

Hugh thought of Fenwick and his association with security and intelligence. He thought of Canville, and the suspicions of espionage which surrounded him. All in all, it seemed not unlikely that this Krasneski was in the same world. Hugh had read enough novels to know that the Polish Secret Police was called the UB, and he wondered if the man were an officer in that service.

It was after one when Jay returned to the hotel. Hugh was waiting for her outside the main entrance. He was surprised when he saw her pay off her taxi one hundred yards away, and walk towards him. His growing anxiety turned to anger.

'Where the hell have you been?' he demanded. 'Have you any idea how late it is? You can't have been at that bloody salon all this time. I've been worried out of my mind. And why didn't you drive right up to the hotel?'

'Dear Hugh,' Jay said mildly. 'I'm sorry. I would have been

back sooner, but after that place I wanted some air and on the way I popped into an interesting-looking church called St Bernadette's and got talking to a priest. Do you know, Hugh, he was Irish, and his name was Ryan.'

'Here, in Warsaw? The Irish are ubiquitous,' Hugh replied.

'Then I couldn't find a taxi,' Jay concluded her story. 'I waited for ages at a rank. As for getting out in the next block, we've got to think of some tale for the Bereski. We can say she was right, and I did need some air, and I went for a walk.'

'I see. Clever,' said Hugh. 'Well, you're here now, darling, thank God. Let's go and have a drink. I need one badly.'

Jay thrust her arm through his. 'I'm sorry I worried you, honey,' she said. 'But I've lots to tell you.'

'And I've something to tell you.'

Hugh produced Urszula's letter, and they discussed it over their vodkas. The obvious answer was to talk to Marek Socha, but in the circumstances they were chary about suggesting another meeting. Jay thought he might not have known that Urszula had written to warn her. But they were more curious than ever about Krasneski. If indeed he were a UB officer, or even some other kind of Polish Government official, it would appear on the surface that he was in strange company with a small shopkeeper and the owner of a beauty salon, if not with Canville and Sam Thaxted.

'Tell me about Beluch's establishment,' Hugh said. 'Did you meet the great man?'

'Oh yes. I met him. He came and talked to me while I was having my manicure. He considers himself a ladies' man – over-charming manners, too well-cut silk suit.' Jay was scathing. 'Not the type to hit you over the head in a dark alley, but quite capable of slipping hemlock into your after-dinner coffee if he wanted to be rid of you.'

Hugh didn't laugh. Jay's language might have been melo-dramatic, but he knew that she meant what she said. She hadn't enjoyed her visit to the beauty parlour.

'He's clever,' Jay continued. 'He asked a lot of questions in a sneaky kind of way.'

'What sort of questions?'

'He asked when we arrived in Warsaw, how long we were going to be here, where we were staying, if we were on a package tour, and then covered up by suggesting a hair appointment before the end of the week.'

'That doesn't sound unreasonable.'

'None of it *sounded* unreasonable,' said Jay. 'But he also wanted to know your first name, what you – or rather Bill Davidson – did for a living, where we lived in London. He tried to worm it out of me without actually exerting any pressure. All I could do was be as vague as possible. Ugh!' Jay shivered at the recollection.

'Did you get anything out of him in return?'

'Not really. The receptionist had told him I knew Monica Canville, and he asked after her and said how sad Sir Rupert's death was. He volunteered that he'd never met Canville. And he'd never heard of the Dzolaks either, or at least he didn't admit it when I mentioned we'd been shopping there.'

'You had quite a chat.' Hugh spoke lightly, though he was as worried as Jay; he hated the idea of his Davidson cousins becoming involved.

'Yes. Absurdly long for a casual customer,' Jay said thoughtfully.

'But, Jay, how on earth could he have suspected you were other than what you claimed to be?'

'I don't know, but I'm sure he did.'

'Then it's lucky you didn't ask him if he knew a Madame Krasneski – that's if we're not reading too much into Urszula's letter,' Hugh said.

'I guess so.' Jay sounded uncertain. 'But, even without worrying the Sochas, we've somehow got to trace this Krasneski, or find out something about him. Hugh, what do you say we try the British Embassy? At least they should know if he's a government official.'

'All right.' Thinking of his passport, Hugh was reluctant. He disliked the idea of playing the part of Bill Davidson at the embassy, but he could think of no alternative. If they didn't pursue this line, they had reached a dead end.

★ ★ ★

189

After lunch they took a taxi to the British Embassy on Alija Roz. It was lucky, they agreed, that taxis in Warsaw were cheap. At the embassy their reception was a degree or so warmer than it had been at the Polish Embassy in Ottawa, but security was as strict.

Asked their business, Hugh said it was a personal matter. This led to a series of queries. Had either of them lost a passport? Had they lost anything else? Had they run out of money? Had they a complaint to make? What sort of trouble were they in?

'No trouble!' Hugh said finally, becoming bored with these questions. 'Look, all I'm asking is that one of your more senior officers should give us ten minutes of his time. I'm sure that if Sir Rupert Canville were still your Ambassador he'd have been happy to see me.'

'You knew Sir Rupert?'

'Yes. And we know Lady Canville. It's not long since we were lunching with her.'

Hugh disliked making use of his acquaintanceship with the Canvilles, but the present impasse had to be overcome somehow. The man behind the Inquiries desk gave him a cynical stare, but reached for his phone.

'If you'll wait over there, sir, I'll do what I can.'

Twenty minutes later 'Mr and Mrs Davidson' were ushered into the office of the Cultural Attaché. Derek Hill happened to be free, and he had known the Canvilles well, before they were posted to Ottawa. A tall, thin, grey-haired man, he was prepared to be pleasant. He drew out a chair for Jay, and beamed at Hugh.

'I gather you were friends of Rupert. How is dear Monica?'

The niceties occupied three minutes, the inquiries as to what they were doing in Warsaw a little longer. The Attaché looked expectant. What could he do for them? Were they sure it wasn't a consular matter?

Hugh explained that a colleague of his in London had asked them to contact a friend, a government official called Krasneski. They were eager to do this, but they had lost the address. It would be embarrassing to return and admit they had done nothing about him, and they wondered –

'If the British Embassy could help.' As Hugh floundered, aware how blank the face he was addressing had suddenly become, Derek Hill completed the sentence for him.

'I'm sorry,' Hugh said. 'It must sound absurd.'

'Not at all, my dear chap,' Hill assured him. 'Though I suspect the simplest thing might be a phone call to your friend in London. But we're used to the most astonishing requests. I suppose you have – er – tried the telephone book?'

'Yes,' said Jay. 'Of course. But the language is an almost insurmountable barrier, and a senior official would probably be ex-directory here, wouldn't he?' She gave Hill a dazzling smile. 'We hoped you would have government lists that would make it easy.'

The Cultural Attaché stood up. 'If you'll wait a moment I'll see what my secretary can dig up.' He loped from the room.

He was away some time. Hugh and Jay became uneasy. Why hadn't he merely summoned his secretary? But eventually Hill returned, shaking his head.

'Terribly sorry,' he said. 'My secretary recalls that there *was* a Viktor Krasneski, rather a playboy, but on the edge of Polish Government circles. If he's your chap, I'm afraid you're out of luck. He's not been seen around Warsaw for over a year.'

TWENTY-ONE

By that evening Dick Fenwick knew that he hadn't been mistaken. He *had* seen Hugh Bigrel and Jay Ryan in the city's old marketplace the previous day, after his visit to Anna Seschki.

Derek Hill had sought him out. The Cultural Attaché was nobody's fool. Though an officer of the British Council rather than the FCO, he had served in a variety of capitals and been around embassies long enough to know that it never did any harm to report variations from the norm. And, in this particular case, he had known Canville and liked him, but he had wondered about the Ambassador's sudden cross-posting to Ottawa. What was more, he had a strong suspicion that Dick Fenwick's alleged function was not his true one. Discretion, however, was second nature to him.

'You busy, Dick?' he had asked, putting his head around the door of the office Fenwick was using. 'Can you spare a couple of minutes for a chat?'

Fenwick was busy, but he laid down his pen. 'With you, Derek, yes. Come along in,' he said.

Hill perched himself on the corner of Fenwick's desk. 'I've just been talking to some friends of Rupert and Monica Canville. People called Davidson. A rather strange pair, I thought them.'

'What did they want?' It was more than an idle question. Any item of information or gossip connected with Rupert Canville interested Fenwick. 'Or was it just a social call?'

'No, it wasn't just a social call. Frankly, I don't quite know what it was. They were presentable enough. Attractive, in fact, but there was something odd about them. Let's put it this way. If I were a customs official, which God forbid, I'd have had them searched down to their skins.'

Fenwick laughed. The name Davidson meant nothing to him

192

in relation to the Canvilles, but Hill was not given to wasting other people's time. He had got to know Derek Hill during and after Sir Rupert Canville's unexpected departure, and he had respect for his perspicacity. Hill's 'little chats' often contained a nugget or two.

'You still haven't told me what they wanted,' he said.

'I don't know that either. They told me a cock-and-bull story about needing to contact a friend of a friend whose address they'd lost, someone called Krasneski.'

'What! Oh, hell and damnation!'

'Ah,' said Derek Hill. 'The name means something to you, does it?'

'Yes.' Fenwick didn't bother to deny it. 'Unfortunately. But if these two are who I'm sure they are, their name isn't Davidson. Describe them, would you, Derek?'

The description was more detailed than Fenwick needed. He was nodding his head after two or three sentences. Hugh Bigrel and Jay Ryan – the latter altered in appearance, but clearly identified by her slight American intonation – were in Poland. What was worse, they were making open inquiries about Krasneski – Viktor Krasnakov – right here, in Warsaw. They were asking to be chopped.

Fenwick had sworn that he'd not bother with them again, that they must look after themselves if they chose to ignore his warnings. But now the situation had changed. They were in a communist country, and after what Anna Seschki had hinted, more than hinted – Of course, he could have misunderstood her, but he didn't believe he had. She had seemed positively to deny compromising Canville, and – He had thought of going back and asking her outright exactly what she had meant, but he knew that she'd have laughed in his face, and denied that her remark had any meaning other than – than, for instance, that people didn't always sleep with their own husbands or wives.

Hill watched him curiously while he cogitated. 'Did you gather where they were staying?' Fenwick asked at length.

'Yes. They said they were on a package tour, and the group was at the Orbis-Solec. It's on Zagórna, near the Vistula.'

'I know the place. It's a favourite with these tours. I'll have to pay this couple a visit there, I suppose,' Fenwick sighed. 'Is there anything else you can tell me about them, Derek?'

'About them, no. Except that they said they were going home at the end of the week. However, I must admit I told them that there had been a chap called Viktor Krasneski in Warsaw social circles at one time, but he'd not been seen around for months. Which, as far as I know, is true. I hope I didn't go too far, and create a problem for you.'

'It shouldn't matter. On the contrary, it may make it simpler for me to persuade them to stop asking dangerous questions.'

Hill stood up. 'Okay. I'll leave you then – to get on with the good work. No need to tell me to keep my mouth shut.'

Fenwick grinned. 'Thanks a lot, Derek. I'm grateful.'

'Any time!' With a wave of his hand Hill opened the office door.

Dick Fenwick looked at his watch. It was getting late. He was tired, and he hadn't eaten yet. After all, the so-called Davidsons were of only peripheral importance, and by now they'd probably done what harm they could. He was tempted to let them wait till the following day.

Madame Bereski had decreed that there should be no engagements after supper that evening. The party, she said, had had a very full day at Zelazowa Wola, inspecting Chopin's birthplace, and she was sure that, with so much to recollect and reflect upon they would like to relax before another early start. In fact, the day had been exhausting, and no one contradicted her.

Jay had explained to her why she and her husband had been out twice that day. The air had done her good, just as Madame had suggested, but she still felt far from well. They too would be happy to retire to their room immediately after a light supper.

Alone, they were despondent. 'I suppose we were crazy to imagine we'd get any answers by coming to Warsaw,' Jay said, 'but it did seem a fair bet.'

'It was. We've learnt quite a lot.'

'But not enough. Sure, we've collected a few more facts, but we're no nearer knowing what it's really all about. We can still only guess.'

'It seems to me that either we give up, or we have another go at this chap Krasneski,' Hugh said slowly. 'But how? We mustn't forget Urszula's cryptic letter.'

'I was wondering if I might go back to the Dzolaks' shop. If I could get the woman by herself, or just with the boy, and speak to her in Polish, I might be able to quiet her fears and learn something worthwhile.'

'All right. I'll come with you.'

'No, Hugh. Let me go alone. She'll be much more inclined to talk if there isn't a man around.'

Reluctantly Hugh agreed, though he found it difficult to account for his hesitation. The Dzolaks, even the husband, had clearly been frightened rather than seriously aggressive, and the shop was a public place. Besides, Jay was a capable girl and, since she spoke the language, probably less likely to get into difficulties in Warsaw than he himself was.

I'm becoming too possessive, he thought, and pulled Jay down on the bed. He gave her a long kiss. 'Let's enjoy the present,' he said, 'and forget tomorrow.'

Viktor Krasnakov was much less ready to forget tomorrow, though he was very aware of the present. He found it strange to be in Warsaw once again. As he sat beside Galinov in the car they had rented at the airport – their presence was unknown to the Soviet Embassy – and let his aide drive him into the centre of the city, memories flooded back. They were not all pleasant, though it was a place where he had been unbelievably happy.

He shifted uncomfortably in his seat. He needed a woman, and his thoughts turned to Anna Seschki, but immediately he dismissed the idea. There were plans to be made and arrangements to be checked, and his duties must come first. He was not in Warsaw for pleasure. Even if he had been, he wasn't sure of a welcome from Anna; he had no idea whether or not she'd forgiven him. It was a pity. He hadn't scorned her, as she'd claimed. He had just fallen in love, and if she was telling the truth when she had said she was in love with him, then she should have understood the inevitability of his actions.

Perhaps Beluch would have laid on a woman for him. At least he could rely on Beluch, he thought. He was less happy about the Dzolaks; he didn't entirely trust them. They hadn't done badly, but they were weak – weak, and obviously frightened, he thought, unconsciously echoing Hugh Bigrel. He doubted if they could be bought, but they might be bullied. They would have to be moved. Not for the first time he wondered what clues had led Bigrel and Ryan to the Dzolaks' shop and Beluch's salon.

'Here we are,' he said to Galinov, as they turned off Nowy Świat into the street that ran along one side of the salon. 'We can leave the car. It'll be parked for us.'

He got out, leaving Galinov to collect their bags, and rang the bell. The door opened at once. A man slipped past him and slid behind the steering wheel. Krasnakov, followed by Galinov, entered a narrow hall. Beluch was waiting to greet them by the open door of a lift. Krasnakov embraced him warmly. He had cause to be grateful to the man. Beluch had served him well.

The lift took them to the top floor of the building. The ground floor of the property was occupied by the salon, but the floor above housed several suites of rooms that had a multitude of uses. Above them was a spacious apartment where Beluch lived. He didn't exactly run a brothel on the first floor, but he accommodated a few select ladies and their lovers. Occasionally, when necessary, he assisted with an operation to compromise some target. He was also able to offer hospitality to persons who preferred that their presence in Warsaw should be unnoticed.

It was all very convenient. There was a large garage at the back, giving access to a lane, and offering a third means of entering or leaving the premises. This ensured privacy for those of Beluch's visitors who desired it – and of course for Beluch himself.

Chance had played no part in the creation of this curious establishment. The site for the salon had been carefully chosen, and the building adapted for its present uses. But the time, effort and money spent on it had been well worthwhile for the

KBG, who had little faith in the love of the Polish people for the USSR, and even less faith in the competence of their opposite numbers in the UB.

'Come along in, Viktor Georgiyevich,' Beluch said. 'And you, Comrade Galinov. Leave the bags by the door and come into the living-room. You have eaten on the flight, yes? Nevertheless, a little something perhaps. And champagne? I have a bottle cooling. Or vodka?'

Krasnakov chose champagne, Galinov vodka. Beluch gestured to the bottles on a side table for Galinov to help himself, and went into the kitchen. He returned with smoked salmon sandwiches, caviare, black bread and a bottle of French champagne.

'Some good things come from the West,' he said, as he opened the champagne.

'And from the East,' Krasnakov remarked, gesturing around the room.

The floor was covered with Chinese carpets. There were a couple of beautiful Russian icons on the walls. The brocade for the curtains had come from Turkey. But the paintings were French Impressionists, and the furniture was European – modern and exceedingly expensive. Galinov, who had never before been inside Beluch's apartment, was goggle-eyed.

Russian-style, he had swallowed his vodka at a gulp, and then eaten a square of black bread. He watched Krasnakov and Beluch eating the sandwiches and dipping into the mound of caviare while they savoured the champagne. Their conversation was casual, but he had the impression that much of what they said had an extra meaning, which only they understood.

Beluch suddenly turned to him. 'You're not eating, Galinov, and your glass is empty. Help yourself, Comrade. Bring the bottle over.'

'But don't get drunk. You'll need all your wits about you tomorrow. We're here on business, remember,' Krasnakov interrupted, and added to Beluch. 'It's time we got on with it, too, Jan. What have you done so far?'

'I've made the rooms ready – separated rooms, so that they can't communicate with each other. And there should be no difficulty in bringing them into the building. Unfortunately, I

have a customer coming tomorrow. He's in the Federal Republic
– the West German – Embassy, and he has a wife and two
children. He's a fool. He even showed their photographs to the
girl he was screwing.'

'Can't you put him off?'

'I'm not anxious to do that. He's provided some useful
information in the past.'

'All the same, try.'

'If you say so.'

'I do. Now, what about snatching them?'

'You want them both? It's essential you have both? As you
know, Viktor Georgiyevich, it's ten times as difficult to snatch
two people as one.'

'I'd prefer both, but Ryan is the first priority. She's a forceful
bitch and, speaking Polish, she'd be able to make more fuss than
he would. Bigrel will go to the British Embassy, but they won't
be able to do anything. On the other hand, until we've found
out what the bloody couple know, we've no means of guessing
how much he could spill.'

'I understand.' Beluch poured more champagne. 'And I've
some bad news for you. Fenwick is in Warsaw. I only learnt
today. Anna Seschki came to have her hair done, and passed on
the news.'

Krasnakov swore. 'You didn't tell her that I – '

'No, of course not. She said Fenwick was trying to tie up the
ends of the Rupert Canville affair.'

'Good. Nothing would please me more than to have them well
and truly tied,' Krasnakov said vehemently.

For a minute there was a heavy silence. Surreptitiously
Galinov poured himself another vodka. Then Krasnakov began
to talk about their plans for the next day in detail. It was after
three when they went to bed, and Krasnakov no longer felt any
desire for a woman.

TWENTY-TWO

The group, under the guidance of Madame Bereski, had set off for the Academy of Fine Arts to view the reconstructed interior of Chopin's last home in Warsaw before he went abroad. A reluctant Hugh Bigrel had gone with them. He had been persuaded to do so only after he had made sure they were due to return to the hotel for lunch.

Jay and he had argued about it, but Jay had claimed it made sense to separate. She would probably do better on her own at the Dzolaks' shop, and his presence with the rest of the party would serve to placate the courier. Jay had promised to be back in plenty of time for a drink before lunch.

So Hugh had kissed her goodbye, joined the other tourists in the hotel foyer, and told Madame Bereski brusquely that his wife still had to rest, and would not be coming with them. To his surprise, this morning Madame Bereski had tended to be sympathetic. Once again she offered the services of a doctor, but she was not obstructive; in fact, as a great admirer of Chopin, she appeared to be genuinely distressed that any member of her group should miss such an important part of the tour. The other members of the party, too, expressed their hopes that his wife would recover very soon, and Hugh did his best to accept these sentiments with a good grace. Though he told himself his feelings were stupid, he was still worried at leaving Jay to make inquiries at the Dzolaks' by herself.

Her charges collected, Madame Bereski had led them out of the hotel. There was no reason why any of them should have noticed a taxi that was parked a short way from the entrance, with the driver concealed behind a morning newspaper. Nor could they know that in fact the man was watching their departure intently through a hole in the paper, or that the cab was fitted with some additional equipment.

Galinov cursed softly as he recognized Hugh Bigrel. He searched for Jay Ryan. This was not so simple. Beluch had described her new appearance, but no photograph of her was available. He counted the group, and by a process of elimination concluded that Ryan was not among them. He decided not to follow Bigrel and the party, but to wait for a quarter of an hour at least, and then if there were no sign of Ryan to phone Krasnakov and ask for orders.

Ten minutes later, as he was becoming restless, a taxi drew up in front of the Orbis-Solec. A man got out, and stood on the pavement paying his fare. Galinov recognized him immediately, and gave a low whistle. The situation was becoming interesting, for the man was Dick Fenwick.

Fenwick entered the hotel. Galinov drew up closer to the main doors, got out of his vehicle and followed him. He was in time to see Fenwick make some inquiries at the reception desk, and then speak to the concierge. Both the receptionist and the concierge shook their heads. Then Galinov observed a young woman sidle through what looked like a service door to one side of the foyer, and move in his direction. Almost furtively she glanced towards the reception desk, as if she wanted to conceal her departure from the hotel. And Galinov realized that almost certainly he was looking at Jay Ryan.

Turning quickly, he hurried back to his taxi. He was sitting behind the wheel, starting the engine, obviously about to drive away, when Ryan came out of the hotel. She ran towards him, waving at him to stop.

'The Old Town,' she said in English, jumping into the cab.

'Taxis aren't permitted there,' Galinov said in Polish.

'I know. Take me as near as you can to the Rynek Starego Miasta.'

This time Jay had spoken Polish too, and any residual doubt Galinov might have had about her identity vanished. He drove off at once, and in his rear-view mirror saw his passenger lean back in her seat and relax. He breathed a sigh of relief. He had hooked one fish with the greatest ease, and it was going to be simple to land her.

Once clear of the hotel Galinov pressed two buttons. One, normal only in taxis for security reasons, locked the car's rear doors on the inside. The second, more usual in certain types of hire car, caused a glass panel to slide up behind the front seat, cutting the driver off from his passenger. Another glance in the mirror assured him that Ryan remained untroubled. He spoke rapidly into his radio telephone.

Five minutes later he drew into the kerb close to a parked car. Jay sat up. She knocked on the glass partition, demanding to know why he had stopped here. But Krasnakov was already wrenching open the rear door and pulling it shut behind him. He pushed Jay back in her seat as the taxi moved off again. The other car followed it at a sedate distance.

Taken by surprise, Jay nevertheless tried to struggle, but Krasnakov, though not a big man, was heavier and stronger. She had no chance. Forcing her into a corner of the cab, Krasnakov produced from his pocket one of those small self-injection syringes issued to combat troops as first-aid against the effects of nerve gas. But this syringe was not filled with atropine, but with a rapid-acting narcotic. He pressed the syringe hard against Jay's thigh. She tensed at the sudden prick, but within thirty seconds her body went limp. Krasnakov put his arm round her, and drew her to him so that her head lolled on his shoulder.

Galinov grinned as he saw the apparently loving couple in the rear of the taxi. He lowered the glass partition. 'All well, Comrade Colonel?' he asked softly in Russian.

'Yes. She'll be out for an hour at least, but the sooner we get her tucked up in bed the better.' Krasnakov gripped his groin, where Jay had attempted to knee him. 'We'll have to be careful with her. She's a bitch – the sort that would scratch your eyes out given any kind of chance.' He dabbed with his handkerchief at his cheek which Jay had raked with her nails, and regarded his torn jacket angrily.

'Then maybe it's lucky we didn't snatch Bigrel at the same time,' said Galinov. 'I couldn't get near him, Comrade. He was with the tourist group, and went off with them, presumably on some sight-seeing visit. Ryan wanted to go to the Old Town. I don't know where exactly.'

'I can guess. To ask the Dzolaks some more questions. She'd have been lucky.' Krasnakov was scornful. 'She's due to answer questions, not ask them.'

'What about Bigrel?'

'We'll leave him for the moment and see how he reacts. Beluch can arrange to have him watched. If necessary, we'll pick him up later or, better, fix a little accident for him. Two separate disappearances would make the British really sit up, and then the UB would start taking notice. That would be a pity. We want this to pass off as quietly as possible.' Krasnakov looked down at the girl he was cradling, and considered her. 'A lot will depend on what Ryan has to say,' he added finally.

From this last remark Galinov understood that he was to be told no more for the moment. He concentrated on his driving, and very soon they were turning into the alley at the rear of the beauty salon. The garage doors were open, and they went straight in. Beluch was waiting for them.

'A good job, Igor Borosovich,' Krasnakov commented to Galinov as he got out of the taxi, letting Jay fall back on the seat. 'Well done.'

It was only then that Galinov remembered he hadn't mentioned Fenwick's appearance at the hotel to the Comrade Colonel. But he decided there was no point in worrying Krasnakov now, when he seemed to be so satisfied with the conduct of the operation.

On another occasion, in company with Jay, Hugh might have enjoyed his morning. For a visitor, Warsaw was a fascinating city and, though Madame Bereski was irritatingly over-authoritative, and too determined that her party should get their money's worth, she was also articulate and knowledgeable. But Hugh was in no mood for sight-seeing, and found it difficult to respond to the interested chatter of his fellow tourists. He was thankful to get back to the hotel not long after noon.

As soon as he entered the foyer he looked around, hoping to find Jay waiting for him. Another tour group, a party of some twenty obvious Scandinavians had just arrived, and there seemed to be some disagreement about the rooms available for them. While their courier dealt with the matter, they stood around in threes and fours, talking volubly, their luggage scattered at their feet. In the confusion Madame Bereski was trying to collect her charges together, so that she could give them their instructions for the afternoon. Hugh couldn't see Jay anywhere.

'Hello, Bill!'

Hugh paid no attention. He didn't connect the name, and the arm upraised in greeting, with himself. Madame Bereski did.

'There is someone you know, Mr Davidson,' she said.

By then Dick Fenwick had pushed his way through the crowd, and was standing in front of Hugh. He clapped Hugh on the shoulders and beamed at him. Then he turned to Madame Bereski, holding out his hand.

'How do you do? You must be Madame Bereski. They told me at the desk. My name's Fenwick. I'm from the British Embassy. Bill here and I are old chums.' He looked Hugh in the eye, defying him to contradict this assertion. 'But I haven't seen him for ages, and there's a great deal for us to catch up on. You'll forgive me, won't you, Madame, if I take him off for a drink and lunch and a good long chat?'

The courier had no reason to object and Hugh, who would have liked to tell Fenwick to go to hell, found himself being led quietly away in the direction of the bar. But when they were out of earshot of his party, he turned on Fenwick.

'I've got to find Jay. I suppose you know she's here in Warsaw with me?'

'Later. She's up in your room at the moment.'

'Is she? How do you know? Are you sure?'

'Yes.'

It was not an intentional lie. When Fenwick had returned to the hotel to await their return, the concierge had told him that Mr Davidson was still out, but Mrs Davidson was resting in her room. And, as Fenwick was debating whether or not to tackle Jay alone, Madame Bereski's party had arrived.

Hugh shrugged, accepting the inevitable. 'Okay. If we're going to the bar, you can buy me a whisky. I'm getting a bit fed up with vodka.'

'And a lot of other things too – including me, I dare say,' Fenwick remarked. 'Whisky it is.'

Fenwick chose a corner table, and a waiter brought their drinks. 'Now,' said Fenwick, 'we'll talk, like two old chums who have just met again. But keep your voice down.' He raised his hand as Hugh opened his mouth. 'I'll begin and I won't mince words,' he said firmly. 'You and Mrs Ryan are fools – fools, do you hear? You have come to a foreign country, a communist country, on borrowed passports – '

'Stolen passports!' Hugh interjected.

'Oh, I see. You mean your cousins deliberately looked the other way while you helped yourselves? All right. Don't bother to deny it.' Fenwick sounded disgusted. 'I've no quarrel with the Davidsons, only with you and Mrs Ryan. Here you are, on passports that aren't your own, under false names and false identities – and, as far as Mrs Ryan's concerned, even disguised for God's sake. Amateurs!' he uttered the last word like an oath. 'The Poles would be justified in throwing you both in gaol on espionage charges.'

'And you propose to inform on us?' Hugh asked coldly.

'Don't be stupid. I don't need to. They'll find out soon enough if you go around asking questions about people like – like Krasneski. For heaven's sake, Bigrel! I've warned you before. Aren't you ever going to understand? You're in danger. This – is – not – your – battle.'

'But it is! That's what *you* refuse to understand, Fenwick. You know as well as I do that someone shot Sam Thaxted and indirectly killed my family. Why can't you tell us the truth about it?'

'I don't know the truth – yet.'

'Oh, come on! Sir Rupert Canville was a spy, and you're covering up for him. Fair enough, since the wretched man's drowned himself and can't do any more harm. I appreciate that it would be tough on poor Monica Canville – and certainly bad for Anglo-American relations – if it became public. But since we

– Jay and I – already know so much, why shouldn't we know the rest of a story that's affected our lives so vastly? You can't believe we'd do any deliberate harm by publicizing it, can you?'

There was silence. Then Fenwick said, 'Have you finished your diatribe?'

'Yes. I know I've been wasting my breath.' Hugh started to rise from his chair.

Fenwick gestured to him to sit down again. 'We'll have another whisky, and damn the expense.' He signalled to the waiter.

In the interval before the drinks came he played with the ashtray on the table between them, and didn't speak. He had no need to reach any decision. The previous night he had made up his mind how far he was prepared to go in trusting Bigrel and Jay Ryan. But he was impressed with the force with which Hugh Bigrel had spoken.

When the waiter had gone, Fenwick sipped his second whisky and said, 'Okay. Before his death Canville wrote me a letter, saying that he had become a Soviet agent. He knew or guessed that I was already on to him.'

'But why?' Hugh broke in; to his surprise he was shocked at this confirmation of his own suspicions of Canville. 'The man could be said to have everything.'

'When he was in Warsaw he had an affair with someone called Anna Seschki. She's a woman who can best be described as a kind of political hostess. Everyone goes to her parties.'

Hugh merely nodded, without remarking that he had already heard of Anna Seschki when he was in Washington. 'And the affair made Canville vulnerable to blackmail. What a fool he must have been! Especially with a wife like Monica. I thought he was supposed to be devoted to her.'

'Maybe. That's irrelevant. What is relevant is that we – the Brits – decided on a cover-up.' Fenwick hurried on. 'The Russians seemed to be all for that solution, too. Unfortunately, Sam Thaxted smelt a rat, and went hunting for it. So he was – eliminated.'

'You mean you – you – '

'No, not me, not the Brits. We don't do that sort of thing any more – much. It was the Russians.'

Fenwick's smile was cynical as he saw the relief on Bigrel's face. He guessed that Bigrel was thinking of Thaxted's daughter. 'After all,' he went on gently, 'the Americans are our allies. You must admit it's only logical that we should have had qualms about shooting one of them on English soil. I'm not sure, of course, but I'd bet it was a man called Viktor Krasnakov who did the shooting, or engineered it. He's known in Warsaw as Krasneski. In reality, he's a Muscovite, a colonel in the KGB. He used to frequent Anna Seschki's parties too.'

Hugh had drawn a deep breath. 'He's not in Warsaw at present, then?'

'I'm told he's in Moscow, but he gets around, so I wouldn't swear to it.' Fenwick sipped his whisky and regarded Hugh Bigrel carefully. 'I doubt if it will ever be proved, so I hope you'll be content with knowing that Krasnakov was to blame for the death of your wife and son. In their case, it wasn't intentional, but a KGB officer is not the kind of man to worry if innocent people get killed. For instance, don't think for a moment that he'll hesitate to kill you and Mrs Ryan if you continue to make nuisances of yourselves. And that's the truth, Bigrel. Now are you satisfied?'

'Yes, but – ' Hugh was frowning. 'There are two points I'd like cleared up. Why should the KGB want to cover for Canville once he was dead and no more use to them? And why didn't you tell us the truth before, instead of a pack of lies?'

The first of these questions had worried Fenwick for many months. Theoretically the Russians should have been pleased by the damage to Western relations that a public airing of the story might cause. But the advantages to be gained would have been small, especially if the revelations gave rise to another round of anti-Soviet spy-mania – or so he had told himself, though he had been able to see no reason for the KGB to have gone to such lengths to conceal the truth as killing Thaxted. Now he believed he knew better.

However, he had to answer Bigrel. He said, carefully, 'Anna Seschki is extremely valuable to the KGB and the Soviet Union.

We know, because of Canville, that's she's a honey-trap to provide material for blackmail. And at her parties she can pick up a lot of snippets of information that may well prove useful when studied and analysed. What's more, we think she may even help to recruit or to control agents, like Beluch of the beauty salon. I'm not certain, but I believe it was to protect the Seschki woman that the KGB have made such a major effort. If her real roles became known, even merely in diplomatic circles, her usefulness to the Soviet Union would be at an end.'

And, as Hugh nodded his understanding, Fenwick thought that he had just added another card to the pack of lies of which Bigrel had accused him. Mentally, he asked Anna Seschki's pardon for maligning her.

He continued. 'As to your second question – well, quite simply, I didn't realize that you and Mrs Ryan would be so persistent. I hoped that a warning to keep off the grass would be sufficient. You had no official standing and no apparent need to know, and it's a cliché that the fewer people who know something the less chance of a leak. Ah well! It's a strange world. You only met the Canvilles once and yet – '

'Actually, I met Lady Canville again, in the UK,' Hugh corrected him.

He explained about the so-called casual luncheon at the Lansdownes' house in the Cotswolds – a meal that had turned out to be a Lucullan banquet, in honour not of him or Jay, nor of Lady Canville who was staying there, but of the other house guest, an American called Worral J. Smith. He added that Jay had remarked that this Smith was a possible Democratic candidate for the next Presidential elections.

Together, Bigrel and Fenwick laughed over the story, and shortly afterwards Fenwick rose to his feet. He said he must leave – they had talked for so long that he was afraid he would have to cut lunch – but if Mrs Ryan had any more questions he could be contacted at the British Embassy until the weekend.

They parted on reasonably good terms. Fenwick watched thoughtfully as Hugh hurried off to find Jay, and suppressed a momentary feeling of envy. He had work to do. He knew by instinct that at last he was in business. The operation had taken a radical change of direction. Cast your bread upon the waters, he thought, and don't be surprised at what may come back to you on the end of the line.

TWENTY-THREE

Talking and drinking with Dick Fenwick, Hugh himself had not noticed how quickly time was passing. Now he was surprised that Jay had not come in search of him before. It was most unlikely that she would wait so long in their room, when she must have guessed the group would have returned. Then the thought occurred to him that, after all the pretence, she really was unwell, and he hurried along the corridor from the lift.

The 'Do Not Disturb' notice in a variety of languages was still hanging on the doorknob where, Hugh assumed, Jay had left it when she went out. Hugh knocked, two, one and then another two, so that she would know who it was. There was no answer. He knocked again more loudly. A maid appeared from a room she was servicing further along the corridor, and pointed to the notice.

Ignoring her, Hugh banged on the door again. Then he tried to explain. The maid spoke only a word or two of English, but she was prepared to be helpful. Giggling, she unlocked the door with her passkey. Hugh brushed past her. The bed was unmade, but otherwise the room was perfectly tidy. He glanced into the bathroom. There was no sign of Jay, and no note. He wondered if she were still out, if she had decided to go on to see the priest, Father Ryan, again, or even pay another visit to Beluch's beauty salon. He told himself not to panic.

He went downstairs and asked the concierge, who said that Mrs Davidson was in her room. When Hugh denied this, he pointed to the hook on which their room key normally hung. The key was missing; therefore, he said, she must be in the hotel because it was forbidden to take keys outside the building. Frustrated, Hugh looked in the restaurant and the café and even the bar. There were not that many places where Jay could be.

Eventually he was forced to appeal to Madame Bereski. And he took back all his uncharitable thoughts of her. He explained that his friend from the British Embassy had had to leave, but that his wife was not in her room. At once Madame Bereski abandoned her lunch, and returned with him to the concierge. Hugh stood by while various members of the staff were summoned and questioned in a barrage of Polish. At last Madame Bereski turned to him.

'Mr Davidson, one of the porters saw Mrs Davidson leave the hotel not long after we did. He says that she seemed in a hurry, which is perhaps why she forgot to leave her key. He believes that she caught a taxi. No one has seen her since.'

Hugh thanked Madame Bereski, who was staring at him curiously. In the circumstances, he reflected, this was less than surprising. Clearly he had lied to her earlier when he had maintained that his wife needed to rest, or his wife had lied to him about her condition. Hugh could almost see Madame Bereski wondering if they had had a quarrel.

'Don't worry, Mr Davidson,' she said. 'Perhaps she went for a walk and got lost, but she knows the name of the hotel. She'll soon be back, I'm sure. Why not come and have lunch with us while you wait?'

Hugh refused, saying he would prefer to stay in the foyer and might get something to eat in the café. He wished he could share the courier's conviction. If Jay had lost her way it would present no problem for her; she could easily ask for directions. If she had been delayed somewhere, she could have telephoned and left a message. She'd have known he would be worried. But what was the alternative? With a sickening jolt he remembered the Sunday in London when Jay had been knocked down by a car, and the strong possibility that this incident had been no accident.

Hiding his anxiety, Hugh thanked Madame Bereski once again, and urged her to return to her own interrupted lunch. She went back to the restaurant, but he found it impossible to wait passively. He wandered about the foyer, and then left the hotel to walk up and down the street outside. A taxi stopped to let off some passengers, and on an impulse he asked the driver to take him as near as possible to the Rynek Starego Miasta in the Old Town. He guessed that this was what Jay had done that morning.

Hugh intended to follow Jay to the Dzolaks' shop. He had no clear idea what he hoped to achieve, but anything was better than inactivity. His guide book was in his pocket, and he had a good sense of direction. Once he paid off the cab, he had no difficulty in finding the street or the shop.

But the woman behind the counter was different. She was younger, and her clothes were modern rather than traditional Polish. She smiled expectantly at Hugh.

'Do you speak English?' he asked slowly.

'A little, sir. How can I help you? A gift for your wife? Your girlfriend?'

She continued to smile as Hugh shook his head, but her eyes were sharp. Hugh had no reason for his antipathy, but he took an instant dislike to this woman. Nor did he like the man who had appeared from the rear of the shop. He was smaller than Dzolak and not at all outwardly aggressive, but Hugh felt that he would have preferred Dzolak's bluster. He sensed that the couple regarding him with apparent benevolence were more astute – even dangerous – than the Dzolaks. Certainly, they were not fearful.

Hugh said, 'Is Mrs Dzolak here?'

They looked at him blankly, and shook their heads in unison. The conversation that followed was ludicrous. No one called Dzolak lived there. They knew no Dzolaks, except a butcher on the –

Hugh interrupted them. He said that he and his wife had been in the shop two days ago, and had spoken with the Dzolaks. His wife had bought a pair of silver earrings. Had she been back this morning?

The man answered. 'We do not know your wife, sir, nor these Dzolaks. Our name is Chowski, Andrzej and Wanda Chowski.'

'And no English lady has been in the shop this morning,' the woman added.

'My wife is – ' Hugh began, and stopped. He had been about to say that Jay was an American, but he realized it was pointless.

They probably wouldn't know the difference. Instead, 'You weren't here the day before yesterday,' he said accusingly.

'We are always here,' Chowski said. 'It is our business.'

'You have mistook the shop,' Mrs Chowski said, as if she had just had a bright thought. 'It is so easy in the Old Town. There must be another one like this, but not the same. You look. It is different. We do not sell silver.'

Hugh looked about him. It was true; it *was* different. It was a gift shop, undoubtedly, but the range of goods and the displays had subtly changed. He didn't remember any leather goods, or dolls dressed in Polish peasant costume. There was amber, but no silver, and he realized that the tapestry behind the counter had become a beaded curtain. For a moment he was shaken, but only for a moment. The one thing that was the same was the location, and he knew that he was in the right street. He had noted its name carefully.

There could not be two similar shops within a few yards of each other; if there had been the Chowskis would certainly have known of the Dzolaks. The proprietors had changed, and a few superficial alterations had been made, but Hugh had no doubt that this was the shop he and Jay had visited the day before yesterday.

The bell above the door tinkled, and suddenly the place seemed full of people. In fact, there were only five – a party of German tourists. But they chattered loudly, and sounded as if they were eager to buy. Hugh realized that he would learn nothing more from the Chowskis. He thanked them, said he was sorry to have bothered them and agreed that he must have been mistaken. In spite of the press of other customers, he could feel their eyes on his back as he stepped out into the street.

He began to walk slowly towards the Rynek. He heard an odd hissing sound behind him, but paid it no attention. Then a small hand plucked at his jacket. He turned quickly, thinking of pickpockets, but at once recognized Tomasz, the Dzolaks' son. He seized the boy by the arm, but the move was unnecessary. Tomasz had no intention of running away immediately. He wanted to speak to the Englishman.

'Mister!' Tomasz pulled Hugh into a deep doorway. 'Not true

212

what we said. We knew the Englishman in your picture. He comes asking questions. He gave me money, like you.'

Tomasz paused for breath. It was clear that he found speaking English a strain. He looked up at Hugh with large brown eyes, and Hugh thought he might be regretting his decision to accost him. He squatted down to be on a level with the boy, and grinned at him.

'And you'll have more money, Tomasz, I promise. First, tell me, have you seen my wife today? The lady I was with before – has she been in the shop?'

'No. Not today.'

'Are you sure, Tomasz? It's very important.'

'Sure! Sure! I watch all day.'

Hugh sighed. If the boy were telling the truth – and there seemed no reason to doubt him – there was no hope of finding Jay here and, after his talk with Fenwick, questions about Thaxted were irrelevant. But he was intrigued by the Chowskis.

'Why has your family left the shop?' he asked.

'Man phones. Bad man, I think. Gives orders. We go. Mama cries, but we always do what he says.'

'Are you all right?' Hugh wondered how much money he could spare.

Tomasz nodded. 'Perhaps we go home later if Jan Beluch allows.'

The boy was becoming nervous. He shifted from one foot to another, and began to cast anxious glances into the street behind Hugh's shoulder. Hugh reached for his wallet, and extracted some notes.

'Your wife,' said Tomasz, eyeing the money. 'She is lost?'

Hugh hesitated. 'Perhaps,' he said. 'At any rate I don't know where she is at the moment. I suppose you wouldn't have any idea?'

'*Nie.*' Tomasz began to edge away.

'Okay.' Hugh held the notes out to him, and the boy's eyes widened. 'Good luck, Tomasz.'

'*Dziękuję.*' The boy thrust the money into the pocket of his shorts and pushed past Hugh. Then he turned back. 'Your wife. Ask Father Ryan. Maybe he know. Bernadette's.'

Hugh watched the young Pole run down the street and disappear. After a minute he continued on his way to the Rynek. He sat at a café table and ordered coffee. He was glad of the cakes that automatically arrived with it, for he was hungry as he had had nothing to eat since breakfast, and the two whiskies with Fenwick had made him feel slightly light-headed. But the first cake nauseated him, and he couldn't face it. He just drank the coffee.

He thought of telephoning the Orbis-Solec to ask if Jay had returned, but was deterred by the language difficulty. And he couldn't face the idea of returning and finding that Jay was still missing. He decided to take Tomasz's advice and visit Father Ryan, though he couldn't conceive how the priest might help. But at least he spoke English, and would perhaps phone the hotel.

Miserably, his mind occupied with fears for Jay, Hugh looked for St Bernadette's in his guide book.

Jay regained consciousness slowly and reluctantly. She had been in the middle of a happy dream, which she tried to recapture without success. As the dream faded she became aware of discomfort. Her head ached. She felt sick and weak. Anxious, she opened her eyes.

She was in bed, in a strange room. Her first reaction was that she had had an accident, and was in hospital, but the room was more like some travesty of a Victorian lady's boudoir than any hospital room she could imagine. Carpet, curtains, bed coverings were a deep rose pink. Apart from the bed the furniture was confined to two chairs, covered in rose-covered velvet. A door, also velvet-covered, was opposite her. All this, and the painting of two girls and a man making love which hung beside the door, were reflected in the mirrored ceiling.

Lying on her back, Jay could see herself, her face pale, her hair intended to resemble Pam Davidson's, her eyes wide and frightened. She made an effort to sit up, and the rose-pink duvet slipped from her shoulders, exposing her breasts.

Involuntarily she started to pull up the duvet to cover herself but, although she was now more or less awake, she found it hard to move her arms. She bit her bottom lip to stop herself from crying out, as a sudden fear that she was paralyzed pierced her. Then common sense reasserted itself. She remembered the man who had leapt into her taxi and her struggle with him, and the prick of a needle in her thigh. It was obvious, she thought bitterly, that he had won, and this was the result. She was suffering from the after-effects of some drug.

She made an effort of will, and forced herself to move first her fingers and toes, then her arms and legs, but sitting up was beyond her for the moment, so she lay, hoping for strength to return and fearful of what was to happen next, her gaze searching the room for some clue as to her whereabouts. Minutes passed. There was no clock and her watch, like her clothes, were not in sight, so she had no means of judging the time or even the date. She only knew that it was during the day, because a little hazy light showed at the edges of the heavy drawn curtains. Her mind was starting to function rationally, and she began to plan how she would act when someone came.

It was Viktor Krasnakov who opened the door, and he was smiling as he entered the room. He had been alerted that Mrs Ryan was beginning to regain consciousness, and he had been watching her ever since through a one-way mirror that was more often used to record scenes for potential blackmail. From what he knew of Mrs Ryan, he considered that so far her reactions had been what he would have expected. She had been upset when she realized her predicament, but she had not panicked. Although clearly she was frightened, she hadn't screamed. By now she should be feeling ghastly, and ready to talk.

'Good afternoon, Mrs Ryan,' he said.

The sight of her abductor was enough to banish Jay's headache and nausea, and replace them with fury, but she had enough sense to feign continued sleepiness. Nevertheless, she knew she must protest.

'What the hell's the meaning of this – this kidnapping?' she demanded weakly. 'And where are my clothes? And who the hell are you?'

In fact, she had instantly recognized her visitor as the man who had attacked her in the so-called taxi. She hadn't realized before how good-looking he was. He had changed his suit, and she remembered with satisfaction that in their struggle she had torn the pocket of his jacket. She had also scratched his cheek; the mark showed livid against his tan. She forgot that she had kneed him in the groin. It still hurt him, and he promised himself that the bitch would pay for it later.

He ignored her questions, and asked politely, 'How are you feeling?' Then he went to the bed and pulled aside the rose-coloured duvet so that Jay's body was exposed. She flushed, and tried to cover herself with her hands, but he merely regarded her, and nodded his satisfaction.

'Nice long legs,' he said. 'Extraordinary how American girls always seem to have long legs.'

He spoke dispassionately, as if he were discussing the length of a plank of wood. But Jay shivered; she was sure he was about to rape her. All she could do was collect saliva in her mouth, and spit in his face. Krasnakov swore, but didn't touch her. Instead, he carelessly tossed the duvet back over her, and went to sit down in one of the chairs.

'It's all right, Mrs Ryan,' he said aloud. 'You're in no danger at the moment. Just realize your vulnerability. Incidentally, when you feel you can move, there's a bathroom through that door, but there is no way out. The door is strong and the windows are shuttered.' To himself he thought, I don't need to take you by force, Ryan; I'll make you come to me, crawling. He crossed his legs, and uncrossed them as his groin hurt. He regarded Jay sardonically.

'You asked who I was. So, let me introduce myself,' he said. 'My name is Viktor Georgiyevich Krasnakov. In Poland I'm often called Krasneski. I believe you've been looking for me in several countries. Here I am. What is it you want from me?'

Jay hesitated, then decided to make the most of the opportunity to learn something, even at the risk of appearing more active than she would have preferred. 'My father was Samuel Thaxted,' she said, her voice shaking a little. 'He was shot when he was driving on a motorway in England.'

216

'Yes. I remember the occasion well,' Krasnakov commented casually. 'A brilliant operation, though I say it myself.'

'What! You don't mean you – '

'Oh yes. I shot your father.'

Jay was more appalled by the calmness with which Krasnakov made the admission than by its content. She turned her head and stared at the Russian. Obviously, he had shot Sam with as much compunction as a sportsman would bring down a clay pigeon, and she knew with absolute certainty that eventually he intended to kill her too.

'Why?' she said. 'For God's sake, why? Just to cover for your spy, Rupert Canville?'

'My poor innocent! Of course not.' Krasnakov threw back his head and laughed. 'Now, no more questions from you, Mrs Ryan. You're about to answer some for me.'

TWENTY-FOUR

St Bernadette's is not one of Warsaw's finest ecclesiastical monuments. Destroyed during the Second World War and rebuilt in its original Gothic form, it has remained a church for the faithful and has never enjoyed great popularity as a tourist attraction. Nevertheless, it was mentioned in Hugh's guide book, and he found it without difficulty.

As the doors sighed shut behind him, he stood for a moment while his eyes became accustomed to the semi-gloom. The building smelt of stale incense, guttered wax, and furniture polish. Close to him a woman was on her knees in front of a statue that he couldn't identify. Scattered among the pews were half-a-dozen worshippers, heads bent in prayer. In a side chapel a child was being shown how to light a candle. A priest in his soutane was directing the arrangement of flowers around the altar.

It was an alien situation for Hugh. Normally his church-going was confined to services at Christmas, Easter, the occasional wedding and the even more occasional baptism or funeral. The thought of funerals reminded him that the last time he had been in a church, other than sight-seeing with Madame Bereski, was in Washington DC, when Sam Thaxted's ashes had been brought to their final home. Impatient with his memories, he strode down the aisle to the altar rail.

'Excuse me!' he called quietly.

The priest came over to him. He was a young man, younger than Hugh, with a pale, expressionless face.

Hugh said, 'Do you speak English – er – Father?'

The priest nodded. 'A little.'

'I should like to see Father Ryan.'

The priest raised his head and gave Hugh a searching look,

then he pointed to the far end of the front pew. He said a few words to one of his group of flower arrangers, and disappeared through a side door, which obviously led to a vestry of some kind. Hugh sat where he had been told, and tried to compose his thoughts. It seemed a long wait.

The priest returned. He was alone, and at first Hugh was disappointed. Then he became annoyed when the priest completely ignored him, and returned directly to his duties at the altar. But a few moments later another man, in a black suit but wearing a clerical collar, came through the side door, glanced round the church and slid into the pew beside him.

'I am Father Ryan. Who are you?'

'My name is – ' Hugh paused. He was at a loss to know how much or how little Jay had confided in Father Ryan. 'Hugh Bigrel,' he said tentatively.

Obviously it had been the right reply, for the response was immediate. 'Good. Come along with me, then, Hugh Bigrel, and tell me what I can do for you.'

The Irish accent was pronounced, and Hugh felt relieved. Father Ryan was small and narrow-shouldered, with a shock of grey hair, a big hooked nose, and squirrel-bright eyes. He looked as if a puff of wind would blow him away. As he led Hugh into an austerely-furnished room with a large crucifix on the wall, Hugh saw that his suit was shiny with wear.

He turned to face Hugh and smiled, showing large yellow teeth. 'I'm glad you're Hugh Bigrel,' he said. 'I'd not want dealings with Mr Davidson. He'd not be trusting me, you see.'

'I understand. It seems that you know something of our – our problem, Father.'

'Something, yes, but I'm not sure I know why you've come to St Bernadette's.' He gave Hugh a shrewd glance. 'There is some trouble?'

'Jay's disappeared.'

It was a bald statement, and the priest listened attentively as Hugh elaborated. From time to time he nodded his head. Clearly he was already familiar with a great deal of Hugh's story. He stood up as Hugh stopped speaking.

'I'll go and telephone the Orbis-Solec at once,' he said.

Father Ryan was away some time. Hugh began to fidget. When the priest came back, one glance at his face was enough to dash his hopes that by now Jay might be safe.

'Jay has not returned to the hotel,' Father Ryan said, 'and there has been no message from her. I have also phoned a friend – a friend whom I trust – at the hospital to which Jay would have been taken if she had been knocked down in the street or become ill in a public place in the centre of Warsaw. I hope it is good news that she is not there.'

'I suppose so.' Hugh was despondent. 'But where on earth can she have got to? I realize that if we were in London I wouldn't be flapping like this, but it's not London and – and, Father Ryan, I'm scared for her.'

'There may not be any need, my son. There could be a simple explanation. However, I'll do what I can, though you must realize I have responsibilities to my people here. For instance, I can't put Jay before the Dzolaks who, from what you say about their shop, may well be in trouble too. Mr Bigrel, you read your newspapers. I don't have to tell you that life in Poland is not always easy or simple. This is a Communist country, but very many Poles are devout Catholics, and Catholics are among those who most dislike their Russian masters. So the Church is on a knife-edge, and there is always tension. We have to take the greatest care.'

'I appreciate that.' Hugh failed to keep the cynicism from his voice; it was clear the priest would not help.

Father Ryan seemed to read his thoughts, and looked at him quizzically. 'I wonder if you do? You met Father Marienski with his flower ladies, but I doubt if you noticed his right hand. He spent a week in prison, as a guest of the UB – the secret police – and all the bones of that hand were crushed. His hand is useless. It's not a pretty sight, and he tries to keep it hidden. Nevertheless, as I said, in spite of the difficulties, I'll do what I can and put out some feelers.'

Hugh swallowed hard. 'I – I'm sorry.' He knew it was an inadequate remark, but there was nothing else he could say. He recognized that the old priest was right. He could pay lip service to the differences between London and Warsaw, but he had no true conception of the reality of Polish life for Polish citizens. And this new, slight understanding made him even more uneasy about Jay. 'Please do anything you can,' he said at last. 'For Jay's sake, if not for mine. And thank you.'

'What are *you* going to do with yourself, Mr Bigrel? Return to the Solec?'

It was a question Hugh hadn't considered. He had hoped against hope that when Father Ryan telephoned he would find that Jay was at the hotel. Now there was only one more place he could try.

He said, 'When Jay had a manicure at Beluch's yesterday, it was suggested that she should come back to have her hair done sometime. I suppose it's conceivable she could be there. At least I could ask.'

Father Ryan was frowning. 'Yes. She told me she had been to Beluch, and met the great man himself. She had disliked him, she said.' He shrugged his shoulders. 'I have reason to believe her instinct was right. I hear a lot of things as a priest. Naturally, the confessional is sacrosanct, but I will tell you that, though the Beluch establishment has a most respectable front, strange things go on inside the building.'

'What do you mean by that, Father?'

Father Ryan seemed to be choosing his words with care. 'Well, I doubt if the place is simply what the world would call a brothel, but it's certainly an illicit meeting-place – what used to be called a "house of assignation". Shall we say a husband will accept that his wife spends three or four hours at a beauty salon, and will suspect nothing?'

Hugh nodded. He told himself that he had no interest in the sexual habits of those who frequented Beluch's salon. What did scare him was the idea that Beluch might be a Soviet agent, who was holding Jay against her will. But could he seriously believe in this theory as a possibility? Put into words, even if unspoken, such fears seemed absurdly melodramatic. Then he thought of the young priest's hand, and of what Fenwick had said about Krasnakov. Involuntarily, he shivered, but quickly recovered himself.

'When she was here did Jay mention anyone in Warsaw other

than the Dzolaks and Beluch, or did you suggest anyone else she might consult?' Hugh asked, rising to his feet.

'Only her cousins,' said Father Ryan.

'Of course! I'd forgotten the Sochas. Perhaps she's gone there again.'

Remembering the note Urszula had left for Jay, Hugh was not hopeful, but at least it was a possibility that needed investigation. He thanked Father Ryan once more, promised to let him know immediately if there was news of Jay, and said goodbye. As he walked down the aisle, he noticed that the young priest was no longer occupied with the flowers.

Outside, he stood for a moment on the church steps, debating his next move. He would need a taxi to go to the Sochas, and Urszula might not be in. The beauty salon was much nearer, and he set off to walk towards it.

There was a different receptionist behind the desk. She greeted Hugh pleasantly, and her expression did not change when he inquiried if Mrs Davidson was in the salon.

'No,' she said at once.

'Well, was she here earlier?'

The girl checked her appointments book thoroughly before shaking her head.

'No. No Mrs Davidson has been in today.'

Hugh had no reason to distrust the girl. She was young, her smile was open and she showed no signs of nervousness. He was careful how he worded the next question.

'Would you know if she had come in just to – to speak to Mr Beluch?'

The girl considered the question for several seconds, and, with his new-found knowledge of the establishment, Hugh wondered whether the pause was because she was unsure of the exact meaning of his question, because she was framing her answer in a foreign language, or because she had received instructions about how to cope with such a situation, in relation to 'Mrs Davidson' or any other client. But when she spoke her answer was perfectly reasonable, and again there was no suggestion that she was lying.

'Except for my lunch I've been here all day, and no one has

requested Mr Beluch. Would you like to speak to Katya? She was on duty from 1300 to 1400 hours.'

'No, thanks.'

Hugh's hesitation had been momentary. He had realized almost at once that, if Jay had been able to do so, she would have returned to the hotel by one o'clock, or at least sent a message. He thanked the receptionist and, as a taxi was depositing an obvious customer in front of the salon, hurried out to catch it. He couldn't remember the Sochas' address, so he asked to be taken to the University.

From there he walked and, by chance, eventually recognized a building as the Sochas' apartment block. He found their name on a list inside the door, and pressed the bell inside it. But there was no answer, and after the third try he gave up his attempts.

Once more he walked the streets, hoping to pick up a passing taxi or to find a rank. He was hot and tired, and all he could do was return to the hotel, hoping against hope that Jay was there, anxiously waiting for him. But the taxis that passed were already occupied and, though the people whom he stopped were friendly, he failed to understand the directions they gave him. At last a young man, who looked like a student, took him by the arm and actually led him to a taxi rank, where he joined a queue.

It was almost seven when he reached the Orbis-Solec. Madame Bereski was hovering in the hall. She buttonholed Hugh at once, almost trembling with relief that one of her charges was safe. But Mrs Davidson had not returned, and nothing had been heard of her.

'Where could she have gone, Mr Davidson? She's supposed to be unwell, but she has been out all day, and there has been no message, nothing to let us – you or me, and I am responsible for her – know what has happened. Why has she done this, Mr Davidson?'

Madame Bereski regarded Hugh accusingly. He guessed what she had been thinking – that it was his fault, that he and his wife had had a row, and that Jay was absenting herself from the hotel in order to punish him. But perhaps by now the courier was beginning to have second thoughts.

'Mr Davidson,' she said earnestly, 'if your wife does not

return soon the police will have to be informed. The hotel will demand it, and I too. I cannot lose one of my group. It would be worth my – my job. You understand,' she repeated, 'I am *responsible* for Mrs Davidson.'

'I understand,' Hugh said, and thought that he'd hit the woman if she mentioned her 'responsibility' once more. But he had to prevent her from involving the police. The last thing he wanted was for 'William Davidson' to be interrogated about his wife. He could even imagine inquiries being telexed to England. He did his best to smile at the courier. 'Madame Bereski, believe me, I do appreciate your position, but before we consider the police – which would be a drastic step – let's wait a little longer.'

Madame Bereski agreed reluctantly. 'Very well. But if she's not returned by the time we have eaten dinner, I must insist.'

'Of course,' Hugh said. 'Now I should like to go to my room. Perhaps you would get me a key.'

Once inside his bedroom, Hugh stripped off his clothes, showered and changed. Afterwards he felt physically better. Mentally, however, he was becoming desperate and he knew he could no longer put off the moment when he must appeal to Dick Fenwick for help. But this seemed an admission that Fenwick's warnings had at last been justified. When finally he did lift the phone it was only to be told that Fenwick was not in the embassy. He thought fleetingly of Derek Hill, the attaché, but decided not to tackle him. He refused to leave a message.

Hugh had no intention of remaining at the Orbis-Solec to be questioned by the police. He went down to the café, where he forced himself to drink a bowl of soup, eat some sandwiches and have coffee. Then he handed in his room key and walked out of the hotel. No one attempted to stop him.

Viktor Georgiyevich Krasnakov was in Beluch's flat on the top floor of the beauty salon. He was alone, and while he waited for Beluch he helped himself to an early pre-dinner drink, sprawled on the leather sofa and considered the day. On the whole it had been extremely satisfactory.

The news from Washington and London was excellent. All

was proceeding according to plan. Not his plan, Krasnakov thought wryly, but his masters', though in practice it made no difference, however distasteful some aspects of it might be to him personally. He hoped there would be compensation later. Meanwhile he wondered if he would be justified in making a quick trip to England once he had finished with Ryan and Bigrel.

Ryan had proved more amenable to interrogation than he had expected. There had been no need for pressure of any kind; the situation in which she found herself had apparently been enough to open her mouth. She had made one demand – for her clothes – which he had ignored. Then she had answered his questions disdainfully, as if they were of no significance, but from her replies it was clear to Krasnakov that the girl had no idea of Thaxted's mission, and no idea why it had been necessary to kill him. Even better, as far as he could judge from her answers, Thaxted had failed to confide in any of his CIA colleagues. Krasnakov could scarcely have hoped for more reassuring information.

And Ryan had got her reward. Krasnakov smiled as he remembered. She had struggled to keep the duvet over her, but he had pulled it away and begun to knead her breasts. When her unwilling body responded, he had laughed at her scarlet cheeks, set mouth and the tears that escaped from her tightly-shut eyes.

He had covered her again, and murmured insultingly, 'Later, perhaps.' But he had also mentioned food and pointed to the bathroom through the pink velvet door. It was the oldest trick in the book, he thought – alternating kindness and threats – but it was surprising how well it worked, even sometimes on professionals.

Krasnakov looked up as the door opened. Beluch came into the room with a frown on his face.

'Something wrong?' said Krasnakov.

Beluch shaped his mouth into a *moue*. 'Probably not of any importance, but – First, Bigrel. I had a girl watching him, but she lost him for a while in the Old Town after he'd visited the Dzolaks' shop, as we'd expected. Then he turned up here.'

'Here?'

'Yes, here. The receptionist on duty was new. To her he was merely an Englishman inquiring after his wife. He went away, apparently quite happy. He didn't ask for me, or make any kind of fuss. He's back at the Solec now.'

'Well, if that's all – '

'It's not all, Viktor Georgiyevich.' Beluch helped himself to a drink. 'This morning a man asked at the hotel for Mr William Davidson – Bigrel, that is, as we know – but Davidson had already gone out with his group. However, the man, who gave his name as Fenwick, returned later, and he and Davidson spent a long time drinking and talking together in the bar.'

'Damn Fenwick!' Now Krasnakov was perturbed.

'This was *before* Bigrel knew that Ryan wasn't at the hotel. He could have had no notion that she'd disappeared.'

'But Fenwick knew Bigrel was there, and that he was posing as Davidson.' Krasnakov was silent, considering. Then he seemed to make up his mind. 'We'll have to forget Bigrel. In the circumstances, with Fenwick keeping an eye on him, it would be too risky to arrange an accident for him. And it wouldn't be worth it. Bigrel and Ryan know less than I feared.'

'What about the Ryan girl? Surely we can't let her go?'

'No. Not now. She must be taken off the board. It's a pity, it's untidy, but it's inevitable if – '

Krasnakov broke off as there was a heavy knock on the door. Before either man could speak a woman came in, blood trickling down her face. Both men knew her as the member of Beluch's staff who had been deputed to watch over Ryan.

'Comrade Beluch! Comrade Beluch!' she exclaimed in Polish. 'I'm sorry – sorry, but I was carrying a tray of food into the American's room when she attacked me from behind the door. She hit me on the head with a – a chair leg, of all things. And – and she got away.'

226

TWENTY-FIVE

'Go away! Go away! And don't come back. We don't know you. We don't want to know you.'

Immediately he opened his front door and saw Hugh Bigrel waiting outside, Marek Socha had attempted to slam it in Hugh's face. But Hugh had anticipated the gesture, and had quickly thrust his foot into the opening. As he spoke, Socha looked desperately from right to left inside the apartment, seeking some implement with which to attack Hugh's leg and force him to move. His intention was obvious, and again Hugh forestalled him. He gave a heave with his shoulder, and burst past Socha.

Urszula came running into the hall. '*Nie! Nie! Proszę! Proszę!*' she exclaimed as soon as she saw Hugh. 'Go, please,' she appealed.

Socha shut the front door. 'If you do not go, I will call the Militia,' he said aggressively.

'Don't be a bloody fool. The last thing you want is the police. You're shit-scared of them.' Hugh had no time for niceties. 'Is Jay here?'

He watched Urszula, guessing that of the pair of them she would find it more difficult to dissemble, but she merely showed surprise at his question. His spirits sank. This was another false hope, he thought, and surely the last.

'No, she's certainly not here.' It was Socha who answered. 'We've not seen her since she came to supper with you, and we don't want to see her again. You come from your country, and you ask questions and you make trouble. Why do you do this to us?' He was still nervous, but his fears had subsided somewhat, and with them his aggressiveness.

'I'm sorry,' Hugh said honestly, 'but Jay – '

'Don't tell us. If we don't know we can't tell.'

Hugh nodded. It was almost impossible to deal rationally with people in this situation, he realized. But he had to ask. 'Have you any idea – any idea whatever of where Jay might have gone?'

'*Nie!*' They shook their heads in unison, though strangely they showed no emotion at the thought of Jay's disappearance.

Nevertheless, Hugh believed them; there was really no reason why they should know anything. He turned towards the front door, but Marek was ahead of him, peering cautiously both ways, presumably to make sure there was no one to see the foreigner leaving. Then he literally pushed Hugh out of the apartment. In other circumstances Hugh might have laughed, but he was in no mood for laughter tonight.

Leaving the building, Hugh walked aimlessly. He could think of nothing to do, except return to the hotel, where the police would probably be waiting to question him, or go to the British Embassy, raise all kinds of hell and demand that Dick Fenwick be sent for. Neither prospect was attractive. The first was not really feasible, not with Bill Davidson's passport. Asked enough questions – and he was sure the police would ask a great many – sooner or later he would be forced into a doubtful or ambiguous answer – and then? Messages to and from London, perhaps. In any case, whatever happened to him it would certainly be of no help to Jay.

So, in fact, there was no choice. It had to be the embassy and, false identity or not, if Fenwick wasn't prepared to help or had suddenly left Warsaw or was just unavailable, he'd make sure that someone in authority listened to him. And if they took the line that Jay was a United States citizen, and thus not their responsibility, a hint of his knowledge of the scandal concerning the late Sir Rupert Canville should bring action. But it was not a part he looked forward to playing with any pleasure.

Finding himself beside another Orbis hotel, Hugh turned in at the main doors. He felt as if he had spent most of the day walking fruitlessly from one part of the city to another, and he needed a rest. In the bar he ordered a double whisky. The place was full, and he heard a variety of languages, including English – which made him suddenly homesick. In spite of this, he drank slowly, enjoying the whisky and the chance to sit down for a few moments. But soon his thoughts overtook him and he found himself contemplating the future that would face him if he never saw Jay again. He knew it would be incredibly blank.

Outside the hotel he was in time to see one taxi drive away, and have another snatched from under his nose by a party of four who pushed carelessly past him. Grimly he set off again on foot.

He had almost passed Beluch's salon before he realized where he was. A shutter had been drawn over the display window, and the only light on the ground floor was that illuminating the sign above the main door. But, glancing up, he saw a faint glow around the windows of the upper floors. Someone was at home. Beluch?

Hugh had never met or even seen Beluch, but Jay's description of the man had been less than encouraging. What was more, his name had been on Sam Thaxted's list, together with Krasneski – Krasnakov of the KGB – and the frightened and mysterious Dzolaks. From Jay's report, it looked as if Beluch would have more in common with Krasnakov than with the Dzolaks, and Father Ryan had made it clear that his establishment was not all it pretended to be.

Beluch's salon was on a corner, and on impulse, instead of continuing along Novy Świat, Hugh decided to investigate. He turned down the street beside the building, and noted the side door. A few more yards and the building became a wall. Soon Hugh came upon a narrow lane which ran parallel with Novy Świat and thus along the rear of the Beluch premises. Here he found another door, and next to it some gates which led almost immediately to a double garage, which looked firmly closed. So were the gates and the door, when he tentatively tried them. Except for a solitary cat inspecting a garbage can no one was about, and Hugh asked himself what he thought he was doing there.

He was on the point of retracing his steps when the door beside the gates opened and a man emerged, quickly but cautiously. The lane was ill-lit, with great patches of shadow, and luckily Hugh was standing in semi-darkness. He drew back as the man approached, and watched him as he passed under a light.

The man was of medium height, squarely-built, and with a heavy stomach only partly disguised by an expensive suit. His grey hair was receding, and Hugh put his age in the middle fifties. But it was his expression that attracted Hugh's attention. He had a wide, cat-after-lapping-a-bowl-of-cream smile, and Hugh was instantly reminded of Father Ryan's comments on the other functions of the beauty salon.

Hugh acted without thought. Three strides, and he was at the man's side. 'Comrade!' he said.

'*Ach, mein Gott!*' The man swung round in horror. '*Was ist?*'

Hugh felt a surge of relief. If they had had no common tongue he would have been able to achieve little or nothing, but the man had instinctively spoken in German, and that was a language in which Hugh was fluent.

'You've enjoyed your evening, *mein Herr?*' he said in German. 'She was good?'

For all he knew the man might have been talking business with Beluch over a quiet drink, but neither his behaviour nor his satisfied smile suggested that as the sole reason for his presence here. And, close to, Hugh could almost smell the sex on him.

'What – what is it you want?' the man asked.

'Just a little chat with you.'

'What about? If it's money, I've scarcely any on me, and I'm in a hurry.'

'I don't want money. But wouldn't you rather I talked to you, than to your wife – or your embassy?'

The last question was more than a guess. They had begun to walk to the end of the lane, and the German, who seemed dazed by the disaster that had apparently overtaken him, had stopped beside a Mercedes with CD plates. Hugh held out his hand for the key, and gestured to the man to go around to the passenger seat.

'Tell me about the set-up at Beluch,' Hugh said, sliding in beside the German.

'What set-up? What do you mean?'

'Don't be a fool, man. You know what I mean.'

'No! I don't! What is all this fuss?' The German blustered for a few more sentences. Then he shrugged. His courage was beginning to return. 'All right, all right. I go to this *Bordel*, very expensive, very discreet. What is it to you? Who are you, anyway? Militia? Vice squad?'

Hugh shook his head. 'I've been told that the salon is also used as a place of rendezvous – for lovers, let us say.'

The German's relief was enormous. 'It's too good to be true. You're a jealous husband!' he exclaimed, and gave a great belly laugh.

Hugh continued to regard him coldly. 'Perhaps,' he admitted. 'But that would make no difference if I were to approach your wife or your embassy, would it?'

The derisive grin, the aftermath of the laugh, faded. The German swallowed hard. '*Nein, mein Herr! Nein.*' His confidence had evaporated again. 'But I have the same girl always. She is a Pole. You are not *her* husband, I'm sure.'

Hugh was growing impatient. He wasn't sure whether the German had misunderstood him or was purposely misleading him. On the other hand, he knew that he mustn't prompt the man, in case he took the obvious route and concocted some story that he thought Hugh might expect to hear.

'When you are in there do you ever see other people? Other customers, for instance?'

'*Nein.* Never. It is, as I say, a very discreet establishment.'

There had been the slightest hesitation before the German's words, and Hugh sensed that he was lying. 'You'll be sent home in disgrace, *mein Herr*, and there could be further accusations. Association with a Pole in a *Bordel*, the owner of which is said to be – what shall we say? – very sympathetic to the Soviet cause.'

Again, on Hugh's part, this was more or less a shot in the dark. The German, he supposed, could well have been a diplomat from the Democratic Republic – East Germany. But the man tensed. He began to stutter a denial of betrayal of anything or anyone other than his wife, but thought better of it. In the confines of the car, his heavy breathing sounded loud. Then, as if resigned, he shrugged. He became business-like.

231

'It's the English lady who was there tonight that interests you? Yes?'

For a moment Hugh was stunned at this sudden confirmation of his unexpressed suspicions. Then he pulled himself together, and merely murmured, 'Probably.'

'Slim, long legs, small-breasted, her pubic hair much darker than the curly hair on her head?'

Hugh nodded. He couldn't bring himself to speak. The description fitted Jay, a naked Jay, her hair lightened and permed to resemble Pam Davidson's.

'How? How – ' he began, but the German continued without prompting. 'I was in the room waiting for my girl when there was a bang outside the door, so I opened it an inch or two, enough to see what was going on. And this lady – your wife – was lying in the corridor. She had no clothes on, but she was clutching a duvet. I think she must have tripped over the end of it.'

'What made you think she was English?'

'Because she said, "Help!" in English, twice over. I heard her distinctly.'

'And you did – nothing?'

'What was I to do?' The German was indignant. 'Her man was bounding after her. He rolled her up in the duvet and carried her back. It was only a game. Englishwomen may seem cold and haughty, but they like sex as much as anyone else.'

Only a game, Hugh thought bitterly. Clearly Jay had been trying to escape, and they had caught her. God knew what was happening to her now. Somehow he had to get her out of that place.

'Tell me about the inside of the building,' he said, forcing himself to speak calmly.

The German did his best, but it was obvious that his knowledge was restricted, and his description of the lift, corridors and rooms he had seen was confusing. He was no more use. Hugh got out of the car, tossing the keys on to the floor, so that the man had to scramble for them. This gave Hugh time to memorize the number plate before the Mercedes shot away. He disliked the German, and mistrusted him; he suspected that he

232

frequented the beauty salon for more than pleasure, and that the West German authorities would be extremely interested in his activities. But all that, he thought, could wait. Right now, Jay was the first priority.

The problem, of course, was what the hell to do about her. He would have liked to contact Fenwick, or someone from the British Embassy, but the German had drawn a chilling picture of Jay's plight, and he could waste no more time.

Direct action was the only answer. There was a bell at the side door of the salon, and Hugh leant on it. When nothing happened, he hammered with his fists. Then he tried the bell again. Eventually the door was opened on a chain, and a man peered out. Hugh seized him by his tie and pulled his head through the gap. The man gagged, but he was trapped and unable to struggle.

'Beluch?' Hugh demanded.

The man produced a flood of Polish, and Hugh cursed his inability to communicate. He reiterated his demand for Beluch. The man seemed to repeat what he had said before, and Hugh guessed that he was denying he was Beluch. The impasse was resolved when a shadow moved behind him, and a different voice spoke.

'Who are you? What do you want?' The questions were asked in Polish, Russian, German, and finally in accented English.

'Are you Beluch?'

'I am Jan Beluch, yes. Let my man go!'

Hugh hesitated before abandoning his only bargaining point, but the problem was solved as Beluch squeezed his man's throat a little tighter in order to release the chain, and opened the door. The man quickly withdrew his head, giving Hugh a vicious glance, and Hugh was left face to face with Beluch.

The latter's initial remark was unexpected.

'Come in, Mr – er – Davidson, isn't it?'

'No, thanks. I'm staying here and you're going to bring out my wife in the next three minutes, or – '

'Your wife is dead, Mr Bigrel.'

For one ghastly moment Hugh thought he was referring to Jay, and he acted without thought, and made a tactical error.

He lunged at Beluch, who was small and slight in comparison, pulled him out of the house, pushed his back to the wall, and banged his head against it. As Beluch screamed, Hugh realized that the Pole had called him Bigrel, not Davidson, and had spoken of Lorna.

But this made no difference. Hugh still pinned Beluch to the wall, and struck him across the face to silence him. Beluch's screams ended in a whimper. Hugh shook him.

'You know perfectly well what I mean! Tell your man to fetch Mrs Ryan. Now! Whatever state she's in. Wrap her in a blanket if necessary. Now, Beluch!'

Hugh could feel hands on his shoulders, trying to pry him off his victim. He stamped backwards, and felt his foot contact a shin-bone. The exclamation this produced gave him positive pleasure; in whatever language, it was clearly a violent curse.

Beluch spoke rapidly in Polish. It sounded like an order. The hands gripping Hugh from behind released their grasp. Beluch seemed to slump, so that Hugh found himself supporting his opponent. At the same time he became conscious of voices, shouts from the main street, a whistle.

'I've told them. She's coming,' Beluch said softly.

There was a pause, then the sound of running feet. Too late Hugh saw Beluch's mouth curve into a spiteful smile. He realized he had been tricked; the orders he had given had not been concerned with Jay. The side street seemed suddenly full of cars and people. Hugh turned his head, but only in time to see the Militia man's heavy truncheon descending towards him. He tried to duck, but it was useless. He felt the blow on his temple, a splitting pain and the hardness of the ground as he collapsed.

He knew nothing of what happened next. He didn't feel Beluch push him out of the way with a contemptuous foot, or the Militia men pick him up and throw him like a sack of flour into the back of a barred van. He knew nothing of Beluch's statement – a statement listened to in respectful silence – about the ridiculous Englishman who, out of his drunken belief that his wife was in the salon, had made a series of unprovoked attacks, first on one of the staff, then on Beluch himself.

All this time Hugh was lost in a nightmare. Jay was crying out to him to save her as she sank deeper and deeper into a bog, and he couldn't move a step to help her.

TWENTY-SIX

Jan Beluch studied his face in the mirror. It was swollen and bruised from the blows Bigrel had landed. His spine, which had been forced against the wall, hurt, and there was a painful lump on the back of his head. 'I'll kill him,' he was muttering through clenched teeth. 'I'll kill him.'

Krasnakov watched Beluch with some irritation. The Pole, he thought, was over-emotional, like all his countrymen. He had not handled the situation with any finesse, but Bigrel had done him no real harm.

'Forget about yourself for one moment, Comrade,' Krasnakov said icily. 'Consider what we must do now. Ryan is here. When Bigrel gets in touch with his embassy, which he will do sooner or later, he'll demand that this place be searched. Fenwick will take him seriously, but the Militia probably won't – or they'll limit themselves to a token search – and I can't see the British Ambassador wanting to make a major incident out of the ravings of one of his nationals, who's entered Poland on a false passport. But you never know. Personally I don't intend to be found here if there is such a search, and I don't intend that Ryan should be found here either. Apart from that, for your own sake you must make sure that to any unwanted visitor Beluch's beauty salon looks like a beauty salon, and nothing else. Now, what suggestions have you?'

Beluch turned from the mirror to look at Krasnakov. 'There is still plenty of the night left, Comrade Colonel,' he said, matching the Russian's new formality by for once giving Krasnakov his rank. 'If you wish, Ryan could be given an injection, and driven out to the Kampinos forest. There are peat bogs there, and a body can lie hidden for a century.'

'No,' said Krasnakov firmly. 'I don't want her killed, not just yet – for a variety of reasons.'

Beluch asked no questions, but merely said, 'Then may I suggest the safe house at Plock? It's about a hundred and twenty kilometres from here, so it's quite convenient.'

'Ah, the religious establishment,' Krasnakov smiled broadly, his temper restored as he thought of the impropriety of such a site for what he had in mind for Jay Ryan. 'Yes, that will be fine. Galinov will take her there tonight. I'll join them later.'

'But you said you wouldn't be staying here.'

'No. I'll phone my embassy and go there. I shall hold you responsible for Ryan's arrival at Plock, so don't make any mistakes. You'd better send a woman with her, as well as Galinov. I'll brief him before I leave.'

'Right, Comrade Colonel.' Beluch accepted Krasnakov's instructions. 'But suppose – suppose Bigrel comes back alone – '

'If he does return send for the Militia again, and play the innocent. But I doubt if he'll cause any more trouble here. His embassy will probably ship him out as soon as possible. Then,' Krasnakov continued thoughtfully, 'if necessary and if he looks like becoming a long-term nuisance, we'll arrange an accident for him – maybe a convenient suicide because he can't bear the loss of Ryan – but anything like that will have to wait till he gets back to Britain.'

Abruptly Krasnakov ceased speaking. He was talking too much. What happened to Bigrel once he left Warsaw was none of Beluch's business.

'Come on,' he said, 'let's get going.'

As Hugh Bigrel regained consciousness his senses became aware of two unpleasant reactions – the smell of vomit, and the pain in his head. He slitted his eyes; the light from the bright bulb behind flush glass in the ceiling was too bright to allow him to open them wide. But almost at once he realized he was lying on the floor of a prison cell, and the vomit was his own.

With great care he raised himself on his elbow and surveyed

237

his surroundings. The cell was small, about ten feet by six, and contained a bed with a thin mattress and a threadbare blanket. The only other furnishing was a bucket in one corner. There was a small, barred window high up in one wall, and a door with a closed grill in another.

His watch had been removed, and he had no means of knowing the time. The faint glow of light beyond the window bars could be either the early-morning sun, or a street lamp. Tentatively he put up a hand and touched his temple. The next instant, drawing a deep breath, he regretted his action. There was a large swelling, and even a feather-like touch had caused him intense pain.

Hugh guessed that he had been unconscious for some hours, which meant that it was probably the middle of the night. He shivered. The cell was cold, with the kind of damp chill that seems to penetrate the bones; he suspected that even at noon the sun never warmed the place. Reaching for the pathetic blanket, he managed to pull it around him. It was a slight protection, but better than nothing. As yet, he couldn't face making the effort necessary to climb off the cement floor on to the bed.

Then he thought of Jay, and immediately his mental distress outweighed his physical pain, and he began to think rationally. In all likelihood his attack – if you could call it an attack – at Beluch's had done her more harm than good. And now he was useless, incarcerated. He bitterly regretted not having contacted Fenwick before he went to the salon, and clearly Fenwick was his only hope now, if Jay was to be saved. The hope was faint, but at least it was a hope, and any action would be better than lying in his vomit and feeling sorry for himself.

He forced himself to go through his pockets. Wallet, passport, ballpoint pen, comb – everything had been removed. His belt had gone also, but he wore slip-on shoes, so there had been no need for them to take away the laces, he thought wryly. But they had left him his handkerchief, and he was grateful for that. He was able to wipe around his mouth, and make some effort to clean himself. He tried to stand, but his head swam and he nearly blacked out, so he gave himself a full minute's rest to allow a modicum of strength to return to his battered body. Then he shuffled on hands and knees to the door.

He knelt up before it, and hammered with his fist. The thick wooden door gave back a series of dull thuds. He continued to bang. As one fist got sore, he changed to the other, and he started to shout.

When he grew tired he rested, but recommenced again as soon as he could. And at last the panel behind the grill above his head slid sideways, more light streamed into the cell, and a broad, angry face appeared at the opening.

The guard growled something. It was obviously an order, and though Hugh didn't understand what it was, it was simple enough to guess its gist. But he paid no attention, and continued to thump on the door, and shout, 'British Embassy! British Embassy!'

Eventually the guard began to nod. 'Okay! Brit-ish Em-bas-sy!' he repeated, and slid shut the panel.

Hugh desisted. There was nothing more he could do for the moment. He could only hope that the guard would take some action and approach his superiors, and that someone from the British Embassy would arrive. If not, he would repeat the performance. In the meantime, his worn blanket round his shoulders, he crawled towards the bed and slowly dragged himself up on to it. It was almost as hard and cold as the floor.

He lay there, shivering slightly, clutching the meagre covering around him. He tried to keep his mind off Jay. Instead, he found himself thinking of Lorna and young David. His head was aching again, but slowly he began to drift in and out of dreams, until finally, in spite of his situation, he was fast asleep.

On reflection, Madame Bereski had not called the Militia the previous evening, and she had persuaded the manager of the Orbis-Solec, who thought highly of her as a tour guide and a customer, to take no action either. But by the next morning they had no choice. Mrs Davidson had been missing, or at least had not been seen in the hotel, for twenty-four hours; it could be longer if her husband had not been telling the truth. Now he, too, had apparently disappeared.

The manager telephoned the Warsaw Militia Headquarters, where no one was yet aware that a drunk called Davidson had spent the night in one of the city's cells. In her turn, Madame Bereski phoned the British Embassy. She outlined the problem to the duty officer; she could not remember Fenwick's name, but she tried to describe him and leave a message for him. Both the Militia and the embassy promised to send officers to the hotel as soon as possible.

The police won. They arrived first, and proceeded to search the room that Hugh and Jay had occupied. Their methods were so damaging that the manager dared to protest. But they found nothing incriminating, and were obviously wondering what action to take next when a young Third Secretary arrived on the scene. He was no help, but he was prepared to listen to Madame Bereski, who had at last recalled Fenwick's name.

Thankful to be rid of the responsibility, the Third Secretary got in touch with Fenwick as soon as he returned to the embassy. By then the Militia had located a man believed to be William Davidson at one of their sub-stations. There was no information concerning his wife, Pamela Davidson. She was not in custody, nor had she been admitted to any hospital.

Fenwick, conscious of the importance of apparent status, borrowed the Ambassador's Rolls-Royce, and instructed His Excellency's chauffeur to drive as fast as possible to the police station, where he found that Bigrel was banging on his cell door again, and continuing to demand the British Embassy. Fenwick threw his weight around and told innumerable lies. He was successful, partly because Davidson's presence was becoming somewhat of an administrative embarrassment to the Militia, and fifteen minutes later he was being driven back to the embassy, with Hugh beside him. The glass partition between the chauffeur and his passengers was shut, so they were able to talk.

'You stink. You need a bath,' were Fenwick's first remarks.

It was not the most auspicious opening to what should have been a friendly interrogation. Fenwick did not mean to be brutal, but was too relieved to have Bigrel safely in his charge to care what he said to him.

'To hell with that!' Hugh responded. He was thankful to be free of the clutches of the police, but felt no personal gratitude to Fenwick. Besides, his head still ached badly and the motion of the car had begun to make him feel sick. 'They've got Jay,' he said. 'That shit Beluch – '

Fenwick let him give his account of events. He listened with far greater attention than his careless lounging in the comfort of the Rolls might suggest, but he asked no questions. Questions could wait, he had decided, studying Hugh Bigrel through half-closed eyes; the man had had a bad time, and was obviously worried sick about Jay Ryan.

'Now, what the hell are you going to do, Fenwick?' Hugh demanded as he came to the end of his story. 'You've said yourself these people don't give a damn. God knows what's happening to Jay.'

'Well, first, we're taking you to the embassy, where I'm staying at present. You can have a bath and breakfast. I'll get your clothes and things fetched from the hotel. Then we'll have a talk.'

'For heaven's sake, forget me! What about Jay? She's at the beauty salon, I tell you!'

'She was,' Fenwick interrupted quietly. 'The one thing you can count on is that she's not there now. Beluch may have the police under his thumb, but your attack on him was pretty public. Even though you're supposed to have been tight, they'll know that the embassy's involved. They'll probably make a show of searching the salon if we request it, so I don't believe Beluch would dare risk keeping her there.'

'You're – you're assuming they won't let her go, after she's told them – told them whatever they want to know?' Hugh spoke diffidently.

'Don't be a bloody fool! You know the answer to that as well as I do.' Fenwick was scathing. 'I told you before that we're not playing some friendly gentlemanly game. It's war of a kind, and if the innocent get hurt, that's too bad. At least we may prevent a holocaust.' He controlled his temper, which was threatening to explode. 'Bigrel, no one asked you or Ryan to stick your fingers in. You insisted, and you were lucky for a while. But now your luck's run out, and you'd better face the fact.'

'Okay. I was a bloody fool. I accept that,' said Hugh bitterly. 'I ought not to have gone to Beluch's place. But what do you expect me to do now? It's Jay's luck that's run out, not mine.'

'Do what I tell you. Clean yourself up, eat and then we'll talk properly.' Hugh glanced up at this somewhat ominous remark, but Fenwick continued. 'Meanwhile I'll tell Madame Bereski that you're safe, but you're leaving her tour. It'll be a bureaucratic nightmare, but I'll manage. Then I'll make some inquiries of my own. Believe me, that's the best either of us can do for Jay Ryan for the moment – if she's still alive.'

And, before Hugh could think of a suitable retort to that, the car had stopped, and Fenwick was urging him out and into a side entrance to the embassy.

Hugh paced up and down, six steps in one direction and six steps back, which was all that was possible. The bedroom was not a great deal larger than his cell, but it was considerably more comfortable, with an adjoining bathroom, well-equipped for an unexpected guest.

He had showered and shaved. His dirty clothes had been removed by an anonymous manservant and, wearing a robe provided by Fenwick, he had eaten the breakfast that the same man had brought him on a tray. Coffee, and some aspirin he found in the bathroom cabinet, had eased his head. And sooner than he expected his bag had arrived from the Solec Hotel, and he had been able to change into clean clothes of his own.

Once dressed, he had filled his pockets with the various possessions which Fenwick had seemingly retrieved from the Militia in a plastic bag. He had checked his wallet and knew that his money was intact, and that he still had the photographs of Sir Rupert Canville and Sam Thaxted. The prints had no names on them, and he hoped that they had not aroused any interest on the part of the Poles. Finally he had slipped on his watch. This simple gesture made him feel more human.

There was no clock in his room, and he had lost his sense of time. He had been surprised to see how late it was, and had wondered what on earth had happened to Fenwick. Impatient, he had gone to the door, and found it locked. He realized that, in a sense, he had exchanged one prison for another, and it was then he had begun his pacing.

By the time Fenwick returned in mid-morning Hugh was furious. He had thought of banging on the door, but decided that here it would be a waste of effort. Some servant would probably appear but, short of assault within the confines of the British Embassy, such a confrontation could achieve nothing. He swore at Fenwick, who brushed aside his complaints.

'What do you expect? Do you think I'm going to let you go again, to create more hell around Warsaw?' he demanded.

Hugh gritted his teeth and remained silent. Fenwick flung himself into one of the two chairs in the room, and motioned Hugh to take the other.

'First, my news, such as it is,' he said. 'Viktor Krasnakov arrived at the Soviet Embassy late yesterday evening. He was alone, though usually he's accompanied by his sidekick, Igor Galinov. He may have been in Warsaw earlier, perhaps staying with Beluch, because a man who answers Galinov's description was seen driving a taxi in the direction of the Orbis-Solec in the morning.'

'And you think – '

'That's how they caught Mrs Ryan? Possibly.' Fenwick nodded.

'It doesn't help much, does it?' Hugh said despondently.

'You can't expect miracles. With any luck, I should know more later in the day.'

'How?'

'Oh, the usual means. Informers. Some Poles hate the Russians. Some will take a bribe.' Fenwick grinned suddenly. 'Which reminds me. I had to pay a whacking fine to get you out of your clink this morning.'

'Damn the money!'

'Okay! Okay! I just mentioned it. I'll try to recover it from secret funds – if you'll co-operate with me. Let's go through everything again.'

Hugh heaved a sigh. 'Fire away.'

'Fine. Let's start with this German, and everything you remember about him. He fascinates me.'

'The German?'

'Yes. The naughty, adulterous German. Try to describe him in detail, and tell me exactly what he said, if you can.'

For a moment Hugh could not believe that Fenwick was serious; as far as he himself was concerned the German was of minor importance. But suddenly his memory came to life, and he said, 'How would you like the number of the CD car he was driving?'

'You're joking?' For his part, Fenwick couldn't believe it was going to be so simple.

'No! I memorized it, because I thought I might want to get in touch with him again, though now I can't imagine why I should.'

'You may not, but I most certainly do.' Fenwick was delighted. 'Bless you, Hugh Bigrel. We'll put you in for a gong yet.'

TWENTY-SEVEN

'That's fine!' At last Dick Fenwick seemed satisfied. 'Now the
problem is what to do about you.' He stared at Hugh thoughtfully. 'What I'd most like would be to put you on the next
British Airways flight to the UK – and I could easily arrange it.'

'If you do, you'll regret it,' Hugh threatened. 'Once in
London I'll raise such a stink about Canville, and your attempts
to cover for him, that the story could be the biggest scandal of
the decade – and there have been some pretty big ones, as you
well know.'

Fenwick laughed. 'I rather thought you'd take that line.
Okay. You can stay on here, but only on condition that you do
exactly as I say, and don't go creating any more personal waves.
You agree?'

'I agree.' Hugh sounded reluctant.

'I mean what I say,' said Fenwick sharply. 'And you should
agree, since I'm being damned generous. You know as well as I
do that you've got no intention of betraying Canville and his
secret, because it wouldn't help Jay Ryan, and it would cause a
good deal of harm to dear old Britain.'

'I said I agreed. What more do you want – a boy scout's oath
or something?'

'Now, now! All I want is to minimize the risk I'm taking for
your sake, by making sure you understand your position.'

'I understand all right. But just you remember that, as far as
I'm concerned, Jay comes first.'

'Okay! Let's leave it at that for the moment.' Fenwick sprang
to his feet. 'Now, we'll go and see if we can trace your German
friend.'

This was not a difficult task, thanks to Hugh. Equipped with
the make and licence number of the car, Fenwick only needed a

couple of phone calls to establish that the owner of the car –
though not necessarily its driver yesterday evening – was one
Herr Otto Schinkel, a counsellor at the Embassy of the German
Federal Republic.

'Now what?' Hugh asked.

'We pay a call on this Herr Schinkel. If we hurry, we should
catch him before he goes to lunch. But scribble on this card in
case he doesn't want to see us.'

Hugh took the card and the pen that Fenwick was holding out
to him. 'So what do I scribble?'

'Something like, "We must continue the chat we had last
night in your car," and sign it "J. Schmidt". That should get us
into his august presence. But when we get there, leave the
talking to me, unless by some ghastly mischance the Schinkel
isn't the right chap. In that case, tip me the wink, and we'll
make a graceful exit.'

Hugh nodded miserably. He couldn't conceive how any of
this, especially another meeting with Herr Schinkel – if it was
Herr Schinkel – was going to help Jay, but Fenwick seemed to
be enthusiastic about his plan. And, Hugh reflected, any action
was better than sitting and staring into space. At least it kept his
imagination in check, and prevented him from giving up all
hope.

He scribbled the words Fenwick had suggested, slipped the
card into an envelope that Fenwick produced, and put it into his
wallet beside the temporary pass to the embassy that Fenwick
had also provided. He had, he thought wryly, become a member
of Fenwick's mysterious army.

They had no difficulty at the West German Embassy. They sent
in the card, and immediately Herr Schinkel agreed to see them.
A charming secretary came down to the reception area to escort
them to his office.

'Herr Schmidt and Herr Braun,' she announced.

'I assume these are not your names,' Schinkel said as soon as
the secretary had gone. 'But you know mine. What do you want
of me?'

'Just a few questions, *mein Herr*,' Fenwick replied in excellent German, 'but I suggest that for your sake it would be advisable to switch off your tape recorder before we begin.'

'Blackmail's a crime!' Schinkel was clearly nervous, but he was prepared to be aggressive. Nevertheless, there was a click as the recorder was turned off.

'And adultery is merely a sin, isn't it?' Fenwick smiled, and studied the nails of his left hand for a moment. Then he looked up, and continued in the same tone of amusement, 'Espionage, however, is a very serious crime, often the fruit of blackmail, I believe, and in most countries it carries a long prison sentence, apart from other inconveniences.'

He returned to the study of his nails, but not before he had noted Schinkel's anguished expression. He gave Hugh Bigrel another good mark for guessing that the German had probably been entrapped by Beluch.

'I – I never – ' The man was red in the face. He hesitated. Then: 'Perhaps I might have occasionally let slip in conversation something about trade prospects, say, or the economic situation – that sort of thing, nothing remotely connected with national security. I'm no traitor.'

'It's amazing what can be of use to a potential enemy,' Fenwick remarked casually.

Schinkel glared. Herr Braun was obviously the more important of his unwelcome visitors, and therefore more to be feared than Herr Schmidt, who had so far remained silent. Schinkel addressed himself to Fenwick.

'I ask you again who you are and what you want, *mein Herr*.'

'And I tell you again, just the answers to a few questions, *mein Herr*.' Fenwick settled himself comfortably in his chair and crossed his legs, as if preparing for a lengthy session. The German frowned.

Fenwick said, 'Let's start with this one. How long have you been patronizing Beluch's – er – establishment, shall we call it?'

'Since I was posted to Warsaw – about three years.'

'Good. Now, when did you first meet Viktor Krasnakov, or do you know him as Krasneski?'

'I've never – never met him. I know no one of that name.'

The German couldn't resist running his tongue over his dry lips. 'I – I only meet the girl who – who attends to me, and – '

'Please keep to the truth, Herr Schinkel. You're a poor liar, and your denial is absurd. You must have met Comrade Krasnakov at the odd diplomatic party, if nowhere else.'

Schinkel had recourse to the oldest line in the book. 'Perhaps. I don't remember. I meet so many people.'

'He's not a man who's easy to forget. I insist you've met him at Beluch's, too.'

'No!'

Fenwick uncrossd his legs and stood up, pushing back his chair and turning towards the door. He glanced at Hugh. 'Shall we go and see Herr Schinkel's Ambassador?'

Hugh shrugged. 'Why not?'

The suggestion was enough. 'No. No, please. I will tell you.' Hurriedly Herr Schinkel intervened. 'It is true I am acquainted with a Herr Krasneski as a result of diplomatic receptions, but no more than acquainted. And – '

'And – ' Fenwick prompted.

'I – I've not actually met him at Beluch's salon, but I've seen him there on two or three occasions. Once he was with Beluch, and the other times I caught a mere glimpse of him, with his – his girlfriend. It was all accidental.'

'Of course, just like last night when you were peering out of your bedroom door. You're full of curiosity, aren't you, Herr Schinkel? Didn't it ever occur to you to turn the tables on Beluch, and try to blackmail him in return?'

Schinkel shivered. By this time he had seemingly given up all attempts at pretence. 'I wouldn't dare,' he said at length. 'He'd have me killed.'

'Really? Nice company you keep.' Fenwick ignored Hugh who had drawn a sharp breath at Schinkel's casual reference to Beluch's ability to arrange a killing. 'Tell us again what you saw last night.'

'It wasn't Krasneski,' Schinkel said quickly. 'The man chasing the Englishwoman, I mean. I think he was a servant – a member of the staff of the place. Anyway, it was just as I told Herr –

Herr Schmidt. I was waiting in my room, and I heard a sound, a kind of bump, outside, and – '

Schinkel repeated his story. He neither added to nor subtracted from what he had told Hugh previously, and Hugh failed to understand why Fenwick listened with such care. Fenwick even made the German continue with a description of his later encounter and conversation with Hugh.

'Right,' Fenwick said when Schinkel stopped speaking. 'Now, if I may use your typewriter.'

While Schinkel watched, and without waiting for permission, he crossed to a metal stand on which was an electric typewriter, held out his hand for some paper, and typed on it busily for a couple of minutes. Re-reading what he had written, he nodded his head in satisfaction. Then he handed the paper to the German.

'Sign it and date it,' he ordered bluntly.

Schinkel gobbled like a turkey. He was sweating, and he ran a finger around inside his collar as if he found it hard to breathe. Hugh wondered what they would do if the German had a stroke or a heart attack. But at last words came.

'How – how did you know?' Schinkel managed to gasp.

'I know a lot,' Fenwick said. 'For instance, I know you have a son at university who hopes to enter your diplomatic service. Of course, if his father were charged with espionage – '

'But it's not true,' Schinkel protested. 'You've typed several times, and it was only two or three. I told you. I saw Krasneski once talking to Beluch and the other twice with – '

'Don't quibble about details. Sign it!' Fenwick repeated.

'Oh God! What's to happen to me?' Schinkel was almost weeping, but he picked up a pen and signed the paper. 'If they find out they'll kill me, I tell you.'

'You should have thought of that before,' said Fenwick tritely. He showed no sympathy as he carefully folded the sheet of paper and put it in his wallet. 'Herr Schinkel, we're leaving now, and if we should happen to meet again we don't know each other. You understand?'

'Oh yes. I understand,' Schinkel said miserably. 'And it's the truth. I've no idea who you are – either of you.'

'Keep it like that,' said Fenwick, 'and you might get lucky. If I were you, I'd acquire an illness, or find some other excuse to ask for a posting home.'

Schinkel had pressed the bell on his desk, and when his secretary appeared to lead the visitors from the embassy, he managed to get to his feet and bid them a polite goodbye. He looked ill already.

In spite of Hugh's protests, Fenwick insisted that the next step should be lunch. He said that the German had left a bad taste in his mouth, which only food and drink could remove. Besides, he needed to think.

'About Jay?' asked Hugh acidly. 'What good did your interview with the wretched Schinkel do for her?'

Fenwick made no direct reply. He had driven to the nearest hotel and, as they went into the bar, he said, 'This isn't the world's greatest restaurant, but it's adequate, and I don't suppose that in the circumstances you care much what you eat – '

'Damn you,' said Hugh.

'Many people have expressed the same wish,' said Fenwick mildly, 'including Herr Schinkel, I suspect.'

'You're not going to let him get away with what he's done, are you?'

'His espionage – treachery, if you like? Yes, why not? I doubt if he's done much damage. Anyway, it can't be undone, and I'm sure he's learnt his lesson. He'll be off back to Bonn as soon as he can fix it.'

'But that's not right. He's admitted he's a traitor. You made him sign a confession.'

'No. No. There you're quite wrong.' Fenwick shook his head. 'That wasn't a confession. It was something much more valuable. And it's why I don't want Schinkel questioned. He might spill the beans to others.'

'What in God's name are you talking about?'

Fenwick grinned. 'Mr Davidson, it's not that I don't trust you, but, believe me, there's information you're better without,

250

at least until this affair is over. And that's putting it delicately. So, let's eat.'

The meal was good, in spite of Fenwick's warning, though neither of them appreciated the food – soup with hot pasties stuffed with cabbage, wild duck with apple. They refused dessert, and settled for tea with lemon. They ate and drank in almost total silence.

Hugh was trying to make some difficult practical decisions. As far as he could tell, Fenwick was more concerned with some ploy of his own than with tracing Jay. To him, Jay was apparently an incidental complication. Sure, he'd make inquiries and help her, but only so long as it was convenient, and didn't jeopardize his own plans.

And he himself was useless, Hugh thought bitterly. He could go to the American Embassy, of course, but how on earth could he explain that 'Pamela Davidson' was a US citizen? He could appeal over Fenwick's head to the British Ambassador, but that would lead to more lies and prevarications and impossible explanations. He doubted whether either course would get him anywhere, and his inability to speak or understand Polish was an insurmountable barrier to action.

Finally he decided that if Fenwick's rather dubious sources didn't produce some positive information that evening, he would go back to England tomorrow. There he would have no language problem. He would have the support of his parents. He could make the right contacts in the FCO. He could tell at least some of the truth. For instance, he could admit that he and Jay had used the Davidsons' passports, and probably the results for his cousins would not be too unpleasant. At least, he would have avoided landing himself in a Polish gaol once more.

If it would do any good, he could fly to Washington and consult Jay's Aunt Hilda and Norman Saint. He could even pocket his pride and appeal to Clifford Di Bianco, who would certainly do anything in his power for Jay.

'I'm thinking of returning home tomorrow,' Hugh said abruptly.

It seemed to take Fenwick a moment to adjust to the idea. 'Good for you!' he said absently.

He didn't inquire why Hugh had changed his plans. He had already made up his own mind that if his masters, as seemed probable when they learnt what Herr Schinkel had put his signature to, ordered him to London or Washington, he couldn't leave Bigrel behind in Warsaw. Bigrel was now an important witness, whether he knew it – or approved of the role – or not.

Fenwick was the first to admit that he owed Bigrel for producing Herr Schinkel out of the hat. He owed Jay Ryan too. In some ways they had been a damned nuisance, but between them they had managed to add several elements to the jigsaw, which he sensed was at last near completion. With any luck, he thought, Rupert Canville would soon be able to rest comfortably in his grave, his secret safe forever – except for a very few whose discretion could be relied upon absolutely. And the appalling damage that might have occurred would have been averted.

'Time to return to the embassy,' he said. 'I've a lot of work to do.'

'Sure.' Hugh was resigned. 'What do you expect of me?'

'We-ll, I'll find you some newspapers and magazines, and a couple of books from our library. I know it's not easy, but you'll have to be patient. As soon as I can I'll bring you what information there is – '

'About Jay?' Hugh demanded.

'Yes, about Jay. By drinks time we should know quite a bit more, but I warn you it may not be news you want to hear.'

Hugh nodded. He knew he must accept the fact that Jay might be dead already, but he had to hope until no doubt remained. And, remembering the deaths of Sam Thaxted, of Lorna and David and the unborn Gemma, even of the unattractive Foxy Worth, he swore that if Jay were to be added to their number, one day, somehow or other, he'd kill Viktor Krasneski or Krasnakov – or whatever the KGB Colonel called himself.

At six o'clock that evening there was a knock on his bedroom door. Hugh threw aside the copy of the *International Herald Tribune*, which he had been reading without interest, and went to answer it. Fenwick came in, carrying a bottle of whisky in one hand, and two glasses in the other.

'Not very elegant,' he said, 'but the best we can do if we want privacy. I hope you don't take ice.'

Hugh glared at him. 'News? Is there any news?'

'Some. Nothing startling.' Fenwick took his time pouring them drinks and taking a seat. 'Cheers!' he said, glancing at the headlines of the newspaper scattered on the floor. 'I didn't know you were interested in American politics.'

'I'm not, not really.'

'You should be. It's important to Britain who becomes the next President of the US of A. At the moment the wind looks set fair for Worral J. Smith, that chap you met at the Lansdownes' place in the Cotswolds, with Lady Canville. Remember?'

'Yes,' Hugh said shortly.

'Worral J. would be fine. He's a great Anglophile.'

'For God's sake, Fenwick! There's only one American I care a damn about at the moment, and that's Jay Ryan!' By now Hugh's temper was on a short fuse.

'I know. I know. Well, she's no longer at the beauty salon. Galinov, Krasnakov's sidekick, together with one of Beluch's trusted girls, took her away late yesterday, as I predicted.'

'Where to? Do you know?'

'I'm told to a safe house somewhere in the vicinity of Plock – a town about eighty miles west of Warsaw. It's a very old, picturesque place that's become something of a Mecca for tourists. Unfortunately, my informant knew no more. He had no idea where the safe house was, or anything else about it. What's more, I'm not sure I altogether trust his information. Anyway, it's too vague to be of much help.'

'I see.'

'Incidentally, Jay Ryan's clothes and possessions have been sent over here from the Solec.'

Hugh nodded. So Madame Bereski had been forced to abandon her, too, he thought. 'Anything else?'

'Yes.' Fenwick rose to pour them each a second whisky. 'This came for you.' He reached in his inside pocket, and tossed an envelope into Hugh's lap. 'Actually it's addressed to William Davidson, but I'm sure it's meant for you.'

'It's been opened,' Hugh said as he took out the single sheet of paper.

Fenwick laughed. 'Naturally,' he said. 'We can't have things going on around here that I don't know about.' He watched Hugh read. 'So what do you make of it? Will you accept the invitation to meet the anonymous author of this missive at eleven o'clock tomorrow in the Rynek Starego Miasta?'

'Yes! It must be connected with Jay.'

'It could be a trap.'

'So what? How did it arrive?'

'Apparently it was thrust into the hand of an embassy guard by a small boy in very short shorts.'

'The Dzolak boy?'

'I'd assume so. But it could still be a trap.'

'I shall go all the same,' said Hugh firmly. 'I expect you can arrange for me to fly out later in the day.' He paused. 'Unless – '

'Unless the meeting leads to anything,' concluded Fenwick. 'I wouldn't count on it. And *we* will keep the rendezvous.' He held up his hand. 'Don't thank me, please. I simply wouldn't trust you on your own.'

TWENTY-EIGHT

Against his better judgement, Viktor Krasnakov had sought solace in the arms of Anna Seschki. He needed comfort and distraction – more profound distraction than that offered by one of Beluch's girls – because belatedly he had forced himself to face facts that had lain at the back of his mind for months – facts concerning the true effect that the operation he was so skilfully conducting would have on his own personal life.

The lengthy conversations with London and Moscow on the embassy's secure lines the previous day should have – in fact at first had – induced euphoria. All the elements of the plan were proceeding extremely well, and events were moving faster than he had hoped. His masters in Moscow were delighted, and initially he had shared their delight.

Then, as the realization dawned that the operation was likely to succeed, and succeed in the near future, he knew at last that it was one thing to plan and plot this master stroke against the West with cool detachment, and quite another to accept that it was about to become reality.

Krasnakov loved Mother Russia, but he had never really faced the implications of the sacrifice he was about to make for the sake of his country. He could only suppose that, in addition to the other major and minor deceptions, he had also deceived himself. The truth was that he had never in his heart believed that he – Viktor Georgiyevich Krasnakov – could really, truly, love a woman. Now he knew that he had been wrong – he had misjudged himself.

He remembered only too well Anna Seschki's first reaction when she originally learnt his secret, and when he had telephoned her later yesterday he had hoped that the passage of time had eased her anger and bitterness. It seemed it had, for she had warmly welcomed his call, and at once invited him to her apartment. And when he was there, neither of them had mentioned what was uppermost in their minds.

Now, Krasnakov propped himself up on one elbow, and looked down at the sleeping woman beside him. She was old, he thought, older than she pretended. The bedside lamp, which had been on all night, was cruel to the skin of her neck and breasts, and etched deep the lines in her face. But she was still beautiful, still desirable.

He reached across her, and put out the lamp, which left the room washed grey with early morning light. It was kinder to her, and desire stirred in him again. He would have to go soon. He should have gone to the safe house at Plock the evening before, but he had felt too miserable. He had convinced himself that a few hours – a day even – would not matter, and there was no real hurry to finish with Ryan. Bigrel had disappeared into the maw of the British Embassy, and Beluch seemed to have the situation at the beauty salon well under control.

Krasnakov began to stroke Anna Seschki gently, teasing her to wakefulness. When she responded he mounted her, and let himself slide into her. He murmured endearments, unaware that he spoke a mixture of Russian and English. He made love slowly. In the dim light, and as the urge to possess her grew, he could imagine that this was another time and another place and, most importantly, another woman, *the* other woman.

He was on the verge of his climax when without warning he felt Anna thrust him away from her. He couldn't stop himself. He spilled on to the sheets and, in that moment of weakness, Anna struggled free of him.

She was out of bed, stamping her naked foot on the carpet. She swore in Polish. 'I hate you! I hate you! You lousy Moscovite!' She was beside herself with anger, her face made ugly by her emotion. 'How dare you make love to me, Anna Maria Seschki,' she cried, 'and pretend I'm that whore of yours. Damn you to hell, Viktor Georgiyevich!'

'Anna, please – ' Krasnakov protested.

Instantly he realized what had happened. Lost in his own fantasy, he had called her by the other's name. It was an easy

256

mistake, and with one of Beluch's girls it would have been of no significance. But with Anna it was different; clearly she still believed herself to be in love with him. Poor Anna! Perhaps, Viktor Krasnakov reluctantly admitted to himself, she had reason to be angry.

'Anna, I'm sorry.'

Anna Seschki paid no attention. She felt dirty, humiliated, and she was determined to revenge herself. She wanted to hurt Viktor Georgiyevich, to make him suffer. Her eye lighted on the bottle of champagne they had drunk in bed the night before; it was still standing in its bucket of ice, which was unfrozen. Anna pulled out the bottle, seized the bucket and poured its icy contents over Krasnakov's lower half. It was a trivial gesture, and Krasnakov grinned at her as he cried out with simulated shock.

The grin infuriated Anna. On impulse, she picked up the champagne bottle and hit Krasnakov in the middle of his forehead.

Krasnakov's cry ceased abruptly. He gave a stifled grunt, and was silent. Anna threw the bottle back into the bucket and ran into the bathroom. She washed and dressed hurriedly, not bothering with make-up and paying the minimum of attention to her appearance. She was weeping as she packed a couple of bags. She could hear Krasnakov snoring and was uncertain whether to be thankful or sorry that she had not killed him. Then, with a last glance around, she left the apartment. She would go and stay with her sister in Cracow, and thus remain safely out of the way if the Russian or his henchmen got any ideas of retribution.

Anna was not long gone by the time Krasnakov began to recover. The blow had been sufficient to stun him, but had done no real damage other than to raise a bump and produce a headache. At once he remembered what had happened, and he cursed Anna Seschki and his own stupidity in coming to her for consolation.

He rested for some minutes before getting out of bed. He showered and shaved slowly, cynically wondering how many other men had used the razor he found in Anna's bathroom. As soon as he was dressed, he telephoned the embassy, and demanded that a staff car should meet him at the end of the road. By now it was mid-morning, and he decided to let Galinov know that he wouldn't be leaving for Plock until later in the day when his head would have cleared completely.

This decision, brought about by Anna Seschki's action, was to save Jay Ryan's life.

Hugh sat at a table in the corner of the Rynek Starego Miasta that the note had indicated. The café was fairly full. He drank the coffee he had ordered, and ate the inevitable rich cake. He waited. There was no sign of Fenwick, but he was sure the man was close at hand. Finally, he ordered more coffee.

A party of eight, speaking what he guessed was Czech, took possession of the next table. One of them came over to him and, with a series of friendly gestures, asked if he might borrow a couple of Hugh's chairs. Hugh nodded his agreement and, while the rearrangements were taking place, a young man slid into the seat remaining opposite him.

'You permit?' he said in English.

Hugh was about to protest that he was expecting a friend, but stopped himself in time. At first glance he had assumed that his visitor, who wore a T-shirt, jeans and trainers, and carried a small rucksack, was a student. Then he realized that it was the other priest – what was his name? Marienski, that was it – from St Bernadette's church.

'Coffee?' he asked.

'That would be nice, if you would pay.'

'Of course.'

Hugh caught the waiter's eye, and they sat in silence until the coffee came. The priest pulled his chair around, so that he was close to Hugh, and began to eat a cake. He used the fork in his left hand somewhat awkwardly, and kept his other hand in his lap. At the next table, the Czechs were talking loudly.

'For God's sake, Fath – ' Hugh began impatiently.

'Hush!' It was no more than a whisper, but it was an order and cut Hugh short. 'My name is Josef – Josef Marienski.'

'I'm sorry.' Hugh felt rebuked.

'Listen carefully.' The priest continued to speak softly, his face showing no expression and his lips moving only slightly. Hugh had to strain to hear and understand the accented English. 'Outside Plock, which is a famous town not far from Warsaw, there is a convent. The nuns belong to an enclosed order, which means they do not leave their grounds. They are of various nationalities, but mostly Poles and, as they cause no trouble, the authorities have so far left them alone.'

There was a burst of Czech laughter, and the priest paused. Hugh was frowning.

'Are you telling me that Jay's at this convent – that that's where Beluch's people took her?'

'Not exactly. I am trying to explain. I want you to see the picture. You cannot go bursting in like a – like a cow in a coffee shop.'

'Bull in a china shop,' said Hugh automatically.

The priest paid no attention to the correction. 'In the grounds of the convent, near the gates so that it's a kind of – what you call? a lodge, I think – there is what used to be a guest house, where relatives and friends of the nuns might come to stay. You understand, the order, though enclosed, is not cut off from the world. They read newspapers, and have radios and television, and a telephone – '

'Jay is in this guest house?' Hugh interrupted.

'Yes. A man and a woman brought her there the evening of the day before yesterday. But it is, unfortunately, no longer a simple guest house. It is now what is called a safe house, for the Russians. People come and go. The UB, our own secret police, ask no questions.'

'And neither do the nuns?'

The priest made a gesture of irritation. 'I thought I had explained to you, Mr Bigrel. The nuns are there on sufferance. That is, they are allowed to remain and continue their religious practices, as long as they do not make nuisances of themselves. You could say they are – are cover for the safe house. That would be true. But they have no dealings with it, no official dealings.'

259

'You mean they look the other way?'

'Yes. They look the other way – most of the time. But let God judge them, not you, Mr Bigrel. If it were not for them, for the fact that they are sometimes prepared to take risks, you wouldn't know that your Mrs Ryan was there, and still alive.'

Hugh shook his head. 'Once more I apologize,' he said. He might have added that he was tired, that he had scarcely slept for two nights, and was worried sick, but it seemed pointless. 'I'm sorry,' he repeated.

'It is not easy to understand this country if you do not belong to it,' the priest admitted. He sighed and continued. 'The safe house is not very big, and it is run by an old couple, who are deaf and dumb, so they are trusted. What the Russians do not seem to realize is that neither of them is blind or stupid, and they have their own means of communicating when they wish to do so. Much that goes on in the house is reported to the nuns.'

'They would help Jay, this couple?'

'They are good Catholics, good Poles, but simple. You will need to speak to the Mother Superior, the Reverend Mother Marie-Theresa. You will have to persuade her to help you.'

'But how – '

'Just go. In my rucksack there is a soutane and one of those hats that priests in Poland wear. They will help to disguise you. It's not unusual for a priest to visit the convent, so no one at the lodge will be surprised to see you pass. Just drive straight up to the main door. I will see that they expect you. And that is all I can do.'

'You've done an enormous amount. How can I thank you?'

'By being careful. Think before you act, so that you do not bring harm to the nuns.' Suddenly the priest smiled, so that his expressionless face became quite different. 'One of them is my youngest sister,' he said.

Hugh nodded. 'I'll be careful. I promise.'

'God bless you then. I will pray for you.'

The young man pushed back his chair and gave Hugh a casual wave. He mingled with the party of Czechs from the next table, who were on the point of leaving the café, and was gone. Hugh waited for a couple of minutes. Then, picking up the rucksack, strolled off, impatient for his rendezvous with Fenwick.

'Don't tell me,' said Fenwick. 'I can see from your face the news is good.'

Hugh was smiling. 'At least Jay's alive, and I know where she is. You were right about Plock.'

He told Fenwick all the priest had said, and Fenwick listened in silence. Then came the questions. What was the state of Jay's health? Was she under sedation? Could she walk? Which room did she occupy? Were the couple who brought her to the safe house still there? Was anything known about them? For instance, were they armed? Had Hugh considered where Jay might be taken, if she could be rescued?

Naturally, the answer to all these questions was that Hugh didn't know. Fenwick said sarcastically, 'I suppose you intend to ride in on your charger, fling a doped Jay Ryan across your saddle, and gallop off into the night. Is that the idea?'

'If it's the only chance of getting her out, yes!' Hugh replied resolutely. 'So if you've got anything constructive to add, go ahead. Otherwise, shut up.'

'Right. In that case, we'll have a quick bite to eat, then go back to the embassy. Since there's a fair possibility that you'll get yourself killed trying to rescue Ryan, you must sign some statements for me.'

'What statements?'

'You'll verify our meeting with Herr Schinkel, for one.' Fenwick had become business-like. 'You'll also change your clothes to make yourself look as much like a priest as possible. No brown suede shoes, for example. I'll inspect you when you're ready.'

'Thanks. That'll be a big help.'

Fenwick continued as if he hadn't heard Hugh's comment. 'Go through Jay's things and pick out something easy for her to wear. She may be able to walk. Do you know one end of a gun from another?'

'Yes. I was in the Cadet Corps at school.'

261

'Good. I'll get you a weapon. And also a suitable car, with a local number plate. And I'll find out exactly where these holy ladies live. All that'll take a little while and I have some business of my own to take care of. So leave at 1700 hours, and your ETA at the convent should be around 1900, which is a convenient time.'

'Thanks,' Hugh said, now meaning his words.

His resolve had not wavered, but Fenwick's remarks and instructions had brought home to him the difficulties that lay ahead, and he felt daunted. But Father Marienski had made it clear that it would be useless to appeal to the police, and a personal assault seemed the only available course of action, if Jay were to be saved. Nevertheless, he wished that Fenwick wouldn't treat the whole thing as a kind of military exercise.

'If – ' Hugh began, but altered his sentence. '*When* I get her out, what should we do? Can we come back to the embassy?'

'It will depend on what chaos you leave behind,' said Fenwick. 'You don't have diplomatic immunity, and if it becomes necessary to kill a Russian or a Pole, you'll need to get out of the country as soon as possible. Anyway, I'll give the matter some thought.'

This time Hugh did not thank him. He merely nodded. He found it hard to believe that he, Hugh Bigrel, who so few months ago had been a peaceful Oxford don with a pregnant wife and a small son, was sitting in a bar in Warsaw, contemplating mayhem and murder and God knew what else, in order to save an American girl whom he had come to love as much as, if not more than, he had ever loved Lorna.

TWENTY-NINE

The car sped across the monotonous Mazovian plain towards
Plock, which is situated on a huge bluff overlooking the River
Vistula, about two hours' drive from Warsaw. The car was
black, as befitted the Roman Catholic cleric who sat in the rear.
The chauffeur was also soberly dressed in a dark suit and a
peaked cap.

'Did you see that stork!' Fenwick exclaimed suddenly. 'On
the roof of the cottage we just passed.'

'No,' Hugh Bigrel said shortly.

Storks, he thought, he could do without. The present situation
was sufficiently unreal and fantastic without adding irrelevant
ornithological detail to it. Bigrel was finding it hard to accept
just what was happening. The alien garments he was wearing
didn't help. Nor did Dick Fenwick, whose mood seemed to vary
between the casual and the cautious. At one moment, they might
have been about to pay a simple social call; at another Fenwick
insisted on seemingly needless precautions. By now even Jay
seemed remote, and Hugh couldn't believe that, if all went well,
he might soon be with her again.

'This is a damned lonely place, but we must be getting near,'
Fenwick remarked after a while, as they threaded their way
along a narrow road. 'When we do get there, I'll go past, turn as
if I'd missed the entrance, and come back. With any luck, that'll
give us a chance to take in the general lay-out of the establishment.' He grinned. 'Cheer up, Father. Stage one should be
simple.'

'Yes,' said Bigrel doubtfully. By now it was nearly dark. The
sky was overcast, with scudding clouds, and the moon, which
would be full in another day or two, gave only a fitful light.

Much longer, Hugh thought, and they wouldn't be able to see a damned thing.

But it was only a few minutes later when they drove past a pair of tall iron gates, set well back from the road. Fenwick cursed. No one had mentioned the existence of gates. But he knew from experience that informants often forgot to pass on essential facts that were well-known to them. Just because they knew them so well, they assumed they would be common knowledge.

The problem, however, remained. Getting in might not be so difficult; although they hadn't been able to catch a glimpse of it yet, the guest house was said to be close by the gates – close enough to act as a kind of lodge, according to that priest at St Bernadette's – so presumably someone would hear the car and come to investigate. But getting out, especially if they had to leave in a hurry, might be another matter.

Fenwick turned the car about half a kilometre down the road, drove back to the entrance, stopped in front of the gates and sounded his horn loudly. Now, shining through the gates, the headlamps of the car showed a longer stretch of drive, and a small stone house about fifty metres along it. The main convent buildings were out of sight, and presumably much further away.

A door in the side of the house facing the drive opened, and a figure in slacks and a loose jacket came out and descended some steps. It was Galinov. He carried a heavy torch, but there was no sign that he was armed.

'Obviously not the old Pole.' Fenwick, who hadn't recognized Krasnakov's aide in the semi-darkness, spoke quietly but urgently, half-turning his head. 'So be careful, Bigrel. Remember you're a priest from Leipzig in the GDR, and if you have to speak, speak German.'

'I'll remember,' Hugh replied, and added under his breath, '*Mein Führer*'. He found Fenwick's assumption of command a little hard to take, though he realized it was inevitable, and had been enormously relieved when Fenwick, who had obtained reluctant permission from his master in London to delay his return, announced his intention of accompanying him. The next moment he forgot everything except playing his part. Galinov had unlocked the gates and come through them, but had made no attempt to open them wide. Fenwick, his cap pulled low to hide his face, had got out of the car. He greeted Galinov in Polish. The Russian, who had been warned that the convent was expecting a visiting priest, grunted casually and moved to the window that Hugh had wound down.

Even Galinov had some respect for clergy. Using his torch discreetly, he peered briefly at the dark, upright figure and the pale face beneath the flat, wide-brimmed hat and, duty done, half-turned away. Then the unfortunate happened; by a quirk of fate, something jogged his memory. He swung back.

'Bigrel!'

The Russian did what he could to redress his former carelessness. In one deft movement he transferred the torch to his left hand and felt for the pistol in his right pocket. He fired through the material. But the shot was hurried, and his warning cry had given Hugh time to fling himself to one side. The bullet lodged in the upholstery somewhere above Hugh's head.

Fenwick's reaction was instantaneous. Galinov sensed rather than heard the movement behind him, and started to turn, but he was much too late. Fenwick's arm came around his neck and jerked back his head. There was a loud crack as his neck broke. Fenwick let the body slide to the ground, recognizing Galinov at the same time.

'You all right, Bigrel?'

'Yes. He missed me.' Hugh was thankful that his voice was steady; for the first time in his life he had been on the receiving end of a shot fired in anger.

'Come on, then! Quick! Leave your bag. They'll have heard that shot in the house.'

Fenwick was already swinging the gates open. He drove the car inside and doused its lights. He'd have liked to turn it for a quick getaway, but the need for haste was paramount. His own gun in his hand, he sprinted towards the door of the guest house, thankful that it had been left open.

Hugh followed, almost tripping over the long skirts of his clerical garb. By the time he reached the front steps, Fenwick was already half-way up the stairs that led from the hall. The doors on either side on the ground floor were closed, and there had been no lights in the windows. Now suddenly the door on the right opened. A woman stepped into the hall, and took careful aim at Fenwick's ascending back. The shots were simultaneous. She fell, Hugh's bullet in her head.

Fenwick stopped and looked down, taking in the situation at a glance – the body on the floor in a widening pool of blood, and the priestly figure staring at his gun as if surprised by the effect of its action.

Fenwick cursed again. He knew he should have checked the downstairs rooms, but he had read too much into the absence of lights, and had thought it a first priority to find Ryan, and ensure her safety. And he had paid for his mistake, though not as expensively as Galinov. As yet Fenwick felt no pain, but he knew he had been hit in the shoulder.

Still, he reflected, he might have been dead. To Hugh he said, 'Thanks,' laconically.

He paused for a moment as Hugh flung open the other downstairs doors. There was no sign of the old deaf and dumb couple or of anyone else, and Hugh joined Fenwick on the stairs.

They found Jay in the second bedroom. The door was locked, but the key was on the outside. As they burst in, Jay sat up in bed. She was wearing a nightdress, but she clutched the duvet to her, as if it might provide protection. In the gloom she failed to recognize either Hugh or Fenwick, but they could see that her eyes were wide with fear, and that she seemed to have difficulty holding up her head.

Fenwick switched on the top light, and Jay, white-faced, lolled back against her pillow. Involuntarily Hugh cried out her name, but she paid him no attention. Fenwick reached her first. Without resistance she let him inspect her eyes and the needle marks on her arm.

'Drugged,' Fenwick said succinctly. He took two strides and threw open a wardrobe. 'Good. Here are her things. Get her dressed, Bigrel, as quick as you can, and wrap the duvet round her too. She'll probably notice the cold outside. Then keep her here till I give you the word. I'm going to find these nuns.'

Hugh did his best, but it was not easy. Jay was no help. It

was worse than dressing a doll, and more like dealing with an unco-operative and uninterested child. By the time he had her seated on the bed, more or less fully clothed and ready to leave, Fenwick was back. With him was a young nun. For a split second Hugh thought he was looking at Father Josef Marienski, but then he realized that this must be the priest's young sister.

'I need your help, Bigrel. Jay'll be okay with Sister – ' Fenwick paused inquiringly.

'Sister Katerina,' the girl said, smiling. She went to Jay and put an arm round her. 'I have a flask of black coffee here. It may help to wake her. But you go, now! The sooner all is done, the better.'

The floor below, to Hugh's surprise, had become a scene of bustling activity. The Reverend Mother was directing operations. She was a small woman with intelligent brown eyes, and she seemed to know exactly what had to be done. The house was to be cleared and cleaned, so that its guests would appear to have departed of their own volition. She had as helpers an elderly couple, to whom she spoke with quick facility in sign language, and two other nuns.

'We must hurry,' she said. 'Jan was told to make up another bed for tonight. He can lip-read a little, and he gathered that a man they called the "Comrade Colonel" would arrive some time about eight o'clock.' Her English was accented, but easy to follow. 'We must be finished and you must be gone before he comes.'

'Krasnakov,' murmured Fenwick.

Hugh made no reply. He was staring at the elderly Pole, who was manoeuvring the body of the woman into a large canvas bag. His wife was standing by with a bucket of hot water and a brush, ready to scrub the strip of carpet and the floor on either side of it.

Seeing Hugh's gaze, the Reverend Mother said, 'We keep a few of these bags to serve as shrouds and coffins for ourselves. We have a small consecrated graveyard within our walls.'

'But you won't bury these characters there,' Fenwick said quickly.

The Reverend Mother smiled, amused that the men who had

caused the deaths, should seemingly be shocked at the idea of burying their victims among the holy. Her own reasons were more practical. 'No,' she said. 'There will almost certainly be a search and an inquiry, publicized or secret, and newly-turned earth would show. Fortunately we have a very deep well, which is not used any more. Jan will see to it. He's old, but he's strong. He's already dealt with the body by the gates.'

As if to confirm her words, Jan heaved the bulging canvas bag on to his back as if it were a sack of coal, and staggered from the house. The two nuns had gone upstairs, and Hugh could hear them moving from room to room. The old Polish woman was pulling at the Reverend Mother's habit. She stabbed her finger at the floor where Fenwick was standing, and made inarticulate noises in the back of her throat.

Fenwick looked down. He saw several spots of fresh blood and, as he moved his arm, more drops fell from his sleeve. He smothered a curse.

'I'm sorry.' He grimaced at Hugh. 'You weren't quite quick enough. She winged me. I think the wretched woman put a bullet in my shoulder.'

'Then I'd better attend to it.' Again the Reverend Mother gestured with her hands, and the old Pole picked up her skirts and ran. 'You wait there,' she ordered Fenwick. He protested, but she paid no attention. She turned to Hugh. 'We can deal with everything except their car. You will have to dispose of that yourselves. I'll show you where it is now, and tell you what to do with it while Maria is getting our first aid box.'

Producing a torch from the pocket of her habit, she led Hugh to the side of the house, where another black car – this time a Zil – stood waiting. The Reverend Mother murmured instructions, and Hugh moved it into the driveway, and then turned their own car and brought it to the front door. As they went in he found himself facing Fenwick's gun. The nun showed no surprise.

'You might have been Krasnakov,' Fenwick said, glancing at his watch. 'The Comrade Colonel,' he explained for the benefit of the Reverend Mother. 'If your information's accurate, he could arrive any time now. We *must* hurry.'

The Polish woman had just returned, clutching a large box. She gave it to the Reverend Mother, and made shushing gestures to move everyone out of her way before getting down on her knees to clean the blood and mess from the carpet.

Again Fenwick protested that attending to him would mean more delay, but the Reverend Mother was adamant. 'A *groszy*'s delay now may save you a *zloty*'s worth of trouble in the future,' she said. 'I probably won't be able to remove the bullet without taking too long, but I'll do what I can.'

The Reverend Mother had her way. And fifteen minutes later Fenwick was grateful for her insistence. In spite of himself he had paled and bitten his lip as the wound was probed and antiseptic poured into it, but once she had bandaged him up he was vastly more comfortable.

By then Sister Katerina had carefully helped Jay down the stairs, and the two other nuns had brought the luggage and a couple of raincoats belonging to Galinov and Beluch's woman.

'All is clear upstairs, Reverend Mother,' they assured her.

'Then we must go,' said Fenwick at once. 'And thank you a hundred times for everything.'

They moved off in convoy. Hugh drove the car in which they had come. He was once more playing the priest and wearing his clerical hat. Behind him Jay was half-asleep, unaware of the bullet hole in the seat in front of her, unaware indeed of anything that was happening.

Fenwick struggled to drive the second car, hindered by his injured shoulder. He was desperately anxious to get away from Plock and back to the embassy in Warsaw. He had been forced to tell the Ambassador of their possible arrival and, needless to say, His Excellency had not been pleased. But a telephone call from London asking – demanding – full co-operation had produced the required result. So once in the embassy they would be safe, he knew, if not welcome, and he could arrange to get them out of the country.

At the moment, however, they were heading in the wrong direction, away from Warsaw, in search of a disused quarry some ten kilometres further on, where the Reverend Mother had told them the car could be pushed into deep water, and remain undiscovered forever. It was an annoying though inevitable detour but, in fact, a lucky one. By taking it, they just missed Viktor Krasnakov as he sped along the narrow road towards the convent.

THIRTY

Viktor Krasnakov drove fast. He was later than he had intended, but it made no difference; whenever he arrived there would be food and drink – and Jan Ryan would be waiting. He hoped Beluch's woman hadn't over-sedated her. He wanted her fully awake, so that she would co-operate with him, however unwillingly. What a change from Anna Seschki, he thought. And at least he could call Ryan any name he liked because afterwards he would kill her – unless he let Galinov have her first.

He reached his destination, and swung his car off the road to face the gates that guarded the drive of the convent. As Fenwick had done earlier, he hooted loudly. When no one answered, he was at first surprised, then alarmed. Galinov should have been expecting him. Cautiously he left his car, and rang the bell that he knew would sound in the main buildings as well as in the safe house.

He waited, tense. Clearly, something was badly wrong. The clouds had thickened and spots of rain had started to fall, so he got back into the car. It was with relief that at last he saw a light moving uncertainly towards him along the drive. Eventually he discerned the old Polish woman, whom he knew to be deaf and dumb. She was carrying an oil lantern, and she took her time about opening the gates. Krasnakov drove through, relieving his feelings by hooting impatiently, though he no longer expected Galinov to appear. The old woman was pulling the gates to, and he cursed the fact that it was impossible to question her.

He reached the safe house, and rang the bell at the front door. The house was in darkness, and there was no answer to his ring. He gestured to the old woman to produce her keys and open the door for him. When she did, he pushed her ahead of him,

simultaneously switching on the light. But there was no attack –
merely silence, broken only by the creaking of the building.

Krasnakov, pistol in his right hand and every sense alert,
could sense that the place was empty. But he took no risks.
Using the old woman as a shield he moved from room to room,
but found neither friend nor enemy. Then from an upstairs
window he saw that the Zil was not parked in its usual place.

Seizing the old woman by the back of her skirt he ran her
down the stairs, and literally kicked her out of the house, so that
she fell on her knees and the lantern, to which she had been
clinging, was extinguished, leaving her in darkness. He slammed
the door behind her, and turned to make a more detailed
examination of the premises. The first thing he noticed was a
dark patch on the strip of carpet in the hall. He touched it
tentatively. It was still damp.

Bending down, Krasnakov took out his pocket knife, and
inserted a blade in a crack between the floorboards beside the
carpet. The first attempt produced only dust, but the second
stained the knife a reddish brown. Krasnakov tried again, and
this time was satisfied that he had found blood.

He went through the house slowly and carefully. The beds
were made. The drawers and cupboards and wardrobes were
empty and contained no clothes. There were no signs of any
bags or luggage. Willingly or unwillingly, Galinov had gone, and
so had Beluch's woman – and Jay Ryan. It seemed that they had
left after a fight of some kind, and in a hurry. In spite of
attempts to clear the house, a high-heeled shoe had slipped
under one of the beds and been forgotten, and in the kitchen
there were signs that preparations for a meal had been com-
menced and abandoned.

These reminded him that he was hungry, and could do with a
drink. He had noticed a bottle of vodka on the sideboard in the
dining-room. Black bread, hunter's sausage and cold venison
were in the refrigerator. He would have liked some hot soup,
but he couldn't be bothered to heat it. He sat at the kitchen
table and made a meal, while he faced his dilemma.

After a few minutes he reached an interim decision. Even if
the nuns had any idea what had happened here in the safe house,

it was a fair gamble that they would simply feign ignorance. It would be pointless to waste time in interrogating them; if necessary, they could be dealt with at a later stage, when events were clearer. Similarly, a one-man search of the area in the dark was out of the question.

No, the only sensible move was to return to his embassy in Warsaw. That was where Galinov, if he were able, would first try to contact him, and he could telephone Beluch, who might have heard from the woman he had sent to assist with Ryan. As for Ryan herself, he must await events. She could be dead, but even if she had escaped and got back to her own people, they would take no action on the basis of any accusations she might make against him. Of course, hindsight showed that it would have been better to have killed her as soon as she had answered his questions satisfactorily, but . . .

After all, he thought, with professional pride, though he had admitted to eliminating Samuel Thaxted, he had given Ryan no hint of the real reason why. He had let her continue to believe that his intention had been to provide cover for Rupert Canville.

Poor, stupid Canville. By taking his own life he had saved them arranging an 'accident' for him later, and fortunately he had died without revealing the truth. But the period immediately after his death had been worrying; he might, after all, have decided to make a last effort to clear his name.

Suddenly Krasnakov felt an unexpected rush of sympathy for Rupert Canville, but he suppressed it instantly. No woman, he told himself, was worth dying for.

In spite of the Reverend Mother's directions, Fenwick and Bigrel had some difficulty in finding the quarry, but at last they reached it and, after some effort, heard a satisfactory splash as the Zil hit the water. Moments later the moon emerged from behind clouds, and they were able to confirm that the car was completely submerged. They could only hope the quarry was as deep as the nun had suggested.

'Fine,' said Fenwick. 'Now, back to Warsaw without passing

the convent, and we'll get the embassy doctor out of bed. He can take a look at Ryan, though I'm sure she'll be fine – '

'Thank God for that,' Hugh said soberly.

'It's she who should thank you. If it hadn't been for your bloody stubbornness – all right, let's call it perseverance – she might not be snoring away on the back seat right now.' Fenwick was equally serious.

He paused before he continued. 'And then the quack can do something about my shoulder,' he added. 'I'd like to get the bullet out as soon as possible. It's getting pretty uncomfortable.' In fact, it was extremely painful, and having to assist with disposal of the Zil hadn't helped. Fenwick was thankful he no longer had to drive, and even more thankful when they left the rutted track that led to the quarry, and were travelling fairly smoothly on a tarmac road. 'A pity you weren't a little quicker with your reaction, Bigrel,' he remarked.

Hugh grunted. He had acted instinctively, and he could scarcely credit that he had actually shot a woman – a woman he had never in his life cast eyes on before. 'I'm not used to this kind of thing,' he said, remembering doubtfully how he had promised himself that if Jay had been killed, he would seek out Krasnakov and kill him in return.

'No, I suppose life at Oxford doesn't train one for it,' Fenwick replied. 'Still, you did well, and we've Ryan with us to show for it.'

For a while they were silent. Jay's rhythmic snores and the steady motion of the car as once more they drove across the plain were making Fenwick sleepy, but the pain in his shoulder kept jolting him awake. Conversation was a distraction.

'I'm flying out of Warsaw on BA's afternoon flight tomorrow,' he remarked. 'I've no choice. I promised my boss. I'm hoping you and Ryan will be with me, but it'll take a bit of organizing.'

'You think it possible?' Hugh had thought no further ahead than rescuing Jay and reaching the safe haven of the embassy.

'I'll do my best, but don't count on it.'

'You mean there may not be seats?'

Fenwick gave a sardonic laugh. 'Seats be damned! I can get people bumped if necessary. That's no problem. But this is

Poland, Bigrel. Will you never learn? You've been in trouble with the police once and, though that was straightened out and your group visa was changed, if Krasnakov or Beluch tipped off the UB that you were travelling on a passport that wasn't your own, they might decide to pick you up. There's also the little matter of Galinov's disappearance, not to mention the woman you shot. If Krasnakov hinted that you had had something to do with any of that – '

Bigrel opened his mouth to ask more questions, but Fenwick's stern appearance deterred him. Instead, he said, 'I see. And all that would apply to Jay, too. Fortunately, her passport – or rather Pam Davidson's – is still in her handbag.'

'Is it? Good. But it still has its group visa, which shows she's over-stayed. She's been reported missing, and with those needle marks on her arms she could be done for drugs, perhaps.'

'Christ! I didn't think of half of that. I thought it – it – '

'Was all over bar the shouting? Well, it may be, so don't worry. But I shall have to do some very rapid footwork in the morning. It may be that we'll have to give you both entirely new passports – '

'But visas – '

'Oh, most things can be fixed here, if you know the right people.'

Fenwick made no further comment. He was wishing he could take his own advice and stop worrying. He felt pretty certain that on reflection Krasnakov would be prepared to cut his losses and let Bigrel and Ryan leave the country. It was what he would have done himself in Krasnakov's place. By now the Russian would have learnt from Ryan that neither she nor Bigrel had the remotest idea of his ultimate objective, so close to accomplishment, he must have hoped. And after their experiences in Poland, he would expect them to be wary of causing more trouble.

On the other hand, Krasnakov had his own masters, and he would have to account for the disappearance of his aide, Galinov, and for the fact that the safe house at Plock had apparently been blown. If he thought that Galinov and the woman with him were still alive, he might decide to attempt to negotiate – the two of

275

them against permission for Bigrel and Ryan to leave Poland unhindered. It was a toss-up, thought Fenwick, and winced as the car started to rattle over cobbles.

Jan Ryan slept for twelve hours. Hugh, who had refused to leave her, dozed fitfully in an armchair in her room until exhaustion overcame him, and he too slept deeply. By mid-morning, however, they were both awake, and in reasonably good spirits, enormously relieved to be together again, and safe in the embassy.

Fenwick, who had been up for several hours, telephoning London and doing what he could to exert pressure in the right quarters to ensure their safe departure on the afternoon flight from Warsaw, regarded them with a jaundiced expression.

'The resilience of youth,' he said acidly.

Jay's smile was rueful. 'Just reaction,' she said. 'If you only knew how thankful I was to be here, Mr Fenwick, and how grateful to you. Hugh's been telling me. You could both have been killed and – and God knows what would have happened to me.' Her voice broke.

'Don't think about it,' Hugh said.

'I'm afraid she must,' Fenwick quietly contradicted him. 'Mrs Ryan, I want to know everything you remember, and I mean everything, especially anything that Krasnakov said to you, or in your hearing.'

'That terrible man!' Jay shuddered. 'He actually boasted to me that he shot Sam.' She drew a deep breath, and regained control of her emotions. 'Okay, Mr Fenwick, I'll sure do my best.

'I planned to go back to the Dzolaks' shop,' she began. 'There was a taxi waiting outside the hotel and . . .'

Fenwick listened attentively. Unknowingly Jay filled in a great deal of background for him. She also described her attempted escape from the beauty salon and confirmed Herr Otto Schinkel's account of the incident. This pleased Fenwick because it showed that the German's information was reliable.

When he was satisfied that she had told him all she could

remember, he said, 'Well, I hope you're happy now, Mrs Ryan. You know who killed your father. You've even met the man.'

'And I want nothing more to do with him, ever. But – ' Jay was frowning.

'But?' Fenwick questioned.

'I still don't understand *why* he killed Sam. When I suggested it was a cover for Sir Rupert Canville, he laughed and called me an innocent. Frankly, I can't see why the Russians should want to protect the reputation of a dead Brit who had been one of their agents.'

For a fraction of a second Fenwick panicked. They mustn't know, they – must – not – know, he thought. Then, of course! God! I must be tired.

'You haven't told Mrs Ryan about Anna Seschki?' he asked Hugh, showing slight surprise.

'I hadn't got around to it.'

'Around to what?' Jay inquired and, when Hugh repeated the lie that Fenwick had fed him, she nodded her understanding. 'I see. At least that makes sense. Poor old Canville. You'd think someone of his experience wouldn't let himself get caught in a trap of that kind.'

'You'd be surprised,' Fenwick said shortly.

Hugh was less charitable. 'He was a fool all the same. Married to the beautiful Monica, he had no excuse to go chasing anyone else.'

Fenwick laughed. 'You've never met Anna Seschki,' he said. 'She's quite a dish too.' He changed the subject quickly. 'Well, barring accidents, you'll both be flying out with me this after-noon. Keep your fingers crossed. There's just one other thing. I'm afraid that when we get to London I shall have to take you to see my boss. He'll want to hear your stories at first hand. Then we'll arrange for you to be taken wherever you wish.'

'That – that's wonderful,' Hugh said. 'We'll be going down to Oxford, to stay with my parents. Incidentally, do you think I could phone them? And Jay would like to call her Aunt Hilda in Washington.'

Fenwick hesitated. He had no wish to tempt fate. He was optimistic there would be no last minute hitches over the couple's departure, but he wouldn't be really happy until they were both on the flight, and the aircraft was out of communist airspace.

'As soon as we get to London,' he said. 'Okay?'

'Sure,' said Hugh and, remembering Fenwick's earlier warning, looked the question he didn't want to ask.

Fenwick shrugged. 'Everything's fine. You'll be home tonight,' he said and he hoped that for once, on this occasion, he was telling Hugh Bigrel the truth.

In the event, trouble at the airport was conspicuous by its absence. Fenwick was aware of watching eyes as he saw his charges through the bureaucracy of departure from a communist country, but they encountered no difficulties. Nevertheless, though outwardly as calm and efficient as Madame Bereski, he was sweating by the time the three of them boarded the aircraft.

What was more, he refused a drink until the Captain made the traditional announcement on such flights – they had reached 'friendly' airspace – when he breathed a sigh of relief. Even the remote possibility of recall or the even remoter chance of interception could now be forgotten. He relaxed and turned to Hugh and Jay, who were holding hands in the seats beside him, to give them a victory sign. Then he demanded champagne.

He thought of Viktor Georgiyevich Krasnakov. He had no means of knowing that the previous evening the Russian had been ordered to return to Moscow as soon as possible, to forget Bigrel and Ryan as unimportant to the main issue and to leave the search for the missing Galinov and his woman companion to the UB.

Even while Fenwick was thinking of him, Krasnakov was in Dzerzhinsky Square. He had just been told that, together with two or three other senior KGB officers, he would be permitted to watch the screen when the man they expected to become the next President of the United States appeared on worldwide television to make the announcement for which they had worked and planned so hard.

THIRTY-ONE

In the book-lined study of Worral J. Smith's mansion in Rock Creek Park in Washington DC., Smith – the man expected to become the next American President – faced the British Ambassador to the United States and Dick Fenwick, who had just flown in from London. They made an unusual trio, but the occasion was unusual.

'I don't believe it!' Smith exclaimed.

But of course he did, Fenwick thought. Worral J. Smith was far too intelligent to doubt what the Ambassador had just told him. He knew and respected the Ambassador as a colleague and friend, and ambassadors didn't tell such tales about such matters in such circumstances unless they were certain of their facts.

Nevertheless, 'I do not believe it!' Smith repeated firmly. 'Sure. I appreciate that you Brits think it's so, but me, I can't accept it. There's been a balls-up somewhere. In other words, you've got it wrong.'

His gaze shifted from the Ambassador, who had given a delicate, almost imperceptible nod of his head to Dick Fenwick. Fenwick met the American's vivid blue eyes, so unexpected in his handsome bronzed face, without flinching. He had anticipated Smith's initial response; it was an automatic reaction to shocking news.

'I'm afraid not, sir,' Fenwick said. 'There's no mistake. Monica Canville is a Soviet agent, and in all probability has been one for many years. She may have been recruited when she went to Moscow as a young dancer on a British Council tour. But I have no proof of that.'

'But do you have proof of any of this?' Smith shot at him.

'You've read the report, sir.' Fenwick pointed to the papers now scattered on the leather top of Smith's magnificent desk.

'Sure, I've read the goddam report. It states that this KGB Colonel, Krasneski or Krasnakov, and Lady Canville were lovers in Warsaw, and that they used to meet at a beauty salon, or above a shop called Dzolak's or something, and that she spied for him.'

'That is correct, sir,' said Fenwick. 'When Sir Rupert Canville discovered the source of the leak in his Warsaw embassy he created a fictitious involvement with a – a political hostess called Anna Seschki, for the sole purpose of getting himself and his wife posted out of Poland. I don't know what story his wife spun him. I doubt if she told him of her KGB lover. I'd guess she wept and admitted to a minor indiscretion, a moment's folly for which she was being blackmailed, and Sir Rupert was prepared to risk his career for her.'

'How do you know that wasn't the truth?' Smith demanded.

'We've got the signed statement of the German, Herr Schinkel, that he saw Krasnakov and Monica Canville together several times at Beluch's beauty salon.' Fenwick spared Hugh Bigrel a grateful thought. 'I agree the evidence is circumstantial, sir, and I'm not sure I'd want to go to court on it. However, there's no doubt that Monica Canville was a Soviet agent.'

'And you've told me this because – '

Smith couldn't bring himself to put his thoughts into words. Fenwick looked at the Ambassador, hoping that he would provide a diplomatic response, and he was not disappointed.

'I was informed, in the strictest confidence, that you were intending to announce your engagement to Lady Canville in the next day or so. That's why we're here, to warn you, Worral,' the Ambassador said gently. He hadn't relished breaking the bad news to the American, but he was delighted that his old friend and colleague, Rupert Canville, was in the clear. 'Officially it's none of our business who becomes the next President, but unofficially I know that London would be most happy to see you in the White House, and – '

Smith nodded dismissively as if he were not interested in what the British might think. His own problems were too overwhelming. He rose to his feet, and began to pace up and down the valuable Chinese rug that covered the floor of his study.

'What about our own people here – the Agency and the FBI? Do they know? If so, why delegate you to tell me?'

'They don't know – yet. And they won't ever unless we're forced to take them into our confidence,' the Ambassador said. 'Worral, the last thing we want is another scandal in London, but we could not stand idly by, and permit – '

Smith raised his hand, as if no more need be said. Fenwick watched him. A man to be envied, he thought, and then changed his mind. At the present moment Worral J. Smith was shaken to the core. He looked ill. He apparently loved Monica Canville desperately, and that wouldn't change in a few minutes or days or even months.

But how desperately did he love her? As much as Rupert Canville, who had been prepared to die in an attempt to save her, accepting her treachery as his own? Fenwick doubted it. There were few men like Canville – foolish romantics some would call them – and perhaps, he thought sardonically, their scarcity was a good thing.

'If you'll excuse me, gentlemen, I need to make a call,' Smith said suddenly, breaking a lengthening silence.

He had addressed the remark to the Ambassador, but it was Fenwick who replied. 'I'm sorry, sir, but that won't be possible.'

'What the hell do you mean? You're not on home ground here, you know.'

'Of course not, sir. But Lady Canville won't be available. She is – er – helping us with information, answering questions – '

'You mean she's being interrogated?'

'Yes, sir, though perhaps "interviewed" would be a better term. She's a British subject, and she's also a Soviet agent. But, of course, as you've gathered, we hope not to prosecute. We hope she'll co-operate in return for immunity, so that there can be a complete cover-up of the whole affair.'

'Okay, okay, Mr Fenwick. I get the picture. No need to underline anything. I appreciate the situation, and for your information I was *not* about to try to contact Lady Canville. So – I shan't keep you more than a minute or two.'

With a slight inclination of his head Worral J. Smith strode purposefully from the room. The Ambassador and Fenwick exchanged glances, but neither spoke. The American was away far longer than he had promised, but when he returned he was smiling sadly.

He said, 'In a few hours I'm to appear on nationwide TV to confirm formally my intention to seek the Democratic nomination for the Presidency. At the same time, I also intend to announce my intention of marrying again.'

Fenwick's head came up sharply. Smith could either pursue his political ambitions, or he could marry Monica Canville. There was no way he could do both. A choice was inevitable.

As if reading his thoughts, Smith said, 'No, I'm not mad, Mr Fenwick. I'm merely an ambitious man. I want to get to the White House more than anything else in this life, partly to satisfy myself and partly because I know I shall make a damned good President. To achieve this I need a wife, a First Lady. The American people expect it. They'd distrust a bachelor of my age, and it's been pointed out to me in no uncertain terms that a widower of nine years, however discreet he may have been, counts almost as a bachelor. In fact, the point's been reflected in my ratings in the polls. That was one reason – and I admit only one, and not by any means the major one – why I proposed to marry Lady Canville.'

Abruptly Smith stopped speaking. All this time he had been standing, hands behind his back, addressing an audience of two. Now, as if to hide his deeper feelings, he went to a cupboard, which he opened to reveal a small refrigerator. He produced a bottle of champagne and glasses. Fenwick was reminded of Hugh Bigrel's description of the luncheon in the Cotswolds when he and Jay Ryan had met Smith with Monica Canville. He waited, trying to guess what decision this powerful American politician had reached.

Smith's next words took both the British by surprise. He said, 'I have just asked a charming lady, a widow of the Vietnam war, whom I've known since childhood, to be my wife, and she's done me the honour of accepting. I shall announce this tonight, and it will certainly quash any rumours there might be around. Perhaps you'll be the first to drink our health and wish us well.'

Shortly afterwards the British Ambassador, accompanied by

Dick Fenwick, returned to his embassy on Massachusetts Avenue. The Ambassador was smiling with relief and satisfaction. 'Splendid!' he said. He glanced at Fenwick. 'Off with the old and on with the new, what? But that's a politician for you. He accepted the inevitable. He may seem a cold fish, but he's a clever man. He'll make an excellent President.'

Fenwick murmured agreement. He was wondering how Viktor Georgiyevich Krasnakov and his masters would receive the news that their plan to plant in the White House a First Lady under KGB control had failed. He scarcely spared a thought for Monica Canville, and he had no idea that Krasnakov had loved her in his fashion, as deeply as had Rupert Canville or Worral J. Smith.

The men in the KGB who had masterminded what had seemed to them a conspiracy to end all conspiracies were as furious as Fenwick could have imagined. Their operation had failed and failed dismally. Characteristically, they demanded revenge. Someone must pay for the wasted time and effort and money.

As the smiling faces of Worral J. Smith and his bride-to-be faded to black on the television screen in front of them, three pairs of eyes turned to Krasnakov. They gave Krasnakov a choice, which was in fact no choice. Like Worral J. Smith, but unlike Rupert Canville, he valued himself more highly than any woman.

Six weeks later, Dick Fenwick, taking a well-earned holiday in the South of France, read in the *International Herald Tribune* of the death of Monica Canville. An intruder had entered her London flat and shot her. It was a strange case; there were no signs of forcible entry, and no indication that theft was a motive.